Pippa Wright lives in London and works in book publishing.

You can find her on Twitter at:
www.twitter.com/troisverres

UNSUITABLE MEN

After eleven years of coupled-up domesticity, Rory Carmichael is single for the first time in her adult life. Her reliable boyfriend, Martin, wasn't the most exciting man in the world, but when she discovers he's not actually dependable Mr Right after all, but a cheater, she's forced to consider that everything she knows about relationships might be wrong. Now, striving to reinvigorate her love life — and her lacklustre career — her mission is to date as many unsuitable men as possible. Toyboys. Sugar daddies. Fauxmosexuals. Maybe the bad boys she's never dated can show her what she's been missing in life. But if Mr Right can turn out to be so wrong, maybe one of her Mr Wrongs will turn out to be just right.

Books by Pippa Wright
Published by The House of Ulverscroft:

LIZZY HARRISON LOSES CONTROL

PIPPA WRIGHT

---◆---

UNSUITABLE MEN

Complete and Unabridged

CHARNWOOD
Leicester

First published in Great Britain in 2012 by
Pan Books
an imprint of
Pan Macmillan
London

First Charnwood Edition
published 2013
by arrangement with
Pan Macmillan
a division of
Macmillan Publishers Limited
London

British Library CIP Data

Wright, Pippa.
   Unsuitable men.
   1. Chick lit.
   2. Large type books.
   I. Title
   823.9′2–dc23

   ISBN 978–1–4448–1379–1

Published by
F. A. Thorpe (Publishing)
Anstey, Leicestershire

Set by Words & Graphics Ltd.
Anstey, Leicestershire
Printed and bound in Great Britain by
T. J. International Ltd., Padstow, Cornwall

This book is printed on acid-free paper

*For Cath and Lisa,
my ideal readers*

Acknowledgements

Love and thanks to:

Cath Lovesey, for insisting on reading and advising on a very early and messy draft even when she was mere days away from giving birth.

Lisa McCormack, for carrying around my first book in a freezer bag so as not to damage the cover, and refusing to allow her friends to read it until they bought their own copies. Also for being a fabulous holiday companion: fish tostadas for ever.

Justin Nicholls, for the loan of his upstairs office space, architectural library and constant supply of chocolate digestives.

Harrie Evans, for generous advice, support and cheer-leading, *Hello!*-reading, Royal Wedding-facilitating and general wonderfulness.

Emily Brooks, who shared with me her brilliant stories of working on heritage magazines, and offered first-draft advice, information and exhibitions of taxidermied kittens.

Nancy Wiese, from whom I first heard the expression 'pert niece'. She remains the finest exemplar of the form.

Jane Southern, for being the most flexible and understanding of employers, for entertaining gossip, and for sending me flowers saying 'The end is nigh' when I hadn't left the house or washed my hair for three days.

Thanks to the lovely Macmillan mafia, especially Jenny Geras, Thalia Suzuma, Sandra Taylor, Ellen Wood, Ali Blackburn, Michelle Kirk and Matt Hayes.

Everyone at Aitken Alexander, especially Andrew Kidd, Sally Riley, Liv Stones and Nishta Hurry.

Tinie Tempah (hi, Tinie, I totally know you're reading this), since I am completely unable to write the words 'my aunt's house' without breaking into a shoddy version of 'Pass Out'. Thanks for the theme tune.

1

I'd only ever had one day off sick in my seven years working at *Country House* magazine, so I suppose it wasn't surprising that my return to the office the day after I split up with my boyfriend of eleven years occasioned some notice. Although my boss, Amanda, knew why I'd been absent, to the rest of the staff my unexpected Wednesday no-show was a fascinating and intriguing mystery, which should tell you everything about what passed for excitement in the daily life of the magazine. I'm not some glowing paragon of health, believe me; I just have a superstitious conviction that if I take time off when I'm not actually near death, I am somehow inviting serious illness to strike me. The way I see it, to take a day off watching reruns of *Come Dine with Me* for a mere sniffle is practically begging the universe to hit you with the cancer stick: not worth it. My office-mate Ticky always complains that it is unfair of me to bring my germs to work, but since I don't see her rushing to pick up the slack, as far as I'm concerned she can just keep on wearing that surgical mask and wiping down her desk with Dettol whenever I cough.

In another office, one with up-to-date technology and remote access, it might have been possible for me to have claimed to be 'working from home', even though everyone knows that is just a euphemism for hanging out in a cafe all day eating cake while occasionally remembering to glance at one's emails. But at *Country House* (established 1886, read by approximately 1886 people, as the ancient office joke went) a blackberry was nothing more than the autumnal soft fruit that appeared in every September issue with a headline such as The Blackberry: Fact or Fiction? or Bramble Jelly: Your Mould Solutions.

The frisson of interest caused by my reappearance would no doubt have delighted someone like our contributing editor Noonoo von Humboldt, who took being the centre of attention as her long-legged, swishy-haired, *Hello!*-photographed due. She strode our office corridors as if they were a catwalk, tossing her head and flicking her pashmina over a shoulder with a nonchalance that must have taken years of practice. But I had always tried to keep my head down at *Country House*, both metaphorically and literally, and today I kept my eyes firmly fixed on the carpet as I hurried past my shared office straight to the staff kitchen. I hoped I might be able to hide there for a few restorative minutes before being interrogated by anyone, but I should have realized that any true gossip hound would have recognized this as prime stakeout territory. And so it proved. Leaping out from behind the fridge, her nostrils flaring as she bore down on me, was features assistant and self-appointed shoulder-to-cry-on-whether-you-like-it-or-not, the Honourable Ticky Lytton-Finch.

'Aurora Carmichael, oh my Goouurd, what

the faahrk is going on?'

'Oh, hi, Ticky,' I said resignedly, unwrapping my scarf from around my neck. There was little point in trying to escape. The most I could hope for was to get away without letting her goad me into complete hysterics. The way I felt right now, it wouldn't take much.

'Don't 'Oh, hi' me, Rory. Where were you? Don't go saying you were sick, I know you'd never miss an opportunity to cough your vile germs all over my desk.'

'No, I wasn't sick,' I conceded.

'But you do look faahrking terrible,' said Ticky, moving closer. 'What's going on?'

'I had a fight with Martin,' I said, feeling my throat constrict. I clamped my lips together so my chin didn't wobble, determined not to cry in front of Ticky, the emotional vampire of the office. Other people's misery and drama were her sustenance. Her beady brown eyes lit up at the very suggestion of tears and she could sniff out a sobbing assistant in the ladies' from fifty paces. For the two years she'd worked here I'd watched her pump her unsuspecting victims for every detail of their emotional lives. Little did they know that her interest in every tiny incident had nothing to do with friendly concern and everything to do with her own vicarious thrills.

'Martin the-youngest-board-director-at-the-accountancy-firm Martin?' asked Ticky, moving still nearer as she detected the possibility of weeping. 'Martin Mr Excel Spreadsheets Martin? Martin your-boyfriend-of-eleven-years Martin? Martin your-only-boyfriend-*ever* Martin?'

3

She peered into my eyes, which I knew were bloodshot and swollen enough to offer her ammunition for a full-on assault on my personal life, and I poured all my energy into not cracking in front of her. I just nodded a silent confirmation.

'But, like, what kind of fight? A splitting-up kind of fight?' she demanded.

'Yes — no, I mean, I'm not sure,' I stammered.

'You're not sure? How are you not sure? Either you have split up or you haven't.'

'I've moved out for a bit,' I muttered. 'It's just temporary.' Of course it was just temporary. This was a moment of madness from Martin. He hadn't meant any of it, I was sure of that. In a few days, when he'd calmed down, I'd be moving straight back home where I belonged.

'Moved out? Where?' Ticky pressed. I wouldn't have been surprised if she'd whipped out a sheaf of paper and started taking notes to pore over later, rubbing her hands together and cackling.

'Just with my aunt,' I said.

'Your aunt in Clapham?' said Ticky, with impressive recall. 'Isn't her house, like, some random hostel full of nutters?'

'It's a boarding house for actors. She's had all sorts of famous people staying there over the years, actually,' I said, stung into defending my aunt's home. Although it is true that I had myself referred to it as a hostel full of nutters in the very recent past, I'd had to swiftly change my tune when I arrived there yesterday with my overnight bag.

'Yah? Who's staying there now, then?' asked

Ticky, her eyes narrowing with interest.

'Well, no one especially,' I admitted. 'Half of the actors have had to move out because of some plumbing problems. That's why there was a room free for me.' I could see Ticky's eyes begin to glaze over as soon as she realized I wasn't about to reveal that George Clooney was hiding out in my aunt's attic bedroom.

'Like, whatever, Roars. Forget the plumbing, get back to Martin. This is totally totally major. *Majorama*. How does it make you *feel?*' She clasped my forearm with both of her hands — you might think in sympathy, but I knew better. It was a well-practised restraining hold designed to stop me from moving away.

'How do you think it makes me feel?' I snapped, trying to pull away.

Ticky held firm. Protected by the thick skin of the supremely posh, she would not doubt for a moment that her interference was, if not wanted, then at the very least necessary.

'Terrible, miserable, awful, dejected. Like your life has ended,' she prompted. 'Unable to eat, lying awake all night sobbing, vomiting at the thought of him with other women . . .'

'This isn't helping, Ticky,' I said, wresting my arm out of her grasp. Trust Ticky to think the worst of Martin. She'd never held back from declaring him to be Mr Boring Spread-sheets Accountant in the past, but now we'd split up she somehow had reimagined him as a treacherous man-whore. 'There is no other woman.'

'Hmm, that's what you think,' she said, with

an infuriating air of knowingness for someone who had met Martin once, six months ago, and seemed barely aware of his existence since.

I rolled my eyes. She didn't understand the kind of stress Martin had been under since he'd been promoted to the board. He'd been working late nights and weekends, coming home exhausted and falling into bed without even uttering a word. Like he had time for another woman.

'Don't keep it all inside, Rory,' Ticky urged, correctly divining that I was not sharing all of my thoughts with her. 'It's so unhealthy. You've got to, like, share it with people? Express yourself?'

'To you?' I asked. In the entire time we'd been working together Ticky and I had never so much as shared a KitKat from the corner shop, yet now she expected me to expose my deepest feelings to her?

'I am, like, a raaahlly raaahlly good listener, actually,' Ticky persisted. 'And, I mean, you need to talk about it because this is maybe the biggest thing ever to happen to you. Isn't it?'

She cocked her head to the side speculatively. I didn't answer. I knew it wasn't a rhetorical question. Ticky would have been utterly thrilled if I had chosen this moment to tell her that there had been a worse time in my life for her to dissect and pore over.

'Isn't it? It's got to be. I mean, wow, breaking up with your first love is hard when you're, like, sixteen, but breaking up with him at twenty-nine? Preparing to turn thirty alone and unloved? Your biological clock going into

6

overdrive? Ovaries shrivelling with every day that passes? That's got to be majorly agonizing.'

I tried to move towards the door with my tea but Ticky barred the way, one hand on either side of the door frame.

'What is *agonizing*, Ticky,' I said through clenched teeth, 'is this conversation. Could you please just leave me alone?'

She paused and looked down at the ground, shaking her head in apparent sympathy. When she looked up she said, as if it were entirely her own idea, 'I think you probably just need to be left alone for a bit, Roars.'

'Thanks *so* much for that.'

'That's okay. I like, totally understand your need for space right now. But when you're ready to talk about it, I am here. Any time. For as long as you like. You can tell me everything.'

As I walked down the corridor to our shared office I saw the editor, Amanda Bonham Baillie, lean out of her office momentarily. Her eyebrows moved fractionally towards each other in a barely perceptible frown — *Country House* was officially anti-Botox, being more a publication read by hearty rural ladies of a certain age whose clothes were always covered in dog hair, but Amanda's inability to express deep emotion on her face had long made me suspect that her cosmetic influences were more West London than West Country.

'Everything all right now, Rory?' she asked, as if it took a mere twenty-four hours to dismantle a long-term relationship, move out of one's shared home, and get over a broken heart.

'Yes, Amanda,' I said dutifully, knowing that she, unlike Ticky, would be appalled if I were to break down and wet her Marni-jacketed shoulder with my tears.

'So sorry about Matthew,' she said kindly.

'Martin. It's Martin, Amanda.'

'Martin, of course,' she said. Her minuscule frown deepened by an atom. 'And Rory, do please try to call me Maaahn.'

No matter how hard I tried, I had never been able to call Amanda 'Maaahn'. The rest of the staff did, but somehow I just couldn't manage it. Not because it felt disrespectful to my boss, but because I wasn't sufficiently posh to get enough vowels into her name. I just ended up saying 'Man', to rhyme with 'can', which always made her wrinkle her nose in polite displeasure. To have tried at all would have felt like putting on a foreign accent, as if I was one of those horribly showy-offy types who calls Paris 'Parrree' and hoicks up the back of their throat when pronouncing any word in German. I simply couldn't manage 'Maaahn' to rhyme with — God, what would it rhyme with? No word in English, that's for sure.

It had taken me years to learn how to deal with the names that appeared on the *Country House* masthead. Who would have guessed that the seemingly innocuous last name Featherstone was not said as spelled, but rather 'Fanshawe'? Or that Amanda's PA, Catherine, insisted her name should be pronounced 'Katrina', just to fool plebs like me (everyone called her Hurricane anyway, obviously, since she was prone to dramatics). Felix Appleby was known as Flickers. Natalia von Humboldt would answer to nothing but Noonoo, and it took me several months to realize that my office-mate Ticky had actually been christened Victoria. There was always some apparently hilarious story behind such nicknames, usually unexplained as most of the staff had known each other socially since infancy. If you escaped a nickname, it would be only because you exulted in a moniker so grand that no one would dare shorten it, literary editor Lysander Honeywell being the prime example.

I had always suspected I'd got my first job here, straight out of university, because the former editor, Old Mr Betterton, whose family had owned the magazine for 150 years, mistakenly believed my unusual name marked me out as one of them. He would never have imagined that my mother chose to call me Aurora after the princess in *Sleeping Beauty*. And not the Grimm's fairy tale either; Mum was strictly Disney-inspired. Since Mr Betterton was always quite happy to take people on surface appearance, he didn't dig especially deep in our twenty-minute interview — much of which I suspected he couldn't actually hear, as his hearing aid whistled alarmingly throughout. Nor did he, I surmised, actually read the CV which revealed that my education came courtesy of the state rather than a trust fund. It was only when I'd been working at the office for a year that I overheard him tell another member of staff that it was his belief Rory Carmichael might not be, after all, one of the Norfolk Carmichaels.

By the time Ticky returned to our shared office my computer was on and I didn't even need to pretend to be buried in work to avoid her questions; there were 167 emails piled up from yesterday and Ticky, true to form, although cc'd on most, had not dealt with a single one of them. Technically, as features assistant, Ticky reported to me. But she spent much of her time 'networking' with Amanda's tacit approval, taking long lunches, skipping off at five to meet 'contacts' (aka old schoolfriends) for cocktails, leaving the office every Friday lunchtime to head out to the country for the weekend or breakfasting at Simpson's-in-the-Strand with aged and wealthy godfathers who Amanda believed might be useful to *Country House* if they might be persuaded to give us access to their rural residences. Ticky claimed this hectic schedule left her too exhausted to deal with the more mundane demands of her job and somehow, despite my being deputy features editor, most of these landed in my in tray.

I knew it wasn't worth telling tales on Ticky's workshy ways; she would be here at the magazine only until she found a chinless husband to whisk her off to her own country house. I'd seen it happen to both of her predecessors. The job was nothing but an interesting diversion for her, with a salary that just bumped up her generous monthly allowance from the bank of Mummy and Daddy.

I must have been looking in her direction because Ticky's head suddenly twisted away from her computer screen.

'Ready to talk yet, Roars?' she asked. 'Maybe a drink after work?'

'No thanks,' I said, turning back to my work.

'Is it because you're skint?' asked Ticky. 'Because I am, like, totes happy to stand you a drink. I mean, February's depressing enough without not being able to afford to drown your sorrows.'

'I can afford a glass of wine, thanks very much, Ticky,' I said crossly.

I supposed I should have been grateful to her for offering, but the not-so-subtle implication that I was an impoverished prole was hard to take. Sometimes I felt like most of the staff at *Country House* regarded me as some kind of a charity project, like an African orphan they'd all adopted to give a chance at a better life. Meaning a life like theirs, of course; none of them could imagine that I might be perfectly contented with my own non-posh existence. Noonoo never understood that I turned down her offers of cast-off pashminas not out of pride, but because I wouldn't be caught dead in one.

The truth was, while I was desperate for a glass of wine — even right now, first thing in the morning — I wasn't ready to talk to anyone about Martin. I hadn't even called my mum yet. I knew in the sitcom version of my life I should have been sitting on a pub sofa surrounded by my girlfriends, having the 'All men are bastards' conversation, but was it worth gathering together my far-flung university friends for what was probably a false alarm? It wasn't like we were all as close as we had been when we were living in

11

each others' pockets in our mouse-infested student house in Warwick. I knew we were all still there for each other even if our meeting up had become a twice-yearly affair, but I hadn't spoken to any of them in months. And, if I was completely honest, I'd always felt that the girls hadn't quite taken Martin to their hearts. Telling them about our fight now might just prejudice them against him later.

Ticky interrupted, refusing to give up. 'You, like, can't keep it all inside for ever, Roars.' Her facial expression suggested a selfless altruism that was belied by the impatient rapping of her pen on the desktop, as if she was marking out the seconds until I cracked.

'You'll be absolutely the first to know when I'm ready to talk about it, Ticky,' I lied. She nodded in satisfaction. Right, I thought. It will be a cold hard day in hell when I find myself so short of friends that I need to confide in you, Ticky Lytton-Finch, you over-entitled emotional parasite.

But that was before the email arrived from Martin. My heart leapt into my throat. Had he reconsidered so soon? Did he want me to come home? My overnight bag sat, zipped and packed, in my room at Auntie Lyd's, ready to return the moment he gave the word.

Dear Rory, the email said:

I will be at my golf class on Saturday morning between 10 a.m. and 12 p.m. I suggest you come to collect your belongings then, as I do not believe either of us wants a repeat of your

12

hysterics yesterday. A clean break will be simpler for both of us.

Best wishes,
Martin

Thirty seconds later I found myself sobbing on Ticky's shoulder as if she was my only friend in the world.

2

'Like I said,' sniffed my Auntie Lyd, as she steered her ancient Ford Escort across two lanes of the South Circular with a blithe unconcern for nearby drivers, 'he's got another woman.'

A small wave of rubbish in the footwell crested and broke over my boots as the car lurched to the left. Mum and I had always called Auntie Lyd's car the Travelling Skip, since she seemed to be blind to the assortment of empty water bottles, cigarette packets and dusty mints that littered the floor, not to mention the layer of cigarette ash that coated every surface, as if the rusting Ford Escort had been recently excavated from Pompeii.

I decided to ignore her insulting speculations. Auntie Lyd had never liked Martin and she had made that still more evident ever since I'd turned up on her doorstep in heartbroken tears. It seemed to me like risky behaviour on her part: I'd seen too many people verbally annihilate a friend's recent ex, only to have the seemingly dead relationship lurch back into life like the villain in a horror movie. Wouldn't it be embarrassing for Auntie Lyd, with her wild speculations about other women, if Martin and I got back together? Although his asking me to move out wasn't exactly encouraging, it was early days. I hadn't given up yet.

'Darling,' said Auntie Lyd, taking my silence

14

as encouragement to continue. 'Surely you can see it yourself? A man who, at the age of thirty, is incapable of ironing his own shirt is not going to get rid of one woman without having another lined up behind the ironing board.'

I sighed and sank down into the seat. I wished I had never confessed that the row that broke up my relationship had hinged on my burning a hole in Martin's favourite shirt. Auntie Lyd's feminist principles had been outraged by the very idea that I might offer to do the ironing in the first place, as if I had done so each morning in high heels and a Playboy bunny outfit instead of my ancient dressing gown and slippers. Her tolerance of other people's domestic idiosyncrasies had been worn down, rather than mellowed, by running her large Clapham townhouse as a boarding house for the last twenty years. As far as I knew she'd never even lived with a man, unless it was one of her paying guests, the PGs as she called them. It was useless to expect her to appreciate Martin's needs.

'He's not incapable, Auntie Lyd. It's not like that,' I said. 'You don't understand.'

'What don't I understand?' she demanded. 'I didn't spend the late seventies stomping around in unflattering hessian dungarees to see my niece, thirty years later, getting dumped for failing to do the ironing properly.'

'You wore hessian dungarees?' I said doubtfully. I'd seen photographs of Auntie Lyd in the seventies. Although the evidence of several family albums suggested that she had indeed burned her bra for most of the decade, her polished look

15

owed far more to Joan Collins than to Greenham Common. Her bob had been darker then, almost black, and if she'd gone without a slash of fierce red lipstick between the years of 1977 to 1983 then there was certainly no photographic evidence of it.

'Well, only for a few weeks, I admit,' huffed Auntie Lyd, annoyed at being doubted. 'How were casting directors supposed to get an idea of my figure in that loose-fitting rubbish? But stop distracting me, Rory. The point remains, what kind of man expects his girlfriend to do the ironing in this day and age? Is feminism *entirely* dead?'

'It's not anti-feminist to do the ironing,' I protested. 'It's just that Martin's job is much more demanding and stressful than mine. So we agreed — well, we never actually agreed it, it was more of an unspoken thing, an understanding — that he'd take care of all the finances and I'd look after the housework.'

Auntie Lyd sniffed her disapproval. I half expected her to whip out a copy of *The Feminine Mystique* from the glove compartment and hit me over the head with it.

'And it wasn't just the ironing,' I confessed, feeling tears beginning to well up. 'He — he said I should make more of an effort with my appearance. I didn't listen to him. I haven't even had a haircut in months,' I wailed, grabbing at a handful of my unruly red curls. I had thought they were charmingly tousled, but now I looked more closely I could see they were bristling with split ends. 'Do you think that's it, Auntie Lyd?

Do you think he dumped me because I'd let myself go?'

Her head snapped round towards me. Auntie Lyd's face was already permanently scrunched up, courtesy of the stream of smoke that rose from her ever-present cigarette, but it puckered even further into a fierce frown.

'It is quite impossible to have let yourself go at the age of twenty-nine, Rory, don't be ridiculous,' she snapped. 'You're still a baby. Never heard anything so stupid. Wait till you're sixty-two and the staff at Waterstone's in Battersea mistake you for Beryl Bainbridge and ask you to sign eight copies of *Master Georgie*. *Then* you can talk to me about letting yourself go.'

I sniffed, looking up. I knew Auntie Lyd. 'Did you sign them?'

' 'Course I did. Their stupid mistake.'

'You do know she's dead, don't you?' I asked.

'*I* know that, Aurora. It's not my problem if *they* didn't. Anyway, dear Beryl would have loved it.'

I squinted at her through her shroud of smoke. It was entirely feasible that Auntie Lyd had known Beryl Bainbridge personally, they both having been actresses in their long-ago youth; you never could tell with my aunt, whose conversation was powered by hints and allusions that she rarely explained. But then again it was equally feasible that she was claiming kinship out of nothing more than a shared similarity of appearance. It was probably the heavy-fringed bob that had confused the Waterstone's staff, but

17

it could have been those cheekbones, so high and rounded they made you think of Inuit tribes in the snowy North. Then again, and less flatteringly, it could also have been the strong smell of stale cigarettes that surrounded her at all times. She fired up another cigarette and inhaled deeply. Then she blew two fierce streams of smoke from her nostrils.

'I know what you're thinking,' said Auntie Lyd. Brakes screeched behind us as she fiddled with the lighter on the dashboard. 'You're thinking this is just temporary. You're thinking he's going to miss you and take you back.'

I pressed my lips together tightly and didn't answer.

'Aurora, he signed his last email to you 'Best wishes'. That is not the behaviour of a man who regrets his decision. It's the behaviour of a man who's already moved on.'

She didn't understand. Martin had always taken refuge in formality, especially at times of high emotion. Hadn't he presented me with a spreadsheet of projected costs saved by living together when he'd suggested I move in with him? It's not that he wasn't romantic — he had sweet little reminders set up on his phone to buy me flowers on my birthday and on our anniversary — but that his feelings for me were expressed in other ways. He provided for me, he took care of the finances, he changed the oil in the car. I didn't need declarations of passion — passion doesn't last. Just look at my mother's four marriages if you want proof of that. It's stability that counts.

18

'Which lane, Rory?' bellowed Auntie Lyd, nudging me with her elbow to get my attention over the rattling engine.

'What? Oh, left — it's the left lane,' I said. She swung the car into the lane without looking and ignored the cacophony of angry horns behind us.

'North Sheen, of all the places,' she huffed. 'What sane person wants to live in North Sheen, I ask you?'

I knew it wasn't a particular prejudice against North Sheen that was annoying Auntie Lyd; it was being forced to drive the car, which usually sat, immobile and gently rusting, outside her house. Auntie Lyd preferred to travel everywhere by taxi — for convenience, she said, but I think also because most of the drivers fondly remembered her star turn as Destiny Devereux in the eighties mini-series *Those Devereux Girls*, and often refused to charge her. The fact she had suggested driving the Travelling Skip at all showed how seriously she was taking my break-up with Martin.

'That's not fair,' I said, determined not to let her get to me. 'North Sheen's lovely, Auntie Lyd — you never even came and visited us there. It's so close to the river, and to Kew Gardens and — '

'I don't need to go there to know what I think of it,' said Auntie Lyd. 'Suburban. In London, but not on the tube. Puh, it's neither fish nor fowl. What is the point of living in this glorious city' — Auntie Lyd waved her cigarette for emphasis, but we were still inching past Wandsworth's distinctly inglorious Southside shopping mall, which didn't really serve her argument — 'if you don't take advantage of it?

'And a new build, too,' she sneered, curling her lip.

'Auntie Lyd, don't be such a snob,' I protested hotly. Our spartan, new, fully insulated and double-glazed house may not have been the romantic tumbledown cottage of my impractical dreams, but it was ours. Mine and Martin's. It was home. People were what made a house a home. Probably Auntie Lyd had forgotten that, running her own home as a business for so long.

'Martin doesn't have time to keep up with the maintenance an old house would need, he's too busy at work. And so am I, actually.'

In truth busyness had very little to do with it. Martin didn't agree with me that architectural quirks gave a place character. Where I saw the patina of the years, he saw the need for a bottle of Cillit Bang. Where I saw original sash windows, he saw draughts and high heating bills. It had taken just one viewing of a Victorian terrace in Putney, with Martin whistling disapproval through his teeth as he tapped walls and rattled window frames, to realize he would never be happy in an older house. I knew I could have tried harder to persuade him, but I also knew that if I succeeded, every roof leak or plumbing issue that came up would be laid at my feet for ever more. It didn't seem worth it. And when Martin found out there was an early-bird discount for buying our home off-plan from the developers, my half-expressed arguments crumbled to dust.

The Travelling Skip lurched around the corner

into the Marchmont estate. I know it sounds like something you might find on the pages of *Country House*, with stables and outbuildings and perhaps even a tennis court, but in fact it was a curving cul-de-sac of self-contained three-bedroomed houses, each staring blankly at the others through its PVC windows. And since the closest I'd ever been to owning a horse was riding a donkey on Salcombe Sands as a toddler, I can't say I had ever found myself lamenting the lack of stabling options.

'It's this one here,' I said. Our house was distinguished from the others by the pot of geraniums I'd put outside the front door, still just alive even in the depths of winter. I convinced myself it was a sign. The geraniums had survived against the odds: there was still hope for our relationship. Auntie Lyd swung into the driveway and slammed on the brakes, making us both lurch alarmingly towards the windscreen before being thrown back against the seats as the car came to a halt. She switched off the engine and released her seatbelt so she could turn to face me.

'These are perfectly nice houses,' she said. 'I'm not being a snob. But they're perfectly nice houses for someone else. Not for Rory Carmichael.'

'What do you mean?'

'I mean, who *are* you? Have you entirely forgotten?'

'I'm — I'm . . . ' I wasn't sure how to answer. I was Martin's girlfriend, that's who I was. I was half of MartinandRory. Without that to define me, who was I?

21

'I'll tell you. You're the niece who used to beg me to take her to the Victoria and Albert Museum when she visited London aged six. You're the girl who preferred touring the cathedral at Rouen to queuing up for ice creams with all the other thirteen-year-olds on the school French trip. You're the girl who asked for membership to the National Trust for her sixteenth birthday — I'm not saying I didn't think it was strange, Rory, frankly I'd rather have bought you a crate of alcopops; but it was *you*.'

I sat silently biting my lip like a sulky teenager while Auntie Lyd ranted on. It was true that I'd always had a passion for old houses and history, even from when I was tiny. While other girls were happy with the ersatz castles sold to them in cartoons, I longed for the real thing, poring over National Trust catalogues as if I might find the meaning of life hidden in the heavy stone fireplace of a medieval manor. Being dragged across the country by my mother as she sought a fresh start with the end of every marriage — until she gave up on England entirely and moved to Spain for love — had made me fascinated to the point of obsession with families who had lived in the same place for generations. I envied that certainty, that absolute knowledge of who you were and where you belonged.

'You're the girl who got a first-class degree in History of Art and an offer for an MA at the Courtauld Institute — which I still think you were idiotic to turn down. You're the girl who spends her working life at *Country House* magazine writing about art and houses that are hundreds of years old — '

'So I suppose you think we should have moved into a medieval castle?' I muttered crossly, sinking lower into my seat as if I might be able to slip down and hide amongst the detritus in the footwell.

'Don't be facetious, Rory,' she said dismissively. 'I am trying to ask why you — Rory Carmichael, who loves everything old, everything historic — why you ever imagined you would be happy here?'

I looked at my hands in my lap. And then up to the bare new brick of the front porch. I'd been planning to grow ivy over it to soften the harsh, just-built corners. So it wasn't the house of my dreams aesthetically, but it represented so much more to me than architecture. We were putting down roots. In years to come we'd be saying, 'We're the Peters family, from North Sheen,' instead of 'I'm Rory from — well, all over really, it's complicated.' That seemed worth a little sacrifice to me. I didn't feel like explaining all of this to Auntie Lyd — while Mum lurched from marriage to marriage, Aunty Lyd had never had a proper relationship for as long as I'd known her. She wouldn't get it.

'I moved here because Martin wanted to,' I said. 'Because Martin wanted to and I love him, and because you have to compromise in a relationship. That's how it works.'

Auntie Lyd shook her head as she ground out her cigarette in the overflowing ashtray. She blew a stream of smoke towards the windscreen; it broke on the glass, spreading out tendrils that obscured the house from view.

'Compromise means meeting in the middle, Rory,' she said, reaching to the back seat to pick up her handbag. 'It doesn't mean giving up your own identity so as to fit into someone else's life.'

She opened her door and brushed ash off her skirt on to the driveway. 'In any case, they'll only despise you for it in the end. Believe me.'

★　★　★

When I let us into the house, pushing open the insulation seal on the front door with a pop, it felt like my vision had shifted in the short time that I'd been staying at my aunt's. Instead of feeling welcomed by the home that I had shared with Martin for the last year, I saw everything as if through Auntie Lydia's eyes. The posters in the hallway of classic Ducati motorbikes (though a poster was the closest Martin had ever got to owning one; apparently the insurance premiums were prohibitively high). The expensive Gaggia espresso machine that took up half the kitchen worktop — even though Auntie Lyd knew I didn't drink coffee and never had. There was hardly a sign that I'd lived there until very recently. It wasn't that Martin had cleared away any indication that I had lived there; it was, I realized, that I had hardly allowed my presence to be felt in our home.

'It's freezing in here,' said Auntie Lyd, wrapping her arms around herself and rubbing her hands up and down to warm up.

'Martin doesn't like having the heating on for

24

more than an hour in the morning and an hour at night to take the chill off,' I said, looking over to the hall thermostat, which showed a chilly four degrees. 'He says anything more is a waste of money. A jumper's already paid for.'

'How cosy,' said Auntie Lyd, rolling her eyes. 'Like a lovely welcoming fridge-freezer. Well, let's get on with it then. Where shall we start?'

'Er, the bedroom?' I suggested. I thought starting with the most painful room would make the rest of it seem easier; like jumping straight into an icy pool rather than shivering hesitantly on the edges.

'Lead the way,' she said, gesturing up the stairs.

As we climbed to the first floor I steeled myself for the task ahead. The bed that we'd shared. The book I'd been reading, and left face down on the bedside table. The wardrobe, full of not just clothes but memories — the dress I was wearing when Martin had first spoken to me in the university library, the cardigan I'd had on when he asked me to move in with him, the dressing gown in which I'd been dumped. I wasn't sure how I was going to get through it without hysterics.

Pushing open the bedroom door, I clenched my teeth together. My heart fluttered in my ribcage as if I expected to see Martin kneeling on the carpet, contrite and begging for forgiveness. Possibly offering marriage. Instead four cardboard boxes sat at the foot of the bed, sealed with brown tape and neatly labelled in Martin's careful handwriting.

Clothing. Linen. Toiletries. Miscellaneous.

Auntie Lyd and I stared at them. The sum total of more than a decade, packed into just four boxes.

'Well,' Auntie Lyd said. 'That makes things easier, I suppose.' She rubbed my arm carefully, as if afraid I might drop to the beige carpet keening and wailing in grief. To be honest, I thought I might. As much as I'd been dreading packing, somehow the sight of those boxes made me feel as if I'd been cheated of the whole experience of saying goodbye to the life we'd had together. Although I couldn't prove that he hadn't shed a tear while sorting through my possessions, from here it seemed that Martin had packed everything up with all the emotion and pathos of a paid-by-the-hour removals firm.

'It's probably a good idea for you to have a quick look around in case he's missed anything,' suggested Auntie Lyd.

'He won't have done,' I said flatly. Martin's ruthless organization had been one of the things that had attracted me to him. After my chaotic childhood with Mum, his certain knowledge about how things should be done, his sheer reliability, had been as head-turningly attractive to me as a six-pack was to other girls.

'Let's have a look anyway,' she insisted. 'I'll check the bedrooms, you take the bathroom.'

She pushed me gently but firmly towards the en suite. As I stepped into the bathroom, the heels of my boots ringing on the hard tiled floor, I heard Auntie Lyd slide open the mirrored

26

doors of the built-in wardrobe.

I looked around the room. There was nothing in here of mine. Nothing at all. I hadn't expected there to be: Martin wasn't dishonest; of course he'd return everything that belonged to me. But there were some things here that didn't look like they belonged to Martin either. A bottle of floral-scented pink shower gel, and one of Herbal Essences shampoo. I turned my head towards the other side of the bathroom, slowly, as if expecting to see something truly repellent. And I did. An eyelash curler on top of the toilet. A packet of make-up-removing wipes wedged down the side of the sink.

It says something about my state of mind at that moment that I had a wild flare of hope that these might perhaps be the possessions of Martin's previously-unknown-to-me transvestite alter ego. Surely I could deal with that? I was an accommodating sort of person; we could work it out. But angry suspicion was slowly replacing the sick feeling in the pit of my stomach.

'Rory!' exclaimed Auntie Lyd, as I stormed past her and ran down the stairs. 'Where are you going?'

I furiously scanned the living room for more incriminating evidence, but everything was just as I'd left it: the huge flat-screen television crouched on the wall, its red standby light winking malevolently. I switched it on just long enough to confirm that it kicked straight in to Sky Sports as usual. The kitchen, too, seemed clean. Until I opened the fridge. Inside were a half-empty packet of fresh raspberries, two skinless chicken breast fillets and a carton of fat-free yogurt from Waitrose. I may as well have found Martin *in flagrante*. Left to shop for himself, he would never venture further than the corner shop or the takeaway menu. These were the supermarket shopping choices of a female of the species.

Auntie Lyd was right. Even bloody Ticky Lytton-Finch was right. He had another woman.

3

It was a bit of a surprise to me to find that I genuinely wanted to talk about Martin to Ticky when I got into work. Perhaps it was because Auntie Lyd was being annoyingly dismissive every time I tried to bring him into conversation. She held up a silencing finger whenever I mentioned his name; I would have got more sympathy from Mr Bits, her ancient marmalade cat. And perhaps it was because I had realized, while gnashing my teeth and wailing into my pillow (thank goodness Auntie Lyd had given me one of the rooms at the very top of the house), that I appeared to have very few friends left who were exclusively mine, rather than mine and Martin's. I couldn't call up Darren and Rebecca, or Anna and Max; for all I knew they were already arranging cosy paired-up evenings with Martin and Whoever-she-was. I was outside of the couple zone for the first time in eleven years, and I couldn't bear that any of them might see me pressing my face up against the glass, pleading to be let back in. I'd called Mum in Spain, where she lived with Steve, husband number four, but she'd been busy heading out to a golf lesson and hadn't had time to chat for long. I had even been desperate enough to consider calling Dad, before realizing that it would alarm him too much if I deviated from our usual scheduled calls at Christmas and birthdays only.

I'd spoken to my old university flatmate Caroline — first-time mother of a three-month-old baby — who had burst into sleep-deprived hormonal tears as soon as she heard my voice. I didn't dare make it worse by telling her about Martin. And by the time I hung up I didn't have the energy to face another rebuff. It seemed that, for all of my defensive insistence that I had plenty of other people to talk to, Ticky was the only one actually available.

Whatever my reasons, Ticky didn't seem remotely surprised by my sudden urge to discuss everything with her. She took it as her due; of course it was only a matter of time before I would volunteer my personal life for her dissection.

'I think this is, like, raaahlly healthy, Roars. First step to recovery and all that. So, like, tell me about the other woman,' she said, propping her elbows on her desk and resting her chin in her hands. 'Who is she?'

I felt my eyes fill with tears.

'I don't know who she is,' I said. 'I don't care.' That was a lie. I was desperate to find out who Martin's new woman was. I'd already spent an unhealthy amount of time on his Facebook page this morning, scrutinizing tiny thumbnail photographs of every woman on his Friends list. I had narrowed it down to a shortlist of ten before forcing myself to de-friend him for the sake of my sanity. But I wasn't about to share that with Ticky; I was too ashamed of my stalker-like behaviour.

'Yah, yah,' nodded Ticky with approval. 'Totes

the right attitude, Roars. There's no point obsessing over his new bird. You'll drive yourself crackers. How long do you think it's been going on?'

'Months,' I intoned glumly. 'He had a weekend away last month and now I think he must have been with her.'

'No *way* — the weekend in Wales? But he said he'd gone with his schoolfriends Paul and Al!'

Ticky's elephantine memory for detail never ceased to amaze me. She could remember everything about people's personal lives to the most ridiculous degree. If you said that you were going to a wedding on Saturday, Ticky would remember immediately, although you had mentioned it only once before, that this was the wedding of Annabel and Marcus, and wasn't she the one whose father had left his wife for her sister, necessitating some complex extended-family seating arrangements? If she ever focused her uncanny talent for recall on her job, she would be unstoppable.

'Yes, I'm certain of it,' I said, although I wasn't. I felt it was true and that was the same thing. I wanted to think the worst of him. It stopped me from wanting him back.

'Utter bastard,' sympathized Ticky. 'Did you really not suspect a *thing*?'

She tilted her head to one side speculatively as I spoke, prompting me with the practised skill of a professional interviewer and leaving tactical silences that I rushed to fill with teary rantings. When I finally ran out of confessional, she leaned forward for a machine-gun burst of sharp questions that, once finished, achieved what I had previously thought to be impossible. It actually exhausted my desire to speak about Martin. It was as if Ticky had wrung me out like a wet cloth. I knew my sense of release was merely a by-product of her blood-sucking; but the effect was astonishingly lightening. I wouldn't have believed that I could actually feel grateful to Ticky Lytton-Finch. Perhaps I had misjudged her all along.

'So, Roars, you're twenty-nine,' she stated briskly, twirling her hair into a bun at the top of her head. 'My sister says all the good men are snapped up by thirty-five. Tick-tock, tick-tock.'

Perhaps I had not misjudged her after all.

'It's far too soon for me to start dating,' I said stiffly. The very idea made me shudder. I'd always gratefully skipped over those complicated women's magazine articles about dating — when to text, how long to leave it before returning an email, whether or not you should have sex with your new man before you'd had the 'exclusivity' talk. It all sounded like a different world to the slow, long-ago unfolding of my relationship with Martin, where our accidental daily encounters in the university library had become less accidental as that first term went on, until, almost without our having ever discussed it, we were a couple.

'Well, Goouurd, of course it is too soon for you to, like, start another long-term relationship,' said Ticky, tossing her thick blonde hair to one side. 'But raaahlly, if Spreadsheets Martin is your only boyfriend then, like, that means you haven't been on a date in eleven years.'

'No,' I admitted. I didn't feel like going on a date for at least another eleven years, to be honest.

'Thing is, Roars, like, you don't have time to waste at your age.' She ignored my glare. 'Saahriously. I'm not suggesting you, like, try to find your future husband or anything, but you do need to get out there and get some practice. Try out a few duff ones to get back in the game, you know?'

'Oh God, I can hardly bear it,' I groaned. 'Duff ones?'

'Yah. You remember Hen Milroy-Pennington?'

'Do I?' I asked, uncertainly. It was never easy to keep up with the huge cast of friends that populated Ticky's social life.

'Yah, you do. Fashion PR? Tall? Dark hair?' That narrowed it down. At least 90 per cent of Ticky's friends, and the female staff of *Country House* for that matter, were blonde. In my early days at the magazine I had naïvely believed that there was some posh gene that bestowed blonde hair upon them, along with an inability to speak quietly and a propensity to turn up one's shirt collars for no reason. Then I had discovered that, with rare exceptions, they owed their colouring to the hand of an expensive hairdresser rather than nature.

'I think so,' I said, not really sure but wanting her to get to the point.

'Yah, right, well, Hen has just got engaged. Eiffel Tower proposal, baguette-cut diamond so big she can hardly lift her hand, announcement in the *Telegraph*: the works.'

33

'Right,' I said, feeling my face pinch up bitterly. 'How lovely for her.' Ticky really was extraordinarily tactless, I thought, bringing up engagements to someone so recently dumped.

'The point is, Roars, a year ago she set herself a proper mission to go out and meet as many men as possible,' said Ticky. 'She went on forty-three dates in the year before she met Hecks. Forty-three!'

'Hecks?'

'Hector Armstrong-Calthorpe? Number eleven in Tatler's Most Invited?' said Ticky, looking astonished that I didn't immediately recognize his name. Ticky and all of the *Country House* staff had a habit of assuming that everyone was as intimate with their social bubble as they were themselves. 'Not actually important, Roars. What is important is that she met a *lot* of unsuitable men before it all happened with Hecks. A lot.'

'Unsuitable men?' I echoed.

'Yah. Use them for practice, you know? Get used to the whole dating scene by going out with people you're not interested in — get the crap ones out of the way, right? Teaches you about what to avoid in future and then you're, like, all chilled and relaxed about dating when you meet a man you're raaahlly interested in.'

'Right,' I said, hesitantly.

'Yah, it's like me and old Fuckwit Farquharson? Totes unsuitable but the bonus is that I absolutely know for future reference that I am not prepared to get down to business with a man who wants to call me 'Nanny' in the sack.'

'Did he?!'

'Oh Goouurd, yes. I had to dump him when it escalated horribly one night,' she shuddered.

'How?' I demanded.

'I don't really want to talk about it,' said Ticky, looking away as if the memory was painful. 'Let's just say I didn't know until then that they made nappies in adult sizes. But now I know the signs, I won't be going there again.'

'What *are* the signs?' I said, in genuine fascination.

'Please — I can't,' said Ticky, holding out her hand to stop me prying further. It seemed her appetite for emotional sharing was strictly a one-way affair. 'Thankfully there is just one Fuckwit Farquharson, but the thing is there are lots of other fuckwits out there and you are bound to encounter some sooner or later, yah? It's good to get them all out of the way so you can get on with meeting someone great. I mean, surely there were some unsuitable men before you got together with Martin?'

'None,' I said, casting my eyes down to my desk in embarrassment. It wasn't like I'd been one of those teenagers who wore a chastity ring and swore to keep herself pure for marriage, but my love of ancient castles and encyclopaedic knowledge of William Morris textile designs were not exactly irresistible to the boys of my youth. When Martin first started talking to me in the university library I'd been as astonished by his attention as I was flattered.

'Sorry,' said Ticky, rolling her eyes. 'Stupido. Forgot he was your first proper boyfriend. But that is all the more reason you need to go out with some unsuitable men. I mean, most girls go out with, like, a series of bad boys in their twenties and then settle down with a nice sensible boy when they hit thirty. But you, Roars, you've spent your whole adult life in a relationship with a sensible man. A boring man, frankly. You, like, totally need to get some bad boys out of your system.'

'Define 'bad boy',' I said, with some trepidation.

'Well, have you ever been on a date with a tortured artist, for example?'

'No.'

'Guy in a band?'

'No.'

'Toyboy?'

'No.'

'Married man?'

'Ticky! No, I certainly haven't. I haven't been out with anyone unsuitable at all. Ever.'

'Well, Goouurd, of course the ultimate irony is the one man you do go out with for eleven years turns out to be unsuitable anyway,' Ticky said, sitting back with a satisfied smile. She was too pleased with her neat conclusion to consider that it might be painful for me to hear.

'Yes, I suppose so,' I said, wincing slightly.

'So you *have* been out with an unsuitable man, Roars — you can tick cheater off your list now.'

'Great.'

'But don't you see this is a good thing?' said Ticky with earnest enthusiasm. 'Getting unsuitable men out of your system is, like, progress. I mean, every nutter and loser you encounter brings you closer to realizing who is really suitable for you.'

'You're not really selling this to me, Ticky,' I said.

'Sahhriously, Roars,' she urged. 'The thing is, everyone's a little bit mental — even the good ones. Even you. But if you don't know what sort of mental is *your* sort of mental, then how will you recognize the right man when he turns up?'

'It's a nice theory, Ticky,' I said, looking at my watch to try to terminate the conversation. 'I'd probably better be getting on with things.'

'Oh faahrk, is it really twelve-thirty?' exclaimed Ticky, grasping my wrist to check the time. 'There's a Stella McCartney sample sale just off Bond Street; I'd better get a faahrking wriggle on. Laters, Roars, and chin up. It could be worse. You could be nearly *forty*.'

She collided with Martha Braithwaite, our formidable features editor, on the way out. A lady whose age, while undisclosed and subject to much office gossip, was certainly well over a decade north of forty. 'Sorry, Marth, no offence,' Ticky carolled as she barged past.

Martha frowned darkly. 'I just came to see how you were doing on the April layouts,' she said, peering into the office.

'Fine, Martha, just fine,' I said, completely untruthfully. I hadn't even looked at them and I could tell from Martha's gimlet-eyed stare that she knew it. 'Getting on to it right now.'

Her eyes narrowed with suspicion. She had always been an exacting boss, but ever since she had been passed over for the editor's job she had become even more demanding. Amanda had been parachuted in above her thanks to a bulging contacts book, impeccable breeding and a private income which allowed her to overlook the relatively impecunious salary. Middle-class Martha, for all her hard-won experience, simply hadn't been able to compete with a glamorous society blonde who was more used to staying in country houses than writing about them.

Even three years later, Martha seemed to feel the need to prove her superior journalistic credentials by leaping on everyone else's errors, as if the Bettertons might belatedly recognize her eye for detail and appoint her to her rightful role. As that was yet to happen, the more insecure she felt, the more she micro-managed the rest of us. Or tried to. Ticky and Noonoo were equally impervious as Amanda and just ignored her. Lysander had little time for her, and nor did Flickers. Which meant that the focus for most of her dissatisfaction was me.

I hadn't helped myself by failing to spot that our art director Jeremy had switched, after a long and drunken lunch, two captions in the proofs for the December issue, so that a Christmas cake was referred to as 'His Royal Highness the Prince of Wales' while our future monarch was labelled 'A nutty organic fruitcake'. The resulting press furore, and numerous cancelled subscriptions, had been probably Martha's happiest time at *Country House* since Amanda's appointment. Jeremy and I had shared the blame, while Martha grabbed the triumph.

These days I checked everything three times and now, under Martha's watchful eye, I bent my head over the proofs once again.

4

Auntie Lyd's two remaining PGs appeared to have a complete inability to sleep beyond the first glimmer of dawn. Despite my being the only person in the house who needed to get up for work on a regular basis, in my short time there I'd discovered I was the latest riser by several hours. I would wake most mornings to the heavy clunk of the water pipes as the boiler warmed up for Percy Granger's usual 5 a.m. shower. This early alarm call told me I had two hours until I needed to get up, but I found I rarely went back to sleep. Although rolling myself back up in the duvet should have felt decadent and lazy, instead I felt trapped in a cocoon of obsessive thoughts about Martin. I found I could whip myself up into a frenzy of fury by remembering everything he ever did to hurt me or betray me; I replayed scene after scene in my head until the repetition made me weep at the very tedium of my own thoughts. I imagined him romping with his new girlfriend in the en suite bathroom — a scene which I enjoyed ending by having them both slip on a fat slug of her Herbal Essences shampoo, injuring themselves horribly. But it was no comfort from the awful truth, which was that the clanking of the pipes woke me, each morning, from dreams in which Martin and I were still together.

This morning I had been woken just after five

by an unearthly scream, which seemed to emanate from the very walls of the house. This was followed by several shouts and a slamming of at least two doors. My thoughts of Martin's perfidious ways were disturbed by an animated discussion on the landing below my attic room — annoyingly I could hear only voices, not actual words. I realized there was no point in staying in bed any longer. Pulling on a baggy jumper over my pyjamas, I headed halfway down the stairs.

I leaned over the banister to see Auntie Lyd, hair piled on top of her head, leaning against the door of her bedroom in a draped Moroccan kaftan. Her arms were folded across her chest as a dressing-gowned Percy ranted at her, his skin a furious red from face to amply exposed chest. I had never seen Percy's hair, usually Brylcreemed into flat submission, standing up on end like that, nor so white. As I got closer, I saw that what I had mistaken for hair was a thick pelt of shampoo bubbles.

' . . . a deliberate attempt on my life,' Percy was protesting.

Even after three weeks at Auntie Lyd's, I still couldn't help myself from seeing Percy as his most famous role, Peter Bennett, the hapless and accident-prone hero of late-seventies sitcom *Whoops! There Goes the Neighbourhood*. Although Percy had only made three series, it had run on the BBC for most of my childhood, and it was a rare day that a repeat couldn't still be found on some nostalgia channel. But these days Percy performed exclusively in the theatre, which he pronounced, in his fruity vowels, 'theee-YAHH-tahh'. Although I was sure he could have afforded his own flat, living at Auntie Lyd's allowed him to indulge in his greatest pleasure: bestowing advice, usually from the breakfast table while clad in his embroidered dressing gown, on the young actors who raced in and out of the attic bedrooms in between auditions and rehearsals. They, in turn, were honoured to receive his patronage and so everyone was happy. The fact that the theatrical youths were no longer in residence meant he was, as far as I could see, in a state of constant fury.

'Who would do such a thing?' Percy demanded, projecting his voice as if he were trying to be heard from the other side of Elgin Square. 'I could have had a heart attack. 'Oh me, my heart, my rising heart.''

'Shakespeare?' asked Auntie Lyd. Percy used so many theatrical quotations in conversation that everyone had given up commenting on them. I suspected Auntie Lyd only did so now in order to distract him.

'Lear,' said Percy, pulling the dressing gown tighter around him. 'A tormented man, Lydia, a tormented man. As indeed, am I.'

'Percy, I think we should both accept it was nothing more than an accidental rush of cold water,' said Auntie Lyd, rubbing her eyes. 'No one was trying to kill you. There's a problem with the boiler, you know that.'

'I know that Avery woman has had her eye on my room for years, Lydia,' Percy sniffed. 'She will stop at nothing to have it for her own. Base, treacherous woman.'

'Percy, if I know her at all, Eleanor is already downstairs at the kitchen table,' said Auntie Lyd, rubbing her eyes. 'She has nothing to do with the hot water going off. It's just a problem with the pipes.'

'I'll give *her* a problem with the pipes,' said Percy, drawing himself up to his full height (not actually very high, especially not in monogrammed velvet slippers). 'Lydia, whether Eleanor is behind this, or whether it is the result of your poor maintenance of this property, I should not wish for my death to be on your conscience. I demand that you address this problem immediately.'

Auntie Lyd yawned. 'I'll call a plumber first thing in the morning, I promise.'

'It is already first thing in the morning!' said Percy, becoming redder.

'It's five o'clock. I'm not about to pay emergency call-out rates just because you had an unexpectedly cold shower, Percy,' said Auntie Lyd patiently. 'Now come downstairs to the kitchen and I'll boil a kettle to wash that shampoo out of your hair.'

'An utter disgrace,' muttered Percy, following her down the stairs. Neither of them had seen me listening to their conversation, but now that I was up I followed them. The company would make a welcome change from my usual solitary morning thoughts.

Auntie Lyd had been right about Eleanor — immaculately made-up, already dressed in beige slacks and a pink sweater, she perched like a small bird on the edge of one of the rickety kitchen chairs, her three-inch heels tucked delicately over the struts. Although she seemed perfectly relaxed, she never leaned back into her chair, or dropped her elbows on to the kitchen table — her posture remained beautiful at all times. I had no idea when Eleanor rose in the mornings, but so far I had yet to come down to the kitchen without finding her in just this position, fully dressed, perfectly made-up, teacup in hand. It didn't matter if I emerged at seven, or ten, or, as this morning, at five. I wouldn't have been particularly surprised to learn that she sat there all night.

Eleanor Avery had been a Pinewood starlet back in the days when the British film industry imagined itself to be a genuine rival to the Americans. Although her star had waned early — though who could forget her saucy vicar's wife seducing the curate in *Not Now, Padre?* — her glamour remained undiminished. These days she sustained herself with a recurrent non-speaking role as a market trader in *EastEnders*. She could regularly be seen in the background, packing fruit and vegetables into brown paper bags with an exaggerated delicacy that, her friends knew, owed less to Method-style immersion than an effort to prolong the life of her pale-pink manicure.

'*There* she is,' said Percy triumphantly, as if he had caught Eleanor with a dripping spanner in one hand and the *Reader's Digest DIY Guide* in another.

'Good morning, Percy,' said Eleanor, delicately sipping from her teacup. 'Good morning, Lydia, Rory.'

'What are you doing up?' said Auntie Lyd, realizing that I was behind her.

'I just heard voices,' I said. 'Wanted to see what was going on.'

'Well, my dear,' said Percy to me, puffing out his chest. 'You've arrived just in time for the show.'

'Show?' said Eleanor uncertainly, her hand trembling a little.

'Yes, you spiteful old crone, I know it was you who turned the water to cold this morning; you may sit here looking all innocent, but I know what lies beneath the surface!'

'The surface?' asked Eleanor, looking to Auntie Lydia for reassurance.

'Don't think I'm not wise to your games, Avery,' said Percy. 'I am on to you. Treachery!'

'Percy, dear,' said Eleanor, her watery eyes widening innocently, 'you appear to have something peculiar in your hair.'

As she spoke the bubbles, which had until now sat on Percy's head as tightly as a shower cap, loosened — perhaps it was the warmth of the kitchen that did it — and the whole mass began to sink down around his ears. Percy's confusion at the descent of the sudsy wig silenced him momentarily and Auntie Lyd took advantage of the situation to manoeuvre him away from Eleanor and towards the deep kitchen sink.

'Now, Percy,' she said, briskly. 'I'm just going to rinse off this shampoo and then it will be as if nothing ever happened, yes? And then I will call a plumber who will sort out the pipes so this doesn't happen again, and *you* will apologize to Eleanor.'

'Over my dead body,' muttered Percy, lowering his head into the porcelain sink. He stopped grumbling as Auntie Lyd ladled warm water from the washing-up bowl over his head, rinsing away the offending bubbles. The soothing sound of the water splashing into the sink brought calm to the kitchen at last.

'It quite reminds me of being a child,' said Eleanor, from her perch. 'Watching my mother wash my little brother in the sink.'

'My mother used to do the same,' Percy's voice echoed from inside the sink. 'I still remember waiting my turn with my sister as the kettle warmed up.'

Auntie Lyd smiled at me over Percy's bent back as Eleanor and Percy engaged in a conversation of gently competitive nostalgia — who had been the last to get indoor plumbing (Percy), who had had to go to school in their brother's shoes (Eleanor), how young people today had no idea how lucky they were. Percy's accusations were all but forgotten. Shortly afterwards we were all sitting at the wooden table, sharing a pot of tea.

'Well, it might have been an earlier start than I'm used to,' said Auntie Lyd, 'but it's worked out rather nicely, sitting here all together like this, hasn't it? It's nice to catch up with you before work, Rory.'

'Aurora, dear,' said Eleanor, turning her pale

45

eyes towards me. 'Your aunt says that you are terribly important at *Country House* magazine these days. Features editor, is it?'

'Oh, er, not quite,' I said. 'Just deputy features editor.'

''Just' deputy?' declared Percy. 'No such thing as 'just' a deputy. Did dear Paul Scofield say that I was 'just' his understudy? Did the audience say I was 'just' Pericles, Prince of Tyre, when I had to take on the matinée performance? No! 'Deputy' means you are ready and able to step into the breach at a moment's notice — there is no 'just' about it.'

Eleanor rolled her eyes at Auntie Lyd, who stared back with the expression of non-committal blankness that she habitually adopted in the face of strong provocation from both sides.

'I'm not sure it's quite *A Star is Born* at *Country House*,' I said, smiling into my tea at the idea that I might some day take over from our Martha in a wild burst of applause and glory, instead of to general indifference.

'I'm sure you are already quite the star, dear,' said Eleanor politely. 'Are you working on anything interesting right now?'

'Rory has her own column, don't you, Rory?' said Auntie Lyd. 'Behind the Rope — all about the hidden highlights of stately homes. I have back issues of every *Country House* since she started it — they're all stacked up in the living room if you want to have a read.'

'What, that big pile of magazines that Mr Bits's bed is balanced on?' asked Percy.

'The very same. Just shove him off if you'd like

46

to see one. I recommend June 2010 on the electric tablecloth at Castle Drogo,' she said. 'Fascinating.'

I stared at her. I'd had no idea that Auntie Lyd even knew I wrote a column, let alone that she had bought the magazine every month to see it. My own mother had never had much interest in *Country House*, and if Dad read it then he had never bothered to say so, but as we were only in touch a few times a year that wasn't a great surprise. Martin, I probably do not need to tell you, thought my column amusing and trivial but failed to see the point of it, much as, I was beginning to realize, he had pretty much failed to see the point of me.

Auntie Lyd smiled back. 'Now,' she said. 'Porridge, everyone?'

Eleanor said she wasn't hungry, and Percy leapt on her, claiming if it weren't for the whisky in her teacup she might find she had more of an appetite in the mornings. I watched, wide-eyed, as Eleanor's trembling hand replaced her cup in the saucer, her lips pursed. Was it really whisky? At five-thirty in the morning? But she didn't deny it. Instead she said that if you asked her, the nearest Percy had ever been to Paul Scofield was watching *A Man for All Seasons* on television, and then that was it — the insults raged across the table once again.

Auntie Lyd just got up and started making porridge for everyone. I went and joined her by the stove, although it hardly needed two of us to stir the pot.

'All right, darling?' she asked.

47

'I'm fine, thanks,' I said, pulling open the cutlery drawer and taking out spoons as Percy and Eleanor sniped at each other behind us.

'Auntie Lyd?'

She turned to face me, the wooden spoon in her hand.

'Auntie Lyd, do you think it's weird that I've only had one boyfriend?'

She smiled. 'It's not weird at all, darling. Haven't you been with him for ever? Why are you worried about that all of a sudden?'

'I just, well, someone I work with said it was weird. That I hadn't been out with anyone else before Martin. Especially not anyone unsuitable.'

'Unsuitable?'

'You know, bad boys, wrong'uns. Non-sensible people not called Martin.'

'Why would you want to go out with 'wrong'uns'?' asked Auntie Lyd, turning back to the porridge. 'It seems to me like you've only just escaped from one of those.'

'Yeah, that's what I think,' I said, reassured that there was no need to follow Ticky's advice. Not that I had intended to anyway.

Auntie Lyd stirred the porridge thoughtfully. 'Although I suppose it is quite instructive to go out with a few unsuitable men in one's youth.'

'Really?'

'Well, darling, look at your mother. I love her dearly, but she only identifies the unsuitable ones after she's exchanged her vows, doesn't she?'

'Mmm,' I agreed. Four marriages was an impressive tally for someone who was not actually a Hollywood celebrity.

Auntie Lyd carried on stirring. 'Have you told her about Martin yet?'

'Yes,' I sighed, remembering my fraught conversation with Mum. 'She said I should never have let such a good one go, and basically implied it was all my fault.'

'Well, that doesn't surprise me,' said Auntie Lyd. 'Your mother is a wonderful woman in many ways, but she does have a tendency to back the wrong horse when it comes to relationships.'

'She got it right in the end,' I said. I rarely felt like defending Mum's love life, but she had been with Steve for fifteen years now, and it seemed like she might have finally settled down.

'She did, darling,' agreed Auntie Lyd. She tapped the wooden spoon on the side of the pan. 'But it took three divorces and a move to Marbella. Yes, I wonder. Maybe things would have been different if she'd just been out with a few unsuitable men instead of always marrying them.'

'So, do you think it would be a good idea for me to date unsuitable men?' I asked hesitantly.

Auntie Lyd considered my question. 'That's up to you, darling,' she said. The hint of a smile hovered on her lips. 'Unsuitable men can be awfully good fun, I suppose. As long as you don't take it all too seriously. Why not?' She shrugged and began ladling porridge into individual bowls.

I handed a bowlful each to Percy and Eleanor, whose argument had slowed not one bit. My own I ate slowly, thinking. It was a strange Venn diagram in which my aunt's opinions corresponded with those of the Honourable Ticky

49

Lytton-Finch. First they had both correctly predicted the existence of Martin's other woman, now they thought I should date unsuitable men: the oddness of receiving the same advice from two such very different people made it harder to dismiss. But it was all far too early. I wasn't ready to start dating anyone yet, let alone anyone unsuitable.

5

The office was oddly quiet that afternoon. Amanda had been seen stalking to the ladies' with Martha hot on her heels. This, we all knew, had nothing to do with synchronized bladders and everything to do with the unspoken rule that the two of them retreated there when their arguments became too heated to be contained within the glass walls of Amanda's office. The ladies' was set apart from the rest of the office and offered, if not complete isolation, at least less danger of being overheard by everyone. But it was a pointless exercise, since it only drew more attention to their arguments.

Ever since Amanda had been appointed editor of *Country House*, the magazine had been moving steadily away from its former incarnation as the home of detailed features on the architecture and art treasures of the nation's finest country houses (never stately homes — only tourists called them that) into a glossy sort of estate agents' catalogue full of well-appointed rural homes with paddocks, swimming pools, good transport links and invitations for offers above two million pounds. These days there were a full fifty pages of property advertisements before you got to a single page of editorial; and when you did get to the meat of the magazine, it was more likely to feature a glittering society gathering than an article on the history and provenance of Harris tweed.

This change in focus, and accompanying change in fortunes, had thrilled the Betterton family, but was to Martha's enormous — and vocal — displeasure.

The staff were so accustomed to the rows that we all took note of how long each one would last. Over her tenure at the helm of *Country House*, Amanda had got her Martha-crushing down from half an hour to an impressive personal best of just three minutes (from the precise second the loo door swung shut behind them to the second it opened again). Yes, of course we timed it; we even bet on it — and you would have too if your usual day was spent working on a feature titled The Moor the Merrier, about whether Exmoor or Dartmoor was, well, merrier.

Bids were kept small, at only twenty pence, but a win could still earn you enough for an afternoon-easing piece of cake, not to mention the esteem of your peers. The excitement of these small stakes was only increased by the fact that all betting in the office had been explicitly banned by the Betterton family after the Great Queen Mother Betting Scandal of 2002, shortly before I arrived, in which Lysander Honeywell had been discovered to be running an office syndicate speculating when the aged royal would go to the great throne in the sky. Old Mr Betterton, who knew the Queen Mother well enough to refer to her as 'Cake' (for even royalty is not immune from the ridiculous nicknamings of the upper classes), had led the office in a more-in-sorrow-than-in-anger school-assembly sort

52

of meeting in which everyone had to swear allegiance to the Crown, renounce the Devil and promise never to commit the sin of gambling while on *Country House* property.

So of course the second the door to the ladies' closed, every single staffer set their watch and made their bet. Everyone kept their heads down, eyes flicking regularly between the ticking clock and the bathroom door. Swearing was heard as the hushed minutes passed. Noonoo's bet on ten minutes evaporated. My twelve minutes were over and still the door remained shut. Only Lysander and Flickers were left in the game, having bet on twenty-two minutes and twenty-five, respectively. Lysander glided past the bathroom door after twenty minutes, holding a piece of paper to try to look like he was engaged in work, but giving himself away by seeming to recall, unconvincingly, something that meant he had to double back on himself to pass back again twice more. I didn't know why he didn't just press a glass to the door and openly listen in; it wouldn't have been any less obvious.

Ticky finally broke the silence. 'Holy macaroni, Roars,' she hissed across our office. 'I am, like, absolutely busting for a waz. What the faahrk do you think they're arguing about this time?'

'Just the usual, I expect,' I said. Noonoo frowned over from her desk with a finger to her lips; clearly she too was hoping to hear something from the direction of the lavatories.

'Saahriously, can't they have their stupid rows somewhere else?' whispered Ticky furiously. 'I am, like, this close to actually buying a chamber pot for our office. And don't even think I am joking.'

'You could always get a catheter,' I suggested helpfully.

'Yah, thanks, Roars, can we just, like, stop talking about wee, it's making me more desperate.'

'So I shouldn't mention waterfalls or gushing taps or anything?'

'Roars, you faahrking cow,' said Ticky, wrapping one leg over the other and squeezing them together tightly.

At last, after twenty-six minutes, the door to the ladies' swung open and Amanda emerged. She glared around the office as if challenging anyone else to dare argue with her, but no one would meet her stare; all eyes were fixed with unlikely dedication upon computer screens. Flickers kept his face impassive, but marked his triumph with an under-the-table air-punch of victory.

'Come oooon, Martha,' hissed Ticky, bouncing up and down in her seat, legs still crossed. 'Pull yourself together and get out of there or I'm going to have to go in.'

The door opened again, more slowly this time, and Martha emerged, her downcast eyes and slumped shoulders telling us, as if we didn't already know, that she had been defeated once more.

Ticky leapt out of her seat and ran to the loo, closely followed by Noonoo, who had obviously also been holding on for too long. They sped past Martha without even looking at her. In fact, out of a combination of sympathy and fear, no one ever properly looked at Martha when she emerged from one of her bathroom battles. She had been known to snap furiously at any attempt to speak to her after one of Amanda's dressing-downs.

So I was pretty surprised when she stopped in the doorway to my office, raising her red-rimmed eyes from the beige office carpet. I waited for her to speak first, in case this was a trick and she was just looking to shout at the first person who made the mistake of attempting to open a conversation. Behind her back, Flickers held out a palm to his office-mates, demanding his winnings.

'Rory,' Martha said finally.

'Hi, Martha,' I said.

'Rory, it turns out that I can't make it to Seaton Hall on Monday after all,' Martha said, pressing her lips together and pausing for a moment. 'Amanda — Amanda suggested that someone else can be more easily spared from the office.'

'Oh, Martha,' I said. I knew she'd been working on this feature on the Duke of Delaval's restoration project for months. Even without the leverage of an aristocratic background, she had persuaded him to allow *Country House* an exclusive preview of Seaton Hall before the official press day, when the usual crowd of gravy-train-boarding journalists would troop from room to room in a recalcitrant pack.

Martha looked up at the ceiling instead of at

me. 'I specifically asked that it should be you who replaced me.'

'That's really kind of you, Martha,' I began. 'Are you sure?' Martha jealously guarded her country house visits, and having been forced to give it up, I feared she would be more critical of me than ever.

Martha straightened up, shaking her head a little and smoothing her black skirt, its cheap fabric shiny with age. 'It is enough that Amanda is sure,' she said, suddenly brisk and efficient. 'It's too late to change the schedule so you'll have to stick to the one I've already set up. Train Monday morning at seven-thirty, meet the photographer there. Staying overnight at the Delaval Arms on the estate, coming back Tuesday on the eleven-forty-five, okay?'

'Okay,' I said. 'Who's the photographer? Nicky Bentworth?'

'No, the condition for exclusive access was that we had to use the duchess's nephew as the photographer, Lance Garcia. You'll meet him up at Seaton Hall.'

'Lance Garcia?' I asked, frowning in confusion. 'I've never heard of him, have you?' *Country House*'s photographers were all from the same upper-class tweedy stable, and practically interchangeable. They were Hugos and Olivers and Barnabys. Never Lances.

'No. The duchess is an American,' sniffed Martha, in much the same way that she might say, 'The duchess has recently escaped from a psychiatric institution.' 'I believe her nephew is from San Francisco. Quite what he will know

56

about photographing historic houses, I do not know. The entire situation will require firm supervision. I hope you are up to it.'

'I'm sure I am,' I said. Actually I was pretty unsure, but the opportunity to get far, far away from London and thoughts of Martin was too good to turn down. Not to mention that I might actually be able to get a hot shower at the Delaval Arms.

'Good. I'll bring you my dossier on Seaton Hall later today,' said Martha. She started to walk away and then turned back. Her face was calm, but her hands betrayed her, holding on to the door frame with white knuckles as if she might rip it away from the wall, Incredible Hulk-style. 'I am sure I can trust you to do me justice.'

I frowned at her departing back, unsure what she could have meant. Was she trying to appoint me as some kind of deputy in her battles against Amanda? A fellow class warrior against the rahs? There was no way I was stepping into anything that might drag me into the bathroom wars. Or did she mean that Seaton Hall was too important to mess up? Like I didn't know that — the entire heritage industry had been itching to get a glimpse of the property for the five years that the duke and duchess had been restoring it. But the duchess had refused to allow anyone access until completion; all anybody knew was that it had cost millions. It was a privilege to be invited to see it at all, let alone before everyone else.

'Kerr-ist,' said Ticky, swinging back into her

seat and exhaling loudly. 'What a relief. I peed like a fricking racehorse.'

'Nice; thanks for sharing.'

'Did I just see Martha leaving?' she asked. 'Tell me she didn't come to share her thoughts on the bathroom argument?'

'No,' I said. 'She's told me I have to take over her visit to Seaton Hall next week. The Duke of Delaval's restoration feature.'

'She gave up Seaton Hall!' Ticky exclaimed, scenting drama. She leaned forward in her seat and propped her elbows on the desk in official listening stance. 'No way! Goouurd, that must have been what they were arguing about. She wouldn't have let go of that without a fight. But why are they getting you to do it?'

'I don't know. Martha said something about me being her specific choice. And she wants me to keep an eye on the photographer — he's not got much experience.'

'Weird,' mused Ticky, putting her feet on the desk and swinging from side to side on her wheeled chair as she stared at the ceiling. 'I wonder if Maaahn let her choose her replacement to soften the blow of not letting her go. Of course Marth would think you're the easiest person to boss around — she can kind of do the feature by proxy through you.'

'Er, or she thought I'd do a good job, Ticky,' I said.

'Oh yah,' she agreed. 'Course you will, Roars, I'm not doubting that. But admit it — Martha's got a much better chance of getting you to do her bidding than she has, like, Noonoo or someone else who'd stick their own ideas all over it and insist on taking the glory.'

'Whatever,' I snapped. Ticky was so pushy and thick-skinned, she didn't see the virtues of doing things my way — carefully, gently, behind the scenes, without causing offence. Just because I didn't get involved in stand-up rows, or insist on doing things my way, it didn't mean I was a pushover.

'Who's the photographer?' she asked, flicking her hair over to one side.

'What's that got to do with anything?' I asked.

'Who. Is. It?' said Ticky, a mysterious smile playing on her lips.

'No one we know — some random relative of the duchess.'

'Male or female?'

'Male. What are you getting at?'

'Name?'

'Lance Garcia,' I said.

'Lance?'

'He's from San Francisco.'

Ticky smirked, and flicked her hair once more.

'Roars, oh my Goouurd, unsuitable man alert!'

'What?' I said. 'Lance Garcia? This isn't a date, Ticky, it's a Monday night in Derbyshire doing a feature.'

'Umm, news flash, Roars. V Day?'

'V Day?' I echoed.

'Yah, Monday's Valentine's Day, Roars, had you really not noticed?' Ticky shrieked with laughter. 'And you're going to be stuck in a romantic country hotel with a totally, brilliantly unsuitably gay man. It's too good. I couldn't make it up. Oh Goouurd, it's priceless.'

'Wait a second,' I said. 'How do you know he's gay? Do you know him?'

'I don't *know* him, Roars,' Ticky sniggered, 'but he's a photographer, he's from San Francisco and his name is *Lance*. Sahhriously. Even *you* should have been able to work that one out.'

Should I? Why was it that, the moment I split up with Martin, it seemed like the world was operating in a way that everyone understood but me?

6

Although I supposedly now lived in one of London's greener areas, it was never more obvious than on leaving the city for the real countryside that Clapham Common was little more than a glorified urban roundabout. The Common's muddy, trodden-down expanses of brown grass, dotted with dog mess and greasy fried-chicken containers, were still barren and wintry, but the windows looking out of the train to Derbyshire showed the first signs of spring. A few stubborn streaks of snow were visible on the tops of the distant hills, but the fields on either side of the track looked fresh and new in the weak morning sunlight. Tree branches, still bare against the sky, were softened and greened by the buds of new leaves; bright yellow daffodils shone out from the hedgerows. As the train made its way north, early lambs could be seen in the fields, huddled next to their mothers. I spent far too long staring out of the window daydreaming, and thinking about last spring when Martin and I had been preparing to move into our new home. It felt like it had been a long, long winter.

Martha had extravagantly booked herself a seat in first class, and the carriage was almost empty this early in the morning, except for a couple of businessmen tucking into their full English breakfasts. The restful journey made me even less inclined to get to work, but after I changed trains at Stockport I ordered a cup of Earl Grey to try to wake myself up, and pulled Martha's dossier out of my bag.

Not for our features editor the clinical efficiency of a PowerPoint presentation. It looked as if she had scooped the contents of her recycling bin into a manila envelope: the dossier bulged with cuttings, Post-it notes and torn-out notebook pages. On top of the bundle of papers, held together by a straining red rubber band, was a memo in which Martha provided a full list of questions for me to ask, stressed various points of history that I should touch on in the feature, instructed me in how to address a duke and duchess (including her recommendation that one should curtsey, but she would leave this to my discretion) and, highlighted in bold, the hot tip (as Martha saw it) that the duchess, the former Bibi Wishart of Marin County, California, had been in her previous life a textile designer, which necessitated as many gushing comments as possible on all fabrics within the Seaton Hall estate. *Compliment the curtains!* exhorted a scribbled note in the margin. Underlined three times was her final comment: *Think Romance! Her Grace intends to hire the house out for weddings.*

Instead of feeling, as Ticky had suggested, annoyed by Martha's micro-management from afar, or affronted at her assumption that I wouldn't know how to behave, I felt grateful and a bit sad. Looking at all the work she had put into the trip made me feel guilty that I was the one who was getting the benefit. Of course I owed it to her to conduct the visit as she would have done (though I drew the line at actually curtseying). The memo also revealed that I would be collected from Buxton Station by a driver. I marvelled at the luxury and felt another pang for Martha.

Usually press trips were an undignified bunfight in which a large group of journalists would be herded from the train into a rackety minibus, the seating on which operated under an unspoken but rigid hierarchy. At the front sat the broadsheet journalists, holding themselves apart from all of us by virtue of their importance and influence, and a certain studied *ennui* that spoke of the many more important matters that weighed on their minds, which we lesser hacks could not possibly understand. In the middle seats sat journalists like me, from small, specialist magazines of limited and dwindling readership, clinging on to the last vestiges of former glory. We had prestige, thanks to the historical reputation of our publications, but no power. And we were glad of the day out; at least, I always was. At the back of the bus, like the naughtiest school-children, sat the freelancers; usually of a certain age, they were here for one thing only: free stuff. Overexcited by the proximity of so many others in comparison to their solitary working-from-home existences, they talked loudly of former trips, the superiority/inferiority of the lunch/tea that had been provided for us, their glory days as features writers for now defunct publications, and the poor state of current heritage journalism. They were to be avoided as much as possible, since they would almost certainly try to pitch a feature to you if you showed the slightest weakness and also because everyone, from the editor of the *Sunday Times* Home section downwards, superstitiously feared that their lowly career prospects might be catching.

There were no such indignities on this trip. I was astonished to be collected not just by a car, but one driven by a chauffeur in a peaked cap and a uniform. I felt like a heroine in a 1930s novel as the car hummed smoothly through the country lanes towards Seaton Hall, although I suspected my ancestors in the thirties would have been found scrubbing pans in the scullery rather than swanning around in motor cars. As we swung through the gates of the estate, the Delaval Arms, where I'd be staying tonight, could be seen across the park, a low stone building that had once been a hunting lodge. It was a full five minutes along a wooded drive before the Hall itself came into view, but it was worth the wait.

Seaton Hall had, as do all the true country houses of England, a history that spanned the centuries with a combination of elegance and eccentricity. It had begun its existence as a Saxon hall, built for defence and warmth rather than beauty, its only windows high slits in the thick stone walls. This was the view that greeted me: forbidding and yet beautiful, with a heavily studded wooden door set deep within the Derbyshire stone. I knew that beyond this hall the house had been added to extensively: there was a Georgian wing, and a Victorian Gothic addition, not to mention a poor attempt, sneered at by Pevsner, at a Palladian walkway on the eastern side. But the mishmash of styles had been saved by the continuity of the local limestone, which gave the building, the dossier said, an overall appearance of harmony. None of this could be seen as we proceeded up the drive; only the ancient hall was visible, presenting a façade that must have hardly changed for hundreds of years. I imagined that the door might open to reveal a rush-strewn floor, the duke and his retinue eating off trenchers and throwing the bones to a pack of rangy wolfhounds by the light of a roaring fire.

But when I stepped out of the car, the door was opened by someone who could only be Lance Garcia, running excitably towards the car in a distinctly twenty-first-century manner.

'Aurora Carmichael?' he asked, flinging his arms around me while I stood stock-still in surprise. 'OMG, I am *so* glad to see you. Bibi wanted you to get the whole aged-retainer-opening-the-door experience, but I said, 'Bibi, this girl is *British*, she is not going to be impressed with a butler like we tragic Americans, she's probably met a million butlers working for *Country House*,' am I right?'

'Hello, you must be Lance,' I said, stepping backwards to see him properly. I wasn't quite sure how to answer the butler question as really it was only rich Americans and investment bankers who had them these days. Most posh British people were too impoverished to afford one.

'The very same,' Lance said, leaning into the car and instructing the driver to drop my overnight bag at the Delaval Arms. With a crunch of gravel the silent chauffeur drove away.

As I followed Lance up the wide stone steps to the open door of the Hall, I had the opportunity to admire his Californian ensemble, as exotic and unlikely in this environment as a bird of paradise in a henhouse. His long, lean legs were clad in lemon-yellow denim, and his feet tripped up the steps in vivid-green Converse. A checked shirt peeped out from under his lime V-necked jumper, and a silver skull ring flashed its diamante eyes on the smallest finger of his left hand. I suspected that Ticky might be right about the duchess's San Francisco nephew.

'Are you ready?' asked Lance, hesitating for one moment to maximize the suspense. I nodded. He beamed as he pushed open the door to a vast hall, the uneven flags of the floor not covered in rushes, but buffed to a dull shine by the wear of generations and lit by a low-hanging iron chandelier which blazed with real wax candles. Although it was still morning outside, the narrow slits of the windows allowed in only a glimmer of light, so the candles lit up the room just as it must have been when it was first built. It was magical.

I stopped on the threshold to stare. Holly and ivy had been wound around the wooden staircase, which led up to a carved gallery that stretched across one wall. Enormous mirrors, spotted with age, hung on the walls and reflected the lights endlessly, as if we were in a series of candlelit chambers instead of just one room. It was not grand in the embellished, fussy style of Versailles; it was sparsely substantial, feudal, imposing. On the bottom step stood the duke and duchess, smiling in silent greeting, and in evident satisfaction at my reaction.

'You love it, right?' said Lance, linking my arm with his and giving me a squeeze. 'I said to Bibi, 'You have got to give her the full candle experience the second she walks through the door,' and now I've seen your face I know I was totally right, right?'

'Totally,' I echoed, entirely forgetting in my awe that I was meant to be admiring the textiles and addressing my hosts in the correct manner.

The duchess stepped towards me, extending her hand graciously. 'Miss Carmichael?' she asked, in a cut-glass voice that did not betray the faintest suggestion of her American background.

'Your Grace,' I said, bobbing my knees and lowering my head completely involuntarily. Somehow the combination of her grand manner and the imposing hall made me feel instantly subservient; perhaps some dormant servile instinct had been awakened, or perhaps the unseen hand of Martha had stretched across the miles to push me downwards into a curtsey.

The duke appeared next to her and shook my hand too, with hearty bonhomie rather than condescension. Now that they were closer, I could see that both of them were older than I had first thought; the candlelight had flattered them both into seeming much younger. He was probably in his early fifties, with a slightly receding hairline and a florid complexion set off with a mustard-coloured cravat. His tweed jacket could have belonged to his father's father and, judging by the frayed leather patches on the elbows, probably had. His red trousers were spattered with mud and what looked like a dog's pawprint.

The duchess seemed to have stepped out of an entirely different story; her accent may have lost any American inflection, but her appearance loudly announced her origins. She could have been any age from thirty-five to sixty, as she had that slightly immobile face that spoke not of youth but of cosmetic assistance. Her blonde hair was highlighted and blow-dried and not one strand dared to wave out of place. Her manicure was immaculate. Although I had to admire her dedication to her appearance out here in the wilds of Derbyshire, I unkindly wondered if she knew that such grooming instantly excluded her from full membership of the aristocracy, despite her title. She would have to get a bit of dirt under her nails to truly belong here; to buy some of her clothes from agricultural shows, like the Duchess of Devonshire, instead of from Net a Porter. As someone who did not fit into this world myself, an observer rather than an insider, I was finely attuned to others who had got it a little bit wrong, and I felt an instant sympathy for her that even her condescending ways could not extinguish. The duchess's shrewd eyes picked up on this immediately, one outsider recognizing another, and her welcoming smile froze into a rictus of distaste; clearly she preferred her guests to be awed rather than sympathetic.

Lance's not fitting in, however, did not count. He was not trying to blend in; nor to suggest that he belonged here in any way. He was a thrilled and awed tourist and his enthusiasm was contagious. While the duke and duchess stood stiffly like paper cut-outs from a book, Lance whisked me through the hall.

'Now you spoke to Martha, right? I loooooove Martha, she is entirely amazing. Devastated not to meet her. The piece you're doing is romance, romance, romance, right? And what better day to do it than Valentine's Day?'

'Yes, absolutely,' I said, glad to have been forewarned. The duke and duchess had restored the house, which had been allowed to fall into disrepair by his disreputable father, at vast expense. Now they had to pay for it and they planned to do that by offering Seaton Hall as a venue for weddings and other large events.

'So I thought we'd start off with the chapel — which I have done out in some darling little lights — and then some pictures in the walkway, which we'll need to have finished before the light begins to go, and we'll finish off with more shots and an interview with Sacheverell and Bibi in the hall. Right?'

Just as he was whisking me out of the door at the far end of the hall, the duke cleared his throat.

'I say, Miss Carmichael, we haven't even offered you a cup of tea. Shall I ask the kitchen to send one up?' he called, his voice ringing in the empty room.

Lance sighed dramatically and exchanged a look with the duchess. 'Darling, there is no time for tea,' the duchess said, supposedly to her husband, but with a warning look in my direction that left me in no doubt I should not even think of saying yes. It seemed clear to me that I was a means to an end to her; she wasn't about to waste time offering me refreshments when there was work to be done.

'Oh no, thank you, I'm fine,' I said quickly, and the duchess offered me a tight smile before leading the duke away up the stairs. 'I love the curtains!' I called, far too late.

'For a country that is so totally obsessed with tea,' confided Lance, leading me through the door to the Palladian wing, 'it is *beyond* impossible to find a skinny soy chai latte anywhere around here. Sometimes I don't know how Bibi stands it.'

'How long has she lived in England?' I asked.

'Oh, years,' said Lance, dragging me through the Victorian Gothic revival wing far too fast — I had no time to look at the imitation fan-vaulting on the ceiling, let alone the crenellated thrones that, although they looked medieval, had (said Martha's dossier) in fact seated a mere two generations of Delavals. 'Bibi came to St Martin's for fashion school when she was twenty and never left. Now you'd think she was born here, am I right? That accent! Uh-mazing, just like Madonna.'

I murmured a non-committal sound of polite agreement; now was not the time to debate Madonna's mastery, or lack thereof, of the

English accent. In any case, I barely had the chance to say anything as Lance rattled through the schedule he had set up and told me how he saw the feature taking shape. I made a few feeble attempts to interject with Martha's instructions, waving the dossier at him as if I could club him into submission with its sheer weight, but although Lance would leap willingly on each idea, he subsequently flattened it in minutes. Since he had been, as he told me, a regular visitor to the house over the five years of restoration, it was impossible for me to deny that he had a far better knowledge than I of how to show it to its best advantage. I wondered if Martha herself would have been able to resist his bulldozing excitability — perhaps she could have steered him towards her own ends, but I doubted it. Even she, I felt, would have realized, in the face of Lance Garcia, that the dossier I waved had now turned into a flag of surrender.

The renovations had been conducted in a way that was guaranteed to thrill the *Country House* reader. The duke and duchess had declined to use a large firm of interior decorators in favour of many small teams of artisans. Father-and-son carpenters had recreated the wooden stairs of the ancient hall by hand. The prayer cushions for the chapel had each been individually hand-stitched to show local landmarks and the Delaval coat of arms. Paints and dyes had been created according to traditional methods — there was woad here, and elderberry, and a yellow made from onion skins. Weaving had been done by two sixty-something women who called themselves,

71

inevitably, Warp and Weft. Lance had spent the last few years photographing the work's progress in timeless black and white: a hymn to craft and tradition. I noted, leafing through his portfolio, that he had even photographed the plumbers, but most likely because they were exceptionally good-looking rather than amazing craftsmen. Despite Martha's instructions, I had to admit that Lance's emphasis on traditional crafts bettered her ideas: his black and white photographs would form the basis of the piece, while he and I would create a few full-colour tableaux that showed off the finished results as romantically as possible to appeal to moneyed brides.

'The chapel, the chapel, the chapel,' chanted Lance, whisking me out of the covered walkway and on to a gravel path that wound through a copse of ancient yew. 'You know,' he confided, 'the family legend says that each of these trees — some of them are over a thousand years old — contains the soul of a knight who laid down his life in battle.'

'Which battle?' I asked breathlessly, looking around me at the looming trees, already captivated by the history of it all.

Lance shrugged. 'Like I know. But imagine the trees lit up with fairy lights, right?' he said. 'Or even, maybe, along the path, flaming torches in braziers? You can see it, right?'

And I could — it would be romantic and mysterious, although perhaps fairy lights were a little undignified a decoration for the hardened manly souls of the tree-bound ancient warriors.

Lance made me stand at the top of the steps to the chapel, which was sunk down in a yew-surrounded hollow, while he ran ahead and switched on the lights. I shivered, pulling my coat tighter around me; even in the light of day this place was a little spooky.

'And here is the *pièce de résistance*,' he announced, and I stepped into the chapel. It had been whitewashed into a stark purity that contrasted with the dark greenness of the yew trees which brushed against the mullioned windows. Lance had eschewed candles here for hundreds of tiny lights which surrounded the altar, leaving the rest of the chapel in almost-darkness. Instead of flowers, it had been decorated with lichen-covered branches which cast their shadows across the walls. Although it was a consecrated chapel there was something pagan and ancient about it; it wouldn't have surprised me if the long-dead soldiers had stepped out of their yews to kneel here in front of us, offering sacrifices to their Saxon gods.

'And here's the thing,' said Lance, interrupting my open-mouthed staring by promenading down the aisle as if it was a catwalk. He stopped at the altar and spun on his heel to face me. 'We just need someone to look a bit bridal in a few shots — and Martha and I think it should totally be you, right?'

'Wh-what?' I said, horrified. This wasn't at all what I had signed up for. I was here as a responsible journalist and representative of *Country House*, not a dress-up Barbie for Lance's entertainment.

'I know, I know,' said Lance, waving his hands. 'Martha said you might be all weird about it, but it's nothing much — no face shots, no full-body shots, just a little bit of human interest. We'll have Sacheverall and Bibi in the Hall and in the walkway, but here we want someone young and bridal-looking. And you're just perfect, darling, with that amazing red hair of yours.'

I felt tears well up alarmingly. I felt so very far away from being bridal. It seemed impossibly cruel that Martha should have lined me up to play that role just after I'd been dumped by the man I had thought I would marry. I wouldn't believe that she had done it on purpose — she must have not thought it through. Luckily the weak light in the chapel hid my trembling chin.

'I — I'm not sure,' I wavered. 'I don't really like having my photograph taken.'

'Oh, Aurora,' said Lance, skipping back up the aisle towards me, both hands outstretched in entreaty.

'Rory,' I insisted.

'Rory,' said Lance. 'It's going to be a few shots of, like, your hand holding on to a man's hand — mine, of course, there's a dire shortage of male models up here, I'm sorry to say. It'll be the back of your head bowed near the altar, that kind of thing. It's not like, *America's Top Model* or anything: no full bridalwear, no hanging from harnesses, no smizing, I swear it. Bibi's going to be in the other photographs and not one of Sacheverell's female staff is under, like, two hundred years old. Please say you'll do it.'

I remembered how hard Martha had worked

to arrange this. I thought about how she had begged me to do her justice.

'Do you absolutely swear that you're not going to put me into some hand-woven wedding dress?' I asked. 'Because I will not put on something scratchy and hempy made by Warp and Weft.'

'Oh, darling,' laughed Lance, 'as if. You don't have to get changed at all; we'll make it work beautifully without any fuss. Just you and me. Trust me.'

7

By the time I got to my room at the Delaval Arms I was exhausted. I had no idea how professional models did it — but then professional models most likely didn't also have to interview a duke and his frosty duchess as well as supervise the photo shoot while being directed in how to assume poses of a bridal nature. I threw myself backwards on to the bed and leapt immediately back up again, having forgotten that Lance had insisted on decorating my hair with holly for the final shots of the day. I picked the spiky leaves gingerly out of my hair and released it from the twist that had restrained it for the afternoon.

I had imagined I'd have a quiet evening on my own at the inn, but Lance had suggested joining me for dinner and, as he had been excellent company all day, I'd happily accepted. Dining with a stranger seemed infinitely preferable to eating by myself on Valentine's Day. On my first Valentine's Day alone for a decade. It wasn't that Martin and I had made a big deal of Valentine's. In fact we'd always stayed in on the night itself because he said all the restaurants put up their prices too much for just one over-commercialized night. His birthday was in March so we had our big night out then, which made sense since Martin liked to really treat us — it was his money after all — and we couldn't have afforded to go to somewhere like Claridge's on two consecutive months. But I'd loved our quiet Valentine's nights at home. Just the two of us, with a special meal that I'd made, and maybe a DVD together afterwards. I didn't need hearts and flowers to love being with Martin.

I caught sight of myself in the mirror, shoulders drooping as I sat on the edge of the bed, the corners of my mouth turned down like one of those Venetian masks meant to represent tragedy. Snap out of it, Rory, I told myself, and forced a smile at my reflection. Martin is no doubt spending Valentine's with his new girlfriend. You are here, at the Delayal Arms, with an oddly dressed, enthusiastic American who would probably prefer to be on a date with someone from Grindr. Both of you are making the most of the circumstances. You owe it to Lance Garcia not to droop all over the table like some half-drowned Ophelia descending into heartbroken despair. It could be worse.

So I made a special effort, as if I was dressing for a proper date instead of — what? A pity date? A business meeting? The evening ahead was strangely undefined, which was maybe what was making me feel weird. I always felt safest when I knew what role I was playing, where I fitted into a particular scenario. Although I'd been intimidated by the icy duchess when I'd interviewed her, I'd known that with enough bowing and scraping, and several compliments on the textiles, I could get her to unbend a little. The duke was easier to work out; he just needed some jolly-hockeysticks teasing and for me to lavish attention on his black labrador. I was the efficient, knowledgeable journalist from *Country House*, respectful and slightly awed. By the end of our interview the duke had invited me to stay for dinner, but the duchess had sharply reminded him of a prior commitment. Thankfully Lance had come to the rescue by insisting on accompanying me to the Delaval Arms; he was probably looking for an excuse to get away from his aunt's romantic celebrations. The former Bibi Wishart didn't strike me as the sort of woman who'd let her husband get away with a DVD and a night in.

I realized as I walked down the corridor to the dining room that I had probably taken more trouble over my appearance for this evening with Lance than I had for the last five Valentine's nights with Martin. I was freshly showered, wearing heels and a pale-lavender dress from Topshop, and had spent half an hour on my make-up instead of my usual five minutes with a mascara wand and a lip gloss. I wondered if it was true what Martin had said, that I'd let myself go with him. I hadn't become obese or stopped shaving my legs or anything, but I had probably stopped making this sort of an effort since we so rarely went out. Shouldn't I have tried a bit harder to keep his attention? Shouldn't I have realized that a man like Martin needed to be proud of the girl on his arm? I shouldn't have taken him for granted. It was weird how I hadn't heard from him at all, except for an efficient cheque for my share of the deposit on the house. Like I had entirely ceased to exist for him, even though his place in my head was still very much occupied. Stop thinking about Martin, I reminded myself, and squared my shoulders, pushing my chest forward and lifting my chin. If I didn't feel confident, I could at least fake it for one night.

Lance was already waiting at the table, dressed in skinny jeans, a checked shirt buttoned right up to his neck and a fitted purple cardigan. His face wore a look of faint amusement as he scanned the room. I wasn't sure exactly what was making him smile: himself, or me, or just the rather improbable situation. We had been given a table that sat slightly raised on a dais at the top of the room, overlooking the other diners, as if on display. I suppose if you were somebody who cared about such things — Michael Winner, say — you would have declared it to be the best table in the house. The maitre d' certainly seemed to think so, leading me towards Lance with a strange combination of deference and condescension that said, quite clearly, *I realize you must be someone of importance to have bagged this table, but I want to make it absolutely evident that I have no idea who you are, and nor do I care.* The room was already nearly full of couples, their faces shining with determination to have a good time. A few of the men looked strained already and I wondered if, from our vantage point, we would be witnesses to any proposals tonight.

'Rory!' Lance exclaimed, leaping to his feet at my approach. I kissed him hello and let the maître d' seat me and, a step too far I felt, shake

79

the napkin out of its fan-shaped arrangement and spread it across my lap.

'Great table,' I said, more because I thought he'd probably arranged it than because I enjoyed being raised above the other diners.

'Mortifying, am I right?' he answered, rolling his eyes at me. 'Sacheverell said we had to have it, nothing but the best for our visitor from *Country House*. Hey, nice dress, I see you got the memo. We totally match — his and hers. Hilarious.'

He had that American way of saying things were hilarious without actually laughing, which I have always found a bit disconcerting. It's almost as if conversation is being appraised rather than experienced when someone comments, 'That's funny' instead of just laughing. I found myself answering in kind though.

'Yes, hilarious,' I said, but smiling to show that I did find it quite funny. With our accidentally matching outfits and our special table of romance — all champagne flutes and tasteful arrangements of roses — we looked like we were being set up for another *Country House* photo shoot. *Were* we being set up for another *Country House* photo shoot? 'We're not being photographed tonight, are we?'

Lance laughed comfortably. He didn't seem to find any of this awkward. 'Your duties are over, Rory, this is just a thank-you from me to you, right? I totally swear we're not going to demand anything from you tonight. Well, not anything you're not prepared to give, am I right?'

His eyes twinkled playfully and, if I hadn't

known that he was gay, I would have thought he was actually flirting with me.

'Ha,' I laughed, nervously.

'No, seriously, we were all kinds of worried when Martha dropped out like that. Not the best sign, you know? But it's been a great day, and I totally know you'll write a great piece. Martha said you were the best journalist at the magazine — she hand-picked you for it.'

'She did?' I asked. How unlike Martha. I wasn't unduly flattered, since it seemed likely to me that she'd said it more to mollify the concerns of the Delaval family than to compliment me.

'Yeah, and I've got to say, you handled Bibi like a dream. She can be an A-one pain in the ass, God forgive me for saying so. But it all worked out.'

The steel-haired waitress, as intimidatingly unsmiling as the maître d', arrived in time to spare me the dilemma of whether or not to agree with him, which seemed rude to my hostess, or disagree and imply that he was indiscreet and treacherous to have spoken like that about his aunt. The waitress carefully lifted a bottle of champagne out of an ice bucket, wrapped it in a napkin and poured out two glasses with her other hand held behind her back, gently bowing as she did so. It was a gesture that suggested, rather than deference, that she was doing us a very great favour by serving us. As I watched her, I caught myself unconsciously inclining my head back at her and quickly snapped back upright in case she thought I had been attempting to condescend to her in some way, as if I was the duchess instead of the duchess's lowly guest in a high-street dress.

The waitress took our order from a short, handwritten menu that was clearly aiming hopefully at a Michelin star — all foams and jellies where I would have preferred a comforting stew of some kind. I let myself be led by her suggestions, partly because I wasn't sure of precisely everything on the menu (salsify?) and partly, I admit, because I hoped it might make her become a little warmer towards us. I felt that she had, correctly, identified me as insufficiently grand for the honour of occupying the top table, and as for Lance, well, insufficiently English was my suspicion. I shouldn't have worried though, because when it was Lance's turn to order he teased and flirted until he'd forced a reluctant smile to appear on her face.

Once we were left alone, Lance lowered his voice to a whisper: 'Unclench, am I right?'

'Me?' I asked.

'No! Jeez, like I'd say that to you! I meant Mrs Danvers over there. I mean, an emulsion of *froideur* served with a foam of disapproval, am I right?'

'You are very right,' I agreed, with relief. 'She has totally terrified me. I don't even know what I ordered — I was too scared to ask any questions.'

Lance leaned over the table confidingly. 'I am so glad to hear you say that — I thought it was just me with my gauche colonial ways that she was objecting to.'

'Well, obviously, if you hadn't started singing 'The Star Spangled Banner' and chanting 'U-S-A, U-S-A' after ordering your starter, she might have been less disapproving, am I right?'

'Do you always do that?' Lance asked, with a gentle frown.

'Do what?'

'Imitate the way people talk.'

'Oh God, did I?' I cringed.

'Yeah, you did,' he said, but smiling so that I could see he hadn't taken any offence. 'You've been doing it all day. Dropping in 'totally' and 'right'. It's okay, I'm not offended or anything. You did it with Sacheverell and Bibi, too — got all *King's Speech* clipped vowels. And then with the waitress — you totally copied her body language when she was pouring the drinks.'

I twisted the napkin in my lap with mortification.

'I'm so sorry, Lance,' I said. 'I didn't mean to be rude, really. I've always done this, ever since I was little. I just pick up on people's accents. It's incredibly embarrassing.'

Lance shrugged. 'Don't be embarrassed. I expect you're just trying to make people feel comfortable around you. That's not a bad thing. And your Californian accent's not at all bad, you know.'

'Oh shut up,' I laughed, but of course I managed to emphasize the 'up' and make myself sound like Paris Hilton.

'Really, you should be an actress,' he teased.

'I can't help it,' I answered. 'We just moved a lot when I was little — all over the country. And you know how mean kids are — I mean children. I had to lose my Geordie accent pretty quickly when we moved to York.'

'Geordie?'

'Er, yes, I don't suppose you'd even know what that sounds like,' I laughed. 'It's from the north-east, a bit sing-songy. Hawey the lads, you know?'

He looked at me blankly. 'I don't know. But I do understand not everyone here talks like the Queen.'

'Except Bibi,' I said.

'The Queen *wishes* she was as posh as Bibi,' grinned Lance.

'Totally.'

'Isn't it, like, not posh to come from the north?' asked Lance. 'Have you been all finishing-schooled to speak properly?'

'Ha,' I laughed. 'Finishing school of life, Lance. I'd just got the hang of the Yorkshire accent when Mum took us to Dorset.' He looked blank again, clearly not understanding the drastic leap of linguistics I'd had to take to adapt to yet another accent, aged nine. 'Ummm, ooo-arrr Thomas Hardy? Hello, my lover?'

'Your lover? You want me to be your lover?' He raised his eyebrow.

I laughed. 'It's just what they say there, to everyone.'

'Sounds like somewhere I should visit.'

'And you can eat a Dorset knob,' I suggested.

'A what?'

I sputtered with laughter at the expression on his face. 'It's a biscuit,' I said.

'Like biscuits-and-gravy biscuit?'

'No — more a cookie. Well, more of a dried-up bit of old bread dough. It's not very nice, actually. But a good name, am I right?'

'You're doing it again!'

'Oh God, sorry. Got a bit carried away with the Dorset knob gag.'

'As anyone would,' said Lance, pursing his lips comically.

By the time our desserts arrived — heart-shaped of course — I had forgotten entirely about trying to play any sort of a role. Lance was supremely hilarious company, so much so that I forgot about who I was meant to be for the evening and just had a good time. It felt as if the pressure was lifted — no matter what Ticky might have said about Lance being an unsuitable man, I hadn't had so much fun on a night out in ages. The interview was over, the photo shoot was done, everyone was happy with how it had gone. Conversation was easy and fun; there was no subtext because we hardly knew each other, and it wasn't like we were on a date or anything, so there was no pressure about whether or not we liked one another *like that* or how the evening would end.

Perhaps it was our superior seating, or perhaps it was because I was having such a good time, but instead of feeling like a sad inferior singleton having a meal with a gay man on Valentine's Day, I felt boozily certain that no one else at the Delaval Arms was having as good a night as me. Except maybe Lance. Because both of us were outsiders here, and because when it came to fitting in I'd rather have joined Lance than any of the other diners, we'd spent the evening like two wildlife-documentary makers studying a watering hole. With our bird's-eye view we had surreptitiously witnessed, with guilty fascination, two arguments — one of the teeth-clenched, words-hissed variety, and one from the school of silently storming-off-to-the-loo. One marriage had been proposed, and accepted, under our noses, to a smattering of applause from other couples, and anxious seat-shifting from a few men. Our favourite couple had failed to address more than ten words to each other over the course of their meal. Lance, who had a better view of them than me, would update me every time a new word was spoken, 'He said, 'Very tasty.' That's up to nine!'

For the first time since I had split up with Martin I saw that life as a single girl did not have to mean moping around on your own, wishing you were part of a couple. I could have fun in the most unlikely circumstances, with someone whose existence I hadn't even been aware of a week ago.

'Is this a traditional English dish, then?' said Lance, pointing his fork at our heart-shaped puddings.

'Pannacotta?' I laughed. 'Hardly. But I suppose they thought spotted dick wasn't very romantic.'

'Are you going to make cock jokes all night?' said Lance. 'I thought Englishwomen were supposed to be all refined, not potty-mouthed.'

'It's a real pudding,' I protested. 'Honestly.

86

Steamed sponge with currants. It's disgusting. Be glad you don't have to eat it.'

'Well, I don't know,' said Lance. 'Who's to say I wouldn't enjoy a soupçon of spotted dick?'

'Oh God, Lance,' I said, 'please can we be new best friends? I really think a gay best friend is totally what has been missing from my life.'

Lance lifted his head and stared at me. 'Gay?' He looked horrified. 'You think I'm gay?'

'A-aren't you?' I asked hesitantly.

'Rory, why ever would you think I'm gay? Haven't we been flirting with each other all night?'

'I-I just thought,' I stammered. 'I mean, you're wearing eyeliner . . . ' I trailed off as he put down his spoon and pushed away the pannacotta. All trace of humour left his face.

'Seriously? Are you that judgy?'

'I didn't mean to upset you, Lance,' I said, flustered. 'I'm really sorry.'

'Oh, don't apologize,' he said, waving a hand in front of his face dismissively.

'It's just my friend at work — she said that you, well, because you're from San Francisco . . . ' I dug myself deeper. I couldn't seem to stop talking. It must have been the champagne. I felt as if I was watching from the outside while a friend of mine made an utter fool of herself. I wanted to kick my own leg under the table, really really hard. 'And — and because your name is Lance.'

'Right,' he said. He put his napkin on the table, and moved his champagne glass an inch to the left while he composed himself. 'Listen. Even if my name was Bender McGaylord and I came from Gayville, Arkansas, I would hope that an entire day and night in my company would count for more than the opinion of someone you work with. Someone who's never even met me. What have I said or done that would make you think I'm gay?'

'It's not an insult, Lance, I'm not homophobic,' I protested.

'Look, I don't think it's an insult to be called gay,' he retorted. 'What, one minute you think I'm gay, next I'm a bigot? I thought you were meant to be this, like, social anthropologist. The girl who moves all over the place and interprets the behaviour of the natives. Seems like you're not all that good at it.'

'I'm sorry, Lance,' I said. From the corner of my eye I could see that all the couples who had provided our entertainment for most of the evening were now shamelessly staring at us, as if we were the Delaval Arms-provided floor show.

He leaned back into his chair. 'Jeez, the gay best friend. That's a doozy, Rory. It really is.'

He smiled tightly at me as I blinked away tears of shame. 'Look, don't cry about it. Seriously. It's not the first time. I don't expect it'll be the last. And, like, you're British, I should have expected it.'

'It's not because I'm British,' I said. 'It's because I'm a total idiot, Lance. Honestly. I — I've just got out of an eleven-year relationship. I don't know anything about men any more. Not a thing. I'm beginning to wonder if I ever did. And I especially don't know anything about men who wear eyeliner.'

He offered me a tiny wintry smile. Of sympathy? I couldn't tell. And in any case my powers of people-reading were clearly entirely lacking, so I wasn't about to trust myself.

'Or men called Lance,' he said, his stony face melting slightly.

'Or men called Bender McGaylord,' I said.

He smiled again, a little less frostily.

'Eleven years, huh?' he asked.

'Yup. We broke up just over a week ago.'

'Jeez,' he said. 'No wonder you're so totally clueless.'

And so it was that my very first date with an unsuitable man was only revealed to be such by the time we got to pudding. Once we'd drunk our coffees — Lance ordered a butch triple espresso, I suspected just to make a point — it was clear that nothing would happen between us. There are some things that quench a man's interest for ever, it seems, and one of those is having his sexuality questioned by a dim-witted English girl. I couldn't say I blamed him.

8

'Er, excuse me, Roars, but why is it my fault that you accused a straight man of being, like, in the gays?' demanded Ticky.

'Because,' I spluttered, trying to save face after relating the whole sorry saga to her, 'because *you said*. You said he was called Lance and was from San Francisco and that meant he was definitely gay.'

Ticky looked quite astonished. But if she hadn't put the idea into my head, would I really have made such a complete idiot of myself? She had to take some responsibility, surely?

'But like, Roars, you were actually there? Like, you met him, you nutter. Couldn't you make up your own mind? What the faahrk did it have to do with me?'

'But, but he was wearing lemon-yellow jeans and a green jumper! I never thought to question it!'

'Darling, can you really not tell the difference between, like, a homosexual and a fauxmosexual?' asked Ticky, her eyebrows almost touching, so deep was her frown of concern. She appeared to have moved from annoyed to anxious in one moment.

'Fauxmosexual?' I asked.

'Yah, like he wears moisturizer and has a cleansing regime and a, like, interest in fashion that borders on the fruity, but he is absolutely all

90

man all the way all the time,' she said. 'You've never even heard of one?'

'Martin didn't wear moisturizer,' I said.

'Roars, you are like, fricking backwards sometimes but, okay, let me explain. The fauxmosexual can confuse some people because he is, like, a stealth straight. Sort of like the Trojan horse of straight men,' Ticky confided, coming over to sit on the edge of my desk as if imparting a valuable lesson. 'Like, he allows women to assume he's in the gays to gain closer access — women don't feel he's any sort of a threat, right? And then, when their defences are down, he lunges in for the kill.'

'Oh God,' I said, shuddering as I remembered once again Lance's horrified face as he had gently explained that he was not gay.

'How do you know all this stuff, Ticky?' I groaned, my hands over my eyes as if I could hide from everything. 'How do I not?'

'Unsuitable men, Roars,' said Ticky. 'I told you. A girl learns about this stuff through encounters with unsuitable men. It's what dating is all about.'

I groaned. If the incident with Lance was any indication of my dating skills, then perhaps a life of semi-seclusion at Auntie Lyd's was preferable. At least it would save me from running around shrieking wild speculations at sexually ambiguous strangers in country house hotels.

'Like, Roars, doesn't this just show how much you need to do this?' asked Ticky, gearing up for another assault on my weakened defences. 'I mean, if you're so dense that you can't even tell who's in the straights and who's in the gays, doesn't that tell you something?'

I wondered what it did tell me. Apart from the fact that I was a bit of an idiot. A judgemental idiot with faulty gaydar. But I wasn't ready to admit that Ticky might be right.

I was saved by the sight of Noonoo, tossing her mauve pashmina over her shoulder as she marched purposefully down the corridor towards the meeting room.

'Editorial meeting!' I said, with an enthusiasm born out of relief rather than any real happy anticipation.

'Oh faahrk,' sighed Ticky. 'Not just editorial. It's the faahrking ideas meeting, too.'

Tuesday's editorial meeting was always the nadir of the week, but this was the worst of all meetings: the monthly call for features ideas for our next issue. In the pre-Amanda days editorial meetings were interminable all-day affairs, in which the merits or otherwise of a piece on carpet beaters could be discussed for an hour or more. Amanda ran a tighter ship — meetings were a less agonizing yet still bum-numbing two hours — but her tactic for shortening the meeting was a fairly brutal approach to rejecting features ideas.

Mollie, the blushing intern who had been with us two weeks, opened the meeting by pitching her first feature. I knew she had been working on it late last night, since I'd been there myself, unwilling to head back to Auntie Lyd's for another dose of tough love and second-hand smoke.

'I — er,' began Mollie, and I knew she was already doomed. Our meetings were like a harsher version of the Just a Minute panel game. Any hesitation or deviation was immediately leapt upon and punished. 'I'm proposing a feature — '

'I know you are, this is the editorial meeting. That's what it's for,' snapped Amanda. 'Get on with it.'

'Um,' said Mollie, the paper in her hand beginning to tremble. 'Wallpaper — from early Chinese hand-painted examples, with reference to Chatsworth, through the archives at Sanderson.'

'Yeees,' said Amanda, tapping at the laptop that sat opened in front of her. She spent most of our editorial meetings catching up on her email correspondence, with only half an ear on the meeting itself.

'We could get advertising alongside from some of the big names, and, er,' said Mollie, bravely persisting even though Amanda had already turned her attention to Lysander and was whispering in his ear.

'The pictures would be beautiful,' Mollie continued.

'Done to death — *including* last February's issue, if you had bothered to check. No. Next?' said Amanda.

Mollie blushed even more furiously and folded up her page of notes, placing it on her lap beneath the desk. Her eyes glittered with tears and Ticky tilted her head towards her with speculative interest.

'Anything else?' asked Amanda. 'We're still two features short for the April issue and I'm not even certain we will get the Pippa Middleton interview since *Tatler* offered her the cover.'

'Sewww,' said Noonoo from the end of the table, flicking her blonde mane like a pashmina-wrapped pony. 'I saw Nickers Stanhope over the weekend? She's opening up an eco-lingerie boutique and teashop at Stokeley? It's, like, a fairtrade, organic Agent Provocateur, but with gluten-free cupcakes?'

Noonoo was a contributing editor, which meant, as far as I could see, that she came into work when her busy schedule of shopping and lunching brought her in the direction of the *Country House* offices, and dropped poorly spelled features about her braying friends into my in tray. Noonoo's ideas always revolved around the lives of herself and her coterie of fabulously wealthy friends, who took up their pens to offer lifestyle features with such down-to-earth tips as 'When clothes shopping, buy three of everything — that way you've got one for each house', or 'Why it's an utter nightmare getting planning permission for a swimming pool in the basement of your Grade I listed home'. There was a time when I had had to stifle my laughter at her pitches — I'd had to resolve never to catch the eye of Jeremy, our art director, as she proposed yet another feature using the word 'mumpreneur' to describe a banker's wife who'd got a sideline in scented candles. But these days, more often than not, I found myself nodding in agreement. Not because I'd had a *Country House* lobotomy, but because I know that this is exactly what Amanda wants. And what's the point in arguing with that?

'Nickers says she and her sister will pose in the undies with, like, a plate of cupcakes?' Noonoo continued, with sublime confidence. 'And she says we can run a special reduced-price entry to Stokeley for the readers — two for the price of one plus a free cake. We can sell the pics to a national for pre-publicity too?'

'Perfect,' said Amanda, her head snapping up from her laptop. 'Three thousand words and get the pictures soonest. Why can't the rest of you bring me stuff like this? Young, fun but still perfectly *Country House?*'

Noonoo bowed her head smugly. I felt Martha's rage next to me. She didn't have to speak for the entire staff to know that the very idea of posh totty in their underwear gracing the illustrious pages of *Country House* appalled her. Amanda's mission to bring a younger readership to the magazine was a direct affront to Martha's years of giving the existing readership what she believed they wanted: scholarly features on aristocratic homes, gardening and art history.

'Ticky?' said Amanda, suddenly. 'You haven't had a features idea for weeks.'

'I, er,' said Ticky, her usual confidence slightly shaken by the direct attack. 'Just been buttering up a few rellies, Amanda, but you know how tricky these old boys can be. I'm, like, this close to getting Uncle Jasper's Mustique memoirs — he was, like, raaahlly close to Princess Margaret back in the day. *If* you know what I mean.'

'Not good enough,' said Amanda. 'I, for one, have heard enough about Princess Margaret's Caribbean exploits to last me a lifetime. Bring me Lady Helen Windsor wife-swapping on the Île de Ré and we're talking, Ticky. Martha?'

Martha coughed and shuffled in her seat. 'I've come up with some ideas for the Marvellous Englishwoman column, as you asked.'

'Let's have them then,' said Amanda, looking up from her laptop, less out of interest in Martha's ideas than in preparation for dismissing them out of hand, as she usually did.

'Vita Sackville-West, Virginia Woolf, Agatha Christie, Dorothy Whipple,' Martha read from a list in her hand.

'Dorothy Whipple?' said Amanda scornfully. 'Martha, sometimes I think you wilfully misunderstand me. While I am sure these women were marvellous in their day, I specifically asked you to find living, contemporary Englishwomen for this feature. Twiggy, Joanna Lumley, Kirstie Allsopp, that sort of thing.'

Martha sniffed as if something unpleasant had been waved under her nose. 'I hardly think Kirstie Allsopp compares to Dorothy Whipple.'

'No,' said Amanda, 'the difference being that our readers might actually have heard of Kirstie Allsopp. I want four new possibilities — living, breathing possibilities — on my desk by the end of the afternoon.'

'Fine,' said Martha, in a voice that indicated she felt it anything but.

'Rory?' said Amanda, her head whipping round to me. I flinched in shock — Amanda didn't usually ask me for features ideas, just relied on me to edit everyone else's articles into shape. I panicked that Lance might have somehow contacted her to report on my mortifying behaviour.

'I, er,' I said, feeling my stock sink with every hesitation. 'I'm working on a new Behind the Rope column — '

'I've been thinking about Behind the Rope,' interrupted Amanda, ominously. I hadn't imagined she ever gave any thought to anything I was involved in, and the discovery that she had was not a comforting one. 'It's tired. Not what the new *Country House* is about. I'm cutting it.'

'But I've got two months' more columns filed!' I exclaimed.

'No,' she said.

I felt myself redden. There was a stifled gasp from Martha beside me. Having my own column was the primary reason I stayed at *Country House*; without it I was nothing but a poorly paid subeditor with a misleading job title. Amanda had already turned to interrogate Flickers on his features ideas when I interrupted.

'Amanda. I don't think we should cut my column,' I said, holding on to the table to stop my hands from shaking.

Amanda looked at me with disbelief and astonishment, as if one of the Betterton family portraits had stepped out of its frame to join the editorial meeting. 'But I do, Rory. And that's final.'

'I — I think I can bring it up to date, make it

more relevant for the new *Country House*,' I said wildly, with no actual idea of how I might achieve this.

'Oh really?' smirked Amanda. 'Do elaborate. After all, this meeting isn't nearly long enough as it is. I am all ears.'

I cast my eyes desperately about the room, where they landed on Ticky, who was looking at me with an expression of horror. Clearly she didn't think I was going to be able to salvage this. She shook her head to warn me to back down. But then I remembered our conversation earlier, and I knew I had an angle.

'I could turn it into a dating column,' I said triumphantly.

'A dating column? What does a dating column have to do with *Country House?*' snapped Amanda. 'Rory, you are wasting everyone's time — '

'Wait, Amanda. You want *Country House* to be more like a women's magazine; a dating column could be just what new readers want; Something fun and light to run alongside the more serious pieces.'

Amanda sighed. 'Rory, every magazine and free newspaper in London has a dating column — why should anyone read this one?'

'Well, I could give it a country house angle, maybe visit a house on a date . . . ' I suggested.

'Boring.'

'No, wait,' I said, in a burst of inspiration. 'I do know how to make it different. I do. Instead of looking for Mr Right, I'm going to be looking for Mr Wrong.'

'Mr Wrong?' said Amanda, turning to look at me with a tiny flicker of interest.

'Mr Unsuitable, then,' I said, looking over at Ticky, whose mouth hung open. 'I'm going to be purposely dating all the wrong types to show our readers how to identify and avoid them themselves — toyboys, lotharios, men who still live with their mums. We can call it *Country House* Dates Unsuitable Men — So You Don't Have To.'

'It's not a bad idea,' said Amanda ruminatively. I thought I might have her. 'But still not quite what I'm after for the magazine.'

'I've already been on the first one,' I blurted. 'A date with a man who seemed like he was gay but wasn't.' I looked at Ticky for confirmation. 'A fauxmosexual. I can write it up straight away, ready for the April issue.'

Amanda considered me. 'I'm not sure,' she said.

I chewed my bottom lip in frustration; I knew when I'd been beaten. If I'd been the Honourable Rory Carmichael of the Norfolk Carmichaels, Amanda would have gone for it like a shot. Someone titled and connected could have dated a packet of pork sausages and Amanda would deem it worth a column; but a nobody like me didn't have a chance.

'You can write it for the website.'

I stopped chewing my lip and stared at Amanda in surprise.

'The website?' I echoed. Despite all the talk of launching the *Country House* website last year, everyone knew that no one actually read it. It existed purely so that Amanda could pretend we were current media players, with an online presence should anyone choose to search for us. In reality *Country House* readers were the Eleanors and Percys and Auntie Lydias of the world, no more interested in the internet than they were in the contemporary urban music scene.

'We need extra material for the website. Forget about the country house thing, just drop that bit. I want a straight dating column, just as you pitched it, dating unsuitable men so our readers don't have to. We'll test it out on the website and, if I like it, we'll move it into the magazine. Five hundred words a fortnight.'

Before I could express thanks or relief or amazement, or any of the other emotions that were roiling in my stomach, the meeting had moved on. Amanda annihilated Martha's latest pitch in record time; Martha stalked out of the meeting without waiting for it to finish; Lysander name-dropped several prize-winning fiction writers before admitting that his review pages this month would mostly focus on the memoirs of Mim, Dowager Duchess of Rutland and (no coincidence this) his own grandmother; Flickers got the go-ahead for yet another piece on country sports; and Amanda's Jack Russell terminated the meeting by asphyxiating us all with stealthy under-the-table flatulence.

In short, the meeting proceeded exactly as it usually did.

9

It took me rather a long time to notice that Ticky was ignoring me that afternoon. In fact, I didn't actually notice until she came over to my desk and cleared her throat loudly for the third time. I looked up from the layouts I'd been proofreading and she glared at me.

'Er, yeah? Not talking to you until you, like, apologize?' she said, wagging her finger at me like the sassy black neighbour in a sitcom; an incongruous look for an old Cheltonian.

'Sorry?' I said, my brain still with one of Noonoo's 'I went to a fun party in a big house' name-dropping featurettes.

'Yah, like, still waiting,' said Ticky, miming looking at her watch.

'Waiting for what?' I asked.

'Rory, I know you are like, having a raaahlly terrible time at the moment. And I know, like, that breaking up with someone can make you mental. Well, more mental than usual. But it is saahriously uncool for you to have taken that unsuitable-men idea and palmed it off as your own.'

'What? Ticky, are you sahhrious — I mean serious? You weren't going to date any unsuitable men yourself — you've got a boyfriend. You told me I should do it.'

'Yah, but I didn't, like, say why don't you go sucking up to Maaahn with my brilliant idea and make her think you're all clever and inventive, when, like, I couldn't come up with any features ideas myself?' Ticky pouted and flicked her hair away from her face.

'Right, okay, well I'm sorry I didn't credit you with a feature idea that Amanda only thinks worthy of putting on the website, which, in case you haven't noticed, is read by pretty much nobody,' I snapped. 'I hardly think anyone is going to be getting promoted over this one, least of all me.'

'But, like, Roars,' Ticky said, and I was surprised to see that she looked properly upset, her mouth pinching up, 'it's all right for you. People already think you're smart, you don't have to prove it all the time. But just for once I'd like Maaahn to think something I did was clever or good, instead of just being, like, 'Oh come on, Ticky, weren't you at school with someone interesting, or, like, isn't your uncle a baron?''

I blinked at her. It had never occurred to me that Ticky, with all of her swishy-haired, expensively educated privileges, might consider herself to be hard done by, either in life or at *Country House*. Surely she knew that class was what counted — here and everywhere? That Martha and I, armed only with what Amanda called 'native cunning', could only get so far. Also, her uncle was a *baron*? I didn't even know barons existed outside of fairy tales.

'You *are* smart, Ticky,' I lied. Perhaps I wasn't lying, perhaps she *was* smart; how was I to know, since she pretty much never did any work? Perhaps, I realized, I too had treated her like a posh idiot, and just let her get away with doing little more than filing her nails in between social appointments.

'You, like, raaahlly think so?' she said, her chin wobbling. 'Mummy always used to say, 'Suffolk-born, Suffolk-bred, Ticky's thick in the arm and thick in the head.''

'That's just a silly saying,' I said. 'I've heard that a million times before — she doesn't really mean you're thick.'

'And I only got a third on my degree,' she sniffed. 'Mummy said they only passed me at all because Daddy made such a big donation to St Andrews.'

I was actually beginning to feel sorry for Ticky; Mummy sounded like a right witch. At least my mother's approach to childcare, while scatty, amounted to nothing more shocking than a benign sort of neglect as she ignored me to focus on hunting her latest husband.

'Ticky, plenty of people who are very smart don't do well academically,' I said consolingly. 'You just need to work with your strengths.'

'But what *are* my strengths, Roars?' she sighed, slumping on to my desk.

'Well, networking is one,' I said, thinking that this was a polite way of mentioning the endless social appointments that kept her from her desk.

'But Roars, I am, like, fucking running out of relatives to milk for Maaahn, and half my old schoolfriends won't invite me to their houses any more in case I try to use them in a magazine feature.'

'Don't they want to be in *Country House?*' I

103

asked; it had never occurred to me that people weren't lining up to show off on our pages. There certainly never seemed to be a shortage of them.

'Roars, duh! They're all way too young. They want to be in *Tatler* or *Vogue*, or get a wodge of cash from *Hello!*. The only time people actually, like, *want* to be in *Country House* is if they're trying to flog the family pile. Or if they're like, *ancient*,' Ticky said.

'What about all of Noonoo's friends? They're not ancient.'

'Noonoo's friends are just, like, total nouveau publicity whores. They'd appear in Readers' Wives if they thought it would get them a bit more attention. No, Roars, the non-nouves, the old-school country house types that Maaahn would kill for, don't want to be in a magazine at all. I totally dread asking them every time.'

I wondered why Ticky and I had so rarely talked properly before. Was it because I was always rushing home to Martin? Because I always had half of my brain tuned in to what he might be doing, what he might need or want? This was the first time since she started at *Country House* that I had even considered that Ticky's diary dates were actually work for her; she no more thrilled at the thought of begging her great-aunt for a favour than I did at copy-editing more of Noonoo's friends' reminiscences.

'Well, aside from networking, you're also very good at getting people to talk,' I said. 'You got me to talk about Martin when I really wasn't sure I wanted to.'

'Thanks, Roars,' said Ticky with a sniffle. 'I guess I'm not entirely useless.'

'You're not at all useless,' I said. 'And I'm sorry for not crediting your idea about the unsuitable men. If it's any consolation, I wouldn't have done it unless I was desperate.'

'Yah, like *totally* desperate,' agreed Ticky, launching herself off my desk and returning to her own with renewed vigour. 'Like, your middle name is desperation. Rory Desperation Carmichael. Desperation, thy name is Rory.'

I rolled my eyes and turned back to the layouts. I pretended to work, but actually I was mostly panicking about the Unsuitable Men column. Ticky was right: to have suggested it at all reeked of desperation. What had I been thinking? Of course, I reassured myself, it was unlikely that anyone but Amanda would read it. But that itself was terrifying. What if I completely cocked it up now that her attention was focused on me for once? You didn't have to attend the management lunches in Old Mr Betterton's fusty old club round the corner to know that redundancies were looming. Advertising was down, other magazines were folding every month. We were protected, for now, by being privately owned — no massive magazine conglomerate was going to axe us in favour of a more profitable stablemate, but the Betterton funds couldn't support us for ever. I had always hoped that I would avoid redundancy by being so far beneath Amanda's notice as to be entirely forgotten about. No longer, it seemed.

At least she had been pleased with the Seaton

Hall piece. Although it had been nearly unrecognizable once Martha had fiddled with it, it still carried my byline, along with a few pictures in which I made my unaccredited hand- and hair-modelling debut. I'd proved I was responsible enough to handle a major feature and, in a gesture of kindness that made me almost tearful with gratitude, the duke had personally written to Amanda to say what a pleasure it had been to host the young journalist from *Country House*. Thankfully he had made no mention of my embarrassing outburst to Lance; perhaps the inherent homophobia of the upper classes had made my indiscretion less terrible in the duke's eyes. Or perhaps Lance had been good enough not to mention it to His Grace at all.

I hoped Lance would also be good enough not to object to my offering him up as the first unsuitable man for the column. No, wait: it wouldn't work if the men in question knew about it. I'd have to keep it from them that they were deemed unsuitable and use pseudonyms for everyone. Even a pseudonym for myself, just in case any of my dates read a copy of the magazine. Though, come to think of it, what man in his right mind, unless in the business of selling private houses worth over a million pounds, actually read *Country House*? It was hardly of interest even to the most unsuitable men I could think of. And even if they did — perhaps they idly flicked through a copy while visiting Nanny in the retirement home — they were hardly likely to go seeking out its website for extra thrills. Still, it was probably safest to keep it all anonymous just in case someone Googled my name and got an unpleasant surprise.

Even as I pored over the magazine layouts, I began drafting my first column in my head. I didn't imagine that *Country House* readers would have heard of fauxmosexuals either. Perhaps my lack of dating experience was going to be a virtue when it came to the unsuitables; it wasn't like I was writing this for a bunch of urban sophisticates. The genteel readership of the magazine would want to be entertained and informed without encountering anything in the line of what Martha called a 'marmalade-dropper'. Nothing scandalous, just good clean fun. And that meant I was surely safe from any expectations that I had to take any of this seriously. It was just a good way of getting noticed by Amanda.

Ticky interrupted my thoughts. 'Roars, I've, like, been thinking. Since you're starting this whole dating thing, do you think maybe it's time to do something with your hair?'

'What about my hair?' I asked. I'd always considered I was one of the lucky ones — my thick red hair may have been a little messy, but I had the kind of curls that could do their own thing without hours of styling. A hairdresser had told me, many years ago, never to brush my hair. I suppose he hadn't actually said never, maybe now I thought about it he'd said only to brush it once in a while, but I had taken his advice to heart. I ran my fingers through the tangled curls

— it wasn't like I had a head full of matted dreadlocks or anything, but I believed my hair looked its best when I let it be free and loose and natural.

'Well, like, when did you last get it cut?' asked Ticky.

I twirled the nearest curl around my fingers, bringing it up close to my face. 'Er, six months ago?' I confessed.

'Six months?' asked Ticky in horror. With her high-maintenance highlights, she could hardly imagine a life that didn't involve a monthly visit to a salon to have her head wrapped in foil like a Christmas turkey.

'My hair doesn't really need that much attention,' I said. 'Curly hair's pretty low-maintenance.'

'Oh, like, beg to differ, Roars,' said Ticky. 'I mean, I totally get the whole natural thing you've got going on, but there's a bit of a diff between, like, Pre-Raphaelite tumbling curls and a head full of frizz.'

I stared at her with frank dislike. If she had set out to craft the insult that would wound me the most, she could not have done better than this. Ever since, as an unconfident teenager, I had first encountered the painted heroines of the Pre-Raphaelites, I had felt an affinity with them. For once the abundant red curls with which I had been cursed, usually scraped by my mother into two tight plaits, were portrayed as beautiful; even as Millais's 'Martyr of Solway' was chained to a rock, the tide slowly rising up to drown her, her unashamedly red hair was gloriously free, falling in thick ropes around her shoulders. Of course, when I was inspired by this painted vision to wear my own hair down, everyone at my new school accused me of having had a perm and I couldn't cross the playground without someone calling me Mick Hucknall and breaking into a rendition of 'Stars', but I took the teasing as my own personal martyrdom. It seemed to me that the look of pained acceptance that I adopted in the face of these philistines only served to increase my resemblance to the tortured heroines I so admired.

Even when I felt that my legs could have been longer or that my hips could have been smaller, I had reassured myself that the glowing beacon of my spectacular hair compensated for all. It was my only claim to beauty and my security blanket, all at the same time. It would be no exaggeration to say that my decision to study History of Art at university, and therefore my entire career (such as it was), was based on my teenage belief that if I stood close to a Pre-Raphaelite painting someone might point out the flattering resemblance (though admittedly no one ever had). And now, it seemed, Ticky was saying that what I had regarded as my crowning glory was in fact a bit of an embarrassment. A head full of frizz?

'I guess I could get some serum or something,' I said, glumly looking at the curl in my hand as if it had personally betrayed me in its fluffiness.

'Look, Roars, don't take this the wrong way, but you are, like, beyond John Frieda Frizz-Ease right now. You actually need, like, John Frieda himself. And probably a team of assistants.'

'Jesus, Ticky, don't spare my feelings, will you?' I sniffed, pulling my hair back into a knot at the back of my head, as if I could hide it away for ever.

'Look, Roars, this is the first time you've split up with anyone, so you don't even know the golden truth I am about to pass on to you. It is a female rite of passage to do something major to your hair when you break up with a boyfriend, yah? Sahhriously, new hair, new you; works every time.'

'But I don't really want to have a haircut,' I said. 'I like my hair long.'

'Nothing drastic, Roars, just a good old trim and a blow-dry. It'll make you feel, like, a million times better?'

'I suppose I could go to that place round the corner,' I said resignedly. I could tell Ticky wasn't going to let up on this one.

'No, leave this to me,' said Ticky. 'I'm going to sort it all out for you.'

'Thanks, Ticky,' I said, allowing her to call her hairdresser ('He's not actually John Frieda, but as good as') and make me an appointment for that very evening.

As she did, I stared at the reflection of my hair in the computer monitor. Even though I had pulled it back, a halo of frizz surrounded my head like a force field. With just one conversation my hair had turned from my pride and joy into a source of shame. In much the same way that I appeared to have gone, in the space of two weeks, from happily settled girlfriend of Martin

110

Peters to cheated-upon frizzy-haired dater of unsuitable men whose closest confidants were an entitled Sloaney office-mate and a bunch of geriatric thespians.

At least it couldn't get any worse.

10

I am sure I need not say that the hair appointment was a disaster. If this was the new me, she was even worse than the old one. Ticky had, of course, been absolutely correct in saying that a haircut is a tried and tested part of the process of getting over a break-up. What she had neglected to say is that so is sobbing over the resulting haircut, believing that you have never looked more hideous, and actually trying to scoop the hair trimmings into your handbag to fashion some desperate homemade extensions. I knew I wasn't really crying about my hair. I was sobbing about Martin and my single status and the way my settled life had slipped out of my grasp before I could do anything about it. But when I looked in the mirror I didn't see a haircut; I saw loss. And a bizarre shoulder-length triangular bob where once there had been waist-length curls.

To compound my misery, Ticky's hairdresser had decided to twist my curls into individual heavily gelled ringlets, which had left me looking uncomfortably like the famous sixteenth-century Albrecht Dürer self-portrait, if only Albrecht Dürer had had the blotchy flushed face of one who was suppressing hysterical tears. I could have told the hairdresser from bitter experience that the immaculately smoothed ringlets would last about as long as it took me to encounter a solitary molecule of water. Even if it hadn't been raining that night, I managed to produce quite a lot of water by bursting into tears as soon as I stepped out of the salon.

I suppressed the tears while I waited for my bus in the rain, convinced I could actually hear my hair kinking around my ears in the moist atmosphere. By the time I got back to Auntie Lyd's my hair was a frizzy mess. I didn't even need to look in the mirror to see how disastrous it was; the sheer volume of fluffy hair around my head felt like I was wearing a comedy wig. I went straight to my bedroom, pulled the duvet up over my head and stayed there until morning.

The house was quiet when I woke up at eight, having slept through my alarm. For once I hadn't even heard Percy having his morning shower. The night had not done my new hairstyle any favours at all — it stretched out beyond my shoulders in a ginger afro that made me look as if I was wearing a Hallowe'en wig. Once I'd washed it, I hoped it would return to some semblance of normal.

I put on my dressing gown over my pyjamas and scowled at my reflection. 'Just be grateful Martin can't see you now,' I muttered. If he'd thought I'd let myself go before, it was nothing to how terrible I looked now.

I hoped, given my late start, that I'd avoid seeing any of the residents until I'd managed to wash my hair. I shared the upstairs bathroom only with Percy — the others used the one on the next floor down — and even though I hadn't heard his pre-dawn shower I knew he'd already be downstairs by now, arguing with Eleanor. But when I put my hand on the doorknob, it seemed like there was noise coming from inside — singing? I hadn't realized this in time to stop turning the handle and, before I knew it, I was staring straight at a man's upended arse.

I should clarify that it was fully encased in denim, but you will appreciate that it was still quite a shock to encounter a strange man crouching under the toilet with his bum in the air, and I don't think I can really be blamed for letting out an enormous scream. Which of course made the man hit his head against the toilet bowl with a resounding crack.

'For fuck's sake!' the strange man swore, pulling his head out from under the loo.

'I know karate!' I said wildly, hoping this would scare off the bathroom intruder, but he just sat back on his heels and rubbed at his dirty-blond hair with a wince.

As he turned around I saw he was wearing a skin-tight T-shirt that read,

Nice legs, what time do they open?

Charming.

'Karate?' he laughed and straightened up to sit on the edge of the bath, checking the palm of his hand as if he expected to see blood. 'Really? Are those your black-belt pyjamas?'

'I mean it,' I blustered, my hand flying to the collar of my pyjamas as I realized how I must look, half-dressed and crazy-haired. 'I'm dangerous. Who are you? What do you think you're

114

doing in my bathroom?'

'Your bathroom, is it?' he said. He didn't seem to be taking my threats seriously. I couldn't blame him: no one was likely to mistake a history-of-art expert for a martial-arts one. He grinned at me, perfectly confident that I would not be breaking into a high kick. 'Because I thought this house belonged to Lydia Bell. And I've already met her downstairs. Which means this isn't your bathroom at all.'

Slightly reassured that he wasn't a burglar — although who knew? Perhaps he was just one who liked to thoroughly research his victims — I allowed myself to relax a little. But not too much.

'Well, it's certainly not *your* bathroom,' I snapped. 'So perhaps you'd like to tell me what you're doing here?'

The man looked at me as if I was insane and gestured to an array of tools on the floor.

'I don't know if you can see anything through all that hair, but I'd have thought it was pretty obvious who I am.'

'Oh,' I said. 'You're the plumber.'

'Yep. I'm the plumber; Jim. And you are?'

'Rory,' I said. 'Lydia's niece.'

'Rory?' he asked, wrinkling his nose and frowning. 'What kind of a name's that for a girl? Bit weird.'

'It's short for Aurora,' I said. I hated having to explain my name. It was a grimly ironic fact that while in my daily life at *Country House* I was regarded as deeply common and only one step away from a council-estate hoodie, the average

115

person encountering my name instantly assumed I was some sort of over-privileged toff.

'Aurora? Like the aurora borealis? Like the dawn?' said Jim, flashing me a cocky grin. He had one of those American sorts of faces: square-jawed, tanned, white-teethed. As if he should have an American football tucked under his armpit and a cheerleader by his side. The obvious kind of good-looking face that said, *You fancy me, don't you? Everyone does.*

I sighed and didn't answer him. It was almost worse when people knew what Aurora meant. Although at least he hadn't guessed the *Sleeping Beauty* connection — that was definitely more shaming.

'Bit of a mouthful, isn't it? I think I'll just call you Dawn.' I think he thought I'd simper agreement or blush or something. He was probably used to charming his female clients with his cheesy grin and his ridiculously tight T-shirts. I could practically see the muscles on his stomach through the thin fabric. He caught me looking and grinned again, distinctly smug. He might as well have said, 'Fancy a bit, do you?'

'Call me — Do you mind?' I said crossly, folding my arms across my chest. 'I don't want you to call me anything. If you'll excuse me, I just want to have my shower and get to work.'

'Oh you can't have a shower, Dawn,' said Jim, still smiling.

'Why not?'

'Because I've turned all the water off. Your aunt said everyone would be finished in the bathrooms by eight.'

116

'But — I've overslept! And I have to wash my hair!' I shrieked.

He shrugged, nodding his head towards the toilet, half of which, I saw only now, was in pieces on the floor. 'Not my problem, Dawn. I can't turn it back on now, I've already disconnected the cistern from the wall.'

'But my *hair*!' I wailed, grasping at the giant afro to make him realize the seriousness of the situation.

'I don't know much about hair,' said Jim, carefully scrutinizing me, 'but I think it might take a bit more than a shower to sort out your barnet.'

'How dare you!' I said, trembling with rage and frustration.

'No offence, Dawn, you're not a bad-looking girl, but have you ever heard of John Frieda Frizz-Ease serum?'

That was it. I was not about to be lectured on hair care by a plumber whose blond streaks were, I suspected, not entirely natural. What sort of man actually gets highlights? The vanity! And for him to stand there, all sweaty in his filthy jeans and a tight white T-shirt with a frankly offensive slogan on it, and actually lecture me on appearance! I stomped back up the stairs to my attic room and slammed the door so hard that the frame shook. I shook, too. I couldn't even, like Percy, rinse my hair in the sink, because there was no water in the entire sodding house. My whole day was ruined. My whole *life* was ruined.

I had already cried more in the last few weeks

than in the last ten years of my life; and with my horrendous haircut I couldn't afford to look any worse. So I gulped back the sobs that were welling up in my chest, and attempted to wrestle my hair into submission. I had to resort to a version of the tight plaits that had blighted my early adolescence — anything else just allowed the frizz to escape and, if anything, it looked worse springing out in irregular patches than when in one huge bouffy triangle. I left the house with two sensible French pleats winding down my head as if it was my first day at Wareham Manor School, aged fourteen, friendless and ginger and the new girl yet again.

'Oh Goouurd, Roars, what happened?' demanded Ticky as soon as she saw my hair. 'What is this freaky hairstyle you've got going on? You look like some spoddy cellist in the National Youth Orchestra, for God's sake. Tell me Marlon didn't do this?'

'No, Marlon didn't do the plaits,' I said through gritted teeth. 'Marlon styled my hair so ridiculously that this is the only way I can wear it today.'

'Oh, like, nightmare,' grimaced Ticky. 'Turn around — let me see. Well, Roars, I can't really see how much he's taken off.'

'Trust me, this is better than it was when I left the salon,' I grumbled.

'Goouurd, Roars, I am, like, so sorry.' She wheeled herself over on her swivelling office chair and propped her elbows on my desk. 'Did you, like, cry and shit? Was it awful?'

'Yes, Ticky, I did cry and shit,' I said as she

nodded encouragingly. 'For about an hour. But I should have realized that I was expecting too much. It was only a haircut. I was never going to have some ugly-duckling-to-swan transformation. This isn't a movie.'

'No, Roars, not unless, like, it's a disaster movie. Like, *Shampoo: The Reckoning*. How did you feel when you looked in the mirror?' She cocked her head to one side in an I-am-listening-attentively gesture.

I had a creeping suspicion that Ticky, for all that she seemed to be trying to help me at the moment, might have somehow engineered my disastrous hairstyle to create more drama for her vicarious enjoyment. Not that I am suggesting she told her hairdresser to make me look stupid, but that arranging a visit to the salon was probably done more in her interests than in mine, even if she wasn't aware of it. Subconsciously it suited her to keep me in a state of victimhood so that she could continue to be the supportive confidante. After all, as long as I was lurching from one emotional disaster to another, her entertainment was guaranteed.

'I hope you didn't pay him,' she said, rubbing my arm reassuringly.

'Of course I bloody paid him!' I said. 'I even tipped him! I didn't want to make a scene.'

Ticky stared at me in amazement. I knew she wouldn't understand. She and her friends were the kind of people who could remain entirely oblivious to the dark looks and resentful mutterings of a pub full of locals as they loudly brayed their way through a Sunday lunch in a tiny village. They believed the world enjoyed listening to their loudly expressed opinions; they had been fed giant helpings of self-confidence along with their boarding-school suppers (never dinners, only common people ate dinners). They had a sense of entitlement so strong that it never occurred to them that not everyone was as delighted with them as they were with themselves.

'Roars,' she said gently. 'It's, like, not making a scene to say you hate what someone's done to your hair. It's just an exchange of money for service, and if that service is crappy you're totally allowed to say so?'

'Yes, I suppose so,' I agreed, to get her off my back. I knew she would have preferred me to have had a screaming row with her hairdresser just so that she had something outrageous to discuss with him the next time she visited for her highlights. My silent seething was not nearly dramatic enough for her purposes. But this was my life, and I was not living it for her enjoyment, I thought bitterly. Although, to be honest, nor did I seem to be especially living it for my own enjoyment these days; more struggling through each day in turn.

I visited the ladies' far too often that day. I wasn't sure what I expected to have happened to my hair each time; it's not as if it would have magically grown back while I sat at my desk answering emails, but I kept returning to the mirror as if it might have improved since the last time I checked. I was turning my head from side to side in yet another despairing analysis when I heard Amanda's strident tones mixed with Martha's equally loud ones in the harsh blend of voices to which everyone in the office was horribly accustomed. And it was heading towards the ladies'. Panicked, I threw myself into a cubicle, locked the door and tucked my feet up on to the loo seat, hoping they would think it was out of order rather than occupied.

I heard the door swing open and two pairs of heels click on to the tiled floor. You could tell which ones were Amanda's — they had the tight plink of spiky, expensive, spindly heels, the impractical kind that suggested (accurately) that their wearer spent more time in taxis than on foot. Martha's were stouter, more clompy, but louder. I had long suspected that she received them as a kickback from the advertisers at the back of the magazine; they looked suspiciously like the truly hideous 'Comfort? Yes! And style, too!' numbers offered by Weldon's of Ludlow. And it would be just like Martha to aim so tragically low in her appropriation of magazine perks.

'First a dating column, and now an agony aunt?' Martha hissed. I don't know why she thought lowering her voice would make any difference now the whole office knew she and Amanda had retreated to the ladies'.

'Martha, I appreciate you are, even after three long years, uncomfortable with the new direction the magazine is taking,' said Amanda wearily, 'but fighting me over every change is simply wasting your time as well as mine.'

'I'm not fighting against *you*, Amanda, I'm

121

fighting *for* our loyal readers,' Martha snapped. 'Forty thousand readers can't be wrong.'

'Forty thousand readers six years ago, Martha,' said Amanda, with a voice of steely politeness. 'Only twenty-two thousand by the time I took over.'

'Twenty-two thousand *very* happy and satisfied readers,' Martha said. 'And you are betraying them all with your silly women's magazine ideas.'

Martha, although she did not have the shell of posh that shielded one from all doubt, had a blind spot all of her own. How did she not see that losing nearly twenty thousand readers in the space of three years was a bit of a problem? Of course there was always the possibility that the ageing readership had simply gone to the big country house in the sky instead of abandoning the magazine for more racy reading, but even so, no other company would have allowed Martha to stay on in any capacity whatsoever. The Bettertons, being a family firm, had only kept her on out of guilt and the knowledge that, after so long at *Country House*, she was effectively unemployable anywhere else.

'Thirty-five thousand readers according to last month's figures,' said Amanda. 'So I must be doing something right.'

'Barely a day goes by that I don't get a letter from a reader complaining about the new changes! Only today I had one asking what had happened to the Janet's Country Ramblings column,' protested Martha.

'Our Letters page is full of people who like the

122

new changes,' answered Amanda smoothly.

'Letters that you've got Ticky Lytton-Finch to write!'

I stifled a gasp from my loo seat. Of course I knew that Ticky wrote half the letters that we published — if you saw the genuine postbag you would see why. I mean, who in their right mind would bother writing to a magazine to say, 'I was most impressed with your new layouts. Keep up the good work'? No one does — they only write to complain when they don't like something, or when they mistake us for the National Trust magazine and send fierce missives deploring the poor standard of cucumber sandwiches sold in the Knole Tea Rooms. But I thought we had kept this fact from Martha, who would never have allowed such a thing when she was Acting-Editor.

'Ticky merely steps into the breach when our correspondence hasn't quite delivered what we need,' said Amanda. 'Much as the Betterton family appointed me when you had failed to deliver what they needed.'

I smothered another gasp — although I thought Martha's one-woman campaign to bring down Amanda was not only pointless but totally misguided, that was one hell of a smack-down. Martha evidently thought so too, because she was stunned into silence.

'Martha. I am as uncertain as you about Rory's dating column. That is why it's been relegated to the website. But I put you in charge of finding an agony aunt for the magazine because I thought you might enjoy the challenge.'

I winced in my cubicle. I knew Amanda had doubts about my column, but it was still hard to hear her say so.

'An agony aunt! Next you'll be asking me to find an astrologer! It's entirely inappropriate,' snapped Martha.

'I can always appoint someone else to do it,' threatened Amanda. 'And any other part of your job that you think 'inappropriate'.'

I winced again; for Martha this time. As much as she was a complete nightmare, I couldn't help but sympathize with her, nearing retirement age in her comfortable and not at all stylish Weldon's of Ludlow shoes, having her entire world turned upside-down by this glossy fortysomething in her Louboutins. Of course Amanda was right, of course Martha had to be made to see it, but it was still painful to hear her be beaten down like this.

'Fine,' said Martha. 'I'll find you an agony aunt.'

'Good,' said Amanda. 'And don't bother asking Honor Blackman — she's already said no.'

Her spiky heels clipped out of the bathroom and in a reflex action I found myself checking my watch — six minutes. Far off Amanda's personal best, but an effective Martha-crushing nonetheless.

Martha's heavy shoes stomped over towards the sinks and I heard a low sigh, then a series of sniffs. I sat very still for a full five minutes until she left the room.

Back in our office, Ticky was counting out a

handful of coins on her desk, and I knew she must have won the latest bet. She guiltily scooped the money off her desk as I came into the room.

'Oh, Roars, it's just you, thank God,' she said. 'Six minutes on the nose. Well done me, eh?'

'Yeah, well done you,' I said.

I wondered if I was losing my taste for the office games that had once helped to pass the time. Sniggering outside the bathroom door in the knowledge that Martha — who had once had such power over all of us — was getting a pasting was totally different from hearing her being humiliated in person. *Country House* was far more than just a job to her; she visited properties at the weekends, she stayed late in the office, she felt each Amanda-sanctioned change as a stab in the heart. She was too close to retirement to find a job elsewhere, but too far from it to be able to look forward to her imminent escape. She was stuck, like a trapped animal, snapping and biting at everyone who approached her. I had the uncomfortable feeling that my sudden sympathy for Martha's situation was not unrelated to the recent unravelling of my personal life. It would have made me a better person to have felt simple empathy for a fellow human being, but I couldn't deny that my pity was tempered by a hefty dose of fear that, if I didn't sort my own life out, Martha's unhappy present might become my future.

11

'Hello, ladies,' drawled Lysander Honeywell, throwing himself into the chintz armchair that sat in the far corner of our office. It was clear that his usual clipped courtesy had been loosened by a certain amount of alcohol.

'Christ, Lysander,' shrieked Ticky, pulling him up from the seat, 'can't you look before you land your drunken arse down? You've sat on Mummy's new fascinator that I just picked up from Fenwick's. She'll kill me.'

Ticky reached behind Lysander for a Fenwick's bag and pulled out a sad-looking jumble of wires and feathers hanging limply from a tiny circle of fabric. I have never got the whole fascinator thing — is it a hat? Is it a hairclip? — but I think that is because I am not of a class that considers the highest possible praise for an item of clothing to be 'fun'. As in 'Gosh, Jocasta, yellow tights! What *fun!*' Instead of, 'Gosh, Jocasta, yellow tights! You have never looked more ridiculously like a garden bird.' But fascinators were indisputably 'fun'; even the most formidable dowager, corseted in stern upholstery, let society know that she was a spirited slip of a gel underneath it all just by wearing one on her steely locks. No posh country wedding was complete unless the congregation fairly bristled with them.

'Yikes, awfully sorry, Victoria,' said Lysander, blushing, or perhaps it was just a boozy flush. 'If your ma complains, tell her I'll buy her a new one. Throw in lunch, too. Haven't seen her for ages.' He slumped back down in the seat while Ticky huffed and sighed as she tried to restore the fascinator back to its maximum fun setting.

'Bloody ruined,' she muttered under her breath.

'Nice lunch?' I asked him. His pale-pink shirt was unbuttoned a bit too low, which almost certainly meant he'd had lunch with a pretty young book publicist. He was of the Simon Cowell generation which confidently believed the sight of an expanse of manly chest inspired as much lust in women as an exposed female cleavage did in men. The bared chest was an incongruous look for a book editor who, I always thought, would surely have come across better literary heroes to emulate than the Mills & Boon cover model. Still, I guessed it worked for him in a way; although he never got anywhere with the publicists, who were all half his age, he rarely seemed to be short of a lady companion.

'Lovely young gel from the Pendragon Press,' he said, settling back into his chair as if he planned to spend the whole afternoon there. Which he probably did. After a long lunch, Lysander rarely returned to his own desk, preferring to while away the rest of the day in idle gossip and office-hopping.

'Where'd you go?' I asked, less out of interest than to prompt the monologue that I knew was already prepared.

Lysander lay back, his hands folded across his

stomach, legs outstretched. His eyes were half closed in fond reminiscence already.

'Just a small place I know, run by an old chum of mine . . . '

I prepared for the clang of a name being dropped.

'Jeremy Wells? L'Écluse?'

'Oooh,' I said politely, as I knew was expected of me. I had been to L'Écluse for a drink before, but it was a little out of my lunchtime price range, and Lysander's. Pendragon must have been picking up the bill. I wondered how soon I could turn my attention back to the computer screen without being noticed.

'I began with the soup of Jerusalem artichokes and bacon, while Leticia had . . . ' Lysander rambled on, going through every dish in immense detail and giving an account of his conversation which, if true, must have bored poor Leticia to tears as it was mostly designed to make her aware of his great importance and his close personal friendships with her bosses and authors.

I let him declaim from the depths of the chintzy chair while I quietly got on with my work. Even though it was he who had got her the job at *Country Life*, Ticky had no patience with Lysander; having known him since childhood she had suffered his monologues for too long already. But I didn't especially mind having him drone on in the background. He was just a rather lonely man who needed an audience and, since he didn't particularly mind if the audience was an attentive one, it felt a bit like having the radio

128

on: you could tune in if it got interesting, and straight back out again when it tailed off.

He had been going for a good ten minutes when Ticky, with her usual want of tact, spoke loudly over him.

'Roars, these unsuitable men. I'm just trying to think if I can set you up with anyone to kick you off. Do you have, like, an age range you want to stick to or just keep it wide open?'

I rolled my eyes in the direction of Lysander, who was looking a little put out at the interruption.

'Lysander, can you just, like, put a cork in it for five minutes while I get on with some actual work over here? Yah, Rory, age range. What do you say?'

'I don't know,' I said, having not really given it any thought before. 'Er, probably around my age?'

'Oh no,' said Lysander, leaning forward in his chair and clutching at the corner of my desk. 'Oh but my dear, you would be ruling out so many interesting men. Men of an older generation have so much to teach younger women.' He pressed a hand to his exposed chest and Ticky stuck two fingers down her throat.

'You may laugh, Victoria Lytton-Finch,' said Lysander with great authority, 'but an older man knows how to spoil a woman, how to treat her *like* a woman. And, my dear Rory, if you don't mind my saying, you look like you could do with a bit of spoiling right now.'

My hand crept to my hair; I knew I looked terrible. He smiled at me with a surprising sweetness. But surely he wasn't suggesting . . . ?

'Lysander, you dirty old perv, there is, like, no way Roars is going out on a date with *you*,' said Ticky, completely disgusted. 'She's young enough to be your daughter.'

Lysander sniffed and sat up very straight. 'Victoria,' he said, 'I will thank you not to speak to me in this manner. I am not a dirty old perv, as you so revoltingly put it, nor am I proposing anything untoward with Aurora.'

I breathed a huge sigh of relief. I mean, there was nominally unsuitable and then there was please-tell-me-you-are-joking-how-would-I-ever-live-this-down unsuitable.

'I am merely suggesting,' said Lysander, turning his back on Ticky to face me fully, 'that by ruling out the older gentlemen, you may be ruling out some perfectly pleasant evenings.'

'Well in that case, you can't rule out the young ones either, Roars,' said Ticky. 'Like, you're going to have to be an equal opportunities dater? And do admit a hot young boy is quite a lot more appealing than one of Lysander's wrinkled old cronies.'

'Er, right,' I said, feeling that actually neither of them was as appealing as someone my own age, someone with a decent job and a home and a shared history. Someone who was the youngest board director at Fairfax Accounting. Someone with a new girlfriend, I reminded myself.

Ticky decided that I should be seeking unsuitable men within an age range of twenty to seventy, which we all finally agreed was quite wide enough to encompass all kinds of unsuitability. Satisfied with her afternoon's work, she decided to pop out of the office to spend her sweepstake winnings on chocolate. Lysander stayed behind, unusually silent in his floral armchair.

'Aurora,' he said, finally. 'I wouldn't normally suggest such a thing, but you are specifically looking for unsuitable men for your column, aren't you?'

'I am,' I said hesitantly.

'Only my cousin Ethelred — '

'Ethelred?'

'We all have unusual names in our family, Aurora,' sniffed Lysander. 'I would have thought *you* would sympathize.'

'Sorry, do carry on,' I said.

'My cousin Ethelred is visiting London from the Highlands this week. Charming fellow, never married. Red-haired, just like you. I'm supposed to be meeting him for dinner at Wilton's tomorrow night, but something has come up — a situation with a lady, if you understand my meaning.'

Oh God, I really hoped Lysander didn't think that, just because I let him run his mouth off in our office, I was offering myself as some sort of confidante for his dirty dalliances.

'Umm, right?' I said.

'So why don't I ring Ethelred and suggest he has dinner with you instead? I can promise he'll be delighted — the old duffer barely sees a woman for weeks on end up on his ruddy estate, let alone a pretty girl of your age. And he's rich as Croesus so you don't need to worry about paying.'

'Oh gosh, Lysander, that's very kind of you,' I said, thinking that really it was anything but; clearly he was just looking for someone on whom to dump an unwanted relation for the evening. 'I think I might be busy tomorrow night.'

'Doing what?' asked Lysander.

I flushed guiltily, as if he could see straight into my pathetically empty diary, its pages free of all social engagements that didn't involve the senior-citizen residents of Elgin Square.

'Oh, just things,' I answered airily, trying to convey such a packed schedule that it was hard for me to remember the specifics. There was no way I was going to allow Lysander to manipulate me into this; there was a significant difference between dating a sophisticated urbane older man of, perhaps, forty, and being forced into proximity to an aged rustic whose only regular female company was, I imagined, a wheezing and arthritic Border terrier.

'Aurora, my dear, I suggest you rearrange those 'things'. Ethelred may not set your young heart a-flutter but I can guarantee that, firstly, he is, unlike your first date, entirely heterosexual. And secondly, may I suggest that you need to consider your readership? A rich, mature land-owning bachelor would be like manna from heaven to them. Manna from heaven. Think of your column and be a professional for goodness' sake.'

'I suppose . . . ' I could feel myself beginning to waver.

Although I considered myself a professional, I wasn't the kind of professional that regularly spent evenings with rich old gentlemen; that was another type of girl entirely. But I couldn't deny that Lysander had a point about our readership. Although I had kept the column about my date with Fauxmosexual Lance very light and tame, Tim from IT had forwarded me a handful of complaints that had been emailed in. He'd kindly kept them from Amanda, but if this column was going to work I needed to be able to show that it was a success with our readers.

'Excellent, excellent,' said Lysander, taking my hesitation for assent. He rocked back and forth a little to get up the momentum to heave himself out of the chair. Once he'd launched himself towards the door he stopped and turned back.

'Cousin Ethelred is *sixty-eight*,' he said, looking immensely pleased with himself. 'Nearly forty years older than you. I think you're going to find him *extremely* unsuitable.'

For the rest of the day, Ticky emailed me brochures for crematoria and care homes. Hilarious. Every time I tried to speak to her about my date with Ethelred she faked vomiting noises. It seemed I had found, in dating an old-age pensioner, the one subject in which Ticky had absolutely no interest. I would have liked to speak properly to Auntie Lyd when I got home, but it was impossible to express the sinking gloom I felt at the idea of my impending date when sat around the kitchen table with my aunt (sixty-three), Percy (seventy-six) and Eleanor (seventy-three). Instead I gave them all a carefully edited version of events.

'An actual Unsuitable Men *column*, darling?'

asked Auntie Lyd, lighting a cigarette. I wasn't sure if her curled lip was from disapproval or smoke. 'As well as Behind the Rope? Won't you be awfully busy?'

'Behind the Rope's been cut,' I said. 'Changes at the magazine, you know.' I tried to sound breezy about it; like it didn't really matter. I'd already given Auntie Lyd enough to worry about, what with the sobbing over Martin and the moving into her house unexpectedly. The last thing she needed was to hear that my work life was a disaster too.

'That's a shame,' said Percy. 'I've been working my way through those magazines under the cat's bed. It's all quite fascinating stuff.'

'Not as fascinating as unsuitable men though,' said Eleanor with a girlish giggle. 'I could tell you a few stories about unsuitables that I have known.'

'If you are going to rehash that pack of lies about Elvis Presley, I shall be forced to leave the room,' said Percy.

Eleanor cast her eyes to the ceiling. 'There was nothing unsuitable about Elvis,' she said, sighing deeply. Percy's mouth set in a tight line. 'Although I find most other men deeply unsuitable in comparison.'

'That is as nothing compared to the perfidy of women,' objected Percy.

'Well,' interrupted Auntie Lyd, turning to me, 'I'm sure you'll do it just as well as you do everything, Rory. I can't wait to read the first one in the magazine.'

'Oh, it won't be in the magazine,' I said.

Auntie Lyd's face puckered into a deep frown beneath her pall of smoke. 'It's going to be on the *Country House* website.'

'Website, dear?' asked Eleanor.

'Yes, you know,' snapped Percy impatiently, assuming an air of great knowledge. 'Internet superhighways, i-telephones, the *broadband*.'

'Ah yes, the broadband,' said Eleanor, nodding in bemused agreement. She took a large gulp from her ever-present teacup.

'A website,' contemplated Auntie Lyd. She tapped the ash from her cigarette into the portable ashtray that she took everywhere. Its lid swung shut as she released the lever. 'Is that good?'

'Yes,' I lied. 'It's really great, just where my writing should be in the, er, age of the information superhighway. I've already published my first piece.' Percy nodded approval. None of them had the first clue about the internet; it was easy to let them believe this new column was a good thing instead of a worrying demotion. Not to mention a whole world of weirdness for my personal life.

'Well,' said Auntie Lyd. 'I don't want to have to get one of those Wii machines just so I can keep up with your writing.'

'You can't read a website from a Wii, Auntie Lyd.'

'I certainly can't,' she answered. 'I will have to find another way of reading it. Well done you, darling. I think you're very brave indeed.'

Somehow that made me feel worse than ever.

12

Wilton's was a restaurant I had visited many times before, as it was a favourite of Old Mr Betterton's, and all of our staff Christmas lunches were held there. To be honest, Wilton's was a favourite of every Old Mr in London; unchanged since it was founded over 100 years ago, it offered a reassuring menu of seasonal wild game from the Duke of Northumberland's estate, followed by stodgy school-dinner puddings. Even though culinary fashion had once more swung in favour of seasonal eating and British classics, the restaurant itself remained resolutely unfashionable, and all the better for it, as far as its patrons were concerned. The night I went there to meet Lysander's cousin Ethelred, I was the youngest person in the dining room by at least thirty years, and one of the few customers who didn't have to be physically assisted to sit down. Ethelred had not arrived yet, which gave me time to look about the room, decorated with hearty hunting scenes, stuffed birds and assorted antlered creatures gazing down on the room with glassy eyes. Underneath one such mournful mounted head an elderly man appeared to be attached to some sort of personal oxygen tank. It hissed gently as he sipped at his dark-brown soup.

It was perfect. *Country House* readers were going to lap this up with their silver spoons.

A few people smiled over as I settled myself at the table, and my hand stole up to my hair in paranoid fashion. With the use of a lot of hair products, and a careful blow-drying technique, I'd managed to persuade my hair back into the loose curls I preferred. But any unexpected glance had me instantly anxious that my hair had somehow rearranged itself into a formation of triangular ringlets. There was a mirror behind me and I turned around for a surreptitious appearance check. Reflected in the dull shine, my hair seemed, if not gorgeous, at least not laughable. In the mirror, I saw the door open behind me. My unsuitable man had arrived.

His flaming red hair, a wide white streak running through the front, gave him away as Lysander's cousin, as did the fact that he looked exactly like Lysander — if Lysander had been inflated to the proportions of a barrage balloon. Ethelred stood in the doorway beaming at the entire room, a smile which was echoed in a waterfall of curving chins that cascaded all the way down to his chest. His vast stomach peeped out from underneath a checked pink and yellow shirt, worn under a suit of yellow moleskin which definitely fell into the category of 'fun'. His largeness was offset by incredibly tiny hands and feet. He opened his arms wide and tiptoed over to me with a delicacy of which I hadn't imagined a man his size to be capable.

'Aurora?' he said, rolling his r's and picking up my hand in both of his. 'Could this vision, this gorgeous vision, be Miss Aurora Carmichael?'

I stood up to shake hands, only to find myself

grasped in an enormous bear hug which lifted me right off my feet.

'How do you do, Ethelred,' I squeaked from within his grasp, remembering Old Mr Betterton's stern admonishment to me in my first week at *Country House* that saying, 'Nice to meet you' was deeply 'doors to manual', the kind of thing only said by lower-middle-class people trying to be genteel. I had never allowed myself to say it since.

'Oh, pshaw,' said Ethelred, releasing me. 'Has that absurd cousin of mine told you to call me that? My dear Aurora, not all of us have chosen to suffer under the heavy burden of our given name, like that dreadful old masochist. Please, call me Teddy.' His eyes twinkled as he lowered himself, with the discreet assistance of a waiter, into the leather armchair opposite me.

'In that case,' I smiled, 'please call me Rory. No one calls me Aurora except for Lysander, and my aunt if she's really cross with me.'

'Ha! I should think not! Ridiculous name!' Teddy laughed, looking positively delighted with both himself and me. 'Excuse me, young man, the young lady and I will each have a glass of champagne to start.'

He leaned over conspiratorially. 'A toast to ridiculous names, don't you think?'

I liked to think that working at *Country House* had trained me well in what Ticky referred to as the 'pert niece technique'. She had, of course, years of practice thanks to her never-ending social engagements with her godfathers and uncles. For me, since my family consisted of

Mum, Auntie Lyd and the occasional visit to Dad and his new family, the technique was something I had had to study and revise like a foreign language, which in a way it was. Although my job was mostly desk-bound, even I had to entertain our more senior columnists or features writers to lunches at times, not to mention attending events where I had been placed next to Old Mr Betterton, who always arranged to sit next to the young female staffers. I had learned that the best way in which to approach such people — men only, of course, the pert niece approach is entirely inappropriate with women — was with a cheeky sort of flirtation that flattered and charmed, without ever being mistaken for anything that might result in an unwanted hand on your knee. A few subtle mentions of 'my boyfriend' usually kept the overly keen at bay.

The aim was that the recipient of the pert niece approach would leave your encounter feeling invigorated, relevant and as if he were twenty years younger, but without the faintest suggestion that you had led him on. You would, of course, feel quite exhausted from having been fascinated by everything he said for hours, but that is why pert niece is a tactic rather than a way of life. Few could sustain it full-time.

Pert niece worked beautifully on Teddy, who volleyed with an excellent 'jocular uncle' of his own. He insisted on ordering for me, something that would have riled me enormously if done by anyone my own age, but which was somehow quite acceptable, gallant even, in these surroundings. I found that I didn't even have to pretend to be fascinated by him as he regaled me with stories of his Highland estate.

'So, Teddy,' I asked, pushing my game pie around the plate in an attempt to hide a heavy slab of pastry crust under a pile of greens. 'Have you never come close to marrying?'

Teddy coughed in alarm. 'Marrying? Oh my dear me, no. Haven't thought about it for decades. Not since before you were born, my dear girl.' He patted his face with the gravy-spattered napkin that he had tucked, like a bib, under his chins. Then his eyes went misty, and he held a forkful of pie suspended in mid-air.

'Not since Fi McKenneth,' he sighed, gazing into the distance.

'Who was she?' I asked, intrigued.

'Fi McKenneth is the finest woman who ever lived,' said Teddy, his chins wobbling for emphasis. He pressed his lips together firmly as if he didn't trust himself to speak, and put down his fork. 'Loved her for years. Wouldn't have me, of course. Sensible woman.'

'But, Teddy, why ever not?' I asked, and I was surprised to find I actually meant it. I was sure Teddy must not always have been quite as spherical in appearance as he was now, and he was so charming and entertaining that I was sure he must have had many admirers in the past. Not to mention he was incredibly rich, which tended to excuse any idiosyncrasies of appearance for many women.

'Not every gel is suited to life in the Highlands, Rory,' said Teddy sadly. 'Takes a special sort of woman to take on an estate. Fi was clever enough to know she wasn't the right kind. I, idiotic enough to believe she was.' He gulped down half a glass of wine in one mouthful. ''Course she ended up marrying; three children. Lives in Edinburgh. Went to her and Snorter's fortieth wedding anniversary only last week. Bloody nice chap.' Teddy picked up his fork and stared at the pie. 'Bloody nice chap.'

'And you never met anyone else?' I asked gently.

'Never wanted to, Rory. Never wanted to. Anyway, the property has kept me so busy . . . ' He trailed off. 'But enough questions from you. It's about time I asked you why a delightful young lady finds herself having dinner with a decrepit old chap like me?'

'Oh.' I hesitated. We had got on so well that I almost wanted to tell him the truth about the column, but it seemed to me that, for all of Teddy's hearty bonhomie, he was a sensitive soul who would be hurt by hearing that he had been offered to me as a dinner companion purely because of his extreme unsuitability. 'Well, I've just split up with my boyfriend and, er, I wanted to start dating again. Lysander said that his cousin was in town and so here we are!' I ended brightly, back to pert niece.

'Well, how thrilling!' said Teddy, rubbing his hands together in delight. 'I had no idea we were on a 'date', Rory. Lysander just said he thought I would enjoy your company. Which I must say I do, enormously.'

'And you've been lovely company too, Teddy,'

I said. He had. In fact I'd enjoyed our evening more than I'd ever expected to. Not that I felt the stirrings of attraction towards Teddy, far from it, but I hadn't wanted to climb out of the bathroom window to escape either.

'A 'date',' said Teddy again, beaming. 'How extraordinary. Who'd have thought it?'

He insisted that we order pudding, followed by cheese, with wines to match. The alcohol hardly seemed to affect him, but the steady flow of wine in this warm room was making me feel hugely sleepy. I longed to lay my head down on the tempting plush window seat at the front of the room. I suppose, looking back, I should have realized that my half-closed eyes and generally languid (okay, drunken) demeanour could have been mistaken for someone who was trying to be all come-hithery, but I had felt safe in our firmly (to me) delineated roles of elderly uncle and youngish niece.

When we finally stepped outside Wilton's, the cold air woke me up just in time. Teddy turned to envelop me in another of his rib-crushing embraces, but this time there was something a little more to it. One of his minuscule hands shot with astonishing stealth under my unbuttoned coat, pulling me against his stomach as he breathed into my hair.

'You've made an old man very happy tonight, Rory, on our 'date'. I wonder if you might make me happier still . . . '

He reached his other hand to the back of my head and I realized with horrible clarity that he was about to kiss me. I froze. I didn't want to push him away too harshly and hurt his feelings, but nor did I want to be kissed by a man who was a full fifteen years older than my own father. But suddenly he stopped and let me go.

'No, Rory, I just can't do it,' he said, shaking his head. 'I know it's what you want, you've made that clear, with your talk of dating and marriage' — *had* I? — 'but one of us has to be strong. I am too old for you. Too old for romance.'

He turned away from me abruptly. I wasn't sure what to say. I didn't think Teddy was too old for romance, just too old for romance with *me*, but I was afraid to protest too much in case he tried to kiss me again.

He turned back, and reached for my hand. While I stood in dumbfounded silence he bent over and kissed my fingers. 'I'm sure you understand, Rory, that I'm flattered by your interest; flattered and honoured. But I think we should part as friends.'

I murmured some polite words of agreement, not sure exactly how I had ended up as the one who was being gently let down. I let him hail me a taxi and we said goodbye on the pavement. I waved out of the window until we went round the corner.

I really wasn't at all sure who had turned out to be the unsuitable one tonight.

13

Ever since I'd moved into Auntie Lyd's, weekends were the worst. The hours from Friday evening until Monday morning stretched ahead of me as bleakly empty as the Arctic tundra. Sometimes the weight of the days to be filled kept me immobilized in bed until nearly lunchtime, hoping that would make the time pass more quickly. I wouldn't want to give you the impression that Martin and I had spent our weekends on exciting European minibreaks, or indulging in extreme sports, or doing anything out of the ordinary. In fact we rarely did anything in particular other than wander round the shops, catch up with friends, watch a bit of TV and fall asleep on the sofa after Sunday lunch. But, I had discovered, a weekend of doing nothing with a partner is entirely different from a weekend of doing nothing alone.

The only good thing about this Saturday was that I didn't have to tell Lysander or Ticky about my date until Monday. I still wasn't really sure if it had been a triumph or a disaster. On one level, I had had a perfectly nice evening with a perfectly nice man who had clearly found me attractive and interesting. On another I had been groped, and then rejected, by a corpulent geriatric. I realized that writing about these dates for public consumption was going to be harder than I'd thought; it was one thing to put my own dating life up for the amusement of the website's limited readership, but quite another to present my dates themselves as inherently laughable. Teddy was a kind man, and I wanted to find a way of conveying that while still being entertaining enough to earn Amanda's approval. At least, I supposed, I had the entire empty weekend to work out a way of doing so.

As I trudged downstairs in my pyjamas and dressing gown, I could hear Eleanor's high, girlish laugh rising up the stairs, suggesting she had a visitor. This was not the kind of laugh she wasted on either Auntie Lyd or Percy. When I opened the door she was sitting at the kitchen table in her usual bird-like pose, her manicured hands wrapped around a glass. Ever since Percy had made us all aware of her early morning whisky habit, Eleanor had switched from a teacup to a brazenly unrepentant cut-glass tumbler. I'd asked Auntie Lyd why she didn't do anything about it, but she had looked at me with stern disapproval, declaring that as long as Eleanor wasn't harming anyone she was welcome to behave as she liked. Auntie Lyd had also, rather unnecessarily I felt, said that as long as I was sulking around the house like a moody teenager, I might want to suspend judgement on how anyone else chose to deal with their own issues. Then she lit another cigarette.

Leaning against the sink, tools laid out in front of him on the work surface like a surgeon's bench, was Jim; clearly the beneficiary of Eleanor's flirtatious giggles.

'All right, Dawn?' he said, smiling in my

145

direction with the overconfident star quarterback's expression that instantly made my hackles rise. 'Do you live in that dressing gown or what?'

'I've just got up,' I muttered crossly. I didn't need a commentary on my morning habits, least of all from him. Surely one of the benefits of being single is being able to keep to your own timetable instead of anyone else's?

'At eleven o'clock?'

'I had a late night,' I said, hoping that this conveyed something more exciting than the truth. Not that I cared what the plumber thought of me, but the whole unsuitable-men project, embarrassing enough in front of my housemates and work colleagues, became even more so in front of strangers.

'Rory was on a date, weren't you, dear?' said Eleanor, patting the chair next to her. 'You must come and tell us all about it.'

'Oh yes,' said Jim, looking highly entertained as he adjusted a spanner. 'You must.' I could see that he had already decided I was the house's most likely source of amusement. Despite the fact that he was the one wearing a T-shirt that said:

Donkey Sherbet's Icy Grill. Playa del Carmen.

Did he have an entire wardrobe full of hideous tops?

'I need tea before I do anything,' I said, ignoring him as I shuffled over to the kettle.

'Sorry, Dawn, no water in the kitchen this morning,' said Jim, leaning against the work surface so that the slogan on his chest was fully visible. I had no idea what donkey sherbet was, but it sounded absolutely revolting.

'Seriously?' I snapped, my hand already on the kettle handle. 'I suppose I can't even have a shower, can I?'

'Don't panic, Dawn,' he said, grinning infuriatingly. 'I left the water on upstairs. Just no tea. You'll live. At least your hair looks better this morning.'

I would not rise to the bait. I would not, I would not, I would not.

'I suppose I'll just have to settle for toast then,' I said. 'Unless you've disconnected the toaster as well?'

Jim just laughed. He'd taken up far too much space with his tools, seeming to have absolutely no consideration for the fact that people might want to make themselves breakfast. I huffed and tutted as I pushed the bread down in the toaster, but Jim didn't even seem to notice as he bantered cheerfully with Eleanor. Watching them together I sulked by the toaster, feeling as if I was the interloper. Even in her seventies Eleanor was still very beautiful and age had not diminished her charm one bit as she flirted with Jim; all flashing eyes and coquettish hand gestures.

'Goodness, Jim,' she breathed, running a finger slowly round the rim of her glass before touching it to her lips, 'are those enormous muscles of yours just from wrestling with pipes?'

Jim looked delighted, although if you ask me he had practically begged for the compliment.

147

No man wears T-shirts that tight without wanting to have his torso commented upon. 'All from wrestling, Miss Avery,' he countered, 'not necessarily just with pipes.'

Eleanor laughed girlishly. 'Oh you are terrible, honestly, but I suppose all this hard work keeps you very fit, I'm sure I couldn't keep up.'

'I'm sure you could, Miss Avery,' laughed Jim, glancing over to me as if I might share his amusement at Eleanor's flirtatious ways. Fresh from my date with Teddy, I felt infuriated by his assumption. Of course it must be a joke if an older woman chose to flirt with a man at least forty years her junior, I thought bitterly, but no one in Wilton's had batted an eyelid at my date with an old-age pensioner. It was a double standard that had me ready to borrow Auntie Lyd's hessian dungarees and wave an angry placard. Jim clearly thought he, with his sprayed-on T-shirt and highlighted hair, was far too good for Eleanor. I glared back at him until he looked away.

'So, Dawn,' he said as I settled down at the kitchen table with a slice of toast and marmalade. 'Tell us about this date, then.'

'Oh yes, do,' said Eleanor, her eyes bright with interest or whisky or a combination of the two.

'Er, it was fine,' I said.

'Who was he?' asked Jim, his eyes twinkling as if he found the very idea of me dating comical. Thank God he hadn't actually seen Teddy in person or he would probably be rolling around on the floor in hysterics.

'Just a cousin of a work colleague. He's a

landowner from Scotland, actually,' I said. 'He lives on a big estate just outside Perth, but he was down in London on business.' I kind of hated myself for showing off about Teddy like this, but it was better than being regarded as a figure of fun.

'Your aunt said he was nearly *seventy!*' said Eleanor, unwittingly treacherous. '*Most* unsuitable, I thought. Well done you.'

Jim's mouth twitched as if he was having trouble keeping a straight face. I stared resolutely at my toast, although now I had no taste for it.

'Nearly seventy?' he echoed, sniggering. 'Sixty-nine, was he?'

'Sixty-eight, actually. I happen to find older men very charming company,' I snapped defensively. I didn't have to justify myself to the plumber.

'And of course Viagra has completely transformed the over-fifties dating scene,' Jim said, very seriously.

'Oh, I *know!*' giggled Eleanor, and Jim grinned at me again.

Auntie Lyd came stalking into the kitchen with Mr Bits following closely behind; I shrank a little into my chair, knowing she would disapprove of my not being properly dressed at this hour. But instead she directed her comments at Eleanor.

'Eleanor Avery, will you please stop sexually harassing poor Jim,' she said, sweeping past the kitchen table and opening the larder. 'I don't know how he is expected to get any work done with you hanging off his arm like that.' Mr Bits wound pleadingly around her feet.

'I'm delighted to be sexually harassed by anyone at all, Miss Bell,' said Jim affably. 'Though apparently I'm a bit on the young side for your niece.'

Auntie Lyd smiled over at me indulgently. 'Morning, Rory. So when you aren't being distracted by my house guests, Jim, how are you getting on?'

He sighed heavily, and then drew in air through his teeth, shaking his head as he looked at the floor: I wondered if all tradesmen were taught this exact sequence of movements at training college, to be used on any occasion but with particular application to queries from women. It conveyed, without a single word being exchanged, imminent difficulty, great expense and the complex, unknowable mystery of the task ahead.

'In words, please,' said Auntie Lyd, sensibly not standing for any of this nonsense.

'In words, Miss Bell, the pipes in your house don't appear to have been touched since the British Empire governed half the planet,' said Jim, shoving his hands into his pockets and shrugging his shoulders. 'I've had a go at patching up the worst bits, but the pipes are just falling apart in my hands. Not to mention I haven't seen a boiler like yours since I was a child.'

Auntie Lyd looked at him shrewdly, as if sizing up his reliability. She was also probably speculating why anyone would voluntarily wear a T-shirt that compressed their internal organs like that.

'So you're saying . . . ?'

'It's all got to be replaced,' said Jim. 'My advice would be that you move out for a fortnight and I can get it all done in one go.'

'Out of the question,' said Auntie Lyd, opening a foil pouch of cat food and tipping it out on to a saucer. She placed it on the floor for Mr Bits. 'Where would we go? Can't you do it in stages?'

Jim whistled through his teeth again, and ruffled his hair so that it stood up in tufts. He shifted from one foot to another, resting a hand on the work surface. 'It'll take longer that way,' he said. 'And that makes it more expensive.'

'Not as expensive as finding alternative accommodation for four people at a moment's notice,' said Auntie Lyd briskly. 'I've already had half of my paying guests move out. You'll just have to work around the rest of us; there's no other way.'

He rubbed his chin ruefully and shook his head again, as if accepting the job was at great personal inconvenience. 'If you say so, Miss Bell.' He offered her a trademark cheeky-chappie grin.

I rolled my eyes; like he was disappointed this job was going to cost an absolute fortune. Replacing the entire plumbing system at Auntie Lyd's was going to be able to keep him in tight T-shirts and cheap blond highlights for the rest of the year.

But Auntie Lyd just smiled. 'Let me have your quote this week, Jim, and please, do call me Lydia.' I couldn't believe even she allowed herself to be charmed by someone as obvious as the pumped-up plumber. And people said I was useless at identifying unsuitable men. At least I'd spotted this one from a mile away, while Eleanor and Auntie Lyd just swooned over his muscles.

I retreated to my room, but the constant banging on the pipes seemed to echo through the whole house; I couldn't hear the radio, or concentrate on reading, so I decided to while away the afternoon in Clapham instead.

Auntie Lyd had moved to number 32 just before I was born, when Elgin Square, now planted with elegant cherry trees and carefully tended floral borders, was the sleeping ground for the local homeless population by night, and centre for drug dealers by day. South London was notorious back then, and that was probably part of its appeal for Auntie Lyd, who rather liked to think of herself as the black sheep of the family, despite the fact that Mum was extremely proud of her actress sister. No one was quite sure how Auntie Lyd had afforded to buy an entire house with her sporadic income as an actress — although it must be admitted that the early eighties had seen Auntie Lyd's finest professional hour, when she and seventies sexpot Linda Ellery had played warring sisters Destiny and Angel in Anglia Television's *Those Devereux Girls.*

Over the course of three years they had bitched and schemed a shoulder-padded path through the wobbly sets that depicted the headquarters of the Devereux Corporation. They struggled with their grief after the death of the family patriarch, Daddy Devereux, and fought for the approval of their cold, wheelchair-bound mother, Ma. They stole each other's husbands and swapped toyboys; they battled corporate takeovers and illegally altered wills; they delivered lines like 'You won't find Ma's love in the bottom of a wine glass' and 'I can't believe he survived the crematorium'. But it was the legendarily mud-spattered cat-fight on Daddy Devereux's grave in the show's final season, with its somewhat incestuous-lesbian subtext, that had won both Lydia and Linda a particular sort of affection in the hearts of the nation. Apart from the odd commercial, Auntie Lyd hadn't acted since, but you have only to mention the name 'Lydia Bell' to men of a certain generation to see their eyes mist over in fond memory.

In her more romantic moments Mum would speculate that Lydia's house must have been bought for her by an admirer — perhaps a wealthy, married one who had to express his devotion discreetly. It seemed to me discreet to the point of downright offensive that a man would buy his television-star lover a house comprising seven dirty bedsits and a basement flat in a neighbourhood that taxi drivers refused to visit. But we would never know, as Auntie Lyd enjoyed cultivating an air of mystery about the whole business and refused to discuss it.

Once the drug dealers had been moved out of Elgin Square and its surroundings, Auntie Lyd's neighbourhood had been colonized instead by small boutiques in which the local residents were relieved of their disposable income in exchange for patchwork cushions, scented candles, Welsh blankets and seashore pebbles painted with expressive words such as LOVE, PEACE or MORE MONEY THAN SENSE. Okay, I made that last one up. No longer having a home of my own in which to display such items, I found that there was little temptation to spend as I wandered around the boutiques that morning; instead I treated the shops like a series of small museums in which you could pick up the exhibits. I flicked through several books on cupcakes and whoopie pies, I tried on expensive cashmere gloves and scarves, I noted the number of bored boyfriends loitering in doorways and told myself how lucky I was to be free of having to indulge someone else's interests on a Saturday afternoon.

When I had exhausted the shops of the High Street and Old Town, and been followed twice round Oliver Bonas by a suspicious security guard, I took myself to the tiny French patisserie that overlooked the Common, grabbing a seat at the high wooden bar that faced the street. The warmth of the cafe had misted up the window, so I rubbed it with my sleeve to see outside, where the light was just beginning to fade. Shoppers walked past the window briskly, rushing to get home before dark, and a few small children played on the muddy strip of grass across the road, next to the shallow paddling pool that had been emptied for winter. The cafe was nearly empty, except for two waitresses speaking in French to the chef. I waved one of them over and ordered a hot chocolate; it wasn't exactly a sophisticated treat but I felt the need for a bit of indulgence.

When it arrived, I was surprised to find that the sight of the tiny pink and white marshmallows bobbing on its surface made my heart sink. I had thought it would remind me of my childhood, and it had, but not in the comforting way I had hoped. Instead I was taken back to the desolate weekend afternoons of my teens, sitting alone in cafes feeling lonely and misunderstood while Mum was off with her latest boyfriend. Of course I should have been off with friends and boyfriends of my own, but the constant moving, as Mum tired of locations as quickly as relationships, had left me drained and insecure. Every new school had a different set of rules: not the ones set by teachers — those were easy to follow — but the far stricter ones agreed upon by the students. The friendship bracelets that were my passport to cool at one school marked me out as a hopeless loser at the next. My skirt was too long at one school, too short at another, and at a third school all the girls spurned the official uniform that Mum had bought me in favour of subtly different trousers and aertex shirts from Pilot.

Is it any wonder that I took refuge in History of Art, where everything not only remained reassuringly the same (a reproduction of Canaletto's 'A Regatta on the Grand Canal' in York was still a reproduction of the same regatta when viewed in Dorset, after all), but also had a clearly delineated context? History was so much safer than the present, so fixed and certain. However, as you can imagine, the ginger-haired new girl with her passion for the Pre-Raphaelites did not find herself at the centre of the popular students, nor even at the centre of the unpopular ones. Before I met Martin I had become used to spending time by myself; I'd even come to believe I didn't mind it. Now, sitting alone again while everyone else rushed past in pairs or groups, I felt it all come rushing back.

I felt a pang for that poor lonely teenager, and wished I could go back in time to tell her that it would be okay. That she'd get to university and make friends there, friends who didn't think it was weird to discuss *chiaroscuro* or egg tempera; that she'd meet people who spoke about church altarpieces with an enthusiasm equal to her own; that there would be lecturers who'd think she was clever, talented even. There would be parties and gigs and a boy who would think she was amazing; she'd fall in love. But then I realized that I'd also have to tell her that several years later the boy would end up cheating on her, she'd be stuck in a menial job with only the most tenuous connection to art history, and she'd find herself facing thirty, single, dating pensioners and living with her chain-smoking aunt and two ancient actors. Probably best to let that poor lonely girl dream of something better, I decided, cruelly mashing a marshmallow against the side of my cup with a spoon.

If Ticky was right, and dating the unsuitables was meant to be a kind of education, what was I supposed to take away from last night? Apart from a bit of a hangover and the memory of Teddy's shiny red face looming over mine. I hadn't really needed to go out with a sixty-eight-year-old man to learn that I was hoping to end up with a younger one. Perhaps, though, the evening pointed to another bit of Rory Carmichael cluelessness — shouldn't I have been able to pick up on the signals before Teddy tried to kiss me? Now that I looked back, his attitude towards me had slightly changed once he realized we were on a 'date'. He hadn't tried anything on in the restaurant — I wasn't so clueless I wouldn't have noticed an attempt at under-the-table footsie — but he had ordered a lot more wine all of a sudden. And maybe there had been a new twinkle in his eye, although my own eyes had been practically looking in two separate directions by then, so it was hard to tell. And yet I'd continued to play the pert niece, failing to respond to any of the clues that Teddy's intentions had changed. Was I really so used to being attached that I'd lost the ability to notice when someone was interested in me?

While I'd been staring out of the window ruing my life, I'd vaguely noticed the same tall guy walk past a few times, glancing into the cafe. He had a guitar case on his back, and a head full of dark curls that almost rivalled my own, and there was a small dog following him, carrying its lead in its mouth. I wondered if he was looking for somebody. He came past again and as he caught my eye he winked and mimed going down a flight of stairs until his head totally disappeared from sight. Then he leapt up against the window, laughing; it was impossible not to laugh back. He mimed 'Shall I come in?' and before I had a chance to answer, he had poked his head around the cafe door.

'Awright?' he said, his disembodied head grinning. 'Do you reckon I can bring my dog in?'

I opened my mouth to answer but instead found myself staring into his astonishingly green eyes, as if hypnotized. I'm not sure you would have called him good-looking — his face had too much character for that — but the contrast between his dark hair and his sea-glass eyes took your breath away. Mine, anyway.

'No!' said the waitress, crossly bustling over from behind the till. 'No dogs allowed. And we're closing in ten minutes.'

'Wait there then, mate,' the curly-haired man said, bending down to speak to the dog. 'It won't take me more than ten minutes to get this lovely young lady's phone number, I'm sure.'

Well. Perhaps I hadn't lost the ability to spot someone's interest in me after all.

The man smiled over at the waitress with an expression that said he was used to charming the reluctant with his deep green gaze. 'Might I get a cup of tea in your remaining ten minutes?' he asked, leaning forward hopefully with his hands clasped.

'Okay, but you'll have to drink it quickly,' she sighed, smiling despite herself, and he settled confidently on the stool next to me, resting his guitar against the window.

'And might I get your phone number in ten minutes, Girl in the window? Only I've gone and told my dog that I will, and Gordon just never lets it lie if I don't actually follow through on these things.' He pointed out of the window to

158

where his dog sat patiently on the pavement, wagging his tail at passers-by.

'Your dog's name is Gordon?' I asked.

'I know,' the man laughed, nudging my shoulder to share the joke. 'They called him that at Battersea because he's brown. I've tried to change it but he won't answer to anything else. Very temperamental. It's a terrier thing — once they've latched on to something they won't let it go, you see.'

The waitress brought over his tea and he leapt up to pay her that instant, for both his tea and, despite my protests, my hot chocolate. He pulled handfuls of loose coins out of his jeans pockets and pressed them on her, insisting she kept the change. It was a sweet gesture, slightly marred only when she returned only a few seconds later to say he hadn't given her enough.

'Here, here, have more,' he said, digging out more coins until the bill was settled and the waitress generously tipped. 'So where were we? I think you were just about to give me your number?'

There was something contagiously confident about his attitude; it didn't seem to occur to him that I might not want to give him my number, and so, oddly, it didn't really occur to me not to let him have it. There was something about the way he looked at me that made my brain stop working properly. I just wanted to stare and stare, as if I could solve the puzzle of his face if I looked at it for long enough. Before I really knew what I was doing he'd punched the digits into his phone, swigged back his tea, promised to call me tomorrow, and left with Gordon.

When he left I realized that not only had I not managed to get either his name or his number, but that this marked a small but significant dating milestone for me. I had never before given my phone number to a stranger, nor actually been asked for it, since men didn't tend to approach you when you were holding hands with your boyfriend. Here was a man — a young and attractive man — who seemed to be interested in me and, look! I had noticed. I had noticed and agreed to an actual date straight away. Mostly because I was too stunned by his eyes to be able to speak in complete sentences, but still. Instead of feeling like a lonely loser drinking cocoa by herself, in an instant I felt like a proper single girl. One who got asked out on dates, and met interesting men at random. One with options; and maybe not all of them unsuitable ones.

14

I'd read enough women's magazines not to expect a call from the man from the cafe; men were mysterious creatures, apparently, who rarely rang when they said they would, or meant what they said. I knew that single women, like me, should be prepared for disappointment; it was enough that I had been asked out. But he did call me, exactly when he said he would: the very next day. And he asked me to meet him for a drink that same evening. And, because I wasn't distracted by his looks on the phone, I managed to agree in words of more than one syllable. My heart leapt with the knowledge that I would be returning to work on Monday ripe with news of two dates in one weekend. At this rate I'd have the column written for the entire year before I knew it. I didn't exactly know that this man was unsuitable — he looked more than suitable, to be honest — but something about the guitar on his back told me he might be.

The curly-haired man, whose name I had discovered to be Malky, suggested we met at a pub just a few minutes' walk from Auntie Lyd's house. Amongst the vodka bars and crowded pizza restaurants of Clapham, the Duke of Wellington on a corner of the Old Town Triangle was a small oasis of old-school pubbiness. They didn't serve cocktails, or tapas, or Thai food, or indeed any food except for crisps in their most basic form (no poncy parmesan-and-rosemary flavour permitted here). It was dark enough that regulars could be distinguished from visitors simply by whether or not they made it through the bar without hitting their heads on the low beams, or the horse brasses which hung from them. There was no music, except for the faint sound of a busker outside. Two men stood at the bar talking in low voices, and the only other people in here were a couple, sat next to each other on a bench and staring out into the room without speaking. I ordered a glass of wine and went to sit down at a table near the door to wait for Malky.

Twenty minutes later I'd finished my wine, been through all the messages on my phone, sent several fake texts in order to look busy, and checked the time on approximately forty-eight separate occasions. So. This was what being stood up felt like. I tried to look as if I was just a casual, cool sort of girl who often popped into pubs by herself for a quiet glass of wine on a Sunday evening. Of course I hadn't been waiting for anyone, oh no. The faces of the couple opposite me were as impassive as Easter Island statues; it didn't look like they were silently mocking me, but I still felt mortified. And worse was the knowledge that I would have to go back to Auntie Lyd's, where she and the actors would no doubt press me for an update on my latest date, since they had all taken an unhealthy interest in the unsuitable-men mission. I decided facing their questions would be better than continuing to sit in the pub by myself.

I'd hardly stepped off the pavement when I heard someone shouting. Sitting on a bench just a few feet along from the pub was a busker, woollen hat pulled low over his forehead, a guitar case open in front of him with a few coins scattered inside.

'Over here, Girl in window, over here!'

'Malky?' I asked, stepping towards the busker uncertainly.

'Where've you been?' he asked, grinning as he pulled the guitar strap over his head. His eyes flashed with laughter as he stood up. 'I've been waiting ages.'

'I was inside the pub, Malky, where we said we'd meet — remember?'

'Oh, right,' he said, leaning forward to scoop up the loose coins. 'I didn't actually say inside the pub, did I, Girl in the window? Just said I'd see you at the Duke — and here I am!'

He threw his arms wide as if I might happily step inside them and consider everything forgotten, but I was too cross. I tucked my chin further into my scarf and kept my arms folded across my chest. It wasn't really my style to have screaming temper tantrums, but I hoped he could tell he was not forgiven.

'Come on, Girl in the window,' Malky said pleadingly; he had the same expression as when he had wheedled the tea out of the grumpy waitress. And, like her, I could feel myself melting under his sea-glass stare.

'My name's Rory,' I said, a final piece of resistance before crumbling completely, and he gave a little start and a nod. I wondered for a moment if he'd forgotten my name until I reminded him of it; but his imploring smile was catching and I couldn't stop myself from smiling back.

"'Course it is, Rory, I know that. Now what are we doing hanging outside like this in the middle of winter, eh? Whose stupid idea was that? Let's get inside. Come on, drinks are on me.'

He pulled at my gloved hand, and I allowed myself to be led back into the pub where Malky, despite his height, ducked past the horse brasses with practised ease.

'You'd better not have brought that dog in,' the landlord warned, stepping out from behind the bar as soon as he saw Malky approaching.

'No, no, no,' promised Malky, holding up a hand. 'He refused to come, Charlie. Still too full of remorse to face you.'

'Remorse doesn't pay to get the carpets cleaned, young man,' said the landlord, retreating back behind the bar again. He frowned. 'You're lucky I don't ban *you* and all.'

'Charlie, I swear,' implored Malky, leaning over the bar to give the landlord the full effect of his grovelling. I wondered if his pretty eyes worked as well on men. 'I can hardly live with the guilt; it's eating me up inside. But bygones and all that. Can't we just have a few drinks and I swear I won't make a mess in the corner, though I really can't speak for Rory here.'

Charlie chuckled reluctantly and began pouring a Guinness for Malky and another wine for me.

'Are you okay here?' asked Malky, ushering me over to the furthest, darkest table in the room. He grabbed two candles off the windowsill and lit them with matches he'd pulled from his pocket. 'This seat okay? You sure you don't want to go and hang out with the fun crew over there?' He nodded his head towards the Easter Island couple, who still hadn't moved except to occasionally raise their glasses to their silent lips.

I laughed, a little uncomfortably, as I recalled evenings that Martin and I had spent together in what I had thought was a companionable, contented silence. Perhaps we'd looked like them. There was no chance of that with Malky, who was still arranging our corner of the pub to his satisfaction, like a dog that has to turn round and round in its bed before it can settle. He found a place for his guitar, pulled off his hat, drew the curtain of the window behind us and moved the chairs closer; he didn't stop talking the whole time.

'So, Rory, are you much into music?' he asked, pausing at last to sip his Guinness.

'Er, a bit,' I said hesitantly. I felt like I was back at a new school, being asked, without yet knowing which answer would condemn me to perpetual squareness, which was my favourite band. I'd spent so many years trying to get the answer right, I'd never really given much thought as to what I actually liked. All the passion that other people gave to music, I'd always given to art history. Like I said, I wasn't the most popular teen. I'd let Martin buy all the music in our house and, since I didn't know how to work our complicated internet radio stereo, he'd always chosen what we listened to.

'Music is my *life*,' Malky declared, placing a hand on his heart. My own heart lightened immediately with the realization that he wasn't going to ask me anything difficult after all. 'If you knew, Rory, the floors I've slept on, the obstacles I've faced, the idiots who've told me I'll never make it. But I'm still here, still making music.'

'That's really great, Malky,' I said, impressed. It was amazing to meet a real musician, a properly creative person; someone so different from Martin. Malky had such presence, it wasn't hard to imagine him commanding an audience. 'So are you in a band, then?'

His hands tightened around his pint glass. 'I *was* in a band, Rory,' he said stiffly. 'We were on the verge of making it pretty big — had a manager, some good gigs, a few record companies sniffing around.'

'What happened?' I asked.

'The guys sold out.' He shrugged. 'They weren't prepared to make the sacrifices I was. But which of us is still a musician? Only me, Rory, only I stuck it out. I wasn't about to give up on fifteen years of hard work like that.'

'Wow,' I said. Fifteen years without getting your big break? I could hardly imagine that kind of dedication. This must be how it felt to be creative, instead of someone like me, who just admired the creativity of others from the outside. 'So, how do you make it work without a record deal? Do you play a lot of gigs?'

I imagined myself coming to see him play: standing in the audience as he dedicated a song to me. All the other girls jealous of his attention.

'The thing is, Rory,' Malky said, leaning forward urgently and jabbing his finger in the air for emphasis. 'Any fucker can strum a few notes on a guitar playing gigs for *money*, but you can only be a *musician* if you feel it in your soul. Know what I mean? It's not all about recording contracts and capitalism and *money*.'

'No, of course not,' I said. I hadn't meant to offend him with my innocent question — as a wage slave I was just intrigued by anyone who managed to live on their creativity alone. I didn't expect I'd have got very far on mine.

'People just don't understand the compromises you have to make for music,' said Malky, sighing and throwing himself back in his seat. 'I mean — I bet you work in an office, right?'

'R-right,' I stammered. He was looking at me with a dark intensity that made my insides flip-flop with nerves. Nerves and, unless I was mistaken — it had been a while — actual lust. I didn't entirely trust my ability to speak without falling over my words. 'I work for *Country House* magazine, it's a family-owned magazine in — '

'Yeah, see, you're working for the Man,' Malky interrupted, with a satisfied nod.

I had to stifle an unwelcome snort of nervous laughter. Malky was pretty passionately worked up and I didn't think it was quite the right time to tell him that I did indeed work for someone called Man. Although not *the* Man, she was definitely married to one of them — a hedge-funder called Hugh who had been at Eton with the Prime Minister.

'And if you take the Man's money, then you've got to live by the Man's rules. Whereas me — I don't take the Man's money, so I get to live by my own rules.'

'Oh, right,' I said, wondering whether a failing magazine about stately homes and art history actually represented the worst of corporate Britain. But I wasn't a creative person, so no doubt I didn't really understand.

Malky pulled open his battered suede jacket to expose an inner pocket. He reached inside and pulled out a handful of postcards, one of which he handed to me with great import. I took it with what I hoped was sufficient gravity, inclining my head to examine it properly.

'It's me,' said Malky, pointing at the picture. It was indeed, though he looked much younger. Those green eyes were unmistakable, though, and the photographer had managed to capture both Malky's brooding depth and the hint of laughter that saved him from being too intense.

'Wow, look at you,' I said, turning the postcard over. In the bottom corner I read *Malky: Smoking Letters, the single, released October 2004.*

'I can sign it for you if you like,' offered Malky.

'Oh yes please,' I said quickly. His apparent confidence seemed less convincing now, more of a veneer over his struggle to make it in music. Strangely it made him seem more attractive to me, rather than less. He'd been prepared to show his vulnerability to me. As someone who was feeling fairly vulnerable herself lately, it made me want to take his hand and tell him everything was going to be fine. And then maybe take that hand and — But since I wasn't that sort of girl — or at least, I never had been before, who knew who I would become once the unsuitable-men project was over? — I went to the bar instead, in the classic British tradition of expressing emotions through the medium of alcohol.

By the time I returned from the bar, Malky's mood had lightened as he waved the signed post-card at me. I put it in my bag for safekeeping.

'Cheers,' he said, raising his glass. 'God, sorry, Rory, I really went off on one there. I just feel so passionate about what I do, you know? It gets me so fired up. Sometimes it just comes across a bit strongly.'

He hit me once again with one of those imploring smiles, and I couldn't help smiling back. He was just so different from the kinds of men I'd met before. One minute laughing, the next so impassioned and angry. So brilliantly unsuitable, I realized. Hadn't Ticky specifically suggested I should date an aspiring musician? This must have been what she meant — the creative temperament, the mood swings, the passion. He didn't have Teddy's impeccable manners, but then he didn't have Teddy's pensioner's bus pass or his extra poundage. This unsuitable man was a lot more exciting. And attractive.

After three more drinks Malky had become a

lot more fun, and so had I. Even the female Easter Island statue had cracked a smile in our direction, seeing us sitting there giggling at each other. Malky was fascinated by the idea of Auntie Lyd's boarding house — I suppose he recognized fellow creative spirits in the actors who lived there — and demanded endless detail about all of the residents, past and present. He turned out to remember Auntie Lyd from *Those Devereux Girls*, and managed a brilliantly accurate impression of Ma Devereux in her wheelchair by scooting himself across the carpet on a wooden stool. He even suggested we run outside to re-enact the famous mud-wrestling scene on the Common, but I persuaded him out of it. Our faces were getting closer and closer with every new story we shared, and it felt completely natural when he put his arm around the back of my chair. It wasn't hard to pick up on the signals this time.

His hypnotic eyes were so extravagantly lashed that I felt almost envious. I gazed into them for so long that eventually I forgot to speak at all.

'Shall we go?' whispered Malky, after we'd been staring at each other for what seemed like hours.

We got up together and moved towards the door; I wasn't looking at Malky, but I was intensely aware that he was following me as closely as if we were tied together. As soon as we were outside, he dragged me round the corner of the pub to the dark alley and pushed me up against a wall. There was no question of me wanting to stop this unsuitable man, but we grabbed at each other almost as if we were fighting. He held my wrists above my head and kissed me until my head ground into the bricks behind me. He hadn't shaved, and his stubble scratched at my chin. It wasn't just like kissing a different man from Martin, it was like kissing a whole different species.

Suddenly I imagined what Martin would think if he saw me here, drunkenly snogging a stranger. Opening my eyes, I saw that Malky and I were grappling by a rather unromantic row of dustbins. It felt sordid and dirty; I wasn't sure if that was exciting or frightening.

'I should go,' I whispered, pulling my coat around me.

'Can't I come back with you?' Malky said, his curly hair brushing against my cheek as he kissed me again.

'No!' I laughed, wriggling out of his grasp. 'I've got work tomorrow. And didn't I tell you there's a bunch of aged thesps at home waiting to hear how my date went?'

'Next time,' he said, pressing me against the wall for one more kiss. 'No excuses.'

'Maybe,' I laughed, escaping to run across the road towards home. But I didn't mean it. I just thought it was probably a bit uncool to say, 'Definitely next time, I am warm for your form, please please call me tomorrow.'

'Next time, Rory!' Malky bellowed across the street, illuminated by the pub lights as if under a spotlight. 'Next time!'

I skipped home with my heart pounding. It had all felt so wrong, so dirty and passionate, instead of the safe routine that was my relationship with Martin. I couldn't imagine Martin grabbing me like that; he'd have been far too concerned about germs and dirt from the bins. He'd have said, 'Why fool around outside a pub when we've got a perfectly good bed at home?' But why was I thinking of Martin when I might have met a man who'd help me to get over him? As confused as I felt in my head, my body had a far more primitive reaction to my unsuitable man. It had been months since I'd felt myself like this, my knees properly weak with the certain knowledge that Malky wanted me and wasn't afraid to show it. Whatever my head felt about Martin, my body wanted Malky too. There was definitely going to be a next time.

15

So certain was I that the entire office would be waiting to hear about my date with Teddy — and so certain too that I would stun them with news of another unsuitable date within forty-eight hours — that I walked across Covent Garden Piazza with a sense of keen anticipation that I hadn't felt since I very first started at *Country House*. It was funny how working in the heart of London blinkered you to all of its charms. Instead of seeing the neo-classical Covent Garden market as beautiful, most days I just cursed how its design caused packs of French schoolchildren to cluster in the narrow walkways, making it impossible to pass. Rather than finding the cobbles a charming link to the past, I deplored how many pairs of shoes they had ruined by trapping my heels between them. It was ironic that while my job was about the beauty of historical architecture, I rarely noticed that I was surrounded by it even on the walk from the tube.

This morning, I noticed everything afresh. It probably helped that the market was free of tourists since it was too early for the shops to be open, and it certainly helped that none of those annoying people who paint themselves silver and stand still all day had yet to emerge. Instead of looking down to avoid catching anyone's eye — it could take ten minutes to cross Inigo

Jones's Italian-inspired piazza once people started asking you directions — I looked up. On the top of each light around the market was a stone pineapple; on my first day at *Country House* I had been thrilled to see this centuries-old emblem of wealth and hospitality, a direct link to the fruit and vegetable market that once stood here. These days most people thought they had something to do with the Pineapple Dance Studio round the corner. I'd walked past them hundreds of times without even seeing them, let alone remembering the excitable new girl I'd once been.

Today, though, I had more than a hint of the excitable new girl about me. Maybe it was the unseasonably sunny day that was infusing every thing with a sense of optimism. Or maybe, let's be honest, it was the memory of snogging Malky last night. The first new man I had kissed in eleven years. Eleven years! Of course he was wildly unsuitable — tempestuous, moody, unemployed; that was the point — but I was beginning to see why so many girls went running after bad boys. Whenever I thought of how insistent he'd been, how passionate, I found I couldn't stop smiling.

When I got to the office, however, Ticky was already muttering into the phone about some weekend disaster involving her boyfriend, Pongo. It was strange to find myself actively wanting Ticky's emotional draining and to be denied it — like trying and failing to be flattened by a bus. I kept attempting to catch her eye but she was too intent on her conversation to notice until

Lysander appeared in the doorway, smirking in a way that suggested he had already spoken to Teddy.

'Auroooooooora,' he said, stretching out my name to extraordinary lengths, and infusing it with layers of meaning and innuendo.

'Lysander,' I said warily. He bounded into the office, checked the armchair for errant fascinators, and threw himself into it.

'Ethelred said he had a delightful evening. You were charming company, I hear, not that I would have expected anything less.'

Ticky, still on the phone, spun her chair around and mimed 'Oh my Goouurd,' trying to keep half an ear on our conversation.

'He was really nice, Lysander, thanks for suggesting it,' I said, still unsure how much of the evening Teddy would have relayed back to his cousin.

'And I hear you were verrrrrrry nice to him, Aurora,' Lysander said, raising one eyebrow.

'What do you mean?' I asked suspiciously.

'He said you made a pass at him, but he had to turn you down.'

Ticky put the phone down instantly, halfway through a sentence. 'You made a pass at Lysander's gopping cousin?!'

'Oh God, no, it wasn't really like that,' I insisted.

'Oh my Goouurd,' said Ticky, 'how revolting. You are, like, practically a necrophiliac, Roars. Yack.'

Lysander stiffened. 'Ethelred is not that much older than me, Victoria. He is hardly a corpse yet.'

175

'I did not try to make a pass at Teddy!' I shouted. Heads whipped round with interest outside our office door.

'Oh, Teddy, is it?' sniggered Ticky. 'Your cuddly old teddy bear.'

'Look, Lysander,' I said, thinking that I would be more likely to get a fair hearing from him than from Ticky, 'I think Teddy must have got the wrong end of the stick. I didn't make a pass at him, but he seemed to think I wanted to. And he, er, he told me that he couldn't do it.'

'No Viagra?' said Ticky, suddenly sympathetic. 'My godmother says that happens a *lot*.'

'That wasn't it at all,' I protested. 'It was all a misunderstanding.'

Ticky and Lysander exchanged amused glances; clearly neither of them believed me. Seemingly, given the choice between my version of events and the version in which I threw myself, panting, on a senior citizen, they preferred the latter.

'Anyway, I went on another date last night,' I announced.

'Another date with Teddy?' asked Ticky. 'Gooourd, there's no stopping you, Roars. One night of pensioner passion wasn't enough, eh?'

'No,' I said. 'A totally different unsuitable man, actually.'

'Roars, you are, like, on a roll,' said Ticky admiringly. 'Was this one from Help the Aged too?'

'Oh shut up,' I said, feeling smug. If they were going to persist in believing that I'd been spurned by Teddy, I was going to keep my Malky

176

story to myself and leave them in suspense. And now that I thought about it, was an anecdote in which I found myself snogging a busker by a row of wheelie bins the best way to salvage my reputation?

Although I ignored them, Ticky and Lysander entertained themselves for a further twenty minutes by loudly discussing how best to sign me up to a Grab a Grandad dating website. Since I'd split up with Martin and proposed the Unsuitable Men column, it seemed that everyone at *Country House* was a little more aware of my existence than they had been. Mostly, admittedly, because they were enjoying a laugh at my expense, but there was still something oddly gratifying about it. I saw how I'd previously been excluded from much of the office banter, not because my colleagues ignored me, but because, stuck within the protective shell of my relationship, I'd held myself apart from them. Without Martin I'd felt new, exposed, raw; and yet somehow that had allowed my colleagues to come closer. Which wasn't something, frankly, I'd ever hoped for, so I was surprised how much I welcomed it. Although there were limits, and if Ticky and Lysander didn't shut up, I might reach them fairly soon.

Still, the saving grace of the unsuitable-men project, I began to realize, was that, no matter how much my colleagues wound me up, I would always get the last word on each date. Ticky and Lysander could tease all they liked; my version of every date was the one that was published. And since everything was anonymous, there was no reason not to embellish just a little. The things I wished I'd said: in my version, I'd say them. The way I wished I'd behaved: in my version, I would. It would be my life, edited by me as it should have been, rather than as it was.

Despite Teddy's rather ungallant behaviour in telling Lysander that he'd had to fend off my advances, I didn't want to stitch him up, even under an assumed name. He had been good company, and I felt sad that he didn't feel he was worthy of romance. So I started work on the piece immediately, amending our undignified fumble into a less embarrassing kiss on the hand from Teddy, and a declaration from him that our love could never be because of my relative youth. It felt like the kindest way to spare both my blushes and his. My five hundred words concluded:

> My second date with a supposedly unsuitable man taught me that I'm not the only one with a set of rules. A man who I found more than suitable turned out to find me wanting. I hope there's a suitable lady out there for Mr X, but sadly it is not me.

I knew it was rather over-egging the pudding, but I also knew Lysander had been right. The very idea of a lonely and immensely wealthy Scottish landowner tortured by the memory of a lost love was straight out of a romance novel. And to discover that he rejected a woman for being too young, that he was that mythical beast, the rich bachelor who actually prefers an older

178

woman — well, I couldn't have invented a story more likely to appeal to the traditional readers of *Country House*. Of course it did make me seem rather pathetic, and it offered my colleagues a lot of ammunition against me, which they would need no encouragement to use, but it seemed a price worth paying for some positive reader feedback that I could wave under Amanda's nose.

At least Ticky had finally given up on the constant grandad jokes. In fact she was nowhere to be seen. I tried not to be annoyed by her regular disappearances — it only annoyed me if I paid attention to how little work she did. But it soon became evident that, far from being idle, she'd been working on something else altogether.

'Yah, so, I hear you're, like, looking for a toyboy,' drawled a voice from the office door.

I looked up from my desk to see a scrawny young boy leaning against the door frame with extremely self-conscious nonchalance, as if he had learned how to be cool out of a book from the school library. I vaguely recognized him as the intern who had been helping Flickers over the last few weeks; I hadn't paid much attention to him since our office was always full of gap-yah or university students getting work experience by doing our most boring tasks for nothing. They stayed for a few weeks, only to be immediately replaced by yet another Jack Wills-wearing doppelganger whose Mummy had begged a favour from Amanda. I found it impossible to keep track of them all, and must admit I'd stopped trying years ago.

'Sorry?' I asked, looking at him more closely. Although he was almost certainly not yet twenty, he seemed, like all the men in our office, to be somehow beyond either age or fashion. He wore light-beige trousers, shiny brogues and a pale-pink shirt, open at the neck. I was certain I had seen him arriving in the office in a sort of sports jacket. If it weren't for an artfully styled fringe, brushed forward across one eye, and the last shreds of a wristband from a music festival, on clothing alone it could have been anyone from Lysander to Old Mr Betterton standing there.

'Like, yah, Ticks said that you were looking for a toyboy for this Unsuitable Men thing?' said the young man, flicking his long fringe out of his eyes. 'So, right, reporting for duty and all that?'

What was Ticky thinking? A toyboy was one thing but I couldn't even look at this boy without imagining him in school uniform. And not in a good way. It made me feel like a paedophile. 'Ticky sent you to me?'

'No,' he said, but his public-school voice made it sound more like 'Neeoohhww'. 'No, Ticks just, like, told me about your mission and I, like, already thought you were totally a MILF anyway, so —'

'A MILF?'

'Umm, you know,' he stammered, flushing deep crimson. 'Mother I'd Like to — you know.'

'I know what it stands for,' I snapped, 'but I don't have any children.'

'It's just, like, an expression for a hot older bird, yah?' he said, shoving his hands in his pockets and kicking at the floor. 'Look, like, this is sahhriously embarrassing. Ticks said you'd totally be up for it. I wasn't, like, expecting to have to beg or anything.'

'Oh right,' I snapped. 'So Ticky said I was a sure thing, did she?'

The boy had the grace to look embarrassed. 'Look, I just thought we might go out for a drink or something,' he said.

I felt a little sorry for him, having been coerced by the emotional steamroller that was Ticky into asking out an older woman who he had probably assumed would be grateful for his attentions. 'Look, um, Luke? Is your name Luke?' I asked.

'Yah,' he said, his face brightening at the realization I had remembered his name.

I wasn't about to admit I'd remembered it purely because I'd seen on the phone list that he was called Luke Home, which sounded like a song by the Proclaimers. Not least because I suspected Luke was far too young even to have heard of them.

'Luke, it's very kind of you, and very brave of you, to ask me out. But I'm not sure we'd have an awful lot to say to each other, given the age difference. So thanks for asking, but I think probably not.'

Luke stopped leaning on the door frame and stood up straight. He took two steps into the office and squared himself in front of my desk. Close up he didn't seem as slight and scrawny. In fact he was quite intimidating.

'Look, Ticks told me that you are meant to be

181

dating unsuitable men, so I think it's, like, pretty rude of you to try to get out of going out with me because you think I'm too young. Too young is, like, the whole point actually.' He crossed his arms and stared at me.

It was true that I had put a toyboy on my list of unsuitable men but I had imagined that this meant a hot twenty-four-year-old. Not a mildly acned boy, whose voice still occasionally betrayed him with a rogue high note. If Teddy had been the extreme end of the older-man spectrum, Luke was about as young a toyboy as I could date without being arrested.

'I'm just not sure we'd have much to say to each other, Luke,' I said.

'I think you might be surprised,' he said, uncrossing his arms and leaning forward to rest his hands on my desk, blatantly staring straight down the front of my dress. 'I think you might be very surprised at what we might have to say to each other. Or do. To each other.'

I was horrified to discover that it was my turn to blush; how had he moved from young boy into sexual predator quite so quickly? Discomfited, I put a hand over my chest to cover up — not that I was wearing anything particularly revealing, but under his lascivious gaze I felt like I was sitting there in my underwear. Luke realized his advantage with a skill that belied his years.

'So we're agreed, yah?' he said, straightening up confidently.

'Are we?' I asked weakly. He stood in front of my desk with his legs wide apart, looking like the hearty captain of games at a boys' school. Which he probably had been only a few short months ago.

'Yah, lunch, Friday. Let's do it.' Luke walked to the door with a new-found swagger and turned to grin at me, back to a young boy again. 'Laters.'

★ ★ ★

When Ticky finally graced our office with her presence, two large carrier bags in hand, she was utterly unapologetic.

'Thought you might need a little privacy, Roars,' she winked. 'Just absented myself for a while for, like, the greater good.'

'Ticky, you are unbelievable. Did you tell that — that *infant* to come and ask me out?'

'Luke Home you mean?'

It turned out his name wasn't a Proclaimers song at all — who'd have guessed that you pronounced his last name 'Hume'?

'Yes, Luke — he's a child. How can I possibly go out with him? Even just for lunch. He'll want to talk about pop music and iPhone apps and, I don't know, things I don't understand.'

'Roars, if we are going to exclude dates on the basis of men talking about things you don't understand, we'd have to rule out, like, three-quarters of the male population of England,' said Ticky. 'You are entirely clueless and these dates are meant to help you with that. No one's asking you to marry him, just have your date and write about it. End of.'

'I wish you'd stop interfering, Ticky. I'm perfectly capable of sorting out dates for myself.'

'Yah?' she asked, disbelieving. 'Not really seeing it, Roars. Left to your own devices you end up on a date with Lysander's ancient cousin. I'm just trying to help you get some balance here. One old-age pensioner plus one toyboy equals one man your own age.'

'I have met a very nice man near my own age already,' I said hotly. 'We've been on one date and we're going to go on another. Soon, actually.'

Ticky looked at me suspiciously. She clearly didn't trust me to make any decisions myself.

'The date from the weekend?' she asked.

'Yes,' I said. 'Malky.'

She nodded thoughtfully. 'Hmm, *sounds* unsuitable, I will admit. No captain of industry goes by Malky, that's for sure. Occupation?'

'Musician,' I said. She nodded again, looking unconvinced. '*Unemployed* musician,' I added.

She looked a little more impressed. 'Age?'

'I'm not sure — early thirties, probably.'

At last she was satisfied. 'Unemployed musician in his thirties — sounds promising, Roars. Totes unsuitable. I fully approve. But nothing wrong with a little back-up, is there?'

'I suppose not,' I agreed grudgingly.

'Rack 'em up, Roars,' said Ticky, beaming at me benevolently like some patron saint of the dateless and desperate. 'Rack 'em up.'

She tapped away quietly at her keyboard for ten minutes before adding, 'Oh, yah, obvs you already know that Luke is Amanda's godson, right?'

16

The house was dark and quiet when I got home on Thursday night; it seemed, for once, that everyone was out. Usually when the house was empty, Mr Bits would be waiting on the stairs ready to wrap himself around the legs of the first person home in a deranged plea for feeding that risked breaking the neck of his potential feeder as they descended to the basement kitchen. But this evening he was nowhere to be seen, so I was able to head down to the kitchen without clinging to the banisters for safety. For a moment I wondered where everyone was, but actually I was rather pleased to be able to kick off my polite smile along with my heels. I hadn't lived in a house share since I'd left university; I'd forgotten what it's like to live with other people who have to be engaged in conversation when sometimes all you really want to do is be silent with your own thoughts.

I still hadn't heard from Malky, and was doing my best to stay calm about it. Ticky had explained that there was a whole game to be played here — Malky wouldn't want to look too keen, and I should remain as cool as possible and absolutely not contact him under any circumstances. But the longer I went without hearing from him, the more desperate I became to see him again. Perhaps I shouldn't have run away from him like that? I thought I was being flirtatious, but maybe he thought I wasn't interested. Should I have let him come home with me like he asked? Surely not: I'd only just met him. If this was a game, it was one at which I felt at a distinct disadvantage. It seemed like everyone else knew the rules but me. I had never subscribed to the belief that men and women were from different planets, but everyone else seemed to think so. Auntie Lyd, who rarely let an opinion go unexpressed, had even gone so far as to say that it was about time I got some experience of the battle of the sexes. I wasn't quite sure how to take this — it's not like Martin had been a hermaphrodite, I had actually been living with a man for over a decade; was she saying relationships between men and women were always a battleground? When I tried to get her to elaborate, she pressed her lips together and left the room in her usual mysterious manner.

The radio was on in the kitchen — Auntie Lyd often left Radio 4 playing when she went out, to keep Mr Bits company, as if he might be fooled by *The Archers* into thinking we were all there, chatting invisibly around the kitchen table. But it seemed to be switched to a sports station tonight, which was weird. A silver laptop was open on the table, which was even weirder — no one in the house owned one, and even if they did, there was no internet access at Auntie Lyd's. Who could it belong to? I tiptoed over towards it to have a nose at what was on the screen when I heard a sound behind me.

I shouldn't have been surprised to see Jim, in

yet another one of his horrible tight T-shirts, although this one just had an innocuous pair of binoculars printed on the front. He practically lived in Elgin Square these days. But I was surprised to see him guiltily straightening himself up as he hastily closed one of the kitchen drawers. I knew for a fact this drawer contained nothing more exciting than a roll of tin foil and a collection of ancient folded tea towels, but his studied sangfroid as he loped towards me across the kitchen floor made me immediately suspicious.

'What are you doing here?' I demanded.

Jim shrugged his shoulders as if it was no big deal that he was hanging out in my aunt's house, not even pretending to be working, nosing around in her drawers. As it were.

'Hiya, Dawn,' he said. 'Nice to see you, too.'

'What are you doing?' I asked again, my hands on my hips.

'Oh, all right, Dawn, call off the search. You caught me red-handed.'

I knew it.

'Yes,' he sighed, raising his hands in surrender. 'It's a fair cop. I was looking for something to eat. You'd better put the cuffs on, guvnor. Be gentle with me.'

'Why were you looking in those drawers, then? If you just wanted something to eat, why weren't you looking in the fridge?'

'Chill out, Miss Marple,' he laughed. 'Jeez, I was just checking I hadn't missed a secret stash of biscuits or anything.'

A likely story.

'I wouldn't have thought you ate biscuits,' I said.

'What's that supposed to mean?' he asked, pulling out the chair and sitting down, his legs stretched out as if he planned to be there some considerable time.

'I'd have thought protein shakes and power gels were more your thing.'

'Is that a compliment on my physique, Dawn?' he asked, leaning backwards to grin at me with his hands behind his head to better display his pecs.

I ignored him as I took off my coat and hung it on the back of a chair. It was rare enough for me to get an evening alone at Auntie Lyd's; it seemed typical that it would be spoiled by the plumber hanging about for absolutely no reason. As I walked behind him I saw that Jim's apparently inoffensive T-shirt was no such thing. The back read:

Sydney Nudist Beach: Security Patrol.

Typical.

'I suppose nothing's working again?' I asked. I'd become so used to the lack of water at home that I had found myself, just this afternoon, turning the taps in the office loos off and on again for a full minute, gazing in wonder at the gushing water like a time traveller newly introduced to modern plumbing.

'Everything's working fine.'

'So you just thought you'd hang out here anyway, did you?' I asked. His presence unsettled me; I wasn't going to be able to relax knowing he was here, and that made all of my irritation and anxiety about Malky and Martin and Luke and work and everything come bubbling up unpleasantly. 'Nowhere else you'd rather be on a Thursday night? No life of your own?'

'That's right, Dawn,' he said, smirking over the top of the laptop. 'I'm hanging out here just so I can get a bit more of your delightful company. Anyway, I don't see you out on the town either.' He was as impervious as Amanda; nothing seemed to get to him.

'Huh,' I grunted. Couldn't he just get the message and leave?

'Remind me again which charm school you graduated from?' he grinned.

I glared at him; how dared he imply that I was rude, when he was the one who was making himself at home in my house, uninvited? Well, Auntie Lyd's house, but still — it wasn't his house, and yet here he was acting like I was the one who was in the way.

'You can't connect to the internet here you know,' I said, as if he wouldn't have realized that already. 'There's free WiFi in the Starbucks on the other side of the Old Town Triangle. You should go there.'

'Thanks for the advice, Dawn,' said Jim. 'But I'm just finishing off setting up your aunt's broadband connection.'

'What?'

'They didn't teach you very good manners at that charm school, did they, Dawn? Didn't anyone tell you it's 'pardon', not 'what'?'

'I beg your *pardon*, Jim, but my Auntie Lyd doesn't even have a mobile phone, let alone a laptop. Why would she want broadband? And why are *you* doing it?'

Jim leaned back in his chair and reached his arms above his head, fingers interlinked as he yawned and stretched. His tight T-shirt rode up a little to show his tanned stomach. In March. I cast my eyes up to the ceiling in disgust. I bet he used sunbeds or, worse, fake tan. The vanity of the man.

' 'Cause she asked me,' he said. 'Happy to help out.'

Of course he was. It gave him an excuse to snoop around her property. He was obviously up to something.

'But you're a plumber,' I said, somewhat pointlessly, since he was no doubt already aware of this fact, it being written in large letters on the side of his white van after all. It made me suspicious — Auntie Lyd knew nothing about computers or the internet, nor did Percy or Eleanor. Nor, let's be honest, did I. They — we — were ripe for being ripped off by this dodgy plumber with his dubious claims of computer knowledge.

'Used to be in IT,' Jim said.

'Oh really?' I said; it seemed very unlikely to me. 'So how much are you charging Auntie Lyd for this?' I wanted him to know that I had my eye on him. He wasn't going to get away with taking advantage of my aunt. Not with me here to look after her.

Jim shrugged. 'No need to get chippy, Dawn.

I'm not charging her anything — just helped her choose the right laptop and broadband supplier. Only took a minute, seeing as I'm here all the time anyway.'

'I don't know why you don't just move in,' I muttered under my breath as I went over to the fridge to see what I could make for supper.

'Aurora Carmichael!' said Jim, in a faux-scandalized voice. 'But we hardly know each other. And anyway, I don't think I'm your type. I've got all my own teeth, for a start.'

'If you are going to go on about the sixty-eight-year-old again,' I snapped, turning around from the fridge, 'that was *one* date. And who are you to judge what my type is?'

'Steady on,' Jim laughed, holding his hands out as if to ward me off. 'Only teasing, Dawn. You date who you like. The care home is your oyster.'

'Actually,' I said, shutting the fridge door so hard that all the bottles inside rattled in alarm. I'd lost my appetite for supper. 'Actually, I'm dating a musician at the moment. He's really creative, and amazing. And young.'

It was probably stretching it to describe my one date and subsequent by-the-bins fumble as 'dating', especially as I hadn't heard from Malky since. And also stretching it somewhat to call thirtysomething Malky 'young' — he wasn't exactly a Luke-style toyboy. But somehow Jim's smug face as he sat at the kitchen table, laughing at me in his hideous clothes with his highlighted hair and his fake tan, made me desperate to prove I wasn't just a tragic dating loser.

'Good for you,' he smiled. I could tell he didn't

191

believe me. He probably thought I was making it all up. He probably thought I'd be living with my spinster aunt for ever, like two generations of Miss Havishams; and if Malky didn't bloody ring me soon, I probably would be.

As if on cue, my phone buzzed with a text message.

'That's probably him now,' I said, unable to suppress a sense of triumph at the opportune interruption, although I was far from certain it would be Malky. But when I read the message from an unknown number, I was relieved that it wasn't. I hadn't read anything that filthy since I'd nicked my mum's copy of Shirley Conran's *Lace* when I was at school.

'Jeez, Dawn, you've gone scarlet,' said Jim, chuckling away smugly as he watched me stare at the screen open-mouthed. 'What's he said?'

'None of your business,' I snapped, turning off my phone immediately. I don't think I could have read the message out loud even if I'd wanted to, and I certainly wasn't about to show it to Jim. I'm not sure I can bring myself to write it down. Let's just say that it expressed a wish to, well, become better acquainted with my arse through the medium of spanking. And I had no idea who it was from. I felt a rising panic — had Teddy decided we would suit after all?

'Aren't you going to reply?' asked Jim.

I was saved from answering both Jim and the anonymous text by the arrival home of Auntie Lyd with Eleanor and Percy, carrying programmes from the National Theatre, where they must have been to a matinée. Grateful for the distraction, I threw my phone into my handbag.

Eleanor's eyes lit up with delight when she saw Jim seated at our kitchen table. At least someone was glad to see him there.

'Ooh, Jim,' she trilled, tripping over to him. 'Is it set up yet? I can't wait for you to show me how to use the broadband. I think I might need some special, private lessons.'

Jim smiled. 'You won't need lessons, Eleanor, you'll catch on straight away, I'm sure.'

Percy grunted from the other side of the table, where he'd settled himself so as to be able to glare at Eleanor. 'Never underestimate how stupid that woman can be.'

'Percy!' admonished Auntie Lyd. 'There is absolutely no need to speak to Eleanor like that — you're just annoyed she got recognized in the foyer and you didn't.'

Percy muttered under his breath, but didn't answer back, so I assumed Auntie Lyd was right about the source of his vicious mood. Both he and Eleanor were fiercely competitive over who got recognized the most, and Percy had even been known to hang about in the Sainsbury's on the high street for no other purpose than a hope he might be spotted by his public, which didn't happen nearly often enough for his satisfaction.

'It's all done, Lydia,' said Jim, closing the lid of the laptop and pushing his chair away from the kitchen table. 'Tomorrow I'll show you how to get online, and then you're away.'

'What brought this on? Why do you want broadband all of a sudden?' I asked Auntie Lyd accusingly.

'Well,' she said, looking surprised at the harshness of my tone. 'I was just talking to Jim about it and he made me see how much we could all benefit from having it set up. Apparently I can order all sorts of things without having to drive out of town. And I can read your new column, too.'

'I could have done it for you,' I said petulantly. 'It's not even that difficult. You should have asked me.'

Two vertical lines appeared between Auntie Lyd's eyebrows as she frowned at me with an expression that told me to stop talking before I made an idiot of myself.

Although really I knew it was already too late; I looked churlish and ungrateful while Jim the dodgy plumber looked generous and kind. But I wanted to be the one who helped her. I felt like a toddler, used to being the darling of the Elgin Square family, disgruntled by a new baby. If that new baby had been six foot three and built like an action hero.

'Don't understand why a young man like you would leave a good job in computers to mess around with people's pipes all day,' muttered Percy, obviously still annoyed and now turning on Jim.

'Have you been speaking to my gran, Perce?' asked Jim, laughing. 'That's just the sort of thing she says.'

'But really,' said Eleanor, resting a hand on Jim's arm and copping a surreptitious feel of his muscles. 'Lydia said you used to be a consultant on the broadband in the City. Don't you miss it?'

'God, no,' Jim laughed. I felt even more suspicious of this so-called IT expert. No one gives up a well-paid white-collar job to become a plumber. Something must have happened. Maybe he was sacked. Maybe he was done for embezzling. Maybe he just wasn't very good at it.

'Seems odd to me,' I said.

'Seems odd to a lot of people, Dawn,' said Jim affably. 'But everything I did started to get outsourced to India and Asia, and I didn't want to compete with that. It wasn't about the work any more — just about how cheaply you could do it.'

'So you just gave up and became a plumber?' I asked.

'I don't think of it as giving up,' said Jim. 'I just took a proper look at my life — always sat at a desk, always commuting, running around according to other people's timetables, competing to do the work for less and less money. It didn't feel like I was giving up a lot when I decided to pack it in.'

'But Jim,' said Eleanor, whose interest in this conversation was excellent cover for the number of times she could touch Jim (she was well into double figures already). 'Surely you were qualified to do something other than plumbing?'

'I suppose,' said Jim, turning to look at her. 'But I like plumbing. Always have. My dad was a plumber, and I used to help him during the school holidays. It's satisfying working with your hands: fixing things, making them better. And if your toilet's overflowing, you don't want to ring a call centre in Mumbai, you want someone to come round and sort it out. You can't outsource a blocked pipe, can you?'

I hadn't thought of it like that. But still, from IT professional to unclogging drains seemed like a weird career trajectory to me. It wasn't like getting a seat on the board, was it? Or a company car, or a performance bonus. You might not be outsourced, but you still spent your days with your hands down other people's toilets. I knew which I'd prefer.

'Mmm, go on Jim, fascinating,' breathed Eleanor, leaning closer. Percy glared at her.

'That's it really,' Jim shrugged. 'I'm in charge of my own time, I take the jobs I want to take, I've got time to go to the gym when I want. It just suits me.'

Unlike that T-shirt, I thought, meanly. I noticed Auntie Lyd was smiling approvingly at Jim; why? She thought gyms were for idiots. And surely Jim was the proof of it — pumped up like a cartoon hero. I bet if you pressed his back his eyes would swivel like Eagle Eyes Action Man. Though Action Man would surely never have submitted to the indignity of blond highlights.

17

When I got to the office the next morning, my email inbox was unusually full. My heart instantly sank with fear that there had been a sudden influx of unsolicited features from mentalists. In the old days they were called green inkers for their usual choice of pen — easily identified and disposed of in the bin. But the broadband, as Percy called it, had changed the entire process, and now every lunatic with a laptop felt qualified to call themselves a writer and submit their rambling thoughts to *Country House* with stern warnings about copyright infringement, as if we had nothing better to do than steal their work and pass it off as our own. There was a terrible inevitability to most of the submissions. I knew without even looking that the latest batch of hopeful contributors would mostly concern themselves with bluebell woods, Easter bonnets and the pagan origins of Easter itself (all too late for the April issue). Those who'd acquainted themselves more fully with our submission guidelines would be aiming for May instead: May queens, may blossom, maypoles, mayflies, may I please bang my head against my desk in frustration. A rare few would be pitching early for the summer and autumn slots; there was yet another office sweepstake, an annual one on how many articles containing the words 'season of mists and mellow fruitfulness' would be submitted for the September issue. Last year's total had been twenty-four, with Amanda's PA, Catherine, declared the worthy winner.

But only four of these emails were unsolicited pitches. The remaining fifteen had all been forwarded to me from Ticky via a website which appeared to be called MyMate'sGreat.com.

'Wow, you sound gorgeous! I am sure I can show you a bit of what you've been missing.'
'Hey Sexy, U R hot. Wanna chat?'
'One Bad Boy, reporting for duty!!!!!!!!!!!!!!!!!!!!!!!!!!!!'
'Bad to the BONE, baby, you know it! Oww-www!'
'Unsuitability guaranteed, call me!'

And so it continued. I had never seen so many exclamation marks in one place before. It was horrifying.

'Ticky?' I said, looking up slowly and trying to keep control of my voice.

She beamed over at me from behind her desk, obviously very pleased with herself. 'Just seen the emails, have you? Not bad, eh, Roars? Your profile only went live last night and look how many replies you've had. Amazeballs.'

'My profile?' I asked as calmly as possible. 'What do you mean my 'profile'?'

'What?' said Ticky innocently. 'I thought we agreed you were going to rack them up? So, like, I just wrote you a little dating profile and look how many men want to meet you!'

'You are unbelievable, Ticky,' I muttered. 'A little dating profile? I can't believe you would do this without even consulting me. These men sound horrendous. I mean, do I wanna chat? How old is he — fourteen?'

'Yah, see, that is totally why I should be in charge of this instead of you.' Ticky tossed her blonde mane. 'Unsuitable, remember? This is not about finding your future husband. Although you never know . . . '

'Ticky, if one of these men is my future husband I swear to God I will bestow on you our first-born child,' I said.

'Like, wow, that's a step of gratitude too far.'

'Not out of gratitude, Ticky,' I growled. 'Because it will be some kind of freaky mutant gremlin child that I will want to get rid of as soon as possible.'

'Um, harsh, Rory?' said Ticky, flicking her hair over her shoulder. 'I'm only trying to help.'

'I really could do without your help. At least let me see what you've written on this 'little dating profile'.'

'Well, like, yah, of course,' said Ticky, picking up papers on her desk and shuffling them around in an unconvincing show of sudden busyness. 'Later, Roars, bit hectic right now.'

'Ticky . . . ' I warned. Trying to use work as an excuse was pretty desperate; she'd have been more convincing if she'd pleaded a vital appointment for morning cocktails with another of her titled godfathers.

'Lots to do, lots to do,' she said, and shot out of the office before I could stop her.

Ticky's reaction made me even more determined to see what she'd written. How hard could it be to find my own profile? I logged on to My Mate's Great and searched for women aged twenty-nine in the Greater London area. There were an awful lot of them, smiling hopefully for the camera in a manner that suggested they were fun and uncomplicated and in no way desperate, unattractive or friendless. I say 'them', but I should have said 'us', because there I was, my profile picture cropped by Ticky out of a group shot at last year's Christmas party. Underneath, the text declared me to be 'back in the game'. With deep foreboding I clicked to open up the full profile.

Rory's friend Ticky says:
Rory is a gorgeous red-headed journalist on a mission. She's just got out of a long-term relationship with a man who thought spreadsheets were a form of foreplay; now she needs a bad boy to show her what she's been missing. Do you have what it takes to show a good girl a very, very bad time? If you think you can release the fiery passion that Rory's been hiding for too long, get in touch.
Unsuitable men ONLY. Nice boys finish last.

That was it. When Ticky came back to the office I was going to wrench that silver spoon out of her over-privileged mouth and use it to beat her to death.

But, perhaps sensing my murderous feelings towards her, Ticky didn't return to her desk for the rest of the morning. I glimpsed her occasionally, rushing past trying to look busy and preoccupied. And at one point I caught her

200

and Noonoo huddled in a corner discussing something in fierce whispers, but Ticky scuttled away down the back stairs as soon as she realized I'd seen her. So intent was I on exacting my revenge that I entirely forgot about my date with the office intern until I received his email just before lunchtime.

I'll come and get you in ten minutes.
Let's go to my club. L

Only at *Country House* would the teenaged intern be a member of a private club. Unless, I flinched with horror, he meant a nightclub? Did teenagers go to actual clubs at lunchtime these days? What did people wear to go clubbing anyway? Surely not the floral dress I was wearing today. This kind of confusing weirdness was precisely why I had been afraid of dating a teenager; a teenager, I suddenly remembered, who was practically related to Amanda. As if it couldn't get any worse.

18

I will say one thing for the public-school system. It may turn out floppy-haired right-wingers with a tendency towards floridity in the cheeks and a distinct lack of presence in the chin department, but it really does teach them excellent manners. It was slightly shaming that the person who effortlessly took control of our lunch date was the one who was not yet out of their teens. Luke picked me up from my office and helped me into my coat. He opened doors, and insisted on walking on the outside of the pavement like a Victorian gentleman concerned with protecting me from the splashes of passing carriages. He asked politely about my morning, and I answered politely back. By the time he ushered me up the steps of a red-brick Georgian townhouse in Garrick Street I was beginning to think this was going to be a perfectly pleasant experience after all.

Nor did Luke turn out to have taken me to a nightclub. Although, as I noticed he signed in as Geoff Home, it appeared more likely this was his father's club than his own. Still, it was reassuringly grown-up — no one was going to expect me to dance on a podium or neck a Wkd Blue or whatever school leavers drink these days. The white-haired maître d' showed us to a table in the centre of the room, but Luke murmured something in his ear and we were led instead to a more secluded situation in the corner. As he presented us with the menus the maître d' gave me an unreadable smile. I wasn't sure what he was thinking, but I flushed guiltily, wondering if perhaps he thought I was one of those schoolteachers who gets arrested for having affairs with her pupils.

We talked about the menu, we ordered, we discussed the work Luke had been doing for Flickers: 'Mostly, like, going to the shop to get him more Marlboro Lights.' It was all completely civilized and actually quite enjoyable, thanks to Luke's impeccable social skills. Why had I worried so much about this date?

Because of the hand on my arse five minutes later. That was why.

'So,' Luke drawled, shuffling his chair around so that he was next to me instead of opposite. 'Why didn't you reply to my text last night?'

'It was you!' I gasped, pushing his hand away. Of course! As horrified as I was to discover that a mere teenager could come up with such filth, I couldn't suppress a little glimmer of relief that the message hadn't been from Teddy after all.

'Yah, totes, who'd you think it was from?' Luke asked. 'The old man you went out with last week?'

'Of course not,' I lied.

'Are you on BBM?' said Luke. 'Only it's much better than text if we're going to be in touch a lot, yah?'

I pushed his hand away again.

'What's BBM?' I asked.

Luke looked at me as if I was one of those

ancient High Court judges who has to be told who the Beatles are. 'Um, like, BlackBerry Messenger? Saahriously, you don't have it?'

'I don't have a BlackBerry,' I confessed.

He shook his head. 'Mental. How do you, like, keep up with people?'

'Oh, the usual ways,' I said vaguely, feeling tragically out of touch. The truth was, it wasn't as if I was so inundated with emails and texts that I'd ever felt the need to be accessible all the time. A gentle potter round Facebook a few times a week was more than enough for me to feel like I was alive to the possibilities of the internet age.

'Only,' said Luke, 'I'd really like to keep up with you, if you know what I mean. I think an older woman has a lot to offer a younger man.' He gave my behind another firm squeeze, as if testing for ripeness. Instead of being outraged by his presumption, I couldn't help laughing at his persistence. I might have considered him a mere infant, but as far as he was concerned, he was quite the debonair ladies' man.

'Luke,' I said, pushing his hand away again, 'will you please take your hand off my backside before I have to report you to your godmother for sexual harassment.'

Luke pouted at me, drawing his hand back to his lap. 'It's, like, not fair to laugh at a man like that,' he said, looking exactly like a small boy who's had a toy taken away.

'I'm sorry,' I said, having to stop myself from patting him on the head like a puppy. 'I didn't mean to be rude. It's just quite hard to take you seriously.'

Luke leaned forward. 'I really think you should take me more seriously,' he said. 'I mean, men my age are, like, at their sexual peak. Just like women in their thirties. It's the perfect combination.'

'I'm *twenty-nine*!' I exclaimed, loud enough that the maître d' looked over with an expression that said, *I can tell you are, my dear. Whatever do you think you are doing with that teenager?*

'God, Luke,' I hissed, mortified. 'Can't we just have lunch without you propositioning me? People are looking at us.'

'Like, saahriously, why are you so afraid of your own sexuality?' Luke asked, his hand sliding once again towards me. 'You're a woman in her prime, I'm a man in his prime, what are you so scared of?'

'I'm not scared of you, Luke,' I scoffed. But I wondered. I wasn't scared exactly — frankly, Luke was still enough of a scrawny teenager that I reckoned I could get him into a headlock if I had to. Uncomfortable, though, I would admit to. I wasn't used to fending off the advances of anyone at all, let alone a horny teenager with wandering hands.

'Yah? Because I think you're afraid of what might happen if you let me seduce you.'

I spluttered into my water glass. I felt like a reverse Mrs Robinson. 'Luke! Seriously. I am not afraid of my sexuality just because I don't want to sleep with you.'

I had to admire his chutzpah though; it never seemed to cross his adolescent mind that I might be rejecting his advances because I didn't find him attractive. He was absolutely certain that if there were any issues here, they were mine.

'Don't, like, fight it,' he urged. 'Ticks said you've been with your boyfriend for ever. Don't you want to know what it's like with someone else after all this time?'

'Look, Luke,' I said. 'I think you might slightly have the wrong end of the stick here. I'm *dating* unsuitable men — just dating. Not having *sex* with all of them. It's not about that.' I shuddered at the idea that I would have had to sleep with Teddy to fulfil my remit.

Luke looked puzzled. 'But, like, why not?'

'Why not what?'

'Why not sleep with the unsuitable men? It's only sex.'

'It's not about sex,' I said. Our main courses arrived and the waiter raised his eyebrow very slightly.

'It's always about sex,' said Luke confidently, unabashed by the presence of the waiter. He lifted a spear of asparagus into his mouth and sucked on the end lasciviously.

'If you think I find that attractive, Luke, you are very much mistaken,' I said, starchy as a schoolmarm.

'I'd find it attractive if you did it,' he leered.

I was beginning to get the feeling Luke would have found it attractive even if I'd been eating an egg sandwich with my mouth open while wearing a polyester fleece onesie. Not that I was so devastatingly attractive that he couldn't help himself, but because he was so full of hormones that he saw every single action of mine as some sort of sexual come-on.

'Well, I'm not going to do it,' I said, sharply cutting my asparagus into small pieces as a warning. A warning he failed to read. It was quite remarkable how he could manage to shovel food into his mouth with one hand while his other snaked around my rear.

Luke tossed his fringe out of his eyes to better look at me. 'But sleeping with unsuitable people is like dating unsuitable people — if you don't try it, how do you know you won't like it?'

'Well, Luke,' I said. 'Would you sleep with another man just to discover you didn't like it?'

'Oh yah,' he answered, perfectly confidently. 'But every time I've slept with a guy, it's made me realize I'd rather be with a girl. See how it works?'

I gaped at him. I'd thought my argument was watertight — weren't public schoolboys supposed to be conservative homophobes? Although perhaps that was just to cover up for what happened at those all-boys schools.

'Yah,' Luke continued. 'Makes sense to try everything at least once, right? Which is why you totes need to be sleeping with the unsuitable men. At least some of them. Just dating is cheating; you're not really putting everything into it. If you know what I mean.'

I wondered if he did have a point. Not that I should be shagging everyone who was unsuitable, but was I holding myself at a remove from it all? Hiding myself behind the 'work project' excuse to protect myself from anything real? Although it seemed likely to me that Luke's argument was less about unsuitable men in general, and more about getting his eighteen-year-old self laid.

'Because, like, you're using the fact that you think I'm unsuitable to stop yourself from really looking at me as a man, yah?' said Luke. 'You've made up your mind already about me being too young, you're just going through the motions on this date. Not, like, allowing yourself to think of me as someone you should deffo be boffing totes *because* I'm unsuitable.'

'Maybe,' I said thoughtfully, more to myself than to Luke. Maybe I *was* using the unsuitability criteria to stop myself taking any of this seriously. That way I could convince myself I was trying to get over Martin while actually remaining as hung up on him as ever. Maybe I did need to get more involved with the unsuitable men than just chaste social encounters in restaurants.

Luke's eyes lit up. 'Captain of Debate Soc at school,' he said proudly, his chest puffed out. 'Knew I could turn you. Are you free tonight?'

'No, Luke,' I spluttered. 'I meant maybe I should be taking the dating more seriously, not maybe I should be shagging you.'

Luke folded his napkin up on the top of the table. 'That's what you say now,' he said, smiling with satisfaction. 'But I can see you're coming round to it.'

'We should be getting back to the office,' I said, pushing his hand away yet again.

'Oh yah,' he agreed. 'Plenty of time, Rory. Don't worry, I'm not giving up on you yet.'

19

Like any dreaded appointment, the editorial meeting seemed to come round far more frequently than a mere once a week. It felt like only hours ago that we last sat in this airless room, looked down on by generations of aristocratic Bettertons from their gilt-framed portraits. Also looked down on by Amanda, but not from within a frame, and for different reasons. There was something about the room, and the fact that it had remained unchanged for decades, that gave me the feeling that, rather than attending a series of editorial meetings over my years at *Country House*, I had in fact attended just one never-ending meeting, in which the same conversations looped endlessly around and around. The speakers might change, editors might be replaced, but the *Country House* calendar was bigger than any of them. Even Amanda's much-vaunted editorial changes, as outrageous as they seemed to Martha, were still constrained within it, almost unchanged from when the magazine had been founded: every year we had to cover the game season and the Game Fair, have a heated debate about hunting (not much of a debate, of course, we were firmly pro), find a fresh angle on Henley, Goodwood and the Derby, and provide sufficient coverage of innumerable charity and society events that our readers could feel, even if they were not in possession of a country home themselves, that they were in some way a part of that world.

So while the very existence of a *Country House* website was enough to have many of our readers clutching at their pearls in horror, our head of IT, Tim, explained to us that it had been specifically designed to appeal to a generation for whom the internet was still a troubling thing. There were no flashing gifs or unsettling use of terms such as ROFL or LOLZ; it was text-heavy, user-friendly and presented in a reassuring palette of cream and English racing green. Amanda beamed broadly, if slightly condescendingly, from the home page, welcoming the *Country House* reader with her dog at her side, a spotty Emma Bridgewater mug in her hand. *See, her smile said, there is no need to be concerned. The internet is a safe and friendly place. Join us.* Leading up to our soft launch, Tim had written a series of articles for the magazine about how to get online, and which websites we recommended — including our own, of course. I had never even thought of bringing these home for Auntie Lyd and her house guests, I realized. Why hadn't it occurred to me that they might have an interest in getting online; in life beyond Elgin Square? Why had the ridiculous plumber had that realization before I had?

Tim answered anxious questions — reassuring Lysander that his identity could not actually be stolen just by having his photograph and a smattering of his book reviews presented on the site; promising Catherine that the pieces she wrote under the name of her Irish wolfhound, Nora, would not be pirated (nor indeed read, but he didn't say that bit); encouraging us all to think of additional content we could bring to the site — behind-the-scenes chats, photographs that didn't make the final edit but were too good to be wasted.

I nodded politely, as we all did, hoping he wasn't going to go on for much longer. Not least because Luke kept making suggestive faces to me from the other side of the table; my spurning of his advances seemed merely to intensify his determination.

Ignoring Luke, who was now mouthing something I didn't want to translate, I focused pointedly on Tim, who was telling us how the website could help shape the direction of the magazine, going forward, by studying the page views to find out which features got the most traffic and therefore resonated most with our readers. He smiled back at me, rather non-plussed by my sudden interest.

'As we've already seen, Rory, with your dating column,' he said.

I opened my eyes wide. Apart from the emails Tim had forwarded to me complaining about the fauxmosexual piece, I'd hardly heard a thing about a response to the column, either inside the office or outside. I strongly suspected Amanda hadn't even read it.

'How so?' said Amanda, and for once I was totally in agreement with her. How so indeed?

'The dating column has by far the most page views of anything on the site,' said Tim. 'And we've had more than twenty emails about the latest piece this week alone.'

'You have? What — what do they say?' I asked nervously.

'Mostly they're women who want to know how they can contact your rich landowner.' Tim smiled at me slightly apologetically, little realizing this had been exactly my hope in writing up the date with Teddy. 'I'll forward them on to you after the meeting.'

'Excellent,' said Amanda, but I didn't know if she was directing this at me or at Tim. 'Thank you, Tim. Now, moving on.'

As soon as I escaped from the meeting I flew back to my desk and opened up my inbox. As promised, there was a message from Tim collating all the emails they'd received about the piece. Fifteen of them offered their contact details to be forwarded on to Teddy, with gentle barbs about how a young filly in her twenties could not expect to appeal to a gentleman of mature years. Of these, seven claimed to be from women within a hundred-mile radius of the Scottish Highlands — two actually resident there. Three complained that a dating column was out of keeping with the *Country House* ethos, but I found it hard to care too much about these, since our readers had an extremely proprietary notion of what the magazine stood for, and a positive mania for pointing it out to us staffers. As they saw it, they were the true keepers of the *Country House* flame, and we the dangerous renegades who couldn't be relied upon not to put out the fire with our incompetent ways. A golden two emails complimented my writing and said they looked forward to hearing about more unsuitable men. Neither appeared to be from anyone I knew, which made them all the more precious. I read them often enough that I could have repeated them, word for word, to anyone who asked; though of course no one did.

I forwarded the emails to Lysander — not to show off about my two complimentary readers, I deleted those first — but to suggest that he might want to send the contact details on to Teddy. I wasn't sure how Lysander would explain away the fact that I'd written about my date for public consumption — although I'd been careful to write it in a way that wouldn't offend Teddy — but it seemed that if there was a silver lining to the date at Wilton's, it might be that Teddy unexpectedly found love as a result. I hoped he would.

Martha swung by my office unexpectedly, claiming to have read my latest column and declaring it 'not bad', which, given her opposition to its very existence, I felt to be high praise. She even went to the trouble of reading, over my shoulder, all of the emails from readers, which was a level of interest that I hadn't anticipated. I wondered if she might be beginning to see the benefits of working with Amanda instead of against her. Of course I'd rather be writing Behind the Rope than Unsuitable Men, but the point was to get Amanda's confidence in me established, and then use it to work the things I was really interested in. I was playing the long game, and Martha would do well to try it, I thought, if only to make her own life easier.

Although I still hadn't heard from Malky, I wasn't going to be able to wait for his promised 'next time' before writing up our date. I'd found it easier to tackle the column about Luke, even though he seemed to think our romantic adventure was far from over; it wouldn't be published until later in the month, but the fortnightly schedule meant I needed to crack on with the write-ups while also finding new men to date. I'd have to end the Malky piece, for publication in early April, by the pub dustbins, just as it had ended in reality. Still, I told myself, that just made him better material for the column: The Man Who Didn't Call. Thinking of him as mere material made me feel a little less despondent. I had been so sure he *would* call; so sure that I would see him again. Had I really mistaken the look in his eyes that night? It had actually made me feel hopeful for the first time in weeks; like he was a real prospect. I guessed this was what Auntie Lyd meant when she said that dating was a battleground. I fiddled with the text a bit more, but the piece wasn't coming together. The quiet fizzle into nothingness was a lot less satisfactory than Teddy's gentlemanly rejection, on the page as in life.

★ ★ ★

On my way home that evening, I walked through the market towards the tube station at Leicester

Square. As any Londoner knows, only tourists and teenagers use Covent Garden tube, with its slow and crowded lifts and queues of confused out-of-towners. It is always infinitely quicker, if you know the way, to weave your way via Garrick Street and escape the slow-moving hordes. Like everyone who works in the centre of town I was used to regarding tourists as little more than the people who wear terrible trainers, ask for directions and need to be reminded that you stand on the right side of the escalator; I hardly even saw them except as an obstacle to be negotiated with my eyes fixed on my path beyond them. But tonight, looking at them all swarming around the market, leaning over the railings to listen to the Royal Opera student singing in the atrium, laughing outside pubs, wrapped up against the cold, I felt unaccountably envious. Not of the tourists as individuals — no, that wasn't it at all, I still didn't want to walk a mile in those ugly trainers — but of their group identity. It wasn't one of those cheesy 'Although I am in the midst of many, I am so alone' moments at all, though I suppose that was part of it. I had thought I, the Londoner, was the one who fitted in here, while they just got in the way. Now I wished with all my heart that I was part of such a group, jostling each other good-naturedly, sharing jokes, so willing to be pleased and entertained. I was lonely, I realized. Properly lonely. Not just for Martin, but for our friends, our life together. For fitting in.

I could feel that I was in danger of letting myself drop into a spiral of negative thoughts, so

I picked up the *Evening Standard* instead and distracted myself in its headlines until the tube reached Clapham Common. When I emerged from the station, I had to pull my hat down against a biting wind that whipped across the bare expanse of grass. Striding down the pavement, head bowed, I heard shouting from the direction of the children's paddling pool, which stood empty and abandoned each winter. I ignored it — there were usually teenagers messing about there with skateboards and I had no interest in what they might be yelling at me. Tonight, though, the shouting was very persistent, and it seemed to be coming closer towards me.

'Hey! Hey!'

I kept walking, looking at the pavement so I wouldn't have to make eye contact with anyone, my face composed into the professional blankness adopted by any Londoner who fears they might be approached by a stranger, especially a stranger who is probably going to ask them for money, or try to take it from them by force.

'Hey! Hey! Rory, hey!'

I lifted up my eyes and there, running towards me, was Malky, his guitar on his back and Gordon skirting his heels.

'Jesus, Rory,' he panted. 'I've been calling you for ages, didn't you hear me?' He stopped in front of me and bent to rest his hands on his knees, wheezing.

'Sorry, I thought it was the boys from over there,' I said, nodding over to the pool. It was too cold to take my hands out of my pockets, even though they were gloved. Also I felt distinctly frosty towards Malky after nearly two weeks of no contact at all.

'I had to run,' Malky said, straightening up with one hand on his chest. I'd forgotten how much taller than me he was. He grinned down. 'Nearly killed me. Not built for speed, me. Now, where have you *been*, Rory?'

'Where have *I* been?' I asked, in a voice as chilly as the wind. I dropped my chin down to my chest and looked at my shoes. I wasn't sure I trusted myself to look directly at his distracting eyes.

'I lost your number, didn't I?' said Malky, lifting my chin and looking at me imploringly. I felt my insides begin to melt under his practised gaze. 'All the contacts on my phone got wiped. And since you so cruelly rejected me the other night I didn't know where you lived — I didn't have any other way of contacting you. I've been desperate for you to call. Desperate.'

'Oh,' I said, instantly disarmed. Goddamn Ticky, I thought, telling me not to contact him under any circumstances. Leaving me feeling all vulnerable and rejected, when all along he'd lost my number. I knew there must have been an explanation; I knew I hadn't mistaken his interest in me.

'I've been hanging out by the Common day and night trying to catch a glimpse of you,' Malky said, stepping closer to me. The corners of his eyes crinkled into a smile. 'I'm so glad to see you. I was beginning to give up hope of seeing you again.'

'Were you?'

'I felt like we had some unfinished business,' he grinned, moving closer, seeing me beginning to thaw. 'Didn't you? Shall we go for a drink now?'

'Now?' Ticky had lectured me firmly on the necessity of never accepting a spontaneous invitation from a man; she decreed all dates had to be arranged in advance to show commitment, even if the man was unsuitable. But she had been wrong about not calling Malky, so I wavered.

'Come on, Rory,' Malky pleaded, linking his arm in mine. 'Haven't I been freezing my arse off out here in pursuit of my lady love? Playing sad songs in the dark like a lovesick troubadour? Are you really going to spurn me now?'

I felt a little shiver run through me at his green eyes close to mine; this was a man who knew the knee-buckling power of an intense stare. But that wasn't the reason I said yes. No, I told myself, I needed a better ending to my new Unsuitable Men column. I wasn't desperate to see him under any circumstances. No. Narrative resolution, I thought. This is just about narrative resolution.

Narrative resolution and more snogging by the dustbins outside the Duke of Wellington, as it turned out. I couldn't honestly tell you how we ended up there again — of course if it had been a planned date I would have tried to steer Malky towards somewhere a bit more romantic, but this was spontaneous and unsuitable and I had decided to go along with it. The evening had passed in a blur of ridiculousness that I struggled to remember clearly the next day — to write down one of Malky's long, rambling stories would be to flatten it into two dimensions. They depended on expansive hand gestures, leaping around the room, constructing mise-en-scène on the table out of crisp packets and horse brasses to illustrate a point. And a lot of alcohol. Martin had never been much of a drinker, confining himself to a few glasses of wine with a meal, so Malky's reckless Guinness-fuelled behaviour was entirely new to me. As was my own, powered by red wine and desire. I floated on a plump cushion of alcohol and attention, both of them equally intoxicating, despite revisiting the tawdry wheelie-bin setting of our first date.

'I'm coming back with you this time,' said Malky gruffly, pulling himself away from kissing me, 'and I'm not taking no for an answer.'

I giggled as he slipped his cold hand under my jumper, but I didn't say yes. I wasn't sure I wanted him to come back to Auntie Lyd's — not that she would still be up, I supposed. The horrendously early rising in our house was matched by an average bedtime of about 10 p.m.

'Come on, where do you live?'

'Malky,' I laughed, 'I hardly know you.'

'You're never going to *get* to know me if you keep saying no,' he urged, pushing his hand up higher. 'I thought you were more fun than this.'

'Stop it, it's cold,' I said, pulling my jumper down. I suddenly thought of Luke. What was stopping me? Was I afraid of my sexuality after all? Was I really making excuses to avoid taking

219

any of this seriously?

Malky hit me with another one of his deep, longing stares. Unbidden, Martin popped into my head again; he hadn't looked at me like that for months. Years, maybe. The bastard. He was probably looking at his new girlfriend like that all the time. I pushed myself away from the wall and kissed Malky fiercely. He looked astonished at my rapid change of heart. I grabbed his hand.

I was, bizarrely enough, going to take the sexual advice of a fiercely priapic teenager.

'Come with me,' I said, and led him and Gordon across the road.

20

When I was at university, my flatmate Abigail had appropriated a cricketing term to describe the sudden doubt that can hit a woman taking a man back to her house for the first time: the Corridor of Uncertainty. I had only experienced it once, long ago with Martin, but in truth I had had so little doubt that he was the right man for me that Abi said it didn't count. From her lofty position of significantly greater experience, she claimed that the Corridor of Uncertainty was always followed by the Kitchen of Truth: the lurking doubts one had in the hallway were either blasted away by the bright strip lighting of our student kitchen (cue snogging and imminent retreat to bedroom) or magnified in its glare (cue sudden backtrack and finding of excuses to kick him out of the house). On one never-forgotten occasion Abi had waved a knife at a particularly persistent suitor after the Kitchen of Truth had spoken strongly against him, and the poor man had run away into the night in terror.

I didn't expect I'd have to chase Malky out of the house with a knife (though remembering Abi made me mentally note the location of Auntie Lyd's cutlery drawer just in case), but I couldn't help a surge of panic that made my hands shake stupidly when I tried to open the door. Was I really going to sleep with someone new? With an unsuitable man I had met only once before, and randomly encountered on the street tonight? It was less than a month since I'd split up with Martin — it felt far too soon, but at the same time it felt like something I needed to do; a sign that I was moving on. Also, what underwear was I wearing? And when did I last shave my legs? These are the common fears of the Corridor of Uncertainty.

It was safe to say that of the many possible scenarios that were running through my mind when turning the key, not one concerned Mr Bits. And yet it was only a matter of seconds until he took centre stage. As the door opened Malky's arm shot around me with such speed that I lurched forward into the hallway, my hand still attached to the key in the lock. Jesus, I thought, what had got into him all of a sudden? But rather than grabbing me in the passionate embrace I'd anticipated, Malky flew past me, entirely horizontal as he sailed over the doorstep to land heavily on the hall carpet, his outstretched hand clinging desperately to his dog's straining lead. Gordon howled and snapped at Mr Bits, who regarded him with disgust from the safety of the stairs.

Malky stumbled to his feet, grasping at the lead, but as he did so Gordon made another frantic lunge. His lead whipped out of Malky's hand and he flew up the stairs so fast that I thought for one insane moment Malky had actually thrown him up there. Mr Bits assessed the situation with lightning speed, allowing Gordon to approach him at full pelt before stepping delicately aside. Gordon's momentum propelled him up several more stairs before he was able to stop. He spun around, snarling, realizing he had been outmanoeuvred. But it was too late.

Mr Bits, who had leapt on to the banister as Gordon passed, dropped with deadly accuracy onto the dog's back, claws sunk deeply in, his orange fur standing on end as if an electric current had passed between the two of them. Gordon shot, howling, up the stairs again and disappeared past the landing, but there was no dislodging Mr Bits, who was still grimly attached when Gordon reappeared, running down the stairs, pursued by Auntie Lyd in a pair of paisley pyjamas.

'*What* is the meaning of this?' she demanded, as Gordon and his feline passenger raced past Malky's still-prone form and disappeared out of the front door into the darkness of Elgin Square like some terrible hybrid creature. '*Who* brought a dog into my house?'

I was too mortified to speak. I stared at my shoes, not sure where to look. Certainly not at Auntie Lyd, whose expression was so terrifying that I thought it might turn me to stone if I faced her directly.

Malky found his feet at last; he'd only been down for a moment but it was a moment in which we had moved with terrifying speed from a seduction scenario to one that could have come straight out of Percy's *Whoops! There Goes the Neighbourhood* sitcom. No wonder he looked confused.

'It's my dog, it's mine,' he said, panicked.

'What the fuck was that?'

'That,' said Auntie Lyd, descending the stairs with regal disapproval burned into every step, 'was Mr Bits.'

'Call him off, can't you? He's torturing my dog!' shouted Malky, peering out into the square, where Gordon's continued shrieks, growing closer, then further, then closer again, suggested he had not yet stopped his desperate running back and forth.

'Mr Bits is a cat, young man,' said Auntie Lyd haughtily. 'Not some slavering dog without a mind of its own. He doesn't take orders from me or anyone else. I'm afraid he'll just hang on until he gets bored. Your dog won't come to any real harm.'

'Real harm?' Malky demanded, grasping at his hair with both hands. 'What the fuck's that supposed to mean?'

'Mr Bits is just showing him who's in charge. He'll drop off once your dog gets the message.'

'What am I supposed to do in the meantime?' asked Malky.

'I don't know,' said Auntie Lyd, fixing him with a fierce stare. His imploring gaze did not seem to affect her in the slightest. 'What were you planning on doing before your dog attacked my cat?'

Malky turned to look at me with meaning.

'He, er, he was just leaving,' I said, finally finding my voice.

'Too right,' said Malky, pulling his coat around himself angrily. 'It's a fucking loony unit in here.'

'I'm sorry,' I muttered to him, low so Auntie

Lyd couldn't hear me. 'I'm sorry, it's all my fault.'

'I know,' he snapped, and left, slamming the door behind him.

★ ★ ★

The next morning, Mr Bits preened himself smugly on the sunny kitchen windowsill. The air of self-satisfaction that usually accompanied him was magnified today. If a cat could have smiled, he would have done. According to Auntie Lydia, who was enjoying telling the story to the entire household, the stealthy dog attack had been his party piece in his long-ago youth; he would sit on the steps outdoors to lure unsuspecting canines towards him, and then ride them out of the square like a cowboy on a bucking steer. Now that he was older, he rarely risked a dog encounter, but clearly he had been delighted with last night's unexpected triumph.

'Good morning, dear,' said Eleanor, raising her whisky to me in a giggly toast. 'We've just been hearing all about last night; you really are a one.'

'Ridiculous dog,' muttered Percy. ' 'Foolish cur, that runs winking into the mouth of a Russian bear to have its head crushed like a rotten apple.' '

'It wasn't a Russian bear, Percy, dear,' said Eleanor, wilfully misunderstanding Percy's quotation. 'It was a dog. And not just a dog, a *man* too, wasn't it, Rory? That's what I'd like to hear more about, Rory: which unsuitable man was *this* one?'

Jim chuckled from over by the sink. Now that

he'd been appointed unofficial house IT consultant as well as plumber, he seemed to be around even more, getting in the way. Every morning found him in the kitchen; I think he actually timed his work to cause maximum inconvenience — I mean, why did he expressly pick early mornings to hang out in the busiest part of the house? As if he saw me glaring, Jim turned and smiled.

'Sounds like a busy night, Dawn,' he said.

'Nothing special,' I said. I was not going to be lured into losing my temper, however much I itched to. 'How about you? Hectic night pumping iron and applying that fake tan?'

Jim looked startled. 'Fake tan?'

'Or do you sleep in a sunbed?' I asked, looking him up and down. He had on another skin-tight top this morning; mercifully slogan-free for once, it was white and long-sleeved but form-fitting enough to allow you no doubt that this was a man who visited the gym often. And probably necked steroids for breakfast. 'Jim, no one is that colour in the middle of winter without a bit of help.'

'Or without a holiday in Thailand over New Year,' said Jim, rolling his eyes and turning back to the sink. 'Lydia, have you had a chance to look at those bathroom catalogues I brought for you?'

'Not yet,' said Auntie Lyd. 'I don't really know the first thing about choosing lavatories; I'm not sure where to start.'

'Well, we need to get the order in soon if you're going to have the bathrooms sorted by the end of the month,' said Jim, ignoring me as if I wasn't there. 'Maybe I can show you a few more options online later and help you choose?'

'Ooh, Jim, you promised to help me with *my* online,' said Eleanor, batting her eyelashes at him a little unsteadily. 'Percy says he's found three websites about himself already.'

'Not just websites,' said Percy grandly. 'They're called *fansites*. Where my fans gather in the virtual realm to discuss my *oeuvre*. Like a stage door in the broadband.'

'Fansites, then,' said Eleanor, tipping her glass up to empty it into her mouth. 'If Percy has three then I am sure I'll have at least that. Probably more.'

'I wasn't able to find a site dedicated to extras on *EastEnders*,' sniffed Percy. 'But perhaps I just haven't trawled the very depths of the broadband yet.'

'Percy,' warned Auntie Lyd. 'I will be using the computer this morning. I suggest you both go to the internet cafe on the High Street if you want to fight over which of you is the more popular.'

'I have *far* better things to do,' said Eleanor, getting up from the stool and stalking out of the room, gently bumping into the door frame as she turned to go up the stairs. Jim exchanged a frowning look with Auntie Lyd. Although I agreed with their silent concern — Eleanor's daytime drinking was worrying — it annoyed me that Auntie Lyd was turning to Jim with her anxieties instead of to me. I was family, not a paid employee. Shouldn't she look to me first?

'I'd better go too,' I said, picking up my toast

and marmalade. 'Got a busy day ahead.'

'Have a lovely day, dear,' said Auntie Lyd.

'Yes, have a lovely day working away in your office, Dawn,' said Jim, waving a spanner at me and smirking. Underneath his seemingly innocent remark I could hear the judgemental subtext: *While you slave in a boring office, I, Mr Spray Tan, am vastly superior in having escaped the nine-to-five. My pumped-up pectorals and I will hang around here, taking advantage of your aunt's generous nature, finding ways to cheat her out of her meagre savings, while you get paid a pittance for being patronized by posh people all day at a magazine that no one reads.*

'And you have a lovely day messing around in other people's poo pipes,' I snapped. Auntie Lyd frowned again, but I was out of the door before she could say anything. She thought Jim was so great, so helpful and kind. She couldn't see through him like I could.

I stomped crossly to the tube. Some mornings the commute was worse than others, and of course this morning was one of those. As if I wasn't cross enough. I knew that Jim's judgement only got to me because I shared it. My love life *was* laughable. My job *was* stupid. Not that I wanted to give it all up to become a plumber or a carpenter or anything — I didn't agree with the suggestion that manual labour was the only key to happiness — but I was beginning to wonder if I'd ever found satisfaction in my work. My main focus had always been on Martin and on our relationship; I hadn't looked to work for any sort of fulfilment other

228

than the chance it offered me to nose around historic properties and view artworks at close range. Now that I had no relationship to speak of, my work life was suddenly lit up harshly, like a vase on a plinth, and in this bright light there was no disguising that this was one shabby, cracked vase. And I was hardly even writing about art history at the moment — my entire focus was this stupid dating column. For all the satisfaction I was getting from work, I might as well be writing for a magazine like *Budgerigars Monthly*; at the very least I'd probably get paid more there.

I took one look at the crowd, five people deep, on the northbound platform at Clapham Common, and decided I didn't have the energy to push my way into the mass. If I went in the wrong direction for a few stops, perhaps as far as Balham, the crowds would thin out and it would be easier to get on a train into town. I turned to face the opposite platform, where a train was already arriving. On the empty southbound tube I picked up a copy of *Metro* and enjoyed the novelty of having a seat, even if only briefly. Sometimes going backwards was the only way you could go forward; wasn't that true in life sometimes, too? I had to believe that these dates with unsuitable men, as ridiculous as they seemed, were taking me somewhere better. That being *Country House*'s dating guinea pig was going to lead me on to better things. Otherwise what was I doing with my life?

21

In the full spirit of going backwards to go forward, I forced from Ticky the password to the My Mate's Great website and accompanied my morning tea with a browse through the available profiles. To be honest it was more about distracting myself from memories of last night with Malky than any genuine enthusiasm for the online offerings. Even if he still had my number, which he didn't, I had no hope at all that he would have called now that his poor dog had been mauled by Mr Bits. At least, I consoled myself, I had a suitably dramatic end to that particular column. Although I would have to write it very carefully: our readers, the postbag told us, strongly favoured dogs over cats. I decided to add on a made-up postscript about Gordon escaping unharmed except for his canine pride.

Surfing through the profiles made for depressing reading. I had had no idea of the sadistic nature of internet dating until now. Of course I had heard the usual horror stories — the twenty-eight-year-old supposed triathlete who turns out to be an obese agoraphobic, the professed six-footer who would make a hobbit look tall — but these, it seemed, were the very tip of a horrific iceberg. I had imagined there would be a smorgasbord of eligible unsuitables for me to choose from, and that it would be a matter of simply choosing who looked the most appealing. Instead my assumptions were shaken by the appearance of something on the website called 'Close Match', by which a man who had looked at your profile could declare, instead of his interest, his lack of it. I was horrified to see that twenty-two men of whose existence I had previously been unaware had chosen to indicate that they were not interested in me. It felt like being tapped on the shoulder in a bar by someone you had not even noticed, and informed that they didn't find you attractive.

But this was significantly less worrying than the quality of the fourteen men who had, instead, picked me as a favourite. I knew that Ticky had set the parameters of my ideal match to be as inclusive as possible, but it concerned me profoundly when I saw the terrifying array spread before me. It was like a game of Guess Who — get rid of all of those unable to write without slipping into incoherent text-speak. Ten remain. Get rid of the men who, despite knowing me to be in London, hope I might be available for a first date in Sheffield or Penzance. Seven remain. Ticky, reminding me of the unsuitable-men agenda, refused to allow me to get rid of the man whose photographs all showed him with his hands cupping his face, or half swathed in a scarf in what we both decided must be an unsubtle attempt to hide a double chin. She agreed, though, that I could delete the astrologer who claimed to be 'uninhibited and adventurous' as it was all too clear that this meant a world of nipple clamps and partner-swapping that was just a little too unsuitable for my remit. Six remained.

I scrutinized their profiles mournfully, wondering if they had looked at mine with the same feeling of deep foreboding. There was a preponderance of IT professionals looking for a 'partner in crime' to 'make the most of all London has to offer', which appeared to mean 'sitting on the sofa sharing a great bottle of wine and a DVD'. Of these I deleted, despite Ticky's protests, the one who offered 'free chocolate and shoes!!!!', as if I were a child whose head might be turned by proffered sweets and shiny things. Sod off, I thought, I can buy my own chocolate and shoes; I can't ever buy back an hour of my life spent in the company of someone so incredibly tedious. Was I their last resort, too? Had I been spoiled by going out with Martin for so long? I had always known I had been lucky to get together with someone like him. Okay, so he was an accountant rather than a film producer or something glamorous — but he was smart, successful, reliable. Perhaps I had been kidding myself for all this time that I belonged with a man like that, when the reality was not only that he had been out of my league, but that I should be grateful for the attentions of a group of men who closely resembled the freakish customers of the bar in *Star Wars*, rather than the Han Solo I had hoped for. It wasn't like I was fresh out of university any more. I was hurtling towards my thirtieth birthday. I guessed this was what people meant when they said you had to make compromises as you got older.

As I clicked open another profile an email

popped up from Luke, whose approaches had become more determined the more I ignored him.

I'll be waiting for you in the stationery
cupboard in five minutes. Hurry.

I deleted it instantly. If anyone saw it they'd be forgiven for thinking that I was actually carrying on an affair with him; in Luke's hormonal imagination I probably was. I shuddered at the thought of Amanda seeing one of his emails — I'd have her attention then, and for all the wrong reasons. I saw Luke lope past my office, smirking suggestively and gesturing towards the room where we kept our supplies.

I ducked my head down and carried on looking at My Mate's Great. The very best thing I could say about the men from the internet, I realized, was that at least each of them was a total stranger, unrelated to anyone in my real life. If our dates were unsuccessful at least I wouldn't have to encounter them again on a daily basis like Luke. Surely that was a bonus?

Despite Ticky's insistence that I should select the most unsuitable of the remaining men for my first internet date, I chose to contact only the ones that I thought had at least the appearance of normality. Once I was a more experienced dater I might be able to brave some of the others, but it seemed wise to me to ease myself into the world of internet dating by going for those who at least seemed like they might be okay; although of course still technically unsuitable in some way.

Dave, twenty-two, was a personal trainer. His profile had been written by his best friend, Bazza, but to be honest I didn't really read it. It was all about the photographs, which showed him smiling broadly as he hung off climbing walls, crossed marathon finish lines, and clasped a surfboard to his bared chest. Unsuitability rating: low. But he counted as another toyboy.

Stu, thirty-one, was a vet. His photographs all showed him posing with fluffy kittens or adorable puppies. It was shameless, but effective. I half expected to see a photograph in which he cradled a newborn baby, but perhaps he had realized that might be taking it a step too far. His veterinary nurse had written a profile for him, which suggested that either she entertained a vast crush on her employer, or he had dictated it to her to cast himself in the most flattering possible light. Unsuitability rating: very low indeed. In fact I quite fancied him. But he was based in Sussex, so got in on a technicality (long distance).

Sebastian, whose profile had been written by his sister, was thirty-nine. He had worked as a war correspondent in Kosovo, Rwanda and Darfur, which suggested both an admirable social conscience and a sense of adventure. He had recently come back to London after fifteen years away and, his sister said, he was looking to put down roots. Although all of his photographs were either cropped at forehead level or showed him wearing a hat, which suggested a lack of hair that his profile didn't admit to, he was attractive in a weather-beaten, sunburned sort of way. Unsuitability rating: another low, but Ticky assured me that single men in their late thirties were all unsuitable commitment-phobes.

As Flickers poked his head into my office I guiltily switched my screen back to a feature on kitchen gardens to disguise my obvious lack of work. Although technically I suppose unsuitable men were work, it still felt slightly embarrassing to be caught perusing the profiles of internet strangers.

'Rory,' he asked, 'have you seen Luke? He disappeared off a few minutes ago and I need him for a mail-out.'

'Oh,' I said innocently, 'I thought I saw him heading towards the stationery cupboard.'

Two minutes later there was a roar of horror from down the corridor. Shortly after that Luke ran past my office pulling his trousers up. And ten minutes after that his work-experience placement was terminated for good.

22

As the days passed, I failed to hear from any of the supposedly unsuitable men I'd emailed. More profiles appeared in the Close Match section. Malky did not get in touch — I tried to tell myself that he would have called if only he'd had my number, but who was I kidding? The only unsuitable man who had seemed to have any kind of potential for suitability had run screaming from my home just like his dog. If this were my own love life, to live as I chose, I would have given up at this point. After all, wasn't there a whole school of thought that said being single was a rite of passage for women? That a period outside relationships was all about finding your own identity? It was the sort of thing that Auntie Lyd went on about constantly: that no woman could truly say she knew herself unless she had spent a significant amount of time on her own. Perhaps Auntie Lyd's often alarming confidence in her own opinions was a result of that very independence from someone else's influence throughout most of her adult life. And yet she'd been so encouraging about my dating unsuitable men. Probably only so that they would act as a vaccine against the truly unsuitable: that the small doses of bad boys would inoculate me from properly falling for the really terrible ones. Or just put me off men altogether, I thought, which Auntie Lyd would probably also support.

But I couldn't give up yet — my column about Malky was about to run and I needed a new date soon. So it was with some relief that, after a week, I finally received an email from Sebastian the war correspondent. I had suggested in my message to him that we might find something in common due to our journalistic backgrounds — I didn't think it was necessary at this stage to let him know that I worked for *Country House*. I would reveal this if it seemed appropriate, much as, I imagined, he would remove his hat to reveal his lack of hair when he felt it was appropriate. He apologized for failing to reply sooner; he had been testifying at a war-crimes tribunal in The Hague. Like many somewhat shallow people, I was fascinated by anyone who dedicated their life to issues with real meaning and importance, although I preferred my social conscience to express itself with a remote and hygienic direct debit to Save the Children. Sebastian could not have impressed me more unless he had revealed that he had personally saved a bunch of orphaned children, Angelina Jolie-style.

He suggested we met on Thursday night outside Covent Garden tube station, and it was immediately clear to me by his innocent plan (I was looking out for discrepancies, of course, anticipating that all internet daters were lying about something; possibly everything) that he had been telling the truth about being out of the country for years. It felt unkind to overrule Sebastian's chosen meeting place, which had most likely been made with good intentions as I had mentioned that I worked nearby, so instead

I agreed, specifying the exact spot in which we should meet, to ensure minimal awkwardness in finding each other. I had no desire to trawl through the crowds accosting any tall, hat-wearing man.

Thursday night was, it turned out, bitterly, bitterly cold and rainy, which made meeting outside any tube station a miserable prospect, but it hardly seemed to diminish the crowds outside Covent Garden. The expectant horde was wrapped up against the harsh weather and every single man who passed the lit-up windows of Oasis was either wearing a hat or hidden by an umbrella. I pressed myself against the window under the smallest of awnings, and looked around me for anyone who might be Sebastian. I was suddenly much too aware of how my face might look to a stranger, and not quite sure how to arrange it — too friendly and approachable and I might attract the attention of random nutters or, worse, the charity muggers who hovered on the fringes of the crowd picking off the vulnerable and signing them up to direct debits (how do you think I got that Save the Children one in the first place?). Too unapproachable and I might scare off the very man I was here to meet. Although, thinking about it, a man who had faced down warlords and similar was unlikely to be frightened by a frowning female journalist of five foot five.

I was still composing my face when a gloved hand touched my arm and a voice asked, 'Rory?'

'Sebastian?' I asked, staring up into a pair of pale-blue eyes, made even paler by the contrast

238

with his darkly tanned face. He had the fair eyelashes of someone who has spent a lot of time in the sun; I imagined that if he had any hair (he was wearing a hat, of course) it would be bleached to the same whiteness. By the weather, I mean: we are talking rugged and outdoorsy here, not Jim-style artificiality.

'I'm glad you're here,' he said, ducking under the awning next to me and regarding me with his grave blue stare. 'Thanks for showing up.'

'Of course I'm here,' I laughed. 'Have you been stood up before?'

'I'm used to disappointment,' he said, looking around him with narrowed eyes as if he expected an attack to come from somewhere in the direction of Neal Street. Perhaps he knew about the chuggers.

'I don't expect you're used to this weather, are you? If you've been out in Darfur, I mean,' I said, shivering in the doorway but not wanting to be pushy and ask where we were going yet.

He looked down at me, his eyes still narrowed. 'You've obviously never experienced a Kosovan winter.'

'No — er, no I haven't. Gosh, no,' I said, feeling irrelevant and idiotic. I should have realized he was not going to be one for small talk. His mind was probably on much deeper subjects.

'This is nothing,' he said darkly. 'Nothing.'

I could see that we could be here for some time discussing the relative harshness of winters across Europe. Perhaps Sebastian was so used to the Kosovan cold that it meant nothing to him to stand here in the rain, but personally I wanted a drink and somewhere warm to sit.

'Did you have somewhere in mind for us to go?' I asked hopefully.

'Somewhere in mind?'

'For a drink,' I said, feeling as if I was speaking a foreign language. I began to wonder if Sebastian had ever been on a date before, or if he just usually tumbled into bed with hard-drinking, combat-wearing female correspondents to a soundtrack of distant gunshots. I understood a lack of interest in small talk, but was my question really so confusing? Surely he knew that most dates were conducted indoors, especially on a rainy March evening?

He looked around him again and his lip curled. 'This isn't really my usual scene,' he said. 'You work near here, don't you? Where do you think?'

Immensely reassured at being given a role to fulfil, I led him through the crowds on Neal Street to the pub on the corner of Shelton Street, but before we'd even opened the door I could see it was hopeless. Just a look through the brightly lit window showed that it was packed; there would be nowhere to sit. Sebastian's tanned face already wore an expression of deep weariness. I couldn't see him being happy wedged into a corner of the bar with our coats and bags squashed by our feet. He sighed behind me as I declared we'd have to go somewhere else. I began to panic. What was I thinking, dragging this noble and principled man, exhausted from a trial at The Hague, on a

240

fruitless and frivolous attempt to find an empty pub on a Thursday night? Everywhere was going to be packed.

I flicked through my mental Rolodex of possibilities and suddenly recalled that Jeremy Wells's L'Écluse, Lysander's favoured restaurant, was just around the corner. Of course it was far too expensive a place to go for supper but, instructed by Ticky that a first internet date should last no longer than two hours, I had already told Sebastian I was meeting friends for a meal at eight-thirty. Even I could afford a couple of drinks in the upstairs bar, which, because it was invisible from the street and accessible only by a lift from the back of the restaurant, was quiet in that expensive-hotel-bar sort of way. I'd only been once before, but it seemed perfect: secluded and grown-up and with, I was sure, enough seats for several convoys of war correspondents.

Sebastian shrugged assent to my suggestion and we hurried across Seven Dials with our heads down to escape the icy sting of the rain driving into our faces. I risked a painful face/sleet interface to note with approval that he was at least as tall as he had claimed to be; in fact I had to add in a slightly embarrassing little skip every few paces to keep up with his long strides. As we approached L'Écluse, a doorman swung open the door in welcome and we were ushered in.

I had forgotten how starkly modernist the reception area of L'Écluse was: all white marble and artfully arranged orchids, with a phalanx of stunning greeters standing behind a desk. The doorman led us towards them before retreating back to his place at the entrance. I smiled at the nearest greeter.

'Hello, we were just hoping for a drink at the bar, please,' I said.

'Certainly, madam, sir. Shall we take your coats?'

Another greeter appeared behind us and as she tried to help Sebastian out of his coat he visibly flinched. I expected in his line of work you learned to be suspicious of the unanticipated rearguard approach, but he relinquished his coat without a struggle once he realized she wasn't about to attack him.

A third greeter glided across the marble floor and asked us to follow her to the lift. As she led us through the restaurant Sebastian looked around as if he was being hunted. The restaurant was quiet so early in the evening, so unless he feared one of the waiters might fly at him with a corkscrew, I thought he was probably safe. I hoped he would be able to relax once we'd passed through the danger zone and sat down with a drink. The greeter called the lift and we rode up one floor in silence, trying to avoid catching each other's eyes in the mirrored walls. Sebastian shifted uncomfortably next to me. He audibly huffed as another greeter appeared to lead us out of the lift.

'Christ, how many people does it take to get a drink around here?'

'I know,' I laughed nervously; it was a bit excessive, and I knew the more staff the higher the bar bill, but it seemed a small price to pay for somewhere warm to sit on a busy night in the middle of London.

At last we were settled in a red velvet banquette with disconcertingly womb-like plush padded walls. In contrast to the harsh minimalist reception, the upstairs bar was like an opulent opium den. There were curtains and swags and cushions and carpets, and vases of exotic flowers, all phallic thrusting stamens, that hid yet more hovering and attentive staff. Although there were a few other people in the bar, the effect of the acres of fabric was to hush everything apart from the tinkling sound of the barman mixing drinks over in the corner. Finally, I thought, running my fingers through my hat-squashed hair, we can relax. Then I saw Sebastian's face. He stared about the room as if contemplating a horrific massacre. Perhaps it was all the red giving him flashbacks of bloodied scenes? When the waiter handed him a drinks menu he actually jumped clear out of his seat.

'Are you okay?' I asked him.

He turned his pale eyes on me and they looked strangely flat in the dim light of the bar. 'I just really hate social injustice,' he said.

I wasn't sure how to respond. I mean, I hate social injustice, too — who doesn't? Maybe some evil dictators or scarily right-wing aristocrats are fans, but surely most fair-minded people hate social injustice. And yet the way Sebastian had said it was almost an accusation; as if social injustice was something I was directly involved in perpetrating. As if I had brought him to this very bar to perpetrate it.

'Mmm,' I said, dropping my eyes to the drinks menu in a panic. 'Me too.'

'I mean, I really hate it,' he persisted, still staring at me, and I feared that yet again my stupid name had led someone to believe I was a card-carrying posh person with a background of debutante balls and riding my pony into crowds of the dispossessed, brandishing a riding crop. I should have taken us to the pub after all; I should have realized that a war correspondent was never going to be comfortable somewhere like this. And nor, frankly, was I.

Sebastian glared around the room, his weather-beaten face contorted into a sneer. 'This kind of place makes me — I don't know. Look at everyone. It just makes me want to get out a gun and mow everyone down.'

I think it was probably at this point that I realized, despite initial appearances, that I was definitely on a date with another unsuitable man. I opened my mouth, but no sound came out. I was saved from replying by the appearance of another waiter — not the same one who had given us the drinks menus, of course, that would have been ridiculous.

'I'll have a beer,' said Sebastian, snapping shut his drinks menu and slamming it on to the table.

'What kind of beer, sir?' asked the waiter, his pen hovering over the pad. 'We have Tsingtao, Asahi — '

I could see he was about to launch into a full list of all beer-related beverages that would no doubt infuriate Sebastian further, but Sebastian interrupted him before he could go any further:

'A beer. In a bottle. Thank you.'

'Madam?' said the waiter, turning to me with only the smallest flicker of a reaction to Sebastian's harsh interruption. 'May I suggest the cocktail of the day? A muddle of raspberry liqueur — '

'Ooh, lovely, yes please,' I gushed, far too enthusiastically, desperate to make up for Sebastian's rudeness, and also entirely unable in my discomfort to make a choice from a drinks menu that contained as many pages as the *Country House* Classifieds section.

Sebastian kept his hat on and, I noticed, had placed himself with his back to the wall to protect himself from rogue greeters and staff.

I ventured a few questions about where he lived and how far he had travelled this evening, which only served to make me sound even more anodyne. I felt like Marie Antoinette in a random social encounter with the leader of the starving peasants outside the palace walls. Brioche, anyone? Sebastian dealt with my questions swiftly and monosyllabically but failed to pick up the cues to ask me anything back. Conversation stuttered to a halt. His hands clenched and unclenched on his lap. Perhaps, I thought, trying to be generous, he was just nervous. I wasn't sure what to say next; I looked hopefully towards the bar but there was no sign of our drinks.

I remembered attending one of Lysander's literary lunches last year, at which the guest of honour was a retired Army general who had just written his controversial memoirs. The general had responded excellently to my employment of the pert niece technique and had regaled me with some enjoyably inappropriate jokes, along with bluff military anecdotes full of acronyms I didn't understand: 'And so I said to the KC, if you don't pass over the M37G then I won't be held responsible for a Code Y7, ha ha ha!' He had spent time in Kosovo and I suddenly recalled, with a flash of inspiration, a joke he had told me about it. Perhaps, I thought, this might lighten the heavy mood that sat between me and Sebastian like a third guest at our table.

'I, erm, I know a joke about Kosovo,' I ventured with a hesitant laugh.

'Do you?' said Sebastian, turning his blank stare in my direction. 'It had better not be the one that ends Slobberdown Mycockyoubitch.'

'No!' I blushed, horrified. I should have realized then that the only thing to do was cut my losses and allow the succession of greeters to relay me out of the building for my own safety, but of course I did not.

'Um, no, it's a different one,' I said, stupidly carrying on instead of aborting my flawed mission. 'So, how many war correspondents did it take to change a lightbulb in Pristina?' I asked.

Sebastian sighed.

'Have you heard it before?' I asked.

'No.'

There was a long pause while he looked at me. I couldn't read anything in his stony face.

'You have to say, 'How many?',' I prompted.

'How many?' he parroted, his voice heavy with disapproval.

'You wouldn't *know*, you weren't *there*.'

The punchline dropped between us like a bird that had been shot out of the sky. I could almost see it twitching its last shuddering breaths on the table. Sebastian's craggy face remained entirely still as he stared at me. Finally, the creases on his forehead deepened into a frown. 'But I *was* there,' he said. 'Are you calling me a liar?'

'Sir,' said the waiter, appearing with such perfect timing that I could have kissed him. A bottle was placed in front of Sebastian, who grabbed it gratefully.

Then, as if I had not already demonstrated myself to be frivolous beyond all hope of salvation, the waiter placed in front of me the cocktail of the day: a vast goldfish bowl of pink liquid on top of which floated an array of exotic flowers. Two silver straws emerged out of the top of the bowl. The waiter leaned forward with a cigarette lighter and lit them both — not straws, after all, but sparklers. Sebastian and I watched in silence, the waiter next to us brimming with the expectation of a delighted reaction, as the sparklers fizzed and sputtered in my drink until they burned themselves out.

Although the date limped on for another painful half an hour I think that was the moment, watching the faint wisps of smoke rise up from the dead sparklers, at which we both knew it was over.

23

I made it home before Auntie Lyd and her paying guests had retired for the evening; the sound of voices from the kitchen, as well as a strong smell of cigarette smoke, suggested it was one of their regular card nights. On these occasions the unofficial house bedtime of ten o'clock had been known to be extended to a daring eleven and, more than once, the PGs and my aunt had stayed up until midnight. It said something about the state of my dating life, and not something good, that I knew an hour's chat with my auntly landlady and her two aged thespian residents would be far more entertaining than the evening I had just endured with an eligible man in a stylish London bar.

The only saving grace of the date was that it had been so perfectly self-contained, and so absolutely final, that I had already started composing my column on the tube home. There was no lingering hope that he might call, nor the likelihood of an unexpected postscript.

Sebastian was unsuitable on all counts — at least, we were unsuitable for each other — but he was exactly suitable for the purposes of my (non-war-related) mission. If I had been truly looking for love, perhaps I'd have been crushed by his evident lack of interest, but as it only matched mine, it was hard to be too hurt. Instead I mostly felt exhausted from the sheer effort of it all.

When I poked my head around the kitchen door I saw that there was a fourth person sat at the table. Of course. Not only did Jim appear to have no proper career ambitions, having given up his white-collar job to become a plumber, but he appeared to have no actual life either. What was he doing spending yet another Thursday evening at Elgin Square? He raised a hand in greeting, as if I were the visitor and he the generously welcoming resident.

'Rory?' said Auntie Lyd, turning in her chair to see what Jim was waving at. 'You're back early, aren't you?'

'Another unsuitable man, dear?' asked Eleanor in her wavery voice.

'Oh, I think it might have been me who was unsuitable this time,' I said, remembering Sebastian's lip curling in disgust at my failed joke.

'You, unsuitable? I should think not, Rory,' said Percy loyally.

'Can I get anyone a drink?' I offered, hoping that I could distract them from further analysis of the state of my love life in front of our resident plumber.

'I think we're fine,' said Jim. 'Why don't you come and sit down?' He had an infuriating manner which, while sounding as if he was including me, effectively excluded me by making it seem as if I was the outsider here.

'Why would you think you were unsuitable, darling?' demanded Auntie Lyd, putting down her cards and lighting a new cigarette. She squinted at me across the kitchen.

249

'Oh, I'm just joking, it was fine really,' I said. 'Bit of a non-starter though.' I wanted to sit down at the kitchen table, but I didn't want it to look like I was doing it just because Jim had said so. Instead I put the kettle on for a cup of tea that I didn't want.

'Oh come on, dear,' said Eleanor, her face radiant from proximity to the plumber. 'You can't leave us in suspense. You know we all positively live for the stories of your dates. Always so entertaining! Do tell us about this one.'

'Yes, do, Dawn,' said Jim, his eyes twinkling over the top of his hand of cards. He was sitting with his legs spread wide apart, a hand on his thigh. That alpha-male pose that says, *I'm in charge here.*

'Was this the war correspondent, darling?' asked Auntie Lyd.

'Yes. Sebastian,' I said. They clearly weren't going to let me get away with not talking about him. 'I'm sure he's a nice person, but he seemed to find me a bit too lightweight and frivolous. I expect he needs a girl who's rather more serious and cerebral.'

Auntie Lyd's brow furrowed as she inhaled deeply on her cigarette.

'Whatever do you mean? You're perfectly intelligent, Rory. If Sebastian couldn't see that in the space of one evening it's hardly your fault.'

'Oh, I don't know,' I said, shrugging. 'I should have realized a tough war correspondent wasn't going to be comfortable in the poncy bar I chose. It was a bit stupid of me not to think it through.'

'Well, he should have had the manners to at least pretend it was okay,' said Jim, interrupting my conversation with Auntie Lyd. 'Sounds like a tool to me.'

Who was he to comment on my love life?

'He's damaged,' I said, goaded into defending Sebastian even though I thought he was a tool as well. 'He's damaged and complex from all the terrible things he's seen.'

Jim raised an eyebrow.

'If you ask me,' declared Auntie Lyd in the voice that presaged a wise pronouncement, 'war zones are full of people who were deeply damaged long before they got there. I wouldn't be surprised if he was the sort of man who masks his own psychological issues by burying himself in dangerous physical situations instead.'

'Such as dates with Dawn,' offered Jim, chuckling at his own joke.

'Ooh, you are terrible,' giggled Eleanor, squeezing his arm for a little too long.

'Rory,' said Auntie Lyd, ignoring them both, 'remember your column is called Unsuitable Men; you are not the unsuitable one.'

'Right,' I said. It seemed strange that she should be so defensive of me, so ready to ascribe the worst motives to Malky and Sebastian and any of the men I'd been seeing, and yet so blind to the way Jim was using her.

Percy's eyes had adopted the faraway look that indicated a theatrical quote was imminent. I saw that Eleanor could see it too; she rolled her eyes at me.

I decided against sitting down. 'I think I'm

going to go to bed,' I said.

I didn't go to sleep for a long time. I couldn't hear the voices of the others from all the way in my attic room, but I knew they were all down there and I felt like they would be talking about me. Then I berated myself for being so self-centred as to imagine they had nothing better to discuss. More likely Jim was being molested by Eleanor while eyeing up Auntie Lyd and her financial assets, such as they were. Somehow the knowledge that all four of them were downstairs laughing and joking and playing cards made me feel impossibly lonely. My chin began to tremble as I thought of Martin. I had never felt lonely with him. Even when I was on my own, the very fact of his existence had reassured me that I was loved and needed. I knew who I was when I was in that relationship. Trying to please one man was so much easier than trying to please a different one every time I embarked on a new date.

★   ★   ★

There was no sign of Jim the following morning and I couldn't work out if this was a good or a bad thing. Maybe he was finally getting a life of his own. Maybe the plumbing job was finished at last. Percy and Eleanor were hissing insults at each other across the table as usual. I tried not to get involved in their morning disagreements, which could be set off by something as minor as someone failing to pass the sugar with sufficient speed. Today's, from what I could glean without

252

looking interested enough to be dragged in on one side or the other, was a reprise of the longest-running argument of all: whose fault it was that Auntie Lyd allowed neither of them to do any cooking. It was one of the few house rules, and the most sternly enforced. Although both were welcome to help themselves to anything from the fridge at any time, use of any electrical or gas appliance (with the sole exception of the kettle) was forbidden. Percy blamed Eleanor for setting fire to the toaster one morning in the distant past, claiming she had done it on purpose to necessitate a visit from the firemen at the station on the other side of Elgin Square. Eleanor insisted it was an accident and that Auntie Lyd had instigated the ban after enduring the odour of Percy's preferred kipper breakfast once too often.

I suspected the actual answer was that Auntie Lyd feared her elderly residents might do themselves some harm when handling her heavy Le Creuset pans, but, whatever the reason, it meant my aunt stood at the stove, as she did every morning, stirring the porridge. I chose to join her there rather than enter the fray at the table.

'Did you sleep?' she asked, correctly diagnosing, from the dark circles under my eyes, that I had not.

'Not really,' I shrugged. There was no point trying to hide it from Auntie Lyd; she would winkle out the truth if I tried to lie.

'I hope you weren't losing sleep over that silly man from last night,' she said, pulling me towards her with one arm while stirring with the other.

'No. Just thinking about Martin,' I muttered into her shoulder, half wanting to talk to her about it and half hoping she wouldn't hear me.

'Oh, darling,' she said, pulling away to look at me. 'Martin? Not *still*?'

'I know,' I said, my eyes cast down to the floor. 'Stupid, isn't it? I'm just tired of the unsuitable men. I miss being with someone.'

Auntie Lyd put down her wooden spoon and took me by the shoulders. 'Aurora Carmichael, you are missing being in a relationship, you are *not* missing Martin. There is a big difference and you need to be clear about that.'

'I know,' I mumbled. Of course I knew that, but however unsuitable Martin might be, at least he wasn't vastly my senior, or socially incompetent or a flaky musician, or, worse, one of the 'U R hawt' internet possibilities. Next to these unsuitables even the man who dumped me for another woman began to look like a prince.

'Rory, I mean it,' said Auntie Lyd, looking at me sternly as if she could actually hear my internal dialogue. 'Martin is a cheater. Worse: a cheater and a bore. You are well shot of him. Trust me, you should be feeling sorry for his new girlfriend instead of yourself.'

'I know,' I said again. And I did — in my head. It was my heart that was the problem; no matter how much I tried to embrace the mission of unsuitable men, my heart yearned for just one, very specifically suitable one.

'Lydia,' called Percy, turning around in his

chair to plead with her, 'do you really permit this *woman* to insult me thus in my own home?'

'It is every bit as much my home as yours, you ridiculous old drama queen,' hissed Eleanor.

'Thou vile serpent,' insisted Percy.

'Porridge, anyone?' offered Auntie Lyd, smiling from her position at the stove as if she had heard none of it.

'Sometimes I think dear Lydia should get her ears tested,' muttered Percy.

'She'd probably prefer to hear nothing at all than have to listen to you,' said Eleanor. 'Wait, is that the doorbell?'

'I didn't hear anything,' said Auntie Lyd.

'You wouldn't,' said Percy under his breath.

'I'm sure it was the doorbell,' said Eleanor, hopping off her stool and moving towards the stairs with whisky-fuelled agility. 'It might be the postman. I'm expecting a few things.'

She returned a few minutes later with her arms full of parcels.

'Who are all of those for?' demanded Percy. 'Is there anything for me?'

'For you?' asked Eleanor, keeping her arms jealously wrapped around the parcels as she lowered them on to the kitchen table. 'Why would there be anything for you? Have you done any shopping on the broadband?'

'Shopping?' asked Percy, sneering.

'Yes, shopping, Percival,' said Eleanor. 'Or have you yet to realize there is more to the broadband than just endlessly looking up your own name?'

Percy coughed uncomfortably and didn't answer.

'What have you been buying, Eleanor?' asked Auntie Lyd. She brought the porridge to the table and Eleanor, less paranoid with her in close proximity, released her grip on the parcels.

'Oh, just things,' said Eleanor. 'Jim showed me how to go on something called the eBay, and you would be astonished at what you can pick up there for next to nothing.' She picked up one of the parcels and weighed it in her hand speculatively.

'Why don't you just open it?' said Percy irritably. 'It's not Christmas, you know. You're allowed to open it without guessing what it is as if you were a child.'

'I think this one might be for you, Lydia,' said Eleanor, tearing open the brown paper and lifting the lid of the white box inside. Her watery eyes opened wide with delight as she pulled out an absolutely hideous green marble table lighter. Carved out of a block of stone the precise colour of the avocado bathroom suite Jim had just removed from upstairs, it was heavy enough to make her hand tremble as she held it. She passed it over to Auntie Lyd and reached back into the box to bring out a matching ashtray.

'Goodness, Eleanor, you really shouldn't be spending your money on me,' said Auntie Lyd, turning the table lighter in her hands, probably considering how long she would have to have it on display before donating it to the charity shop.

'It looks lethal,' said Percy, his eyes narrowed in suspicion, no doubt believing that the treacherous and untrustworthy Eleanor, despite the fact she could barely hold the lighter, would find a way to stove his head in with it.

'This one is for you, Rory,' said Eleanor, pushing a large opened parcel across the table towards me. 'I hope you like it, dear.'

Inside the polystyrene curls nestled an enormous yellow and brown flowered lampshade, fringed with brown tassels. Eleanor must have hit a rich vein of seventies cast-offs in her eBay explorations.

'Wow,' I said, lifting it out to see it more clearly, but it was no more attractive out of the box than it had been in it.

'Your room is so bare, dear,' smiled Eleanor sweetly, and I felt a painful stab of sadness as I realized how true this was. I had thought I would only be in the attic bedroom for a few weeks so it hadn't seemed worth making an effort. And yet I had already been there for nearly two months. And it felt like I might be there for ever.

'There is nothing in there that shows your personality, dear, no personal touches,' Eleanor continued. 'I wasn't sure what to get you, but dear Lydia said you just love anything that is a bit old.'

Auntie Lyd made a face at me behind Eleanor's back which I think was an attempt to deny all responsibility for the choice of the lampshade.

'Must be why Rory doesn't mind living with you,' said Percy. 'Seeing as you're so old yourself.'

'Percy,' admonished Auntie Lyd, frowning at him.

'If you speak to me like that, Percival, I shall

257

keep your present for myself,' declared Eleanor. She picked up her whisky and sipped at it, her watery eyes issuing a mild challenge to Percy, whose expression changed from indignant to grudgingly expectant. If I were him, having seen the presents Auntie Lyd and I had received, I would have let her keep it.

'I do apologize, Eleanor,' he said at last. 'Quite unnecessary of me.'

'Mmm,' Eleanor agreed, putting her whisky down. She reached into the pile of parcels for the smallest one; a short brown tube with plastic caps fixed on each end. Placing it in front of her on the table, she appeared to scrutinize the label for a few minutes.

Percy coughed and crossed his legs, obviously itching to grab the parcel out of Eleanor's reach, but attempting to be patient.

'Here you are,' she said, finally pushing it across the kitchen table. It rolled towards Percy, stopping when it hit his bowl of porridge.

He picked it up with such studied non-chalance it might have been a drama-school exercise: pretend you are an excited elderly thespian who doesn't want to admit he is dying to see what his female nemesis might have bought him. Do not let your nemesis suspect your interest in the gift.

Opening the tube, he pulled out a battered magazine. He unfurled it, smoothing the pages out in front of him to show the cover. I could just read, upside-down, the *Radio Times*.

'Eleanor,' Percy said, in a voice barely above a whisper. 'Is it . . . ?'

I raised my eyebrows at Auntie Lyd, but she just shrugged. Clearly she had no idea what was happening either.

'It is,' said Eleanor, settling back in her chair with triumphant satisfaction. 'It is the *Radio Times* from the 14th of May 1979.'

'May 1979?' I asked, trying to decipher the looks that were passing between Eleanor and Percy. I was astonished to see that the deep lines around Percy's eyes were wet with tears.

'The first ever broadcast of *Whoops! There Goes the Neighbourhood*,' he said in an unsteady voice. All of his usual bluster and pomp had dissolved, replaced with a hesitant excitement. 'I'm not certain, but I think in this issue there might be . . . ' He started to flick through the magazine.

'A full profile of you?' said Eleanor. 'Page twenty-six.'

'Eleanor, what an absolutely lovely thing to do,' said Auntie Lyd, beaming at this rare moment of residential harmony.

'I know,' said Eleanor, looking immensely pleased with herself. 'I even outbid the Ashby-de-la-Zouch branch of Percy's fan club to get it.'

'I have an Ashby-de-la-Zouch fan club?' sighed Percy, blinking away more tears. His white-knuckled hands gripped the tattered copy of the *Radio Times* as if he would never let go of it.

There was a sound from the stairs, and the kitchen door swung open to show Jim standing in the doorway, beaming as if expecting a rapturous welcome.

'Morning, all,' he announced. I felt unkindly

pleased that everyone was too engrossed in looking at Percy's *Radio Times* to pay Jim the attention he thought of as his due. He seemed to think we'd all start genuflecting just because he'd walked into the room.

'What's going on here?' Jim asked, sauntering over to the table where Percy had opened the magazine to the full profile. 'No way, Perce, is that you?'

We all stared at the glossy photograph of a much younger Percy Granger, smiling confidently from under a bird's-wing sweep of chestnut-brown hair that preempted Princess Diana's feather cut by years. He wore a lemon-yellow V-necked jumper that would not have shamed the wardrobe of Lance Garcia, but which, unlike Lance's, was worn without a hint of irony. A golden chain glinted from within a tangle of dark chest hair.

'In my prime,' whispered Percy, gazing at the photograph. 'In my prime.'

'Christ, you were a good-looking man, Perce,' said Jim, leaning down to look at the picture more closely. 'Still are, I mean. But look at you there — I bet you were mobbed by the ladies wherever you went.'

Percy sat up a little straighter in his chair, a lone tear drying on his cheek. 'I certainly didn't want for female company,' he agreed.

'Oh, he was absolutely gorgeous,' said Auntie Lyd, pulling the magazine towards her to look at the photographs. 'I remember when Linda and I were filming the first series of *Those Devereux Girls*, we got thrown off the set of *Whoops!* for

260

trying to sneak into Percy's dressing room.'

'Auntie Lyd!' I said. 'You stalked Percy!'

'*Did* you?' asked Percy, regarding Auntie Lyd with great interest.

'Oh yes, but you were far too grand to be bothered with two silly girls like us,' she laughed. 'Lin ended up going off with one of the security guards instead and I — Well, never mind what I did.' She laughed again but it seemed that, for just a second, her face darkened.

'Well,' declared Percy, his chest distended with pride. 'I am very flattered. Very flattered indeed. Stalked by Linda Ellery and Lydia Bell.'

'There are men all over London who'd love to have been in your shoes, Perce,' said Jim, nudging Percy's shoulder.

'Oh honestly, Jim,' said Auntie Lyd, blushing. She picked up her porridge bowl and took it over to the sink. It wasn't an act — she didn't seem to enjoy talking about her time as an actress, unlike Percy and Eleanor, who could speak of nothing else.

'It's true, you know, Lydia dear,' said Eleanor, nodding her head in agreement. 'I tried to buy you a copy of the *Sunday Times Magazine* from 1983 with the big mud-fight photo shoot of you and Linda Ellery, but it seems it's a collectors' item these days. I simply couldn't afford it.'

'Really?' said Auntie Lyd, looking over her shoulder. 'How bizarre.'

'It was such a shame you retired from acting so young, dear,' said Eleanor.

'Too young,' agreed Percy, looking up from his *Radio Times*. 'You weren't even thirty-five. Even

261

now I barely meet a man whose tongue doesn't fall half out of his head when I say I board with Lydia Bell.'

Auntie Lyd smiled dismissively and turned the taps on full in the kitchen sink, drowning out the sound of the latest compliment.

'You are all far too kind,' she insisted, and snapped on a pair of yellow rubber gloves. She turned back towards us with a closed-mouth smile that discouraged further flattery. 'Now what more needs washing up?'

This didn't seem a good moment to remind Auntie Lyd that she owned a dishwasher. I stacked the finished porridge bowls on the kitchen table but before I could carry them over to the sink Jim took them out of my hands.

'I'll take those,' he said, intercepting my path to Auntie Lyd with a smile. 'You know, you look a lot like your aunt used to, Dawn. You really do.'

I flinched away, not sure what he meant. Auntie Lyd had been stunning; famously so. We might have shared the same large brown eyes, but that was where the resemblance stopped. What was Jim playing at by trying to flatter me all of a sudden? Had he guessed I was suspicious of his motives towards my aunt?

'Yeah, right,' I said.

Jim shrugged. 'Learn to take a compliment, Dawn. Not everyone's out to get you.'

Was he on some mission to win me over as well as my aunt? Well. He might have wormed his way into Auntie Lydia's affections, but there was no way that dodgy plumber was going to fool me.

24

Ticky was out of the office all morning at an interview. Her first interview, which I'd insisted she take on, had been an extraordinary success. We all should have realized years ago that the combination of her emotional vampirism and her magnificently thick skin meant she would confidently wade into depths that other interviewers dared not plumb. Amanda was astounded when Ticky emerged from her meeting with Araminta 'Minty' Clinchmore with not just the anticipated personal tour of the Clinchmore estate, which was about to go up for sale for the first time in its four-hundred-year history, but with Minty's on-the-record admission of her husband's gambling debts and cocaine addiction which had forced the sale. Apparently the story had been common knowledge in the circles in which Ticky moved, and she refused to accept Minty's vague allusions to downsizing and not wanting to open the house to the public. What was intended to be a quiet puff piece that would help to sell one of the grandest private houses in England turned into a genuine society scoop that could not have thrilled Amanda more if she had personally photographed Octavius Clinchmore with a coke straw up his nose.

Although I was delighted that Ticky was now going to take on more of the interviewing duties, it meant she was in the office even less, and yet more of her menial tasks fell to me. Amanda didn't appear to notice. At least she had deigned to comment that my column remained the most viewed regular feature on the website, but even with Amanda's current approval, I wasn't sure enough of my advantage yet to push for the column to be promoted into the proper magazine. It wasn't just a lack of confidence that stopped me from demanding it. The longer the unsuitable-men project went on, the more I wondered how much longer I wanted to continue.

I had arrived in the office to an email from Sebastian, tersely wishing me the best in life and announcing that he was leaving the country shortly and would not be returning for some time. I hoped, uncharitably, that a war had broken out somewhere far away, rather than that I had scared him out of England with my shameful frivolity. I hadn't wanted to see him again either, but his emailed rejection meant I would have to return to the depressing unsuitables from the My Mate's Great website. If Sebastian had been the best of them, how much worse would the others be? Malky had been the only one of my dates with whom it had all been easy and fun, the only one who I thought might actually replace Martin in some way; and he had seemingly disappeared off the face of the earth since Mr Bits had attacked his dog.

I knew that Auntie Lyd was right: just because I hadn't yet met anyone new didn't mean I should be giving up. Even less did it mean that I should still be pining for Martin. But as time went on, I seemed to be thinking of him more, instead of less. I tried to fight it. Whenever I found my mind drifting dangerously back to Martin I threw obstacles in front of my daydreams. I remembered that if I ever wanted to watch something on television he made me watch it upstairs so I didn't interrupt his sports viewing. I felt Auntie-Lyd-like rage when I considered the domestic drudge I'd been — even though, there was no point denying it, at the time I hadn't minded at all. Back then it had felt like a down-payment on a future together. Now I wished I'd charged for my services like a cleaner.

Martin had never seen the point of History of Art, either. Of course he respected the practical application — like my former classmates who had gone on to work at Christie's and Sotheby's. Martin understood that because it made a lot of money, but it was impossible to get in there without family contacts, and so I hadn't tried. Martin liked art that looked like art — pictures that were famous and respected and framed in a gallery with a Perspex box next to them that gave a neat summary of what one should know about them, no more, no less: This is a picture of the King of Spain's daughter and her court, painted by Velázquez in 1656, containing a self-portrait of the artist at work. And, oh look, is that a dwarf standing next to the Infanta? When we had gone to Venice for the weekend a few years ago, revisiting my student field trip, Martin had looked interested only once: when I pointed out the resemblance of a Venetian courtier in a fresco to Phil Collins.

Instead of insisting on my own interests, I'd danced attendance around him, trying to keep him happy, divining his moods. I glared at my reflection in the computer screen. Why was it that every time I tried to hate Martin, the person I ended up hating was myself, for having been so weak for so long? If our relationship had ever had a chance, I'd thrown it away by becoming the worst kind of doormat. A spineless pushover. No wonder he'd moved on to someone else. I bet his new girlfriend didn't even know where the ironing board was, unless it was to use it for some kind of acrobatic sexual act.

There was a brief rap on the door and Martha came striding into the office. Without saying hello, she sat down in the chintz armchair. She crossed her legs and clasped her hands girlishly around her knees, smiling at me expectantly as if it was I who had interrupted her work.

'Hi, Martha,' I said, trying to make it sound like a question without rudely demanding what on earth she wanted this time.

'Hello, Rory,' she said innocently. But there was nothing innocent at all about her supposedly casual arrival. Since I'd deputized for her on the Seaton Hall piece, Martha had, apparently without Amanda's influence, suggested a few other projects that I might like to take on in her place. It hadn't escaped my notice that each of these country house visits had been scheduled for a weekend. I'd managed to escape so far by pleading prior commitments, but there was a gleam in her eye that suggested she was back for another try.

'That was an excellent piece you wrote on Luke Home,' she said. 'Most amusing.'

'Thank you,' I said carefully.

There was something different about her. Instead of being slumped in the chair, resentfully looking out for Amanda, Martha sat on the very edge of the cushion, bouncing her top leg in a jaunty manner quite at odds with her sensible shoes.

'Yes, very jolly. He really was like a dreadful dog that wouldn't stop humping the furniture, wasn't he? How terribly embarrassing for Amanda.'

I tried not to take offence at Martha's suggestion that Luke regarded me as little more than a chair-leg on which to rub himself. She was always at her bitchiest when she felt herself threatened.

'Amanda was perfectly happy with the piece,' I said.

Which was true. Although I think her praise had been mostly out of gratitude for my not mentioning in print Luke's trousers-down stationery-cupboard indiscretion. His undignified departure from our office might have made a good ending to a column, but I knew that to use it would have been tantamount to writing my own letter of resignation.

'Oh, of course, Rory, you're quite the golden girl these days, aren't you?' said Martha, with what seemed to be a completely genuine smile. Maybe she wasn't being sarcastic at all. Something had definitely changed.

'Have you had your hair cut, Martha?' I asked.

Perhaps that would explain it.

She raised a hand to the back of her head and patted her stern grey curls. 'Just a little trim. How kind of you to notice.'

I felt suspicious. Why was she being so nice instead of snappish like normal? It had to be a particularly bad trip that she was trying to foist on me: somewhere far away and unpleasant, with rude owners and a minibus full of the most mental freelancers for company. I kept silent and waited for her to speak.

'Rory,' she began at last. 'I find I've double-booked myself for this Sunday.'

'Oh, have you? That's a shame,' I said. There was no way I was actually going to offer to cover for her. I resented the implication that I would have no weekend plans of my own, and I resented still further being regarded as some kind of kindred spirit to Martha just because both of us were single women without a trust fund between us. And yet the most I could hope for if I stayed at *Country House* was to someday fill Martha's Weldon's of Ludlow shoes. I shuddered.

'I thought you might like to cover for me at Hartley House on Sunday,' she said, getting straight to the point. 'This dating column seems to be taking up so much of your time. I thought you'd be grateful for the chance to get back to what *Country House* is really about.'

'I think the dating column is very much what the new *Country House* is about,' I said, warningly. I didn't want to be drawn into any kind of battle against Amanda's changes.

'Oh yes, of course it is,' Martha agreed hastily. 'I know everyone's very keen on it. Well done you. But I thought you'd always loved a country house visit? And Hartley is only an hour out of London; a quick whizz-bang on the minibus at ten and honestly, Rory, you'd be back in time for *Antiques Roadshow.*'

'No,' I said. Martha looked astonished. I felt quite astonished myself. I'd never said no to her outright before. I think it was the insulting implication that I would want to be home to watch *Antiques Roadshow* that forced the refusal out of me. And the realization that I had been a pushover too long — in all areas of my life.

'But Rory,' she pleaded. 'It really won't take long. No interview, no photo shoot, just a short presentation about the new altar screens and you'll be away.'

'No,' I said again, rolling the word around in my mouth like a toffee. It was such a satisfying novelty to say it.

Martha inched forward on the chair, her hands gripping the arms. 'Rory, please. I'll even write the piece for you afterwards. Just go on the trip so they know *Country House* has been, take a few notes and I'll do the rest. I beg of you, don't ruin my weekend.'

'Martha, I'm sorry, I can't do it,' I said.

She stood up and brushed down her skirt; it was a soft tweed one that she had been wearing quite a bit lately. One of several new items in her wardrobe, I realized.

'Well, I'm sorry to hear that, Rory,' said Martha, tight-lipped, straightening her soft

269

purple twinset. That was new too. 'I had thought you would be willing to help. I thought we had an understanding, both being outsiders here. I see a lot of myself in you, you know.'

If she had thought that would weaken me, she had thought wrong. Nothing was more guaranteed to stiffen my resolve than to hear Martha express my deepest fear, that I might turn into her: bitter, angry, frustrated and unhappy.

'I'm so sorry, Martha,' I said firmly. 'I hope you can find someone else.'

'So do I,' she said, so kicked-spanielishly mournful that I nearly backed down, but I dug my fingernails into my palm to stop myself.

I watched her walk down the corridor back towards her office. I'd never paid much attention to Martha's clothes before — they were usually variations on a theme of smart black business-lady suits from Next that dated her as effectively as if she'd gone around wearing a badge with her age on it. But lately, although you still wouldn't call her a stylish woman (those shoes), she had begun to experiment with the gentle palette of a Scottish hillside — all lavenders, greys and pale greens. I wondered what had brought about the change. Perhaps she'd had her colours done — it was just the sort of suburban eighties treat that would appeal to her.

25

It might have been saying no to Martha that lifted my spirits, or it might have been getting out of what sounded like a fairly dire day trip to Hartley House — I might love a bit of art history, but it was hard even for me to get excited about altar screens — but I found myself heading home with a smile on my lips. Perhaps, too, it was the praise I'd been getting for the new column — if it had even led Martha to be complimentary then I knew it was working in some way. It was strange to realize that, for all my talk of keeping my head down and working away in the background, being singled out for attention had the power to entirely change how I felt about my professional life. From being despondent about the unsuitable-men project, I began to see how, even if it wasn't transforming my love life, it was making a difference to how I was seen at work. And maybe that was more important in the end? Maybe I hadn't paid enough attention to my job in all the years I was with Martin; the scales had always been so heavily weighted in his favour. If I could change my office persona from meek proofreader to dating-columnist in just a few months, then maybe I could change it still further. I had my share of the house deposit from Martin sitting in the bank. I could retrain; go back to the Courtauld Institute and take that Master of Arts that I'd turned down nine years ago. Or apply for one of those Guggenheim fellowships in Venice. I had no real ties any more. Where I had seen problems — no relationship, a job I wasn't sure about — now I was beginning to see possibilities.

As I turned the corner into Elgin Square, I heard a shout from the pub garden. I didn't pay any attention as it was a noisy pub, frequented by a young and boisterous crowd that, if I was honest, intimidated me a little. The outdoor heaters kept the smokers warm enough that the pub garden, which opened out on to the street, was as busy in the winter as at the height of summer. The pub had even set up a small outdoor bar, which did a brisk trade in mulled wine and cider. Not that I had ever been there, but I walked past it often enough to feel like a bit of a local.

'Oi,' shouted a voice. 'Oi!'

I ignored it, certain that whoever it was couldn't be calling me. I don't consider myself a snob, but I like to think I don't know anyone who would choose to call me by shouting oi.

'Oi, Rory! Wait!'

Evidently I was mistaken. I turned around to see a man struggling to emerge from the row of potted bushes that separated the pub garden from the street. Rather than exit through the actual gate, he had chosen to force his way out between the branches, pushing them apart with his hands and wincing as they flew determinedly back into his face. If it was a battle between man and bush, I would have bet on the bush. Malky's face grinned from within the greenery. Even when he looked ridiculous he looked gorgeous, his eyes reflecting the vivid colour of the leaves.

'Rory, Jesus, help me, would you? These fucking bushes are determined to make me stay. I think they're in the employ of the landlord.'

'I'm not sure you're going to be able to get out that way,' I said, ineffectually holding back a small twig so that I could see Malky more clearly.

'Then you'd better come in here instead, hadn't you? I think the bushes are making their wishes plain. Let me buy you a cider.'

'Oh, Malky, I'm not sure,' I said, feebly. I felt like the universe had been trying to tell me, through the medium of Mr Bits and Gordon, that any relationship with Malky was a non-starter. No matter how much his eyes might plead. 'I was on my way home. I'm a bit tired, it's been a long day.'

'Jesus, woman,' said Malky, with his beseeching look, 'will you not even come in and let me tell you the story of Gordon's miraculous recovery? Don't you owe me that much at least?'

'Is he okay?' I asked, peering through the bushes to see if the dog was visible.

'Gordon's off out with a mate of mine tonight,' said Malky. 'You get twice as much money busking if you've got a dog with you, so I lend him out every once in a while for a share of the profits. He actually made me a bit more money when he was bandaged up after that mental cat attack, so I feel like I owe you a drink in a way.'

He could see I was hesitating, though in truth

I was tempted less by Malky than I was by the feeling that I wanted to be somewhere where other young single people were hanging out. As far as I could tell, Malky was alone, but wouldn't it be more fun having a drink with him, unsuitable as he was, rather than going home to Auntie Lyd's, where no doubt Jim would be holding court to his retinue of aged admirers? That decided me.

'I'll come in for one, okay,' I agreed. 'But I think I'll give the bushes a miss.'

'You might have to pass my drink to me through the verdant growth,' said Malky, struggling. 'I'm not sure it's going to let me go.'

But the bushes did let him go in the end, even if I had to spend five minutes pulling leaves out of his tangled hair and agreeing that the scratches on his hands and face were surprisingly deep and almost certain to become dangerously infected. Malky insisted that, as this might be his last night before developing a life-threatening case of bush-induced gangrene (and yes, he made every possible bush-related joke you can imagine, but I will spare you from repeating them all here), we had to drink deeply to his very good health. It was warm underneath the glowing heater, and warmer still after two pints of mulled cider, but Malky said he had to sit right next to me to make sure I didn't take a chill.

'Rory,' he said, looking into my eyes very seriously as his leg pressed against mine. 'Rory, I feel like there's something between us.'

'You do?' I asked. It seemed rather early in the

evening for him to be putting the moves on me. He shuffled a little bit closer.

'I do,' he said. 'Something tangible. Something . . . vibrating.'

'*Vibrating?*' I may have had limited experience with unsuitable men, but this didn't seem like something that was in any kind of a romantic script.

'Yeah,' he said, picking up his cider and taking a large swig. 'I think it's your phone going off in your pocket.'

'Ohhh. Oh right.' I'd felt my phone buzzing, but had ignored it. I thought you weren't meant to look at your phone when you were out with someone — wasn't it a bit rude?

'Aren't you going to check it?' he asked. 'Mightn't it be someone interesting? Not more interesting than me, mind. But a little bit interesting. Of minor interest. I'll go off to the bar while you have a read — same again?'

'Thanks, that'd be lovely,' I agreed. I had no expectation that it would be anyone of interest at all. Most likely it would be Auntie Lyd asking me to pick up some milk on my way home, or Martha having another try at getting me to visit Hartley House for her. But Malky didn't know that, and I was rather enjoying the feeling of sitting in a pub with an attractive man, having my phone buzz away as if I was a girl in demand.

I had three messages from an unknown number. When I read the first message, I gasped. When I read the second one, I blushed crimson. When I read the third, I began to have the distinct feeling that my teenage toyboy was trying to re-establish contact. I'd thought — I'd *hoped* — he'd given up on me; I hadn't heard from him since I'd seen him running down the office corridor with his trousers around his knees.

'Looks like that was from someone interesting, young Rory,' said Malky, sitting back down next to me with two steaming pints of mulled cider. 'You've gone all red — who's been sending you dirty texts then?'

'How — how did you know?' I demanded. Had he read them over my shoulder? Might other people in the pub have seen them? How completely mortifying.

'Ha — really?' he laughed, his eyes sparkling. 'No way, I was just kidding. Let's have a look.'

'No!' I exclaimed, pulling my phone to my chest. I was going to press delete and pretend I'd never received them. It was best to just ignore Luke and hope he'd get the message.

'Aw, come on,' said Malky, putting his hands over mine and grabbing for my mobile. 'Don't be a spoilsport. I want to see just what sort of filthy messages a nice girl like you gets.' He wrestled the phone away from me and stood up, holding it way above his head so that I couldn't reach it.

'Malky,' I hissed, keeping my voice low. 'Give it back.' I didn't want to draw too much attention to myself. I wouldn't have put it past Malky to read the messages aloud to the entire pub garden. It was just the sort of thing he would find hilarious.

'Oh good Lord, no,' Malky laughed, holding on to his ribs. 'Jesus, no, this is brilliant. You dirty bitch — who is he?'

'I hardly know him,' I protested. 'He was one of the interns at work; he's just a teenager.'

''Lyin on my bed thinkin bout u,'' Malky read. ''Thinkin bout u', hey? That's romance right there, that is. Lyrical. Gorgeous.'

'Shut up,' I said, pulling on his belt to try to make him sit back down. 'Just shut up, this is mortifying.'

''Thinkin wot I'd do if u were here 2. Hard.' Now that's beautiful, isn't it? Almost poetic. Should I tell him that if you were there too you'd have set a deranged cat on to him by now and chased him out into the street?'

'Oh God, don't. Please just give me the phone back,' I begged, clutching at his coat now.

''Wot wud u do 2 me, MILF?' Well, Rory,' Malky sniggered, 'what *would* you do to him? And why didn't you tell me you had kids?'

'I don't! I don't have kids. He's just a ridiculous hormonal teenager.'

Malky read through the messages again, his shoulders shaking. I let go of his coat and steadily drank my way through the cider, hoping if I drank more it would be less mortifying.

'I'm going to answer,' announced Malky.

'No, Malky! You can't. Just ignore it. Give me back the phone.'

'Aw, come on,' Malky said, sitting down again, but still holding the phone out of my reach. 'It'll be hilarious. He won't know what hit him.'

'Malky, please don't,' I said weakly.

'Rory,' said Malky, pleading. 'I won't if you really don't want me to, but come on, this is

277

genius. We can write it together. Let's wind him up. He's not going to know what hit him.'

His face shone with barely suppressed laughter. I wondered how it must feel to be like Malky, only really interested in the here and now, never worried about consequences or the future. For once, after nearly three pints of cider, I thought it looked like it might be fun. It wasn't like I'd ever see Luke again anyway.

I picked up my cider and finished it. 'Go on then,' I said. 'Let's do it.'

'Brilliant. Let's keep it simple,' said Malky, his eyes shining. 'What about licking — something about licking — will that do it?'

'I don't know! I've never sent sex texts to anyone in my life!'

'Sexts,' corrected Malky, waving an admonishing finger. 'I believe the youth call them sexts, Rory. I think licking, definitely licking.' He'd no sooner tapped out a reply than an answer from Luke arrived.

'Nooooo!' exclaimed Malky. ' "Treat my cock like an ice-cream cone." '

'What? How absolutely revolting.' I grabbed the phone out of his hands to check he wasn't making anything up.

'Right,' said Malky. 'Your turn. Come on.'

'Ice cream,' I said, tapping the phone on my chin as I considered my response. 'Ice cream. Hmm. What about something to do with a rock-hard Magnum?'

I suspect that if Luke could have seen the giggling and jostling and fighting for possession of the mobile phone that ensued, he would no doubt have dismissed me and Malky as hopelessly immature. And completely unerotic. But no matter how ridiculous we got, Luke replied immediately and filthily. The more we drank the more hilarious it all seemed, until Malky and I were almost sobbing with laughter on our shared seat. My phone vibrated once more and Malky grabbed it.

'Oh my God! Oh my God! We've got a penis!'

'What?'

'A penis! A picture of an erect penis!'

'No, you are not serious,' I shrieked, snatching for the phone. 'Argh, no, full frontal! That is absolutely disgusting!'

'What shall we send back?' asked Malky, his eyes bright with hysteria. 'Wait, wait, I know.'

He took the phone back and opened up his shirt, exposing his hairy chest. He brought the phone in close to his chest. 'Let him guess what *this* is,' he said, burying the phone camera inside his shirt.

'No, no, stop,' I begged. 'I can't bear to see what he'd send after that. That's enough.'

'Oh go on, just one little picture. Are you worried he'll think you've got a bushy old seventies beaver?'

'I might have known we'd get back to talking about bushes.'

'Come on, Rory,' pleaded Malky. But the picture message was enough for me. I put the phone down on the table and he left it there, glancing hopefully at it every now and again, but it remained silent.

'*Do* you have a bushy old seventies beaver?'

asked Malky, squinting his beautiful eyes as he tried to focus on my face.

'Oh shut up. Wouldn't you like to know?' I snorted with laughter. My ribs were actually aching; it felt like a long time since I'd laughed like that. Not since my last date with Malky, to be perfectly honest.

'I would, actually,' said Malky, running his hand up my leg. He hooked a finger under the hem of my skirt as if he'd tear it off right there. 'And I don't have my dog with me tonight, so I think I should, don't you?'

I looked up at him. It felt right. If earlier I'd thought the universe was keeping us apart, tonight it felt like fate had brought me past the pub. Fate had made Malky see me, had made Luke send the stupid messages that had made our evening so hysterical, like a winged pervy Cupid with a bow and arrow in one hand and a red-hot mobile in the other. Malky was the man who was going to get me over Martin. This time we wouldn't be interrupted.

'Do you promise not to text me a picture of your penis at any stage of the proposed sexual encounter?' I asked, as seriously as I could manage.

Malky placed a hand on his heart. 'How many times, Rory, must I remind you that it's 'sext', not 'text'? But you have my word. No digital penises, I promise.'

'Let's go back to yours,' I said, casting my eyes down towards the table, suddenly a little shy despite the revolting suggestions we'd spent the evening texting to Luke.

'Oh, er, not really possible tonight,' said Malky, scratching the side of his face and looking away. 'It's not that I don't want you there, honest. It's just a bit of a tip where I live; I wasn't really expecting anyone to come over tonight, you know. I haven't tidied up or anything.'

'I don't mind,' I said. I didn't. My body fizzed with desire. I honestly thought at that moment that I'd happily have shagged him by the pungent wheelie bins outside the Duke of Wellington.

'Come on,' begged Malky. 'I live miles away — and your house is just around the corner. Don't make me wait any longer; let's go there.'

I checked the time on my phone. Eleven-thirty. There was no chance of seeing Auntie Lyd tonight. All the signs were auspicious. 'Let's do it then,' I said.

Malky stood up and offered me his hand. When I rose to my feet I realized just how much I'd had to drink. The ground pitched beneath me and I had to reach for the table to steady myself. I hiccupped.

'Oops, hold on,' Malky said, scooping up my things from the table. He linked my arm through his and I leaned on him gratefully. We left the pub garden with only one slight detour into the shrubbery, which, given the quantity of cider we had dispatched between us, was pretty good going.

26

All the lights were off at Auntie Lyd's and there was no sound to suggest that anyone was awake apart from us. I warned Malky to be quiet with a tipsy 'Sssh' that came out far louder than I'd intended. He shushed me back by placing his finger on my lips. I started laughing, and he covered my mouth with his whole hand to muffle the sound, looking wildly up the stairs as if he expected Auntie Lyd and Mr Bits to come thundering down at any second. Which of course just made me laugh all the more, remembering him prostrate on the hall carpet last time. Malky's green eyes crinkled up as he started to laugh himself, and then he pulled his hand away and covered my mouth with his own.

He tasted of cider and roll-up cigarettes. There was a part of me that felt like I would never get used to kissing someone who wasn't Martin; Martin who smelled of Smints breath fresheners and clean laundry. Clean laundry that I had always washed myself, come to think of it. The thought of Martin just made me more determined to exorcize the role he had taken up in my head by supplanting him with someone else. I kissed Malky even harder.

'Steady on, young lady. Time for bed,' he whispered, pulling away. Before I knew what he was doing he'd dropped to his knees and hefted me over his shoulder into a fireman's lift.

For someone so lanky he was surprisingly strong.

'Oof, Malky, ow, put me down,' I giggled, as quietly as I could while dangling down his back.

'I'll put you down on your bed and not before, young Rory. Where's your room?'

'Malky, it's right at the top of the house, you don't have to do this,' I hissed, kicking my legs enough to offer a protest, but not so much that he might drop me from his unsteady grasp.

'Jesus, it would be,' he sighed, and started off up the stairs, my head narrowly missing the wall with every step upwards. 'Here we go, Rory, on the stairway to heaven.'

There was no corridor of uncertainty this time, and not just because we were in a stairwell instead. Perhaps Malky and I had got all the awkwardness out of the way the first time he'd come round, or perhaps I was just too inebriated to question anything. This time, as we went up the stairs, instead of finding it funnier, I felt myself becoming quieter and more serious the nearer we got to my attic bedroom. Malky, too, had stopped his whispered commentary, but judging by his wheezing breath this might have been because the effort of climbing to the top floor with me on his shoulder was more than he'd anticipated.

He pushed open the door to my room and instead of throwing me on the bed as I'd imagined, he laid me down very gently, as if I was terribly fragile and delicate. His face quite grave, he smoothed my hair away from my face and carefully laid himself on top of me, both of us still buttoned up in our winter coats, with scarves wrapped around our necks. Malky rested his head in my hair, his cold cheek on mine, and I could hear the sound of his breathing slowing as he recovered from the climb. I lay staring at the ceiling, unsure what to do, as I heard his breath soften and settle into a rhythm. I didn't want to pounce on him before he had recovered, but this sudden change of mood, from giggly and foolish to quiet and still, had thrown me into indecision. Just as I had decided to try to wriggle out from underneath him, a snore ripped out of his throat right next to my ear and I leapt into the air.

'What? What?' said Malky, rolling off me and rubbing his eyes. 'What's going on?' He stared about him wildly as if he had already forgotten where he was.

'It's okay, Malky, you're in my bedroom. I think you just fell asleep,' I said, rubbing his shoulder reassuringly and trying not to be offended at his apparent lack of interest in tearing my clothes off.

'Fell asleep?' said Malky, rolling towards me with an irresistible grin. 'Impossible. Not with you right here. What kind of a chump do you take me for?'

'The kind of chump who snores in my ear,' I teased. Malky rolled on top of me again, and brought his mouth close to my ear. He took the lobe between his teeth and pulled at it gently. I could feel from his breath on my face that he was starting to laugh again. He began to place delicate kisses all along the shell of my ear from bottom to top, and then, just as I was beginning to think that things were progressing nicely, he let out another tremendous snore.

'Malky!' I hissed, hitting his shoulder, but he was creased up with laughter.

'Joke, joke,' he insisted, holding up his hands in defence. 'Jesus, Rory, just a joke this time. Now why don't you get out of those clothes and show me what you wouldn't show to that poor young hormonal teenager earlier?'

So I did.

★   ★   ★

When I woke up in the morning, he was gone. I wasn't sure if I should have been grateful or sorry not to see him next to me in bed. I felt a momentary sense of outrage that he should have left without saying goodbye, but that was replaced almost immediately with a fear that he had sneaked out as quickly as possible out of horror at finding himself in bed with me. And then there was, above both of those, a sense of relief that at least I would be spared the possibility of a morning shag because honestly, last night had been just appalling.

I had thought my sex life with Martin was fairly pedestrian — after eleven years together it was never going to be swinging from the chandeliers every night; I could have predicted his every move on the rare occasions we didn't go to bed wearing pyjamas and reading our books side by side until we turned out the lights. Right hand on my right breast, crush and squeeze a little (actually quite painful, but it was far too late to tell him so), move to left breast, then a hand on each breast, squeeze together as if trying to create one large 34F breast instead of two 34Cs, move right hand down below, fiddle for thirty seconds, cursory lick of left nipple, entry, thrust, thrust, 'Are you nearly there?' and then that was it. But compared to Malky, Martin was a master of foreplay; a bedroom Baryshnikov.

I hadn't realized it, but Malky's lying prone on top of me fully clothed was merely the precursor to phase one of his seduction method: lying on top of me naked. Which he seemed to believe was sufficiently erotic to drive me into a frenzy. After five minutes I had become embarrassed just lying there doing nothing — but there was nothing to respond to except the sound of his heavy breath in my ear and all that did was make me tense myself for another loud snore. So I'd started to try to move and make encouraging noises, but Malky had tensed and hissed, 'Stop distracting me,' and the next thing I knew, he had moved on to phase two, the pressing his groin against mine. Although it was having no effect on me, it was evident that this technique was working perfectly well on him.

Phase three lasted a merciful matter of seconds, and then Malky rolled off me.

'Amazing,' he sighed. I didn't know how to answer, certain he couldn't have imagined it was amazing for me. I'd hardly had time to compose my face in an expression of interest, let alone ecstasy.

'Amazing,' he said again, nestling his head in

the pillows and pulling the covers right up to his chin. 'Thanks, Rory.'

Thanks? Thanks?! Before I could answer, Malky had let loose another snore, fast asleep already.

I lay staring at the ceiling as he rumbled noisily beside me. I wondered if he had used up all of his sexual energy in texting and flirtation and cider-drinking. When it came to, well, coming, Malky had nothing left at all.

So it wasn't the worst thing in the world to wake up and find myself alone. I rolled over to reach for the bedside table where I kept my phone — what time was it anyway? I felt around without raising my head; my fingers negotiated a glass of water, a paperback book lying opened with the spine up, an old tissue and a magazine. But no phone. Sitting up made my head swim horribly but I managed to quickly look on the table, and on the floor. Still no phone. I lay back on the pillows, trying not to feel sick. From downstairs I could hear the sound of the new power shower as someone used the bathroom. If that was Percy then it must be around six. Further downstairs I could hear a door open and close, and the gently bubbling voice of Eleanor floated up to my bedroom. With great effort I turned my head towards the window, where a faint light filtered through the thin curtains. It must still be early. Not time to get up yet. My phone was probably in my coat pocket or something. I pulled the duvet up over my head and went back to sleep.

* ★ ★

The house was quiet when I woke up again, and sharp blocks of bright sunlight patterned my bed, breaking through between the curtains. There were sounds from Elgin Square outside — children playing on the swings, cars revving as they negotiated the speed bumps. I pushed the duvet away and opened one eye experimentally. The light made me wince, but my head no longer hurt; perhaps I'd managed to sleep through the worst of the hangover. I swung my legs down to the floor and sat up, rubbing my eyes. Pulling open the curtains allowed light to flood the room. As I stood at the window, looking down into the square, I caught sight of the tiny faraway figures of Percy and Eleanor on the corner, turning towards Clapham Old Town. I wondered where they were off to, and together too. At least their new-found *entente* meant I would be spared their arguing over the kitchen table this morning.

I pulled on my pyjamas and dressing gown and stumbled downstairs. The door to the first-floor bathroom was closed as I descended the stairs — I could hear the sound of *The Archers* from inside, which meant Auntie Lyd was taking one of her long baths. Now that the bathrooms were finished at last, she had taken to staying in hers for hours — perhaps because it was the only place she could escape the demands of her paying guests.

In the kitchen, Jim had dismantled the sink and stood straddling it, his front spattered with dirty water.

'Hi,' I grunted. It surely couldn't be long before Jim moved on to sponge off some other family. The bathrooms were finished, the downstairs loo had been replaced, and he seemed to have been working on the kitchen for weeks. Although I hadn't caught him rooting around in Auntie Lyd's belongings again, I suspected he was just making up jobs now to get more money out of her.

'Rory,' said Jim, putting down his toolbox and wiping his hands on the front of his tight T-shirt. 'I need to talk to you. Sit down.'

I was so surprised that he'd called me by my real name that I forgot to object to his peremptory command, and sat obediently on one of the kitchen chairs. I pulled my dressing gown tighter around me and held it protectively at my neck.

'Rory, do you know anything about the man I found leaving your house this morning carrying half the contents of your aunt's fridge?'

'What?' I asked, entirely confused.

'He seemed to know you. He said you'd told him to help himself.' Jim stood over me with his arms folded. His eyes had narrowed into dark slits and I felt as if it had been me who was caught sneaking out with a load of food.

'I — I didn't,' I began.

'But you did invite that man into your aunt's house?' demanded Jim, towering above me intimidatingly.

'It's my house too, you know. I can invite anyone I want back here,' I protested. 'Anyway, he was probably just hungry. He's allowed to have a bit of toast; stop overreacting.'

'Rory,' said Jim, sighing and running his hand through his highlighted hair. 'Helping yourself to a bit of toast is not the same thing as loading up a carrier bag with a loaf of bread and two pints of milk. What sort of man does that? He even had a tin of cat food in there.'

'He's got a dog,' I said feebly. Malky probably thought it was the least I owed him after Mr Bits had attacked Gordon. It wasn't as if he'd been caught taking money out of Auntie Lyd's purse. It wasn't as if Malky was going to overcharge my aunt for unnecessary plumbing work. It wasn't like he'd been found going through my aunt's private belongings, actually. I crossed my own arms defensively. 'And anyway, it's not really any of your business, Jim.'

'I'm just looking out for you, Rory. For you and your aunt.'

'It's really not necessary,' I said stiffly.

'No. It's not. But I can't help worrying about you, Rory. I know you've got this stupid thing about unsuitable men, I get what you're trying to do, but you need to be careful. Don't get yourself into dodgy situations just because you're trying to prove something.'

'I'm not trying to prove anything,' I snapped.

'Really? Seems like it to me.'

'Why would you — No.' I held up a hand. 'I'm not interested in what you think, Jim. You may have my aunt fooled with your sucking up, but I know what you're up to. You've got a nerve telling me to look out for dodgy situations when you're — you're — '

Jim's eyes glittered dangerously. 'When I'm what?'

'I don't know exactly,' I warned. 'But I don't trust you. What sort of man spends so much time hanging out with a bunch of pensioners — evenings, weekends — without an ulterior motive? I want you to know I'm watching you. You won't rip off Auntie Lyd on my watch.'

'Rip her off?' said Jim, taking a menacing step towards me. 'You think I'm spending all this time here to rip her off?'

'Well, why else would you have dragged this job out for months? You might have Auntie Lyd fooled, but you haven't fooled me.'

'And what exactly is your evidence for my great rip-off scheme?' demanded Jim. 'What proof do you have that I've done anything other than help your aunt out?'

'For money,' I pointed out. 'You aren't helping her out, you're working here for money, actually.'

'Of course for money, I don't work for nothing — do you? Come on. Prove it. If you're going to make serious allegations like that you need to be able to back them up.'

'I caught you looking through the kitchen drawers!' I stood up to face him.

'That's it? One time I was looking for biscuits and suddenly I'm a thief? That's all you've got?'

'It's all I need, Jim,' I said, feeling myself beginning to shake. I didn't need an incriminating sheaf of bank statements to know that his behaviour didn't add up. 'I've got my eye on you. Don't think you'll get away with it.'

Jim's face was thunderous. He strode towards

291

me as if he was going to take hold of my shoulders and shake me; I ducked away from him and ran up the stairs. I could hear him shouting behind me, so I grabbed my coat from the rack in the hall, shoving my feet into a pair of Auntie Lyd's shoes that had been left by the front door. I buttoned the coat as I ran into the square, but when I turned back to check, there was no sign of Jim. Most likely he was panicking now he knew I was on to him. He was probably already trying to get Auntie Lyd on his side, whispering lies to her through the bathroom door. It was like he was trying to protect his investment by driving me away.

Now that I'd flounced dramatically out of the house, I wasn't sure what to do. I didn't have any money and, feeling in my pockets, there was still no sign of my phone, so I couldn't have called anyone even if I'd had anyone to call. Once I would have rung Auntie Lyd if I found myself in an upsetting situation, but Jim had wormed his way into her trust, and I honestly wasn't sure if she would take my side against him. Although I was annoyed with Malky myself — for an unsatisfactory night and for running off without saying goodbye — I couldn't believe that he would have stolen food from us. Jim was so quick to judge, I bet he'd just found Malky leaving the house with a sandwich and had turned it into some great big drama to try to alienate me from Auntie Lyd. All part of his plan, whatever his plan was.

As I stomped towards the Common I fumed with anger. Auntie Lyd's house, once my only refuge, had turned into a place where I felt barely welcome. I'd hardly had a moment to see Auntie Lyd alone for weeks. Jim was always there, in the way, cosying up to her, excluding me. If he was going to be a permanent fixture at Elgin Square, it was time I moved on.

Tears of self-pity sprang up in my eyes as I contemplated the alternative: moving into a shared house with strangers. Fine in your twenties, but at my age? At nearly thirty? I should have been making a home with someone, settling down. Who had I been kidding with this unsuitable-men thing? All it had done was unsettle me. Everyone had said it would be a learning experience, but all I had learned was that I yearned for a suitable man. One who would be kind and reliable. Within ten years of my age. And who wouldn't steal the food from my aunt's house. I knew there would have to be compromises, but it was time to acknowledge that I was not a girl who craved exciting adventure. I could leave that to other girls. It was time to give up the unsuitable men and get on with finding one who was suitable.

Scowling at the ground while pacing my angry strides meant I hadn't taken note of how far I'd walked. When I looked up I saw that my steps had taken me to one of the quiet ponds at the top of the Common, ringed by trees that hushed the sound of the constant traffic. On an island in the middle of the pond primroses and crocuses spread under the trees, protected from walkers and dogs. A sign ambitiously referred to 'the lake' and advised of the wildlife that might

293

be seen. I caught sight of a heron, folded up like a newspaper, sitting motionless on a branch while a family of ducklings swam under it. Looking past the birds, I stared into the murky water as if I might scry a more positive future for myself in its depths.

Suddenly I felt a hand on my arm and I flinched. I was so certain it would be Jim, having followed me out of Auntie Lyd's house, that for a moment I just stared blankly at the couple who stood smiling expectantly next to me.

'Rory?' said the woman. 'Rory, it's Anna. How are you?' She tilted her head to one side with concern and I had a horrible realization of how insane I must look to her, unmade up, hair all over the place, wearing a coat over my pyjamas and dressing gown in public in the middle of the day.

She beamed next to her husband, her cheeks shining. I had been at their wedding six months ago, hand in hand with Martin, wondering if we would be next. It felt like a lifetime ago.

'Ah, hi, Rory,' said Max, clearing his throat. 'Good to see you. Sorry we've been out of touch.' He shuffled his feet and looked to Anna for reassurance.

'We've been a bit preoccupied,' she confided, wrapping her arm around Max's waist. 'Rory, we're having a baby.'

The tears that I had only just suppressed came dangerously close to the surface again. In truth I was happy for them both, but I was terrified they would report my deranged appearance and my tears at their news to Martin, who would no doubt read something far worse into them. I should have been looking amazing, gorgeous, pulled together. Why hadn't they bumped into me when I was flirting in the pub garden with Malky last night, confident and laughing?

'Congratulations,' I said in a strangled voice. 'Wow, really, congratulations. What lovely news. When are you due?'

'August the 10th,' they said in unison, and burst out laughing. Max bent his head to kiss Anna's hair.

'A summer baby, how lovely,' I said dutifully.

'And how are you?' asked Anna. It was clear from her worried expression that she had already made up her mind: Rory has become a crazy lady who is no longer even capable of dressing herself.

'Oh, you know,' I said as breezily as I could manage. 'Just trying to walk off a hangover — bit of a big night last night. You know how it is when you're single. Busy, busy. Out all the time. Dating, that sort of thing.'

'Gosh yes, exhausting,' agreed Anna. 'I feel quite glad I'm excused from all that these days, don't you, Max?'

'I'll say. Getting a bit much at our age,' said Max, as if he was ninety-five instead of thirty-two. 'Ah, that's to say, for us old married types. Different for you, Rory, obviously. Different for you.'

'We do miss you, Rory,' said Anna, her eyebrows knitted sympathetically. 'I shouldn't say it, but I think Martin does too.'

I wasn't sure how to answer. I had spent so

much time imagining Martin cavorting with his new girlfriend that I had hardly considered the possibility he might actually miss me. I had thought that missing the ex was my role to play, not his.

''Course he does,' blustered Max. 'That Melinda girl's a total princess. Pain in the arse if you ask me.'

'Max,' warned Anna, nudging him sharply with her elbow. 'I'm sure Rory doesn't want to hear about that. She's clearly moved on, from the sound of it. Haven't you?'

'Yes,' I said, a bit too fast. I didn't even want to admit to myself the masochistic desire to hear everything about Martin's new girlfriend. Safer for all of us that the conversation changed before I began begging for information. 'Yes, absolutely. Moving on.' I made a half-hearted little pointing gesture with my hand and they both laughed politely.

Max looked at his watch and cleared his throat again.

'I really should be going,' I said, rushing to fill the awkward silence. 'Look at me, not even properly dressed. What a disgrace. It was lovely to see you both, and congratulations again.'

Anna reached towards me for a hug. Between us I could feel the gentle swell of her stomach, and I hugged her tighter. Max patted my back hesitantly as we pulled apart, as if I were a small dog they had encountered on their walk.

'We must get together soon,' he said. I made noises of agreement, but I think we all knew that we wouldn't be meeting up again. They were part of my life with Martin and that was over now. He and Melinda would see the new baby when it was born, not me.

I turned around as I walked away from the pond. Anna and Max stood together by the water's edge, his arm protectively around her shoulder. They waved sweetly at me, already looking parental, as if I was their small child heading off on its own for the first time, in need of encouragement. It felt like goodbye.

27

I walked away from Anna and Max and cut directly across the Common back to Auntie Lyd's. I didn't want to be seen by anyone else like this, unkempt and red-eyed and a figure of sympathy. Seeing Martin's friends made me realize that it was time I took charge of myself. No more sulking about a relationship that was over. No more feeling sorry for myself. No more unsuitable men either; that column had served its purpose. And it was time to admit it was never going to bring me the love of my life. I'd learned all I needed to from the wrong men; now it was time to start looking for the right one. I was going to sort my life out, get back to being who I should be. I'd make changes at work based on my own skills and talents, not just the comic potential of my so-called love life. I felt renewed with the vigour and resolve of a new start, a new beginning. I would move out of Auntie Lyd's. A house share wasn't scary; it was the right thing to do. I'd meet new people that way, make friends my own age. Things were going to be different.

Turning my key silently in the front door, I hesitated on the doorstep, straining to hear any sound that might suggest the presence of either Jim or Auntie Lyd. Hearing nothing untoward, I tiptoed up the stairs to the bathroom. For all that Jim was an unwanted presence in the house, I had to admit he had transformed the plumbing.

Gone was the trickle of rusty liquid that had passed for a shower before; now jets of steaming water beat a tattoo on the top of my head as I stood still, eyes closed. I grabbed a loofah from the side of the bath and attacked myself with it, scrubbing everywhere until my skin was pink and raw. I felt that I was scrubbing away the past, cleaning myself up for a future in which I would be better, stronger, different.

Out of the shower, I wrapped my hair in a towel and shrugged my dressing gown back on, ready to face a new world. When I opened the bathroom door, though, what I faced was Auntie Lydia, looking thunderous on the landing.

'Aurora Carmichael,' she said. 'Where have you been? I've been ringing your phone for an hour.'

'I — I think I lost it,' I said, discomfited by her harsh expression.

'Or you have been ignoring me.'

'No, honestly, I lost it last night,' I said. 'I can't find it anywhere.'

'Fine. I would like you to explain, right now, why you have been hurling wild and insulting accusations at Jim.'

'Auntie Lyd — ' I started.

'Yes?' she frowned, her lips pursed so tightly that the skin around her mouth puckered and whitened.

'I just don't trust him. I — I think he's trying to rip you off. I think he's got an ulterior motive, hanging out here all the time.'

'Do you?' said Auntie Lyd, her voice heavy with sarcasm. 'Please enlighten me further. I assume you have some evidence for this accusation?'

'Auntie Lyd,' I pleaded. 'It's just a gut instinct — he's up to no good. I've found him going through the kitchen drawers when you were out, and he's made this job last way too long. I'm just trying to look out for you.'

She looked furious. I should have known Jim would have got to her first; poisoning her mind against me.

'Excuse me for being confused, Aurora, but I am not quite sure what role I am playing in your ridiculous fantasies about Jim. Should I assume that I am the confused old lady, too senile to be aware of a nefarious plot against her?'

'No, no, Auntie Lyd, that's not it at all,' I protested.

'Oh really? Because with all of your talk about looking out for me, Aurora, you have caused nothing but difficulty since the moment you arrived here. Bringing strange men into my house to attack my cat and steal my food, sulking around the place being moody. I thought you'd come here to sort yourself out, but you just seem to be getting worse.'

'I'm not,' I insisted. 'I *am* sorting myself out. You're not giving me a chance.'

'I've given you plenty of chances,' snapped Auntie Lyd. 'I thought you were going to embrace a new life here, but instead you've wasted your time going out with extraordinarily stupid men — '

'You said you thought I should go out with the unsuitable men,' I said, my voice beginning to wobble. Auntie Lyd had been a defender of the whole idea from the beginning, and now she was using it against me.

'I thought you might derive some amusement from it, Aurora. A distraction to get you over Martin. Not that you would use it as an excuse to feel sorry for yourself, sulking over Martin — still — and being appallingly rude to Jim whenever you encounter him.'

I knew she would bring it back to Jim, I just knew it.

'I should have known you'd take his side,' I muttered.

Auntie Lyd's eyes flashed with anger. 'It is not a matter of taking sides, Aurora,' she said. 'What do you think this is, the playground? We are all adults here, and it's time you began behaving like one.'

'I just know he's taking advantage of you, Auntie Lyd,' I said. I could feel that I had started snivelling like a child, and that my argument was as pathetic and ill-thought-out as a child's, too. 'With his highlights, and his horrible T-shirts, and this never-ending plumbing job that's costing you a fortune.'

Auntie Lyd stiffened in fury. Her nostrils flared as she pulled herself up to her full height.

'Jim is an honourable man who has been very kind to all of us, Aurora. He has been supportive and helpful while you have flounced around like a spoiled brat. And for you to stand there and be such an unconscionable snob about him disgusts me.'

I bit my lower lip hard to stop my chin from

wobbling. I was afraid if I tried to speak I would dissolve into tears.

'I'm so disappointed in you, Rory,' said Auntie Lyd, shaking her head. I'd never seen her look at me like this; all the warmth had gone out of her eyes. 'So very disappointed.'

She turned and walked down the stairs towards the kitchen. Her quiet disappointment was a thousand times more hurtful than her shouting had been.

'I'm not a snob,' I called out, but she'd already gone. 'I'm not.'

I got changed in my room, hiccupping with sobs. Auntie Lyd had been the one constant in my life, after Martin. More reliable than either of my parents, and certainly more present. And now she had turned on me, just like Martin had. I couldn't believe she had accused me of being a snob — me! The girl who was treated like some kind of proletarian serf at work. The one without a trust fund or an ancestral home or a family tree going back to William the Conqueror. My chest heaved with the unfairness of it all. I had to get out of the house as quickly as possible, and stay out for as long as I could.

I sneaked down the stairs with stealth, picking up my handbag, which had been hanging on the banisters since last night. Scouring its depths, I still couldn't locate my phone. Laughter rose up from the basement kitchen as I closed the door behind me and I felt even more desolate than before. Worse than Auntie Lyd and Jim discussing their anger at me was this, their evident shared amusement at my misery, their hilarity while I was still crushed.

Compounding my unhappiness was the fact that the man behind the bar in the pub said no one had handed in a phone last night. It was as if the whole world was conspiring against me. I could only think of one solution to it all: to hide away for as long as possible. If I had been braver I expect I would have run away somewhere; turned up unexpectedly at a faraway friend's home for the weekend, or booked myself into a hotel for the night. But the best place to hide on a grey March afternoon, for one as risk-averse and cash-strapped as me, seemed to be the cinema.

I settled into my seat in the darkened theatre, hardly aware of what film I was going to see. I'd chosen it purely based on the fact that it started in the next few minutes. The sparse audience — a few pairs of thirtysomething women, a couple of men on their own — suggested this was no blockbuster, or perhaps it just suggested that people with real, active lives didn't go to the cinema in the middle of the day. A few months ago I'd have been horrified at the idea of going to the cinema by myself. I'd have thought everyone would have pointed me out as the sad single girl on her own. Today, though, it felt like a blessing: a place to hide out by myself, unseen by anyone. And who cared what anyone else thought? As the adverts boomed out of the speakers I shrank down in my cushioned seat so that I could rest the back of my head against it. The wall of noise was strangely soporific, drowning out my own thoughts and replacing them with a comforting blur of meaningless sound. I felt my eyelids droop before the film had even begun. It turned out to be something with subtitles — I think it might have been Polish — but I struggled to concentrate. Instead I let myself drift off to the accompaniment of incomprehensible dialogue.

I stirred awake to the soft thump of cinema seats springing back into position. Lights flickered on. Two women walked up the aisle wiping their eyes. I caught the words 'searing' and 'masterful' as they passed me. The man in the row in front blew his nose loudly. I felt a little relieved to have been spared what had obviously been a draining cinematic experience.

Outside it was still light, and I wondered if this day was ever going to end. I had hoped to return home under cover of darkness, when I could sneak up to my room, pull the covers over my head and believe that my new beginning would come tomorrow. There was a French restaurant across the road from the cinema — I'd been there with Auntie Lyd often as a teenager for moules marinière and rough red wine, which my aunt insisted that I was old enough to drink from the age of fifteen. I knew it was dimly lit and staffed by waiters who rarely condescended to notice their customers. It was just the sort of place to while away an hour without being disturbed, or indeed noticed. When I stepped inside, the white-haired owner looked up from the bar and motioned me over to a corner table, so dark that I couldn't read the handwritten menu. I asked for a glass of wine, and he returned with a squat tumbler filled right to the top.

'Extra for you,' he confided, unusually friendly. '*Extra pour la nièce de Lydia Bell. Ah, les belles filles Devereux.*'

He waltzed back towards the bar, humming a tune that I recognized as the theme of *Those Devereux Girls*, sung by Auntie Lyd's co-star, Linda Ellery. I turned the tumbler in my hands, watching the play of candlelight on its surface. It was always strange to be reminded of Auntie Lyd's celebrity, faded though it might have been. I suppose with the selfishness of youth I had grown up thinking of Auntie Lyd as someone who belonged to me, instead of seeing her as a person in her own right, with a public identity in which she was no one's aunt. I sipped my wine slowly, letting its warmth spread through my chest. I thought of Auntie Lyd's house, where she always seemed to be on her feet, cooking or cleaning or gently offering advice. Where she kept the peace between Percy and Eleanor without ever taking sides. Where she'd offered me a room, rent-free, without question, never asking how long I would be staying or making me feel that I was in her way. I remembered the pile of *Country House* magazines in her living room; she'd read every column I'd ever written and subscribed to a magazine in which she had no interest, just for my sake.

And I'd repaid her by being selfish and thoughtless and rude. She was right: I'd assumed that my brave and clever aunt was some doddery woman to be made a fool of by the conniving

305

plumber. Whatever Jim's motives, and I still suspected them, Auntie Lyd could take care of herself. More than that, she took care of everyone else, too. I owed her a proper apology. I left the rest of my wine sitting on the table and said goodbye to the owner, who called after me to send my aunt to see him soon.

The afternoon light was just turning to dusk as I turned the corner into Elgin Square. One street light cast an orange glow from the far side of the children's playground, but the rest of the square squatted in a murky gloom. On the white steps of Auntie Lyd's house I could see the figure of a man, sitting with his head held in his hands, his dark coat spread out on either side of him. I had imagined this sight so many times that I doubted what I was seeing, certain I must have hallucinated it. I stopped still. Even from this distance, even with his head buried in his palms, I knew that figure better than any other. I would have recognized him from twice the distance. Martin.

As if he had felt my eyes on him, Martin raised his head up, and slowly got to his feet. My legs carried me unsteadily towards him. His hand reached for the wrought-iron gate at the bottom of the steps just as mine did, and for a moment we both stood there, the gate between us, our fingers touching.

'Rory,' said Martin, putting his cold hand over mine. My first thought was to snatch my hand away, but instead I stayed still, waiting to hear why he was there. We were standing so close that I thought he must be able to hear that I had almost stopped breathing.

'Yes?' I whispered.

'Your aunt's had a heart attack. I'm here to take you to the hospital.'

28

It felt both entirely familiar and perfectly surreal
to be at Martin's side in his car again. As
if nothing at all had changed, and also as if
everything had. Martin explained all that he
knew: Auntie Lyd had collapsed at the butcher's
this afternoon. The butcher had found a
next-of-kin card in her wallet and, failing to
reach me by the mobile number listed, had
called the number marked 'Rory: home'. Thank
God Martin had been there to take her call. He
told me he had driven to the house and found
that no one knew where I was. The plumber had
taken Percy and Eleanor to the hospital to wait
for news, while Martin had sat alone on the cold
steps waiting for my return. I was sick with
shame. As if I hadn't already felt guilty enough
about taking her for granted, now my proud aunt
had collapsed in a butcher's shop, all alone,
taken away in an ambulance by strangers with no
way to contact her nearest relative. While I
self-indulgently slept in a cinema, and drank
wine afterwards, feeling sorry for myself.

Martin glanced at me as I huddled in the
passenger seat, not speaking, dry-eyed with fear
of what I would find at the hospital. He rested
his palm on my thigh, stroking my leg with his
thumb as he drove. When we were together I
used to tease him about this dad-like move,
calling it the Reassuring Thumb-Rub, but I

didn't feel reassured at all by it today. I let him carry on, though; it felt rude to pull my leg away when he'd come all this way to help me. I just wanted to see Auntie Lyd and make sure she was okay. Martin had said she was going to be fine, but what did he know? I cursed myself for losing my phone yesterday. How could I have been so stupid? It proved to me what I should have realized long ago — messing around with unsuitable men, trying to be someone I wasn't, brought trouble not only to me, but to the people I cared about. After all, who had ended up coming to the rescue but Martin, my once-suitable man? Didn't that tell me something important about the sort of person I should be with? It wasn't like Malky had rushed to my aid, with his guitar on his back and his dog at his heels.

Martin dropped me off at the hospital entrance and went to park the car once I'd given him some cash; luckily I had a lot of pound coins in my purse because apparently the parking charges were astronomical. Outside the hospital two thin old men stood in their dressing gowns, attached to drips which swung, full-bellied, next to them. They passed a cigarette between their yellowed fingers.

'Can you tell me where the cardiology unit is?' I asked as the automatic doors slid open ahead of me.

The man nearest me coughed into his sleeve and wheezed, 'G Wing, dear.' His companion gave me a wan smile of sympathy.

I took the stairs, not willing to wait a moment

for the lift to arrive, and feeling, too, that I wanted to punish myself in some way for letting Auntie Lydia down. I forced myself to run up the four flights until I felt that my lungs would burst. My chest had only just stopped heaving when I pushed open the door marked CARDIOLOGY WAITING ROOM. There, looking pathetically small on the hard yellow plastic chairs, were Eleanor and Percy, their hands clasped. I had grown so used to seeing them both every day that I registered with a shock, in this unfamiliar environment, how frail they both were. Here in the harsh, antiseptic surroundings of the hospital, uncertain and confused, they looked elderly and frightened.

'Rory,' Eleanor quavered, standing up with difficulty. 'Rory, my dear. You mustn't worry. Lydia is going to be quite all right.'

'Is she?' I asked, grasping her hand. 'Have you seen her?'

'None of us has seen her,' said Percy, rising up from his seat to stand next to Eleanor. 'But Jim spoke to the doctor. He said it was a very minor attack. Lydia will have to stay in for a few days, but she is going to be just fine.'

'I want to see her,' I said, looking around for a nurse. 'I want to see her. Where's Jim? Is he with her?'

Eleanor and Percy looked at one another. 'I'm not sure where Jim is, dear,' said Eleanor, leaning a little on Percy.

'He said he had to sort out a few things, didn't he, Eleanor?' said Percy. 'He said he'd be back soon.'

'How long has he been gone?' I asked. 'How long have you been waiting here?' It seemed outrageous to me that Jim would just leave these two frail pensioners alone in the hospital. Eleanor's face was lined with exhaustion and worry; they should have been at home.

Percy waved his hand dismissively. 'A few hours. It's nothing; nothing.' He stumbled a little at Eleanor's weight on him.

'You both sit down,' I said. 'My boyf — I mean Martin, my friend Martin is here. That is, he'll be here any minute. I'm going to get him to take you home. You shouldn't have had to wait here all this time.'

'But we wanted to, dear, for Lydia,' insisted Eleanor, sitting back down gratefully.

'Auntie Lyd would want you both to be at home. I can call you if there are any updates. You're both far too good to have waited for so long. I don't know what Jim was thinking of, leaving you here with no way of getting back.'

'We could get the bus, dear,' Eleanor suggested gently.

'I wouldn't dream of it,' said a voice from the door. Martin glided into the room, extending his hands to Eleanor. I remembered suddenly how charming he could be when he tried; my mother had always adored him. 'Eleanor Avery, how is it possible that you don't age like the rest of us? And Percy Granger? How marvellous to see you again, sir.'

Eleanor's eyes swept from Martin to me, trying to assess the situation. I silently wished her luck with that one, since I had no idea what

311

was going on myself. It had been extraordinarily good of Martin to come all the way to Clapham to find me; it seemed quite bizarre that he was still at my side instead of driving back to North Sheen and his new girlfriend.

'If Percy and Eleanor need a lift home then I insist on taking them,' said Martin, executing a Reassuring Thumb-Rub on my shoulder. Behind him I saw a nurse passing the waiting-room doors.

'Thank you,' I said distantly, distracted by the nurse, who failed to turn into the waiting room as I'd hoped. I turned back to him. 'Yes, that would be brilliant. Thanks so much, Martin, it's really kind of you. Thank you.'

Martin helped Percy and Eleanor up and led them towards the doors. When he'd ushered them out he took a step back into the waiting room and wrapped his arms around me. Before I knew what I was doing, I buried my head into his shoulder, inhaling the familiar scent of his coat.

'I'll drop them there and then I'll come back to wait with you,' he whispered into my hair. 'You shouldn't have to wait on your own.'

'I'm fine. I'm really fine. You've done more than enough,' I said. I pulled out of his embrace before I got too comfortable there. His behaviour was confusing me. As was my own. Why was he here? And wasn't I supposed to be shouting at him? Furious and angry? Not just falling gratefully into his arms as if we were still together.

'No, I'm coming back,' Martin insisted. I

started to protest, but he placed a silencing finger on my lips. 'Anyway, I've got a twenty-four-hour parking permit so I shouldn't waste it.'

When they had gone I stepped out into the corridor, but the nurse had gone. There didn't appear to be anyone else I could ask about Auntie Lyd, so I went back into the empty waiting room. It seemed to have been designed to keep anyone waiting in maximum discomfort — the plastic chairs were welded on to a metal rail so that they couldn't be moved, and their ergonomically designed curved edges discouraged any position other than sitting sharply upright. No wonder Percy and Eleanor had looked so drained by their hours here. I appreciated there was probably some important medical reason why everything needed to be wipe-clean — superbugs or something — but it felt as if all the grief and fear was magnified and reflected in the harsh, unrelenting surfaces of the room. I shuffled to the edge of the row, where a Formica table-top offered a selection of reading material; when I got closer I saw that it consisted entirely of NHS leaflets about looking after your heart. I picked up one about giving up smoking and put it in my bag, hoping if I gave it to Auntie Lyd she would be weakened enough not to use it as a weapon against me.

I hated to think of her, somewhere in this hospital, on her own. I should have been with her to hold her hand, to tell her I was sorry. I wanted to talk to a doctor, to take charge somehow. It had hurt to hear that the person who had spoken to the doctor was Jim; it should have been me. I should have been there. But I had only myself to blame. Who else should the doctor speak to when a woman is brought in, unconscious, with no relatives, accompanied only by her tenants and a plumber? Poor Auntie Lyd.

As well as making the waiting room relentlessly uncomfortable, whatever sadist had been in charge of the decorating had neglected to provide a clock. Perhaps it had been kindly meant — trying to spare anxious relatives the torture of the slowly ticking hands. But without my phone, a clock, or even a window to show the passing of time, it was impossible to gauge how long I had been there. When the waiting-room door swung open at last, I looked up gratefully.

Instead of the nurse or doctor that I'd hoped for, it was Jim's highlights that I saw peering round the door. Seeing me, he edged into the room quietly, as if fearing I might launch straight back into the argument we were having when I last saw him. He was carrying a Marks & Spencer's bag and I felt a rush of fury towards him — he'd left Percy and Eleanor here, all on their own in the hospital with no way to get home, so that he could go and do some light shopping? I sat on my hands and counted to ten. It would help no one to lose my temper with him again. Auntie Lyd would want us to get on, especially now.

'Rory,' he said. He hadn't stepped fully into the room, but hesitated by the door, rubbing his head so that his hair stuck out in all directions.

'Rory, Jesus, thank God you're here. We were so worried when we couldn't get hold of you.'

'Martin found me,' I said. 'He's been great. He's taking Percy and Eleanor home right now. They were really tired after waiting so long on their own.' I didn't mean it to come out accusingly, but it obviously did as Jim pressed his lips together into a tight line.

'Martin, right. Okay. I was just coming to take them back. I didn't know it was going to take so long to pick up a few things.' He held the bag out to me as if I might want to inspect his shopping. I didn't need to take a look. It would no doubt contain a new supply of T-shirts a size too small, and I'd seen enough of those over the last few months.

I shrugged.

'Don't you want it?' asked Jim, shaking the bag at me. A bit aggressively, actually. 'I expect you'll be the first to see her when she wakes up.'

'What do you mean?' I said, flinching backwards away from the bag.

'The stuff I got for Lydia,' sighed Jim crossly. 'Where do you think I've been? Just hanging out at the shops?'

'No,' I mumbled, shamefacedly since that was exactly where I had thought he'd been. Why did I always feel that Jim caught me at a disadvantage with everything he did?

'Look, Dawn,' he smiled, seeing my embarrassment. 'I know you're going to think I've got some evil reason for doing this, that it's just part of whatever dastardly scheme you think I'm up to, but the truth is when my mum was in

315

hospital I remember how much she hated wearing the hospital gowns and eating their sorry excuse for food. I didn't want to root through Lydia's stuff at home — I know how you feel about me going through her belongings — so I just went out and got her a few things, okay? Nothing sinister; no evil plan. Here. Have a look.'

Jim dropped the bag on my lap. I peered inside and saw a soft flannel nightgown, a muted plaid with buttons that reached up to the neck. It wasn't her sort of thing at all, but I knew Auntie Lyd would be grateful for it. Under the nightgown was an assortment of ready-made snacks — pasta salads and chopped fruit and some breadsticks.

'Thanks, Jim,' I said, my head bowed. 'You didn't have to do that, I could have sorted this out.'

'I thought you probably had enough going on already,' said Jim. He settled himself in the chair next to me and stretched out his legs as if he was planning to stay for a while.

I twisted the plastic bag between my hands, wrapping it round and round until the tips of my fingers went white. 'What — what exactly did the doctors say, Jim?' I asked.

'Oh Jesus, sorry, I thought the others would have told you,' he said, drawing his legs up to sit straight. He turned around on his unforgiving plastic chair and slung his arm around the back of my own. 'She's going to be fine, Rory. She really is.'

'Are they sure?'

'They're just keeping her in for observation,

they said. And a lecture on giving up smoking, I expect. If they're brave.'

I sniffed and nodded. Somehow I trusted Jim's word more than Percy and Eleanor's. Maybe because he had spoken to the doctor directly. I didn't feel like he was just offering me empty assurances to settle my mind. If there had been terrible news, I felt he would have been able to tell me. Let's face it, he didn't usually hold back from telling me things I didn't want to hear, like how bad my hair looked.

'She'll be okay,' Jim said. 'Don't worry. The doctor said they were running a few more tests, but they should be done by six. Then you can see her. I'll wait with you if you like.'

'I'll be all right,' I said. I leaned back a little, until I realized it seemed I was trying to lean into his outstretched arm on the back of my chair. I straightened up again. 'Martin's coming back later, he said. You don't need to stay.'

'Oh, Martin, great. Shall I wait till he gets back?' Jim looked at me with real concern and I wondered if the hard yellow chairs made me look, as Percy and Eleanor had, fragile and in need of tender care; but that couldn't be the case since Jim himself looked anything but frail with his pumped-up musculature.

I shook my head. 'I'm fine. Thanks, Jim. Really, thanks. You should go.'

He pulled his hand away from the back of my chair. His hands pressed flat on his thighs as he pushed himself up to standing. 'Okay. You can call me any time though. I mean it. Any time you need anything.'

'Lost my phone,' I said, looking at the ground. It came out more churlishly than I'd meant it to. As if I was making an excuse for not calling him, instead of being embarrassed to have lost it in the first place.

Jim put his hands in his pockets and hunched his shoulders in a shrug. 'Okay,' he said. He rubbed at his hair again as he walked to the door. When he was halfway out of the room he stopped, frowning.

'Dawn, doesn't your aunt usually cook for Perce and Eleanor in the evenings?'

'Yes. Oh God, yes, I hadn't even thought about that. Don't worry, Jim, I'm sure they can sort themselves out just this once. Surely Eleanor can't set fire to the toaster twice.'

Jim laughed and gave me a little salute as he left.

The doors swung shut behind him and I was on my own again. The plastic chairs seemed to have become even harder. I bundled my coat into a pillow and stretched myself out across three chairs. I'd hardly slept last night, and despite my nap in the cinema, suddenly I felt exhausted. Trying to ignore the hard edges digging into my side, I closed my eyes.

29

When I woke up it took me a few seconds to remember that I was in the hospital. The harsh yellow chairs reminded me as soon as I opened my eyes, as did the insistent pressure against my ribs. I stretched my legs out across the plastic and yawned. I remembered making a pillow out of my coat before I lay down, but now I could feel that the coat was spread over me like a blanket, tucked right up to my chin, while my head rested on someone's lap. I turned my head to look up, squinting into the light of the fluorescent tube overhead.

'Jim?' I murmured sleepily.

Martin frowned down at me. 'Jim?'

'Martin!' I exclaimed, sitting up immediately. 'Sorry.'

'Jim? That plumber at your aunt's house?' said Martin. His frown deepened. He edged forward on his seat and suddenly winced, a hand on his lower back.

'Are you okay?' I asked. 'It's these horrible chairs. Have I been asleep for ages?'

Martin arched his back, biting his lower lip. 'A little while,' he acknowledged.

'Oh poor you, Martin,' I said. 'Your poor back. Here, let me put my coat behind you. Is that better?'

'Thanks,' he grunted, leaning backwards, but I could see he was still in pain.

319

'Martin, I really appreciate your being here, please don't think I don't,' I said, 'but it's fine if you want to go now. You've done more than enough. And there's no need for you to suffer on these chairs when you don't have to.' In truth it wasn't just concern for his back that made me think he should go home. It was doing my head in having him here, acting like we'd never broken up.

'What kind of man would I be to leave you alone in a hospital?' asked Martin. 'I want to help, Rory. Please let me.' He winced again as he shifted on the chair.

It didn't make any sense to me that he was here at all, but I wasn't ready to initiate that conversation when the doctor was due to arrive any minute. Unless — had I slept through it?

'What's the time?' I asked, standing up anxiously. 'Has the doctor been already?'

'Rory, Rory, Rory,' said Martin, rising up from the seat and reaching his hands out towards me with the indulgent smile I remembered so well. He put his arm around me and led me away from the door and back to the row of bolted-down chairs. Pushing my head on to his shoulder, he smoothed my hair with a heavy hand. 'Rory, Rory. No need to get hysterical. It's going to be okay. I'm here.'

I was too agitated to be comforted. Especially by my very recently ex-boyfriend. The nervous energy of waiting for news of Auntie Lyd made me incapable of sitting still — now I understood why films always showed expectant fathers pacing the hospital corridor; at least moving helped you to feel like you were doing something. When the door to the waiting room opened, I was glad of the excuse to pull my head away from Martin's grasp.

'Miss Carmichael?' asked a nurse. Not the doctor after all. What did that mean?

I nodded, and gripped the sides of the plastic chair.

'Don't look so worried,' she smiled. 'The doctor says she's going to be fine. He's been called away to an emergency but he says it's okay for you to come and see her.'

I nodded again, silently. Martin put his arm around me.

'Shall I come with you?' he asked. I shook my head, then remembered the M&S bag and grabbed it from the floor.

In the corridor the nurse walked briskly in front of me and I was grateful to her for it. If she had been sympathetic I think I might have fallen apart.

'The doctor's going to keep her in for observation,' said the nurse over her shoulder. 'But he's pleased with her progress so far.'

She stopped outside a pair of double doors. The room inside was darkened.

'Your aunt is sedated,' she explained, her hand on the door. 'So don't expect her to wake up. And don't be alarmed by the machines that are attached to her — we just need to monitor her overnight to make sure all is as it should be.'

She pushed open the door and I followed her into the room. There, on a spindly looking metal-framed bed, lay Auntie Lyd, her chest rising and falling under the thin blue weave of a hospital blanket. A drip was taped to the back of her hand, and a monitor behind her pulsed a regular red light that, as instructed by the nurse, I tried to find reassuring instead of alarming. Auntie Lyd's face looked calm, but a purpling bruise on her jaw made me catch my breath. Had she fallen on her face when she collapsed? Had the doctors done this by accident? I took hold of her fingers and they clutched my own.

'It's involuntary,' said the nurse, hovering at my shoulder and indicating Auntie Lyd's clasping hand. She moved a wooden stool to the side of the bed for me to sit on. 'She's not really aware you're here. I'm going to leave you now, okay?'

I looked up from Auntie Lyd, realizing I hadn't spoken one word to the nurse since she'd come to find me. 'Thank you.'

'She'll be all right,' smiled the nurse. 'The doctor was a big fan of your aunt's back in the day. We all were. We'll be looking out for her. You should go home and get some sleep and come back in the morning, okay?'

'Okay.' I nodded. I heard the soft squeak of the nurse's shoes on the linoleum and the door's muffled swing with her departure. Auntie Lyd breathed calmly on and I had the strange feeling that although she was unconscious, it was she who was a comfort to me instead of the other way around. Guilt weighed heavily on me; even now, while she lay on a hospital bed, I was taking strength from Auntie Lyd instead of supporting her.

I smoothed the hair away from her forehead; with the expressive dark eyes closed, she looked much older. Her forceful personality lent her the illusion of youth, and I had grown used to thinking of her as a woman in her prime. Here, so still and silent, I saw her for the first time as she would be when she was truly old. The thought of losing her clutched at my heart. I would do anything to make her well. I'd caused her nothing but difficulty since I'd moved in. The best thing I could do to help Auntie Lyd would be to stop being a drain on her. I felt her fingers flex in mine. As soon as she was better I would move out; let her life go back to normal. It was time to stop being selfish, and to think of what was best for Auntie Lyd for a change.

30

'I'll come in with you,' said Martin, when he stopped the car in Elgin Square. It was dark outside and light from the kitchen window glowed welcomingly from the basement. Percy and Eleanor would be inside waiting for news.

'No.' I surprised myself with my answer. I'd been thinking about Auntie Lyd and it came out more harshly than I'd intended.

'It's okay, Rory,' Martin reassured me, leaning closer. 'I want to be here to support you. You don't have to do this alone.'

I shook my head, trying to shake my thoughts into order. Of all the strange things that had happened today, Martin's continued presence was the most inexplicable.

'Martin,' I asked, 'what are you doing here?'

'I'm here to help, Rory,' he said, his voice puzzled. 'I just want to help.'

'But why?' I stared out of the windscreen. I was afraid if I looked at him I was in danger of bursting into tears. In all of my frenzied post-break-up imaginings, I'd always thought I'd be furious and angry with Martin if I ever saw him again. I'd rehearsed my cutting remarks and vicious put-downs until I thought I had them off by heart. But now he was here, sitting next to me in his car, the script was all wrong. He wasn't supposed to be being helpful and kind; I wasn't meant to be exhausted and emotional. A few drops of rain landed on the glass and started to slide downwards.

'Well, I got the phone call and it — it just seemed the right thing to do,' Martin stammered. 'I thought you'd be grateful for some help.'

'I am grateful,' I said, still staring ahead. I had to stay calm and not start wailing about why he was torturing me by being all helpful and boyfriend-like. 'I am. Thank you. You didn't have to do any of it. But I don't understand why you're still here. Why you want to come into the house.'

'Rory, I know,' he answered, clutching the steering wheel tightly as if he was going to wrench it off the dashboard towards his chest. 'I know I ruined everything. I've been a total arsehole. I wish I could tell you how much I regret it. It's just — I got the phone call about your aunt and it seemed like a sign. A sign that I could make things up to you; make you see how sorry I am.'

My head spun. What was he trying to say? And why did he think my aunt's heart attack had anything to do with him? As if she'd only collapsed to allow him some kind of emotional epiphany about his ex-girlfriend.

'It's okay,' I said. 'I can see you're sorry. But I think you should go now. Back to your new girlfriend.'

'No, Rory, you don't understand.' Martin clutched at my elbow to try to get me to turn around. I cast my eyes downwards. 'Me and Melinda — it wasn't really anything. It took you moving out to make me see that was nothing more than a stupid fling. It's all finished now. Rory, please, I need you to forgive me. I need you to come home.'

I couldn't take it in. For two months I'd dreamed that moving out would make Martin miss me and beg for my return. I'd imagined him turning up at the house, pleading for forgiveness. I'd fantasized about it endlessly. When I hadn't been imagining dark acts of revenge, of course. But not like this. Not now.

'I miss you, Rory,' he said softly. 'I miss everything about you. I want you to come back. I want our life back.'

'Oh, Martin,' I sighed, so incredibly tired. I felt dizzy. It had been hours since I'd eaten. Perhaps that was why I even felt a bit sick. 'I've got to go.' I started scrabbling at the door handle to get out.

'Can't we at least talk about it?' he asked, holding on to my arm and looking at me imploringly. He was usually so in control, so dominant; I wasn't used to seeing him like this, pleading and apologetic. That was usually my role.

'Not now,' I said. 'It's too much.' I was trying so hard to be strong, to push him away, but the truth was I was so tired and confused that I was afraid I was just going to bury my head in his chest and let him look after me like he'd always done.

'I know it's too much right now, Rory,' said Martin, lifting up my chin to look into my eyes, sensing me weakening. 'But I'll be back tomorrow, and the next day. As long as you need me. And as long as it takes for you to realize that I still love you, and you love me, okay?'

'I don't know,' I mumbled. I wasn't at all sure it was okay.

'I know you're angry. I deserve it. I'm going to make it up to you, I promise. At least let me come and take you to the hospital tomorrow?' Martin pleaded, his hand on my thigh. 'Please?'

It felt too tiring to carry on arguing with him. And it would save me getting the bus to the hospital. 'Okay,' I agreed, pulling away and opening the car door. 'Thanks, Martin.'

'It's the least I owe you, Rory. Sleep well. I'll be back tomorrow.'

He waited in the car as I crossed the pavement and climbed the steps up to Auntie Lyd's front door; they seemed to shift and slide under my feet like an escalator, unbalancing me. Or was it knowing Martin was watching my every move that was so unsettling?

I closed the front door behind me and leaned against it for a few breaths before I went downstairs. I knew I would have to plaster a reassuring expression on my face for Percy and Eleanor, and give them the news in the most encouraging way. They had waited at the hospital for so long, supporting Auntie Lyd when I had been nowhere to be found. They deserved my full attention and I had no right to plead tiredness. I had to banish all thoughts of Martin from my head, no matter how much they clamoured for attention.

From downstairs a clatter of plates indicated

the paying guests were fending for themselves in the kitchen. There was no smell of burning, and no shouting either. In fact I thought I could discern the smell of something spicy, and I wondered which of them had discovered a previously hidden ability to cook. Eleanor's wavery voice floated up the stairs.

'Was that the door?'

'It wouldn't be the postman at this hour, Eleanor,' snapped Percy.

'That's enough, Perce. I thought you and Eleanor were bosom buddies these days,' said a voice that I recognized, to my surprise, as Jim's.

'There is a viper in *her* bosom,' I heard Percy say.

'As if *you'd* know what was in my bosom, Percy Granger,' said Eleanor. I guessed their peace agreement, always fragile, had been stretched to breaking point by the stress of Auntie Lyd's sudden illness.

I trudged down the stairs, straightening my shoulders as I entered the kitchen. 'It was the door; it was me,' I said.

The kitchen table was covered in foil containers — Percy stopped with a spoon halfway between one container and his plate. Mustard-yellow curry dripped from the spoon on to the table. Eleanor's eyes filled with tears and she clutched nervously at the neck of her blouse. Jim pushed his chair away from the table and stood up.

'It's all okay,' I said, coming into the warmth of the room. 'She's sleeping. She's going to be fine. We can all see her tomorrow.'

Percy lowered the spoon on to his plate and, his argument with her forgotten, put his arm around Eleanor, whose shoulders were shaking. Jim ushered me to a chair as if it was me who had been hospitalized.

'Have you eaten anything?' he asked, crouching down at my knees once I'd sat down. 'You look pale; do you feel okay?'

I suddenly felt as if I wouldn't be able to stand up if I tried. It must have been coming home that made me relax to the point of narcolepsy.

'I'm fine,' I said. It made me embarrassed to get all of this attention while it was Auntie Lyd who was really ill. Anything I was feeling was nothing compared to that. 'How are you all doing? I'm glad you ordered in some food.'

'It was Jim, dear,' said Eleanor, drying her eyes with a handkerchief that Percy had pulled out of his cardigan pocket. 'He ordered it on the broadband. Isn't it amazing what you can do these days?'

'You should try to eat something,' insisted Jim to me, pushing himself up to standing. He picked up a plate and began to load it with rice and spoonfuls of greasy curry. When he placed it in front of me my stomach turned at the pools of oil that spread out to the edges of the plate.

'Thanks,' I said, and began to move the curry around the plate with my fork, hoping no one would notice if nothing made it into my mouth.

Eleanor and Percy exclaimed over the curry like it was the last supper, praising Jim's choices as if he had cooked them with his own hands. Only a certain tightness around Percy's mouth, and Eleanor's anxious eyes flicking towards Jim every few minutes, revealed how hard they were trying to keep the flow of light chatter going. I managed a few mouthfuls of dry rice, which sat heavily on my stomach, and joined in the conversation as much as they would allow, but it was as if their dialogue was scripted to spare either Jim or me the effort of having to speak. Jim poured me a glass of wine; I was pathetically grateful for it. He didn't seem to be eating much either, but he topped up his own wine steadily and drank with a sense of purpose, as if he was dosing himself with medicine.

I wasn't surprised when Percy and Eleanor both declared, at only eight-thirty, that they would be retiring to bed early. I almost felt as if I should applaud their performance, but I didn't want them to feel obliged to stay for an encore; they both looked drained and weary. I hugged them both before they went upstairs, and promised we would all go together to see Auntie Lyd tomorrow. I knew that I could expect to see them both dressed and ready by sunrise, waiting hopefully at the kitchen table for a lift.

Percy patted Jim matily on the arm as he left, but Eleanor insisted that he stood for a hug. She circled his waist with her thin arms and ran a hand lasciviously up his back — by now it was almost a reflex action, despite her exhaustion — before being dragged away by Percy. We could hear her protests, and his admonishments, as they went up the stairs.

Jim started to clear away the plates, scraping the leftovers back into the foil containers.

'You can leave that, Jim,' I said. 'I'll do it. You've been amazing, you don't have to do any more.'

I was surprised to find that I really meant it. He *had* been amazing. Especially for someone who, only hours earlier, I'd accused of being a dodgy con artist out to defraud my aunt. I wondered if, yet again, my powers of judgement had been wrong. I couldn't stop myself from thinking that it was weird for a young man to devote himself to a house full of aged thespians with no ulterior motive, but I had to admit that Auntie Lyd was right: what evidence did I have that Jim was anything other than a supportive help to her? First my cheating ex-boyfriend turned out to be a repentant saviour, now the dodgy plumber seemed like he might be nothing of the kind. Had dating the unsuitable men taught me absolutely nothing about how to identify the good from the bad?

Jim didn't stop clearing up, just scooped the rubbish into the bin and took the stack of plates to the dishwasher. ''S not a problem,' he shrugged. 'I'd feel bad if I didn't help out. Your aunt's been so good to me.'

His eyes flicked in my direction for a second, and I realized to my shame that he was anticipating some sort of unpleasant response from me. Some accusation about his using Auntie Lyd.

'I'm sorry, Jim, I've been so rude to you,' I said, my tongue loosened by wine and guilt. 'I don't know why. I think I just felt jealous of how close you got to Auntie Lyd. It's childish. I'm really sorry. You've done nothing but be kind and helpful since you got here. Auntie Lyd wouldn't know what to do without you.'

Jim closed the dishwasher door and came to sit next to me. He poured himself another glass of wine and drank deeply. 'You don't need to apologize,' he said. 'I knew you needed your aunt's support, with your breakup and everything. I shouldn't have taken up so much of her time. She's just really helped me with a few things. She gives good advice.'

'She does,' I agreed, turning my wine glass in my hands. 'Tough love a speciality.'

'Yeah,' he laughed. 'She's good at that.'

We sat in silence for a while. Auntie Lyd would have been glad to see it. Perhaps we weren't ever going to be best friends, but at least we could sit in the same room without sniping at one another.

'I owe her a lot,' said Jim suddenly. His voice was unsteady.

'You do?'

'Yeah,' he said quietly. He drained the wine bottle into his glass, shaking out the last drops.

'Jim,' I hesitated. 'You said your mum was in hospital a while ago.'

He nodded, not looking up.

'Is — did she — was she okay?'

Jim didn't look at me. He just shook his head.

'Oh, Jim, I'm so sorry,' I said. My hand hovered over his back, not sure if I should comfort him, afraid to intrude into his thoughts. He sat up suddenly, his mouth a tight line.

'It's fine, it was a few years ago,' he said. 'Just

— hospitals, you know? Horrible places. Brings it all back.' He stared at the far wall, but it seemed like he was looking much further away.

'Lydia's been really good to me,' he continued. 'She's got me to talk about my mum loads. My sister's not been handling it at all well, and it's left me without anyone to talk to properly. I hadn't realized how much it had been building up until she asked me about it. I'd kind of been relying on Lydia lately. Too much, probably. So, Jesus, for her to end up in hospital too.'

He dropped his head into his hands, his shoulders hunched.

'She's going to be okay, Jim,' I said, and this time I did put my arm around him. He seemed so vulnerable, far from the cocky plumber I was used to. 'She's going to be out of hospital in a few days.'

Jim leaned into my shoulder, and rubbed at his eyes. 'It shouldn't be you comforting me, Rory, this is all wrong.'

I stroked his hair. Close up it didn't look highlighted, just naturally blond, like a child's. When he lifted his head up, it didn't occur to me to take my hand away.

'Rory.' His voice was low and urgent. I knotted my fingers in his hair as if to hold on tighter. Everything seemed to slow down. I couldn't have told you which of us moved first, only that we both seemed impelled together until our lips were touching.

It was only the smallest, lightest of kisses. Innocent, the kind you might give to a sleeping baby. But I hardly had time to acknowledge the strangeness of it — I was kissing the plumber! — before Jim leapt away from me as if he'd been stung.

'Sorry, Rory, sorry. We shouldn't — ' He ran his hands through his hair and pushed his chair away from the table.

'S-sorry,' I stammered back, not sure which one of us should be apologizing. Or if either of us should.

'I'm drunk,' he said, wiping his mouth as if to get rid of the touch of my lips. 'I've had too much to drink, and you're all over the place after the day you've had. This is all wrong.'

'Is it?' I asked, in a quiet voice. I didn't understand. He hadn't seemed drunk. I didn't feel like I was all over the place. In fact sitting with Jim had been the calmest I'd felt all day.

'You need to go to bed, Rory,' said Jim sternly. He strode to the far side of the kitchen and flicked on the kettle, although I was sure he had as little interest in a cup of tea as I had. He just wanted to get away from me. 'You're tired and I don't think you're fully aware of what you're doing.'

I rose to my feet and my head swam with confusion. I was sure I hadn't mistaken the look in Jim's eyes, but he had clearly thought better of it.

'G-good night then,' I said.

'Night,' he muttered. I waited for a moment, watching his broad shoulders hunched over the work surface, his head bowed. He didn't turn round.

31

I had expected to lie awake for most of the night, worrying about Auntie Lyd, thinking about Martin wanting us to get back together, puzzling over Jim's behaviour in the kitchen. Instead I slept dreamlessly, waking to the shrill ring of the alarm clock at eight. I sprang up in bed, breathing hard, as if I had been sprinting around Clapham Common: Auntie Lyd. Like a fool I had forgotten to check what time visiting hours were at the hospital. What if she was awake already? Would she be afraid, on her own? In pain? I remembered her furious defence the day before that she was not a frail old lady to be patronized. She would not submit easily to the passive role of patient, no matter how ill she was.

I pulled on my clothes from yesterday, not bothering to shower or wash my face; I just wanted to get to the hospital as soon as possible. I could always wait in the cafe until they let me see her. Downstairs in the kitchen, Eleanor and Percy sat at the kitchen table — I was surprised to see that Eleanor held a cup of coffee between her hands instead of her usual whisky. And there was not a tremor to be seen. In the corner of the kitchen, Jim had his back turned to the room. I hadn't expected to see him here on a Sunday morning, and I wondered why he had come here at all if he was going to ignore me like this, until I realized he was on the house phone. My heart leapt into my throat — what if it was the hospital? Had Auntie Lyd taken a turn for the worse?

'No comment,' he said, and then, more crossly, 'I *said* no comment, and I meant it.'

I looked at Percy and Eleanor with eyebrows raised in silent enquiry.

'Journalists,' whispered Eleanor with a fastidious grimace. 'Someone at the hospital has told the papers about Lydia. This is the third phone call this morning.'

Jim slammed the phone down. 'Jesus,' he snapped. He turned around and saw me standing by the table. I wasn't sure if the flicker of annoyance I saw was intended for me or for the person he'd just hung up on.

'Hi, Jim,' I said, feeling a blush creeping up my neck.

'All right, Dawn,' he smiled. 'Don't worry about the papers — they'll be on to another news story soon.'

'How strange,' I said. 'It's not like Auntie Lyd gets mobbed by paparazzi every day.'

Jim shrugged. 'I suppose they've got to write about something. Ambulance chasers.'

I stepped over towards the kettle, out of earshot of Percy and Eleanor. 'Jim,' I began, my voice as low as I could make it.

He smiled. 'I've got something for you,' he said quietly.

'Have you?' I asked, feeling a flutter of alarm in my chest. What did he mean? Was he going to kiss me again? In front of Percy and Eleanor?

'Oh yes,' he said, stepping closer and reaching

336

into his pocket. 'At least, I think it's yours. I had to read some rather interesting texts to work out who it might belong to.'

He held my mobile phone out to me, flat on his palm like an offering. A sardonic smile twitched on his mouth. Oh God, the texts from Luke. Worse, the replies from me and Malky.

'Wh-where did you find it?' I asked, taking it from his hand while avoiding looking at him directly. What must he think of me, exchanging filthy texts with one man, sleeping with another, hanging out with my ex-boyfriend and kissing Jim in the kitchen? I hardly knew what to think myself.

'It was posted through the door,' said Jim, unable to stop smirking. 'I found it there when I came in this morning. It was with this.' He handed me a worn and dirty scrap of lined paper that had obviously been torn from a notebook. Scrawled across it was a brief message: *I found this in my pocket. Sorry. Malky.* I frowned at the note, hardly caring why he'd had my phone in the first place. I was just grateful to have it back.

I deleted all the missed calls from yesterday and checked my messages. There was just one new one, from Luke, clearly frustrated at the sudden termination of our conversation on Friday night. 'If you had a shred of decency,' his message read, 'you would at least send me a picture of your tits.'

Before I could ask Jim anything more, the home phone rang again.

'I'll get it,' said Jim, scowling. He snatched the phone from its cradle and barked a terse 'Yes?'

Percy, Eleanor and I watched him expectantly. While I would rather not have seen him this morning, my head still spinning from last night, I had to admit that I was grateful to him for being here. He had obviously already made breakfast for everyone, somehow steered Eleanor away from her morning whisky, and now he was dealing with phone calls from the press. I hadn't considered that Auntie Lyd was famous enough, so long after her heyday, that journalists would hound her family for updates on her health.

'Right, mate, hi,' said Jim, nodding into the phone. 'Did you want to speak to Dawn? I mean, Rory? Okay, I can pass on a message. Yup, yup. How did you — ? Okay, fine, yup. Thanks, mate, see you in a bit.'

'Who was that?' I asked, as soon as he hung up.

'Martin,' said Jim. 'He said to tell you he's nearly here — he checked with the hospital and your aunt is doing well. He'll take you straight there.'

'He rang the hospital . . . ?' I began. I should have called the moment I'd woken up. It shouldn't have been Martin who made the call; that was my responsibility.

Jim interrupted as if he'd read my mind. 'He said he was family.'

I felt irrationally annoyed by Martin's presumption. I was Auntie Lyd's family, not him. I knew I should have been grateful that he was giving up his time like this, and sparing me the bus journey, but if I was honest, I'd woken up this morning thinking that I would have preferred to travel there on my own, anonymous and unnoticed on public transport where I was free to think. I wondered if Martin would have been so keen to help me if he knew I'd been kissing another man in the kitchen last night. That aside, I didn't want to be obliged to consider his feelings when I got to the hospital, to have him at the back of my mind when I wanted to give all my attention to Auntie Lyd.

'Everything all right, Rory, dear?' asked Eleanor, tilting her head at me, bird-like.

'Oh fine, fine,' I said. The others didn't need to be burdened with my worries. They had enough of their own.

'Will we come to the hospital with you?' Percy asked.

My heart sank a little. I shouldn't deny them the chance to come and see Auntie Lyd themselves, but I so longed to see her on my own.

Jim interrupted before I could speak, seeming to read my mind. 'I think we should all stay here this morning, let Rory see Lydia by herself first. Best not to crowd the patient, don't you think, Dawn? I can bring us all for afternoon visiting hours.'

'Well, yes,' agreed Eleanor. 'If you think that's best, dear. I'm sure we don't want to be any trouble, do we, Percy?'

'You're no trouble,' I said to Eleanor. 'I'm sure Auntie Lyd will want to see you both as soon as possible. But maybe Jim's right — this afternoon's better.'

I smiled at Jim gratefully and he shrugged.

Turning away, he started to empty the dishwasher, stacking plates and bowls noisily on the side. Although it was kind of him to help, I couldn't help wondering if he was using household chores as an excuse to keep me at a distance. As if I might pounce on him again. Obviously Jim thought last night had been a huge mistake. Of course he was right. What had we been thinking? We'd both drunk far too much, and now it was clear he regretted it. Fine. It wasn't like I even fancied him.

'Call me,' said Jim gruffly, his head buried in the dishwasher.

'Sorry?' I asked.

'Call me to say if she wants afternoon visitors, and I'll bring Perce and Eleanor to the hospital,' said Jim, glancing up. I couldn't work him out. One minute he was laughing and teasing, the next serious and grim. It made me nervous. Suddenly I wanted to get out of the kitchen, out of the house. Martin would be here soon and then I would lose my only chance to be alone.

'Okay,' I said, backing slowly towards the kitchen door as if I imagined the others would forcibly restrain me there if they suspected my motives. 'I — I think I'm going to wait for Martin outside. I feel like I could do with some fresh air.'

Jim stood up, looking annoyed. He gestured towards the kitchen table and the spread of plates in front of Percy and Eleanor.

'You haven't eaten anything,' he said, hands on his hips.

'I'm not hungry,' I said apologetically. Jim

glowered at me as if he were a devoted housewife and I the ungrateful husband spurning the meal she had spent all day preparing.

'You hardly had anything last night. You need to eat,' Jim insisted. He picked up a banana from the fruit bowl and thrust it at me, almost angrily. 'Take this.'

I took it from his hand and muttered my thanks. I could feel Percy and Eleanor watching the exchange with interest. Everything between me and Jim seemed oddly charged with significance this morning; as if the banana was a symbol of great meaning instead of just a fruit. It *was* a little phallic, I thought. Perhaps they would have been less intrigued if he had offered me a satsuma or an apple instead.

'I'll call you as soon as there's news,' I promised, backing out of the kitchen towards the stairs, waving the banana. Upstairs I tucked it into my coat pocket, where I knew it would become bruised and black and inedible within hours. I'd find somewhere to get rid of it at the hospital.

Outside I sat on the step where Martin had waited for me only yesterday. Now I waited for him, tucking my chin into my scarf even though the day was already warm. At the bottom of my handbag I found my sunglasses, unworn for months. The spring sunlight was far from bright, but putting my shades on darkened the square pleasantly, as if I was now under a protective shield. I propped my elbows on my knees and allowed my head to sink down into my hands. It was a relief to be alone, even if just for a moment. My face hidden, I didn't have to pretend. Although I didn't know how I would have coped without the support of everyone around me, there was a sense of obligation, a need to be visibly grateful and appreciative for everyone's efforts, that weighed almost as heavily on me as the worry for Auntie Lyd. I was glad of this brief interlude in which I could just feel like crap without inspiring anyone to feel they must cheer me up.

My rest was interrupted by the beeping of a horn. I looked up to see Martin's car turning into the square. He'd bought it when he got promoted — a large new Audi estate which I'd taken, at the time, as a sign that he was beginning to think about a future that might involve marriage and children. It was a family car, after all. But then I discovered, thanks to a spreadsheet on his desktop, that he'd made the purchase purely because of the Audi's excellent fuel economy. He loved this car, washing it and painstakingly waxing it every Sunday morning; I had often thought this weekly display of ritual devotion was almost his version of church. The fact Martin was here at all, instead of attending to his usual routine, was significant. I could see how hard he was trying. He pulled up outside Auntie Lyd's house and wound down the window, leaning out with his elbow tucked over the door. He kept the engine running.

'What are you doing outside?' he shouted.

'Waiting for you,' I said, coming down the steps.

I got into the passenger seat, dropping my

handbag into the footwell.

'How did you sleep?' he asked. I looked at him: the hopeful expression, so anxious to please, so concerned with my approval. It was such a reversal of our usual dynamic that I almost wanted to laugh in his face. The stress and grief were obviously affecting me more than I knew.

'Fine, thanks. Can we go?'

'Of course,' he said.

He clicked on the radio as we left Elgin Square, obviously realizing that I wasn't up for much talking. I knew I should probably be more amenable; try to acknowledge my gratitude by making conversation. But as we drove, Martin sang along to Magic FM with a cheery enthusiasm that seemed to suggest he wasn't offended. I glanced over at him and he smiled back; that indulgent grin again. It was odd to think of how many years I had spent modifying my behaviour to ensure I didn't upset or annoy him — I'd anticipated his every need, believing this was what kept our relationship going — and here I was distracted, monosyllabic, and he didn't seem to mind at all. It only seemed to make him more eager to please me. Perhaps I should have been like this all along.

When we got to the cardiology unit Martin hovered solicitously at my elbow, ushering me towards the waiting room.

'I'll go to find a nurse,' he said. 'You wait here.'

'No,' I said, pulling my arm away. The thick, soupy air of the hospital felt stifling, recycled

343

through the lungs of the unwell. 'I know where she is. I'm going straight there. I hate that waiting room.'

He looked surprised at my insistence, and agreed without demur, stroking my arm to pacify me. 'Okay. Show me the way. Let's go.'

He started to follow me. I turned and put my hand on his chest, moving him to the side of the corridor to let a gurney pass. He looked down at me with such an anxious expression that I felt guilty for wishing him to go away.

'Martin. I need to see her on my own. Please.'

He held up both hands in mock surrender. 'Of course you do, Rory. I'll give you some time alone.'

He shooed me down the corridor as if I was a naughty child: 'Go on.'

The closer I got to the ward, the more nervous I felt. Martin had assured me the doctor had said Auntie Lyd was much improved, and he had actually been satisfied with that answer and not asked any further questions, as I would have done. It wasn't Martin's fault. He was trying to spare me any anxiety, but really he had made it worse: I didn't know what to expect. 'Much improved' could mean that she was still uncon- scious, or it could mean that she was already sitting, dressed, on the end of her bed waiting to be brought home. Hospital staff marched purpose- fully through the corridors, chatting cheerfully, in contrast to the drawn and anxious relatives and friends who shadowed them in silence. I won- dered how Auntie Lyd would react to seeing me. She had been so angry the last time we spoke. Maybe I should have allowed Percy and Eleanor

344

— or even Jim — to see her first. I didn't want to upset her again.

I took a deep breath outside Blue Ward. While I tried to compose myself, I could hear laughter coming from inside, and before I could push the door it swung open from the inside and a hospital orderly emerged waving a piece of paper. 'I got her autograph,' he beamed as he passed me. I grabbed the opened door and peered in. In the midst of a small group of nurses I could see Auntie Lyd sitting up in bed, leaning on a stack of pillows, dressed in the plaid flannel nightgown that Jim had bought. She was surrounded by flowers, vast ostentatious bunches that had been deposited in an assortment of hospital-related receptacles, the ward's supply of vases obviously being exhausted by such floral bounty. Auntie Lyd was pale, with two vivid spots of red on her cheeks, as if someone had rubbed on paint with a fingertip. She smiled at everyone politely, with an expression that I recognized as the faintly embarrassed yet dutiful one she wore on the occasions she was stopped in the street by people who recognized her. Unlike Percy and Eleanor she did not invite the attention of fans, but rather tolerated it.

Her head turned slowly in my direction and her colour heightened. She raised herself up a little and I rushed over to the bed to stop her from exerting herself.

'Rory,' she said weakly.

'Auntie Lyd.' I clasped her hand between both of mine, and this time her tight hold was not an involuntary reflex. I blinked away tears.

345

The doctor who had been sitting on the end of Auntie Lyd's bed stood up, and I saw him silently indicate to the others that they should leave. The small crowd dispersed obediently, gossiping and giggling as they left the ward. I felt reassured that they wouldn't be so flippant if there was anything to worry about.

'How do you feel?' I asked.

The doctor cleared his throat noisily, still standing at the foot of the bed.

'Doctor Prasad, this is my niece, Rory,' Auntie Lyd said.

'Ah, Rory.' He nodded in greeting. 'Your aunt is perfectly well, apart from a non-ST segment myocardial infarction.'

Auntie Lyd smiled dutifully, but I had no idea what he was on about.

'Minor heart attack, very minor,' the doctor explained, seeing my puzzled expression. 'She'll be ready to come home in a few days. But she's going to need a very calm, tranquil environment when she gets there. Rest. No excitements, no disturbances. You'll have to make sure of that.'

He cast me such a forbidding look of warning that I wondered if Auntie Lyd had told him how difficult I'd made things over the last few months. Did he know about Malky's dog and Mr Bits? About my arguments with Jim? My teenage sulking over Martin? I flushed guiltily.

'Rory is a very great support to me,' said Auntie Lyd, squeezing my hand again. She was so loyal. I didn't deserve it.

The doctor promised to be back on his rounds in the afternoon, adjusted the beeping machine

346

next to Auntie Lyd to no apparent purpose, and left the ward. I drew the curtain around the bed for privacy. When I sat down next to her the red spots had left her cheeks and she looked worryingly grey. She offered me a wan smile, sinking back on her pillows.

'I'm so sorry, Auntie Lyd,' I whispered, hanging my head in shame. 'I haven't been a support to you at all, I've been terrible. I'm sorry I argued with Jim. I'm sorry for everything.'

'Oh, Rory,' she sighed. 'This isn't your fault, you silly girl.'

'It is,' I sniffed.

'Must I remind you again, Aurora, that not everything is about you? According to the doctor it is all about *me*, and my tobacco habit.' Although her voice was still weak there was a touch of asperity to it that reassured me more than anything the doctor had said.

I decided to change tack and instead admired the flowers that had been sent this morning. Auntie Lyd turned her head to look at them too. Reading the cards, I was surprised to see that several were from newspapers and magazines. There must have been some Press Association briefing about Auntie Lyd for everyone to have reacted so quickly; it was less than twenty-four hours since she'd been admitted to hospital. It was weird to imagine that someone, seeing a woman collapsed on the floor of the butcher's, must have thought, *What I must do in this situation is inform the press.* The more blunt of the floral tributes from magazines and news-papers had asked outright for an interview when

Auntie Lyd was better, which made me think that even those who had been more subtle probably had the same objective in mind.

Auntie Lyd shifted uncomfortably on her pillows as I picked up the card on a small pot of primroses, sunny and somehow appealingly innocent next to the blowsy bouquets that dwarfed it.

'Who's Paul?' I asked. The card was signed, *These still make me think of you. Be well.*

Auntie Lyd turned her face away. 'Someone I worked with,' she said. 'A long time ago.'

When she turned back I saw the vivid colour had returned to her cheeks and her eyes had become glassy. I tucked the card back into the primroses and decided not to push it. Auntie Lyd enjoyed keeping her mysteries and this was not the time to press her for confessions.

The curtain surrounding the bed twitched and, with a clatter of curtain rings, opened to reveal Martin framed between the hangings. Auntie Lyd gave a start of surprise, and pushed herself up to sitting, glancing over at me anxiously as if I would be equally shocked by his presence.

'Lydia,' Martin said, coming inside to stand next to me. He pulled me protectively in to his side and I tried not to resist, although I wished he'd given us longer before interrupting. 'How are you?'

Auntie Lyd looked from Martin to me in astonishment, lifting her head from the pillows. The doctor's warning about the need for calm and tranquillity rang in my ears. I knew she had taken against Martin after I'd split up with him, and his unexpected arrival in the hospital must be a shock to her, but I didn't want her to start worrying about me.

'Martin took the call about your heart attack, Auntie Lyd,' I reassured her quickly. 'He drove Percy and Eleanor home yesterday; he's given up his time to bring me here today. He's been really helpful to all of us.'

Auntie Lyd said nothing, just rested her head back on her pillows, her eyes wide in her pinched face.

'I know, Lydia,' said Martin. 'You're surprised to see me here. But I wanted to let you know that Rory's being looked after while you're here. I wouldn't let her go through this alone. We're putting our troubles behind us now. Everything's going to be okay.'

'Is it?' said Auntie Lyd, looking at me searchingly.

'Yes, of course,' I said, although I was far from sure. I felt like a Tory wife posing for the press with her husband hours after his numerous affairs have been revealed. Loyal but wary, and rather forced into a position of solidarity with Martin thanks to his appearance at Auntie Lyd's bedside.

'I'm tired, Rory,' said Auntie Lyd, lowering her eyelids slowly. She exhaled, or perhaps it was a sigh. 'I think I need to sleep now.'

'Okay,' I said, coming to sit down next to her so that my face was level with hers. 'I'll come back this afternoon. Do you want me to bring Percy and Eleanor? Jim?'

'Lovely, darling,' she said. I wasn't sure if she had really heard me. Her eyes stayed closed; I could see them flickering faintly beneath her papery eyelids.

'We'll all see you later,' I whispered, and kissed her forehead. I think she was already asleep.

32

There was a Turkish cafe opposite the hospital, and Martin insisted on taking me there for something to eat, claiming he could see me growing thinner by the minute. I still wasn't hungry, but I thought Martin probably could do with the break so I let myself be persuaded to leave the cardiology unit. The banana Jim had pressed on me thumped reproachfully against my side in my coat pocket as Martin led me via the car park so we could renew the parking permit. I'd run out of coins this time, and suggested that I pay for the food once we got to the cafe; that seemed fair. He'd already been so generous, and hadn't even asked me to contribute towards his petrol from driving over from North Sheen. Martin kissed the top of my head gratefully; I could see he was glad I'd offered. He wouldn't have asked, but I knew he'd have his petrol costs worked out for the month and all of this extra mileage would eat into his budget. It was funny how you remembered that sort of thing, even after months apart.

The cafe was already busy, even though lunch was still hours away. Two young nurses in their pink surgical scrubs stood patiently in the takeaway line, pointedly ignoring the comments of a rowdy table full of paint-splattered builders. An elderly Turkish man balanced on the corner of a spindly metal fold-up chair next to the till, occasionally sipping from a tiny cup of thick black coffee. He tapped away at a calculator while the pile of receipts at his elbow fluttered worryingly with the breeze every time the door opened. There was a smell of fried food, and the chefs, visible through the kitchen hatch, looked harried. Most of the tables were full but the waitress, squeezing past us with plates held high above her head, nodded us towards a space at the back. Martin took the cushioned seat that faced out into the cafe and peeled a sticky laminated menu off the table. I pulled out the other chair and sat down. When the waitress reappeared, untucking a pad from her apron and whipping a pen from behind her ear, Martin surprised me by, Teddy-like, ordering for both of us.

'We'll have two coffees, please,' he said, handing her the menu. 'The full Turkish breakfast for me, and my girlfriend will have the fruit plate.'

I stopped the waitress before she left. 'No coffee for me,' I said. 'Please can I have an English breakfast tea instead?'

'Sure,' she shrugged, and scrawled it on to her order pad.

'Rory, be adventurous,' smiled Martin. 'Turkish coffee is amazing stuff. You should give it a try.'

'I don't like coffee, Martin,' I reminded him tartly. My anger at his barging up to Auntie Lyd's bedside was beginning to build. I had suppressed it for her sake but now, safely away from the ward, it had returned. 'I've never liked

352

coffee. And I'm not your girlfriend.'

Martin stuck out his bottom lip petulantly, but his eyes sparkled as if I had said something funny. Under the table his hand found my leg and he smoothed his thumb across my thigh over and over, as if calming an anxious pet. I tried to pull away but he held on tightly, the pressure of his fingers gently but forcefully restraining me.

'It's okay, Rory,' he soothed, seeing my annoyance. 'I know you need to put up a fight, make me suffer a bit before you take me back. I understand. I know you, Rory.'

'Things changed while we were apart, Martin,' I told him. I finally wrenched free of his grasp and crossed my legs away from him. 'You might not know me any more.'

'I know I need you, Rory,' he insisted. 'And you need me. You can't do this alone. You don't need to. I can take whatever you want to throw at me.'

I considered the ketchup bottle on the table. He saw where I was looking and laughed.

'Even that. But throwing things isn't your usual style. Unless you really *have* changed.'

He did know me. I had never been the type to have tantrums. Perhaps I should have been. I smiled reluctantly.

'When all this is over, when your aunt's better, I want you to come home,' said Martin. 'It hasn't felt like home since you left, Rory. Not for a minute.'

'Probably because you moved someone else in straight away,' I said, turning my knife over on the table. He surely wouldn't think I was going to just come back without even discussing the reason why I'd left.

'Melinda never moved in,' he answered. 'She didn't. No matter what you might have heard.'

'I didn't hear anything, Martin,' I said quietly. 'I saw it for myself when I came to collect my stuff.'

Martin's eyes narrowed. His hands stopped their relentless movement as he gripped them into stillness on top of the sticky table.

'You saw what she wanted you to see, Rory. She never moved in — she tried, oh yes, she tried. Leaving things at my house to try and stake a claim. But she couldn't, Rory. She couldn't because it was always our house. Yours and mine. She didn't belong there. She could never have replaced what you and I had.'

I looked down at the wood-effect tabletop. I couldn't take in everything Martin was saying — he'd destroyed our relationship for a fling with someone who didn't mean anything to him? My mind seemed to close off, as if unable to even try to understand him. I felt my attention drift to the patterns I could discern in the smeared surface of the table. On the edge of the table, missed by the cloth, a clot of ketchup mingled with a dull yellow smear — mustard? It made me think, in a way that would have infuriated Martin if I'd been foolish enough to admit to it, of the Abstract Expressionists — giving a physical form to feelings and emotions that can't be expressed figuratively. If only there was a way of speaking like that, blurting it all out at once without trying to form it into proper sentences, saying everything I'd been thinking for months. Everything I thought of saying at this moment sounded flat and clichéd — 'You cheated on me,' 'I don't know if I can trust you again,' 'I need some time.'

Or perhaps I just really did want to throw the ketchup in Martin's face. He stretched his hand across the table and lifted my chin up so that I would look into his eyes.

'Rory, Rory, Rory,' he said. His face softened with sympathy. 'It's okay to be angry with me. I've been a terrible boyfriend. I don't know how I can make it up to you. I just know that I want to. Please let me. I'm trying.'

I dropped my eyes down, although his fingers still tilted my face upwards.

'I — I don't know,' I whispered.

'Rory,' he said firmly. I felt his fingers twitch under my chin as if he was about to shake my head to rearrange the contents into a form he found more amenable. 'I know this is hard, but you need to think about your life. You're thirty — '

'*Nearly* thirty,' I insisted. Had he forgotten my birthday was in September, on top of everything else?

'Nearly thirty,' he conceded. 'You need to think about your future, Rory. Our future. It's lonely out there, Rory, lonely and difficult. Remember how your aunt had to be taken to hospital alone? A single woman all on her own? Is that what you want for yourself?'

I pushed his hand away furiously. 'Auntie Lyd is an amazing woman. She's not a figure of pity,'

I snapped. But hadn't I been guilty of thinking just the same when I'd accused her of being a victim of Jim's supposed con-artistry?

'Not pity, no,' said Martin. His voice seemed to become softer the more agitated I became. 'Your Auntie Lyd has made choices in her life. And they've had consequences. I just want you to think about what sort of choices you are making in your life. That's all. I'm thinking of you, Rory.'

'I'd be happy if I was like Auntie Lyd when I reached my sixties,' I declared, jutting out my chin. 'You saw her on the ward, all those well-wishers, everyone sending her flowers. She's got a brilliant life, I don't care what you say.'

'Rory,' he said sorrowfully, his eyes sympathetic and pitying. 'You really think that's what you want? To live alone with strangers for the rest of your life? Never to have a family of your own? You're not like her.'

'I — I — ' I saw suddenly and horribly that I didn't want that. I loved Auntie Lyd, but I didn't want to be her. I did want a family of my own.

'And what if your aunt hadn't got better?' he asked, gently. 'Where would you be then? All alone, Rory.'

I blinked at him, unable to speak. I didn't want to think about the possibility of life without Auntie Lyd. Martin leaned closer, his voice low and persuasive.

'You have a right to hate me, Rory. I understand you're angry. But please, don't throw away everything we once had out of pride.

356

Without even thinking about it.'

I looked away from him, studying instead my reflection in the smeared surface of my knife. What if I said no to him now and that was it? What if I never met another suitable man again? It wasn't like I'd met anyone really wonderful in the time we'd been apart — if it was a choice between Martin and Malky or Teddy or Luke or Sebastian, then it was impossible not to see that Martin was superior to all of them. Would I torture myself for the rest of my single Auntie-Lyd-like life, remembering the morning when I sat opposite Martin and said no to the security and stability — and the family — that I'd always wanted? When I settled instead for one of the terrible men off the internet, would I think of this moment?

'I — I need more time,' I said. He was right. I should at least think about this properly.

'How much time?' There was an almost imperceptible edge of impatience to his voice. Imperceptible unless, like me, you had spent eleven years listening out for it: the first tiny creak before the ice collapses.

Hot tears sprang up in my eyes. He'd forced me into presenting a united front to Auntie Lyd before I was ready, and now he was accusing me of leading him on. The waitress looked over from the counter with a sympathetic expression. I expect she was used to emotional customers coming over from the hospital.

'It's not even been twenty-four hours,' I said, to the table. My eyes swam so that its surface was hardly visible.

'Well, I've just had to buy a second twenty-four-hour parking permit, actually,' Martin said, and there was no answer to that. He was always right. I didn't need to check my watch to know he wouldn't have made a mistake.

He raised his reassuring thumb to my cheek, where he wiped away a tear. 'I didn't mean to upset you. It's just because I love you, Rory. I want us to be together again. Happy like we used to be. Remember?'

I did remember. I remembered how he had taken care of me, how much simpler my life had been when I was with him. I hadn't been tortured by indecision and confusion when I was Martin's girlfriend; he was so sure of everything, so confident, that it calmed all of my anxieties. He made the decisions, and that made me feel safe. It would be so easy to go back to that. Not to have to start all over again with someone new. Not to have to get used to someone else's quirks, and have them get used to mine. Martin was so tolerant of my weaknesses; would another man be so understanding? And we had been happy, we really had. It would be hard to trust him again, but perhaps it would be hard to trust anyone again. I could see how much he was trying. And he was being more patient than I had any right to expect. I couldn't make him wait for ever.

'I do remember, Martin,' I whispered, picking at the label of the ketchup bottle. 'But I do need time.'

'As long as it takes for you to decide you're coming home, Rory,' he answered gently.

The waitress shimmied past our table, her fringe damp with perspiration, her arms stacked with dirty plates. Martin clicked his fingers sharply to get her attention.

''Scuse me, over here — what's happened to our food? We haven't got all day, you know.'

33

Stepping out into the hospital corridor on Sunday afternoon, I called the office to leave a message on Amanda's phone.

The doctor had said Auntie Lyd would be in hospital for at least another two days, although her recovery had been significantly better than expected. Already she had been able to take an assisted shower, having haughtily declined the offer of a bed bath, and she had been persuaded to eat some of the snacks that Jim had bought yesterday. Now that Dr Prasad had revealed himself as a fan of *Those Devereux Girls* I had a slight suspicion that he was keeping Auntie Lyd in as much for his own satisfaction as for medical observation. He became quite giddy in her presence, especially when she had signed the DVD box set that he had promenaded proudly into the ward.

More flowers had arrived this afternoon, including a bouquet from Amanda Bonham Baillie and the staff of *Country House*. I was touched by this unexpected show of thoughtfulness from my employers. Given that they were already aware of the situation, leaving a message for Amanda was really only a courtesy call; I was sure she wouldn't be surprised to hear that I had to stay at my aunt's side until she was out of hospital. I dialled the office number and waited for the beep that would tell me to speak. Instead the phone was picked up and Amanda's voice barked, 'Yes?'

'Oh, er, Amanda, hello,' I stammered, surprised to encounter a real voice at the end of the line at the weekend.

'Who is this?'

'Amanda, it's Rory Carmichael,' I said. 'Sorry to interrupt, I didn't expect you to be in the office.'

'Well I am. What do you want on a Sunday evening?' She seemed rather blunt, given her likely knowledge of why I was ringing, but then I would probably have been more surprised if she had gone all Samaritans-helpline on me.

'I — I just wanted to say that I won't be in the office for a few days, Amanda,' I said. 'For obvious reasons. I have to wait for my aunt to be out of hospital.'

'Your aunt? What about her?' Amanda snapped impatiently.

'Yes, my aunt,' I said, now utterly muddled. Had I misread the card? Had the flowers been from *Country Living* instead, or *Country Life*, or maybe even *Country Pursuits?* There were so many rural publications it was easy to mix them up. 'My aunt, Lydia Bell. She had a heart attack. You sent flowers.'

There was a long pause. I heard Amanda's hissing intake of breath, as if she was inhaling through a straw.

'Your aunt is Lydia Bell,' she said slowly. 'Of course, Rory, of course. Do forgive me. I'm a little distracted. A few things are — well, some things are going on here.'

'Is everything all right?' I asked. All thoughts of the office had been wiped from my mind over the weekend; instantly the spectre of redundancy tapped me on the shoulder, reminding me it had been there all along.

'Yes, yes, everything under control. Nothing for you to worry about. Take as long as you need. And please do send my best wishes to your aunt.' In the background I could hear the clicking of computer keys. I could imagine Amanda now, phone tucked under her ear, her thoughts already moving away from this conversation and back to work.

'I will,' I said. 'Thank you for the flowers. It was really kind of you.'

'Please don't mention it,' said Amanda, sounding embarrassed, and she hung up abruptly. I wondered if I would ever understand how her mind worked. Why send flowers to Auntie Lyd at all if she was going to be embarrassed about it? I supposed she didn't like to be seen as having any kind of emotions, in case they revealed a weak spot in her armour.

Back on the ward, Auntie Lyd sat with Percy and Eleanor on either side of her bed, Jim kneeling on the floor next to her. The two actors gazed at her with devotion, and Auntie Lyd beamed back at them both like a beatific Madonna for aged thesps. You couldn't mistake this woman, surrounded by her friends, for someone who was sad and alone, I thought, still troubled by Martin's words. Although she was pale, Auntie Lyd was magnificent. She laughed at something Jim said and leaned over to ruffle

his hair. He was in another one of his dreadful
T-shirts —

It's What's Inside (Your Pants) That Counts

— and I wondered what on earth had possessed
me to kiss him last night. He was so not my type.
Of course he was attractive — you'd have to be
blind not to see that — but he was pretty much
the definition of unsuitable. A cocky wide boy
who probably had a different dolly bird every
week. Seeing Martin standing at the end of the
bed, sleek in his expensive grey coat, just
reinforced the difference between them.

Martin's dark head was bowed as he tapped at
his iPhone, no doubt taking care of important
work business. Even in his weekend clothes he
exuded authority. You didn't need to know that
he was a board director to see that he was
unmistakably someone to be taken seriously; a
grown-up. It wasn't just me who thought so. This
afternoon I had noticed that the nurses
addressed most of their comments to him, as if
his was the opinion that counted. He had subtly
taken control of the situation, taking responsibilities out of my hands, offering to drive Auntie
Lyd home later in the week even though it
meant time away from his busy job. I might be
unsure about Martin himself, but at least I
was certain that this was my type — safe,
confident, assured. He looked up as I approached
the bed.

'Rory,' he said, slipping the phone back into
his pocket. 'Visiting hours are nearly over. I'm

going to take you home, and I'll take Eleanor and Percy too.'

Jim looked up from his kneeling position next to Auntie Lyd. 'I can take Eleanor and Perce back, if you like, mate. They might want to stay a little longer.'

'They might indeed.' Martin smiled down at him, close-lipped. 'But visiting hours, as I said, are nearly over. I'll take them home with Rory now.'

'Okay,' said Jim, shrugging. 'Up to you.'

Martin cleared his throat. 'I think I speak for the family, Jim, when I say that we are all grateful to you for your help over the weekend.'

Jim gave an embarrassed chuckle and looked up at Auntie Lyd. She patted his hand. 'No problem,' he said.

Martin continued. 'Now that the immediate danger has passed, Jim, and now that I'm here to look after everyone, please don't feel that you need to spend any more of your time at the hospital. I'm sure you have a busy week ahead of you with your — plumbing business, is it?'

'Don't worry, mate,' said Jim. 'I've finished at Lydia's and I'm still waiting for the next job to be confirmed. I'm happy to help out while I'm free.'

'But it's not necessary,' said Martin sharply.

Auntie Lyd pulled herself up to sitting, her mouth set firmly in a manner that I knew well. Jim moved as if to help her, but she brushed his arm away. 'I believe I speak for my family, Martin, when I say that whether Jim's help is necessary or not, I am happy to see him at any

364

time, either in hospital or in my home. I hope that is clear.'

'Of course, Lydia,' said Martin, conceding obediently. I was glad to see that he wasn't going to argue. He draped his arm heavily over my shoulders and nudged me very slightly towards the door as a signal we should leave.

'Rory,' said Auntie Lyd, holding out her hand towards me. 'Would you mind very much staying for a little while? Just you?'

I stepped forward to the side of her bed. 'Of course not, Auntie Lyd, I'll stay as long as you like.'

Martin coughed behind us.

'Martin,' I asked, 'is it still okay to take Percy and Eleanor back? I'll catch the bus, it'll be fine.'

'Well,' said Martin, discomfited by this change to his plans, 'why doesn't Jim take them back and then I can stay here with you?'

Out of the corner of my eye I saw Eleanor's hand steal into Percy's, embarrassed at being an inconvenience.

'Of course,' said Jim, straightening up to standing. 'My pleasure, mate.'

'I'd like Jim to stay too,' said Auntie Lyd quickly.

Martin smiled tightly. 'In that case I'd be delighted to escort Eleanor and Percy home. At your service, Lydia.'

I helped Martin gather up Eleanor and Percy's belongings, and walked with them to the lift. Martin's polite affability didn't hide from me the fact that he was annoyed. It seemed that his keenness to offer help was less deeply felt when I

365

wasn't its direct recipient. I made sure to kiss him goodbye, on the cheek, and he said he'd call me later.

When I went back to the ward Auntie Lyd was alone.

'Where's Jim?' I asked.

'I sent him off to get us some tea,' she said, settling back against the pillows. She straightened the yellow blanket and pulled it up her lap.

'Now,' she said. 'Are you going to tell me what's happening with Martin?'

Trust Auntie Lyd not to pussyfoot around the issue, I thought. And here I was trying to keep everything calm and serene around her.

'He wants you back, doesn't he?' pressed Auntie Lyd, when I failed to answer immediately.

'Yes,' I admitted.

'And what has happened to Miss Bathroom Products?'

'He says that's over. He says it didn't really mean anything to him at all.'

'Is that enough?' she asked.

I sighed. 'I don't know, Auntie Lyd. It shouldn't be. But I've missed him so much.'

She nodded and said nothing.

'He's been really great this weekend,' I offered. 'So supportive.'

She nodded again.

'Do you think he's changed?' she asked.

'I don't know,' I said. 'Can people ever really change?'

'Yes,' she said, to my surprise. 'They can.'

'Right,' I said uncertainly. I had expected her

to be firmly against giving Martin a second chance, and yet here she was seemingly encouraging me to get back together with him.

Auntie Lyd turned her head away from me and looked at the flowers that surrounded her bedside. The small pot of primroses had, I noticed, been moved to the table next to her.

'Auntie Lyd, who's Paul?' I asked, very quietly, so that she could pretend not to hear me if she didn't want to answer.

She answered without looking back. 'Someone I used to work with, darling, I told you that.'

'Someone — someone you were in love with?' I asked carefully.

'Yes,' she said.

If I had been Ticky I would have pushed my advantage here; gone in for the kill. This was the most I had ever heard Auntie Lyd speak about her personal life; I hadn't dreamed she would answer my questions. Instead I stayed still while she continued to stare at the flowers.

Her head turned slowly towards me, and her eyes were oddly bright, almost feverish. 'You ask me if people can change. Paul is the reason I know they can.'

'Who was he, Auntie Lyd?' I asked.

Auntie Lyd sighed deeply and smoothed the blanket again on her lap. 'Paul Johnson was my agent,' she said softly, her eyes gazing at the ceiling. 'Linda's too. Quite the big shot at the time.'

Her voice drifted off and her eyes half-closed. I wondered if she was falling asleep again. Outside the drawn curtains the ward doors opened and a trolley rattled in, someone asking if anyone wanted snacks; it seemed to startle her out of her reverie. Her eyes snapped open.

'Married, of course,' she said, her voice no longer dreamy but harder. 'But unhappily so, he told me, he only stayed for the children. I know, I know how it sounds, but it's hard to see these situations when you're in the middle of them. For four years I waited for him to leave her. For four years we made plans. He bought the house in Clapham for us, you know? Put it in my name as a sign of his commitment to me. He was going to move in when he left, far away from his family home in Kensington. Make a new start together.'

She closed her eyes again for a brief moment.

'We'd named our children, even. Of course I felt terrible about his wife, but I told myself these things happen. People marry the wrong person. You can't stop a love like ours. Silly lines straight from *Those Devereux Girls*. He wasn't a man cheating on his wife, he was a man in love. Our passion was too strong. Ridiculous, really.' She laughed bitterly.

'Only Linda knew the whole story. I hid it from everyone, even your mother. Then Linda told me Paul had made a pass at her. I didn't believe her, and we had a terrible fight. She said he was cheating on me, too, with anyone who'd have him. I said she was jealous, wanted him for herself. I walked out of *Those Devereux Girls* — told them I wouldn't work with Linda any more.'

'What did Paul say?' I asked.

'Furious, of course,' said Auntie Lyd. 'Not just

368

about Lin's accusation but, well, there went his ten per cent when the show got cancelled. But I told him I'd done it for us. I thought that showing him I would give up Devereux Girls for him, that I'd make a huge sacrifice like that to show my loyalty to him, would make him leave his marriage at last.'

'Did it?' I asked.

Auntie Lyd looked at me and smiled wearily. 'Yes, Aurora, that is why you see me here happily married to Paul with those children that we named way back when.'

'Sorry.'

'Linda was right, of course,' she continued. 'He'd been sleeping with half of his client list all along, all those eager young actresses like me, desperate to be loved. I was just one of many.'

'But he bought the house,' I said. 'He must have been serious about you to have done that.'

'What he was serious about, Rory, was putting his money where his wife couldn't find it if they got divorced. She'd been threatening him for years; he was the one begging to stay. It was her money that had set up his agency, of course.' She sighed again, but she was quite still and quiet, not agitated at all. 'I was just a back-up plan. I expect he had several — he was always one to spread the risk.'

'So what happened?'

'I left the agency, of course. And when I did, I checked over my statements. I'd always let Paul do that before. There were some — irregularities there. It seemed he'd not only been cheating on me emotionally, he'd been defrauding me out of money for years.' She let out a long hissing breath. 'So . . . '

'Did you sue him?' I asked.

'Aurora,' chastised Auntie Lyd gently. 'Now it is you who is making up scenes from soap operas. I did not sue him. You will understand, I'm sure, that despite everything, in some awful way I still loved him. And I had no desire to drag both of our names through an ugly legal battle. All of the details of our relationship would have been splashed all over the papers.' She shuddered. 'It would have been too humiliating.'

I nodded and waited for her to start speaking again.

'I told him I was keeping the house instead of demanding back the money he owed me. Since it was in my name he would have had some difficulty proving it belonged to him without revealing a lot of things he preferred to keep hidden. He was so grateful I wasn't going to cause a scandal that he just let me have it.'

'And you never heard from him again?'

'Of course I did,' she said, smiling at me sadly. Her eyes returned to the primroses next to her bed. 'I still do sometimes.'

'But, you said he changed. Was he truly sorry? Did you ever forgive him?'

'I don't know if he changed, Rory,' said Auntie Lyd, frowning slightly at my misunderstanding. 'I haven't spoken to him for thirty years, despite his efforts. Perhaps he did. I expect not. No, darling, I mean that the person who changed was me.'

34

When Jim arrived back, balancing three polystyrene cups of tea on a cardboard tray, Auntie Lyd
was already asleep. He lowered the tray on to her
bedside table and looked over at me, running his
fingers through his hair, making it stand up in
all directions. It was weird to me that he'd go
to the trouble of getting highlights and yet be so
unconcerned with how his hair looked most of
the time.

'Why do I get the feeling Lydia was just trying
to get me out of the way with that little errand?'
he asked quietly, smiling over at her while she
slept. 'She didn't really want a tea at all, did she?'

'No,' I admitted. For someone who was still
unwell, Auntie Lyd had managed to engineer her
discussion with me most efficiently. 'She just
wanted to have a talk with me on my own. Sorry
to send you off for nothing.'

'Do you want yours?' Jim whispered.

'It's okay,' I said. 'I don't need it. I think we
can leave now, if you're ready?' Auntie Lyd
seemed deeply asleep now, her breath steady and
even. It didn't seem like she would be waking
any time soon.

Jim helped me clear up the cubicle, moving a
water bottle within reach and leaving her reading
glasses near her hand in case she woke up in the
night and needed them. Once we were sure
Auntie Lyd had everything she might need, we

left the ward, tiptoeing out silently so as not to wake her.

I offered to get the bus home, but Jim wouldn't hear of it. He cleared the passenger seat of his van of the Sunday papers and a half-empty crisp packet, apologizing the whole time for the mess.

'So,' he said, as we turned out of the hospital car park.

'So,' I answered. This was the first time we'd been alone since last night. I wasn't sure if I should be saying something about it.

'So your ex has come back,' Jim said. He kept his eyes on the road, changing lanes as the van struggled up the hill. 'That must be weird.'

'It is weird,' I agreed. It was even weirder to be discussing Martin with a man I'd been kissing just hours ago.

'What's going on there then?'

'I don't know,' I said. 'He thinks we should get back together.'

'Do *you* think you should get back together?' Jim asked.

I looked out of the window. Two little girls pushed their scooters up the hill, leaning in towards the pavement with the effort of it. What *did* I think about it?

'It's exactly what I thought I wanted,' I heard myself saying.

Jim was silent for a while. 'Oh?' he asked, at last.

'Exactly what I wanted when we first split up,' I explained. I twisted a curl of my hair in my fingers. 'Now I don't know.'

'How long were you two together?'

'Eleven years.'

Jim whistled through his teeth. 'Long time,' he said. 'Do you still love him?'

I considered the question.

'I think so,' I said. It was bizarre to be having this conversation with Jim, of all people, but he was oddly easy to talk to. Steering the van back towards Elgin Square, he seemed to be able to prompt me to talk about everything without betraying any Ticky-style enjoyment of the drama. I guess sometimes it is easier to talk freely to someone who's almost a stranger than to the people you're closest to.

'Really?' said Jim. He sounded surprised.

'You can't just turn your feelings off like a switch, can you? But I can't work out if it's just nostalgia that's making me feel all of this, the memory of the relationship we had, or if it's a sign I should give him another chance.'

Jim exhaled through his teeth again. 'What does your aunt say? I can't imagine Lydia doesn't have a strong opinion on it.'

'Funnily enough she hasn't,' I said. I tucked the curl of hair behind my ear. 'I thought she'd try to talk me out of even thinking about getting back together with Martin, but instead she just talked to me about people changing.'

'Do you think they can?' asked Jim, echoing my own question to Auntie Lyd earlier.

'I do now,' I said, thinking of my aunt. Thinking of myself. The question was, could Martin change?

'Well. It sounds like you've made up your

mind,' said Jim. The van pulled to a halt at a set of traffic lights.

'Does it?' I didn't feel remotely close to having made up my mind. If anything I was more confused than ever.

'Listen to yourself. You've got that shared past, you still love him, you think people can change. What's stopping you?'

I turned to look at him, but he stared steadfastly ahead. I wondered how we could have this talk about me and Martin and yet fail to even discuss what had happened between us in the kitchen.

'Jim,' I said. 'About last night.'

He revved the engine and we pulled away from the junction. 'Forget last night,' he said. 'We'd both had too much to drink. You were very emotional.'

'I wasn't — ' I began.

'Rory,' he insisted. 'You owe it to yourself to think about your relationship with Martin properly. You can't let yourself be distracted from a decision about the rest of your life by one drunken kiss.'

'One drunken kiss,' I echoed. Of course that's all it was, I knew that, but did he have to say it so harshly? It wasn't like I'd ever entertained the idea that I'd have some sort of relationship with Jim — why was it necessary to make it so very obvious that he had absolutely no interest in me? It felt like one of the My Mate's Great unsuitables made flesh — Jim was closing a match that I'd not even seriously considered.

'You've got a lot going on right now, Rory,'

said Jim. 'That's all I mean.'

We turned into Elgin Square and he stopped the van in the middle of the road outside Auntie Lyd's house, the engine still running.

'Aren't you coming in?' I asked, picking up my handbag. 'I'm sure Percy and Eleanor would love to see you.'

'No,' he said abruptly. 'I've got to get on.'

I let myself out of the van, sliding down off the high leather seat on to the road. Jim smiled at me as I swung the door shut. It was the kind of smile you might give to a child riding her bike without stabilizers for the first time: encouraging and protective, but with a little hint of anxiety about the outcome.

'Good luck, Dawn,' he said.

35

I wish I could say that the day we drove Auntie Lyd back home to Elgin Square was a day of glorious spring. It would sound so promising and positive to say that her arrival was heralded by sunshine and a chorus of birdsong, but unfortunately the weather that welcomed us was a thick grey mist that threatened, without ever doing so, to turn into rain. I chewed my fingernail anxiously, fearing it might be a bad omen. Not that I believed in such things, of course, but recently I had found myself descending into the sort of magical thinking where I seemed to see portents everywhere: if I threw this banana into the waiting-room bin without getting up (I had found it in my coat pocket yesterday, so black and squashed as to be inedible) then I should get back together with Martin. If I missed the bin, I shouldn't. A black cat outside the hospital — was that good or bad? Auntie Lyd would have scorned it all if she had known; she who thought reading your horoscope in the paper was the act of a credulous fool.

I glanced at her. So strong in the hospital, determined to come home, she seemed now to have shrunk into the passenger seat of Martin's car, diminished somehow. It may have been just how she appeared from where I was, in the back behind the driver's seat and awkwardly angled so I could keep an eye on her. Only Martin looked truly comfortable, legs stretched to full length, his strong hands grasping the steering wheel as he manoeuvred us confidently around the corners of the square. The wipers slid across the windscreen, revealing in the cleared glass a hand-painted

Welcome Home Lydia

banner streaked and spotted by the weather.

Auntie Lyd laughed. 'Is this your handiwork, Rory?'

'Of course not,' Martin laughed back a little too heartily, grasping the opportunity to share a joke with her. 'Rory's no artist. But I expect she can make up some waffly art history bollocks about its provenance, can't you?'

He turned in his seat to negotiate the car into a space just outside the house, and made a face at me to show that he was joking. I smiled back, latching on to the availability of a parking space as the good omen I'd been seeking. Everything was going to be okay.

'Absolutely,' I said, in a posh radio announcer's voice. 'Note how the artist creates the work, and then allows nature to penetrate it by exposing it to the elements. The smeared letters remind us not just of impermanence, but of transformation and transition. The free brush-strokes reveal a confident artist at the peak of his powers.'

'So it was Percy!' exclaimed Auntie Lyd.

'Eleanor too,' I said. 'And Martin hung it up before we left this morning.'

Auntie Lyd smiled politely at him as he helped her from her seat but I could see it was going to take a bit more than a helping hand and a shared joke to get her to drop her defences entirely. Although she had refrained from expressing any opinion on whether or not I should go back to Martin, it was clear that she herself had yet to completely forgive him.

I rang the bell to allow Percy and Eleanor to answer the door, as they'd asked. Martin had said it would be too cramped in the car for them to come to the hospital to pick up Auntie Lyd, which seemed not quite honest given the roomy interior of the Audi, and they had been a little hurt at the exclusion. Hence the idea for the banner and for the official welcoming committee, which I had hastily conjured up to create a diversion. It was bad enough that Auntie Lyd retained some of her suspicions of Martin; I couldn't have everyone at Elgin Square against him or we would never be able to visit again if I moved back in with him.

Eleanor flung open the door, stretching her arms wide. She had chosen to celebrate Auntie Lyd's return by donning one of her best dresses, a floral Laura Ashley number that was probably older than I was. Its Victorian high neck and floor-length skirt gave her the appearance of having escaped from a period drama, except for her vivid blue eyeshadow. Behind her Percy stood back, as if in a receiving line, his hands clasped formally behind him. While Eleanor threw her arms around Auntie Lyd so hard that I put my hands out in case they toppled down the stairs, Percy remained so absolutely still that I wondered if he was feeling unwell. But as Auntie Lyd stepped over the threshold he burst into shuddering sobs, his hands flailing helplessly in front of him, and I saw that his previous restraint had only been an attempt to keep himself together. Auntie Lyd let him weep on to her shoulder, while Eleanor rubbed his back consolingly.

I had been so worried about Auntie Lyd, and about myself, that I hadn't given nearly enough thought to how frightening this must have been for Percy and Eleanor. Auntie Lyd was more than their landlady, she was their only family. If I had been anxious about what would happen to me without Auntie Lyd, I with a job and a regular salary and youth on my side, then how much more precarious an existence was it for the two of them? They had probably been kept awake with fears of the kind of places they could expect to live if they had to move, of council-owned residential homes, of trying to find rooms in shared houses at their age. I saw how brave they had been to hide all of this anxiety from me every day in favour of making sure Auntie Lydia's niece wasn't concerned about them. Their cheerful acting had been convincing enough to fool me, and I was ashamed of it.

'Bloody actors,' whispered Martin's voice behind me. 'Always a drama, isn't it?'

Before I could answer he raised his voice to address us all: 'Right then, enough of this. I think it's time we got our patient back into her sickbed. In we go, Lyd.'

I flinched as I saw Auntie Lyd's shoulders tense. Martin meant to be kind, but he was so used to being in charge of everything that he didn't see how much Auntie Lyd would resent being dictated to in her own home. Not to mention calling her 'Lyd', which only family were permitted to do. Percy, sniffing, let Auntie Lyd go, and retreated backwards to dab at his eyes with his shirtsleeve.

Auntie Lyd turned around; no longer shrunken, she seemed to grow in front of us.

'Martin. How kind you have been to Rory. I'm so grateful. And for driving me home today. Thank you.'

Martin smiled with satisfaction, putting his arm around me as we stood framed in the open doorway. I couldn't believe he couldn't hear the frost in Auntie Lyd's voice. If I were him I would have been putting up my hands in self-defence.

'But I am, as you rightly say, a poor old lady invalid who needs her rest. And for that reason I would like to spend my first night at home with just family. I'm sure you understand.'

'Rory?' asked Martin, looking down at me with puzzlement. Auntie Lyd didn't wait for an answer, but allowed herself to be escorted into the house by Percy and Eleanor.

'Martin, it's her first night home. She'll come round,' I said. 'Just give her time.'

'Give you time, give her time, it's like I'm a fucking watch factory,' he snapped, and then stopped when he saw my shocked face. 'Sorry, sorry, Rory, sorry. I shouldn't have said that. It's just getting to me, all of this.'

'Look, I've talked to Auntie Lyd about us,' I began.

'So you think there is an us?' he asked quickly.

'I don't know, Martin, it's been a strange week. I haven't had time to think about it properly.' Martin frowned; it was clear he felt that four days was plenty of time. 'Time on my own, I mean. Can we just — I don't know — can't we just agree that we won't contact each other for a few days, and then I promise I'll make a decision? Just give me until — until the end of this week, okay?'

'Friday,' he said.

'Saturday.'

'Friday's the end of the week.'

'There's going to be a lot going on this week. Saturday is better,' I insisted. 'I want to think about this properly, Martin. I owe you that at least. Please don't rush me.'

Martin took my hands and looked at me with such intensity I worried he might be in physical pain.

'Saturday,' he agreed, crushing my fingers in his own. 'Please come home then, Rory.'

36

There is a school of thought that says work can be a place of refuge during difficult times in one's personal life. And in some ways I can see that might be true — my colleagues had at least offered some sort of distraction from everything when I'd first broken up with Martin. Getting up and dressed every day, catching the tube and sitting at my desk had forced me to carry on, instead of just sobbing under the duvet. And finally writing up my piece about Malky had been quite cathartic, drawing a line under our fling. Yet going back to the office the day after Auntie Lyd came out of hospital felt far too soon to me; but she had become irritable when I said I'd stay with her, and insisted she was hardly going to come to harm in her own home. So although I went back to *Country House* mostly to make her happy, I will admit that I thought I could at least get some headspace there to think about what was happening with Martin. I had imagined it would be an easy decision — he had cheated on me and betrayed me, and that should mean it was over. But it wasn't that simple to think about throwing away a second chance at a relationship that had once meant everything to me. Life wasn't black and white, I knew that. It's just that I wasn't sure if I was able to deal with the exact shade of grey of the new relationship Martin was offering. At least at *Country House*, where things were reassuringly always the same, I could allow myself to think about it all properly.

But when I got in to work, although things looked the same, it turned out that everything was different.

The first thing that struck me on walking into my office was that Ticky's desk was suspiciously spotless. For one scary moment I thought the feared redundancies might have started already, but when I opened one of her desk drawers it was reassuringly still full of expensive make-up and low-carb chocolate bars. Instead of the usual scattering of papers, *Heat* magazines and pink heart-shaped Post-its, Ticky's desk was empty but for a lined pad with a neat list in her rounded handwriting:

Marvellous Englishwoman???
URGENT Layouts — to Man for final approval 11/04
Freelance subs for emergency cover — no from Binks
Hamilton & Lara Brooks. Still to try:
  Savannah Fitzroy
  Zelie Brennan-Leigh
  Rollo Morris?
  English Heritage press briefing for 2012 — 05/05.
    Noonoo?
  Armdale Gardens — visual direction?
    Brief to Jeremy

If it hadn't been in Ticky's hand I wouldn't have believed her capable of a list that demonstrated not only a thorough grasp of what needed to be done in my absence, but actual forward planning and initiative-taking. It seemed a little excessive to be looking for a freelance sub when I had only been out of the office for a few days, but I couldn't fault her for trying. Despite this demonstration of efficiency, Ticky wasn't here on time, of course, though I actually found this a bit of a relief. Otherwise I would have suspected some sort of body-snatching Stepford scenario.

Lysander arrived in my office before Ticky did, which was even more peculiar, since it was far too early for one of his post-lunch office perambulations. Something was up. He reclined in the chintz chair in a manner that said he intended to be there a while. Settling himself comfortably, he rested his elbows on the arms of the chair and tented his fingers like the pensive detective in a murder mystery. Perhaps he was about to tell me someone had done away with Ticky after all.

'What a week, Aurora, what a week,' he said. When I failed to take the bait he seemed to remember that he had yet to acknowledge that I had been out of the office for personal reasons. He hastily added, 'I can't tell you how relieved we all were to hear that your aunt is making a full recovery.'

'Thank you,' I said. 'She's doing well.'

'How well I remember her in *Those Devereux Girls*,' Lysander said. 'A glorious woman. Indeed, how well I remember meeting her at Annabel's in, oh, it must have been about '82.'

'You knew Auntie Lyd?' I asked, goggling at him. 'Really? You've never mentioned this before.'

Lysander leaned forward. 'No need to 'freak out',' he said, making quotation marks with his fingers in a move he believed helped him appear down with the kids. Even though the kids today had not been born in '82, let alone hanging out at Annabel's. 'I had no idea Lydia Bell was your aunt until Amanda said so on Monday — none of us had.'

'So you, Lysander Honeywell, are a friend of my aunt's?' I asked, unconvinced. 'How come I've never heard her mention you?'

He waved a hand dismissively before resuming his crime detective position. 'Oh, not a friend, Aurora, no. I cannot claim that privilege. We just met the once. But I've never forgotten. A marvellous woman.'

'She is,' I agreed, but his misty-eyed reminiscences over Auntie Lyd had already ended, replaced by the expression that I knew preceded the telling of gossip.

Lysander rubbed his hands together, building suspense. 'Item two,' he said. 'Martha's left. Resigned on Friday night, gone already.'

'What?' Was this why she had been trying to get me to cover for her over the weekend? Had my refusal caused her to entirely lose the plot?

'Oh yes, Aurora, it's been busy here while you've been away. And you will never, not ever, imagine where she has gone.' His eyes sparkled with amusement. Wherever it was, Lysander was delighted by it.

'Wait — she's left? Just like that? Without giving notice?'

'Well . . . ' Lysander leaned forward again and

385

I could see how much he had been delightedly anticipating my return to the office. Not for my own sake, but for the opportunity to tell the story to the one member of staff who didn't already know it. He had probably been lying in wait for me this and every morning to ensure he got to me before anyone else. 'She told Amanda that she'd consulted an employment lawyer. She was going to sue for constructive dismissal and age discrimination, but instead she'd settle for a year's salary and no notice period.'

'What — but — a year's salary? She's been here for twenty years, that's nothing!' I wasn't sure why I was leaping to Martha's defence since she had done little but make my life difficult over the years, but how could she give up her job — her life — like that? How would she live? Surely she'd find it impossible to get another job? What about her retirement plans, her pension?

'Ah,' said Lysander, his face breaking into a broad grin. 'She doesn't need money where she's going.'

'Of course she needs money, Lysander,' I snapped. With his rich family he had no idea what it might be like to be a woman of a certain age facing a penniless future. None. Martha did; that had been why she worked so hard. 'Unless — no, she's not — she's not joining a *religious order*, is she?' It would be just like her to leave in a manner that implied not only that she was on to better things, but that by remaining at the revamped circulation-chasing *Country House* we were all in some way morally inferior. Also it would neatly do away with the need for a pension.

Lysander shrieked with laughter, slapping his knees. 'A religious order!' he exclaimed, wiping at his eyes. 'A religious order! Oh my. Aurora, no, it's not a religious order. Quite the opposite.'

I was beginning to feel annoyed by his hints and allusions. It wouldn't have surprised me if he'd whipped out a fan and hidden behind it *Dangerous Liaisons*-style. 'A brothel?' I asked facetiously.

Lysander's smile dropped. 'Please do not speak like that about my future cousin,' he said sternly. 'I do not care to have the Honeywell name brought into disrepute.'

'Your cousin?' I echoed. Light slowly dawned. The softer colours she had been wearing. The weekends away. Hadn't she even brought a tin of Scottish shortbread into the office one Monday morning? I had been blind. We all had. 'No! Teddy?'

Lysander beamed again and leaned forward, rubbing his hands together in delight. 'Yes! Ethelred! She offered to pass on the contact details of the women who wrote in to the website about him, apparently to save me the bother, but she got rid of all of them and contacted him herself instead. *Et voilà — l'amour!*'

I nearly clapped my own hands together. It was like a fairy story. Martha was going to be the lady of the manor.

'Amazing,' I said.

'Oh faahrk,' snarled Ticky, waltzing into the office, swinging her handbag off her shoulder.

'Lysander, are you still going on about Martha? Jeez, get, like, a life, would you? Get a life and get out.' She stood over him in a stance that was made even more intimidating by her high stilettos, knee-length skirt and blouse. I was so used to seeing her dressed head to toe in Jack Wills that I couldn't stop staring at this new, business-like Ticky. 'Out!'

Lysander leapt up obediently from his seat, muttering, 'Sorry, Victoria,' and fled the office.

'Christ, Rory, am I glad to see you back. Faahrking major nightmare,' sighed Ticky, dropping into the space just vacated by Lysander. 'Martha walks out, you're nowhere to be seen; like, absolutely everything has landed on my desk.'

'Well, it's not been a particularly great week for me either, Ticky,' I said stiffly.

'Oh Goouurd, sorry, Roars,' said Ticky, slapping a palm to her forehead. 'Like, how rude? How's your aunt? Maaahn says she's like, some sort of famous bird from back in the day?'

'She's fine, thanks.' I wondered if I should have some sort of T-shirt made that said,

> Lydia Bell is much better now,
> thanks for asking.
> Yes, she was quite famous once.

'Look,' said Ticky, 'I don't mean to be, like, an insensitive bitch here' — which was in itself a surprising admission — 'but we are having a faahrking horror with the new issue: print deadline is next week and I really need to start handing stuff back to you, like, pronto-saurus.'

'Sure, sure,' I answered, astonished that Ticky, of all people, would steer the conversation away from personal gossip and towards work. I gestured at her desk. 'It looks like you've got everything under control, Ticky, thanks so much.'

'Yah,' she said, rising up from the chair and flicking her hair over her shoulder. 'It's, like, actually been sort of *fun*.'

'Really?'

'I know, Roars, I know. Fun in, like, a totes 'mare sort of way. But Maaahn's had to, like, trust me with shit, you know? And nothing's gone completely tits-up yet, so, yah. It's been quite good.'

'Is that what the new look's in aid of?' I asked.

'Well, like, dress for the job you want, yah? Not the job you have. That's what Daddy always says, you know, although he completely meant *Please dress in Country Casuals like Mummy does and stop walking around in denim cut-offs distracting the gardener.* There are going to be some changes round here and I'm, like, dressing up for them.'

Ticky's revelations were almost as amazing as Lysander's. The workshy public schoolgirl had suddenly turned into an ambitious career woman. I had the strange feeling that I was about to be professionally leapfrogged by my own assistant. And the even stranger feeling that I wasn't sure I cared. Seeing Martha's unexpected escape made me think. I had assumed my only choice was to follow in her Weldon's of

Ludlow footsteps up the *Country House* ladder; what if I should instead be following her out of the door?

'Roars, like, are you listening?' demanded Ticky. 'I said Maaahn wants to see you at eleven.'

'Does she?' I asked. 'What about?'

'Well, obviously she sat me down in her office and explained precisely why she wanted to see you,' said Ticky, rolling her eyes at me. 'Then she told me all about the state of her marriage and lent me a tampon. Jeez, Roars, like I know. She just said go to see her at eleven. End of.'

I supposed it was only to be expected that Amanda would want to see me now that Martha had left. But it made me nervous. With the features editor gone I was now officially the odd one out. Martha had never been my ally, of course. In fact, we had probably avoided each other rather than clung together, fearing that our lack of poshness would become magnified by proximity, but in some way I had felt that there was one person on the magazine who understood what it was like to be in this world but not of it. I knew she valued my dedication where others just wondered at my lack of useful contacts or blonde highlights. Without Martha there I felt exposed and vulnerable as the hour of my meeting with Amanda approached. Clearly I wasn't the only one to think that I might be in trouble. Flickers and Noonoo were huddled together in a corner, whispering and casting looks over towards me. When they saw me looking back they both waved with unconvincing

390

nonchalance. The pointing and whispering just added to my sense of foreboding.

I kept my eyes fixed on the carpet as I walked to Amanda's office at the appointed hour, but even so I could feel the frisson of interest that accompanied my progress down the corridor. It wouldn't have surprised me to discover that I was the subject of the latest office sweepstake. In fact, it would have surprised me more if I hadn't been.

Catherine bustled over as soon as she saw me approaching. 'Oh, poor dear Rory, what an ordeal. I am sorry.' I wasn't absolutely sure if she meant Auntie Lyd's heart attack or the impending meeting, so I just smiled politely and said thank you to cover both eventualities. Catherine ushered me into the editor's office.

Amanda, who had her chair turned outwards to the window, spun around and stood up, smiling ingratiatingly. She motioned to the chair opposite her desk and I sat down, folding my hands in my lap to prevent any nervous fidgeting. It wouldn't do for her to see that I was anxious.

'Rory, how *is* your aunt?' she asked, nudging a box of tissues on her desk closer to me.

'Much better, thank you,' I said. 'And thank you again for the flowers, we were both touched.'

Amanda waved away my thanks. 'Oh really, a mere gesture. What sort of employers would we be not to acknowledge such a difficult time in your family?' Well, I thought, the sort of employer who has never before taken an interest in my personal life. The sort of employer who had reflexively sent flowers to a former celebrity having no idea that she was the aunt of one of her employees.

I left space for Amanda to speak. It was best to let her take charge of a conversation from the very beginning, I found, since she was bound to do so in the end anyway.

'Although it was a surprise to me that you hadn't mentioned before that your aunt was Lydia Bell — after all, she would be a wonderful candidate for the Marvellous Englishwoman interviews.'

'She — she's not really a public person these days,' I answered. 'It didn't occur to me to suggest it.'

'Rory, you need to think more like a journalist,' Amanda said. 'Lydia Bell is always going to be a figure of interest to our readers — she's the right age, the right demographic. Everyone remembers *Those Devereux Girls*. You should have told me about her before. I mean, who else are you hiding?' She tapped her pen briskly on her desk as she looked at me, and I realized this wasn't a hypothetical question. I felt like Ticky, forced to squeeze her contacts at every opportunity.

'Er, Percy Granger and Eleanor Avery?' I offered, unsure if she would be impressed by either.

'Eleanor Avery from *Not Now, Padre?* Percy Granger from *Whoops! There Goes the Neighbourhood?*' she asked, eyes narrowed. 'Why didn't you say so before?'

'I wasn't sure you'd be interested,' I said, although the truth was it had never occurred to me to offer them up for publicity in order to further my own career.

'Think. Like. A. Journalist,' Amanda enunciated, tapping her pen sharply on the desk with every word. 'Rory,' she said, and she too tented her fingers as Lysander had earlier. I wondered if it was a technique they had been taught at public school: position to be adopted when conveying difficult news. 'Rory, you will no doubt be aware that Martha has decided to leave us.'

'Yes, I had heard that,' I admitted.

'Very sad,' said Amanda, unconvincingly. 'For us, I mean; of course it's delightful for Martha, and we are all so happy for her. And for those of us left behind it means some changes. Which is why I asked you here.'

Amanda seemed to be looking at me as if for the first time. I wasn't sure what such intense scrutiny was in aid of. Get on with it, I thought, digging my nails into my palms. Stop acting like you're about to reveal whodunnit. Just tell me you're making me redundant.

'Rory,' she said. 'I have yet to decide who is going to replace Martha. I'm sure you will appreciate that it's not simply a matter of just moving everyone up a level. There is a real opportunity for change here and I need to think about it seriously.'

'Of course,' I said, wishing she would hurry up and put me out of my misery.

'I'm going to be changing around some responsibilities. Taking this chance to shake up the editorial team. That being said, I'd like you to apply for the position of features editor.

Formally, I mean. You've surprised me lately, Rory. The Unsuitable Men column has been fun — witty. Very different from the staid art history pieces I'm used to from you.'

'Thank you,' I said cautiously, suspecting that my stock had risen in her eyes less because of Unsuitable Men than because she had discovered that my aunt was once well known. I tried not to be offended that she considered my previous work staid.

'Did I offend you in some way, Rory?' Amanda asked, raising a supercilious eyebrow.

I felt oddly emboldened, by what I don't know. Usually I would have muttered, 'No' and seethed about it in private. But audiences with Amanda were so rare I knew I would regret it for ever if I didn't speak up properly.

'Amanda, I like writing those art history pieces. That's why I work here. I like visiting country houses, and researching the artworks, and finding out the history behind things. I — I don't think I'm the right person for this job if my value to you comes only from writing a dating column, and being related to someone who was once famous. I think, actually, it might be time for me to move on from *Country House*. I think I should find somewhere that I fit in better.'

Amanda gripped her pen between her fingers and stared at me crossly. 'Firstly, Rory, the person who decides what makes a good features editor is not you. It is me. Which is why you will apply for this as I asked.'

I started to speak, but Amanda raised her hand to stop me.

'Secondly, baby. Bathwater.'

'Sorry?' I asked.

'Rory, you have invested a lot of time at *Country House* and, whatever you might think, you are valued here. Don't go throwing the baby out with the bathwater because of some silly notion that you don't fit in. I've told you there will be changes here. Write me a proposal. Tell me how you propose to integrate the old *Country House* with the new — how you can keep the art history but bring in new readers. Pitch me an idea for an advice columnist. Baby, bathwater. Think about it.'

'But . . . ' I felt my grand gesture had been swept under the carpet. I thought I had just resigned, but Amanda didn't even seem to notice.

'End of conversation, Rory,' said Amanda, turning back to her computer screen. 'Let me have your pitch by Monday.'

I left her office stunned, hardly able to take in what she had been saying. Amanda considered me a valued member of the team? She thought I fitted in? She was considering promoting me, and not dismissing my ideas out of hand? I had gone in there expecting to be made redundant, ended up offering my resignation, and now I was leaving not only still with a job, but with the possibility of a promotion that I wasn't even sure I wanted. My shocked face was like a lure to Ticky, who sprang to my side out of nowhere as I passed the kitchen.

'Roooooars,' she drawled, deeply sympathetic. 'Was it appalling? What did Maaahn say? Are you okay? How are you feeling? When do you leave?'

'Leave?' I asked.

Ticky nodded. 'Yah.'

I noticed how the office seemed to have stilled, waiting for me to answer. They all thought Amanda had called me in there to get rid of me. That she would fire me the day I came back from the bedside of my aunt.

'Roars,' said Ticky suddenly, clutching at my arm. 'It's faahrking shit. Maaahn is insane. This place would, like, fall apart without you.'

Lysander appeared on my other side, holding his fooling-no-one piece of paper. 'Aurora, please say it's not true. Isn't there something we can do?'

Noonoo's head rose up above Lysander's shoulder like a pashmina-swathed moon. 'I raaahlly can't believe she'd do it, Rory. Who's going to make all of my friends sound like they can actually string a sentence together if you're not here?'

Jeremy came striding down the corridor from the art department, squaring his dark-framed glasses determinedly with his hand. 'I'm going in there, Rory. I'm going in there right now and telling her we won't work until you're reinstated.'

'Wait,' I said. 'Wait, all of you. I'm not leaving.'

'You're not?' said Ticky. 'Faahrking hell, Roars, way to make the lot of us have, like, a collective faahrking heart attack.'

Lysander glared at her and she hastily continued, 'Oh yah, sorry, no offence to your aunt, Roars.'

Jeremy looked enormously relieved, placing a

palm flat on his chest and exhaling loudly. 'So I don't actually have to go in there? Oh thank God, Rory, because I don't know if I really could have done it.'

'So what's going on then?' asked Flickers, drawn by the knot of people in the corridor.

'Is the sweepstake ruined?' I asked.

'Rory,' he said, looking wounded. 'There are some things that even *I* won't bet on.'

Later I saw him returning pound coins to a few people. But by then I didn't really mind. Amanda had told me I was valued at *Country House*, but I had thought it was just to stop her losing another member of the team when she was already short-staffed. The reaction of my colleagues, however, had astonished me. I did have friends here. I was of value. I was going to write that proposal. I was going to get that job.

37

Auntie Lyd's house was still full of flowers, although some of them had started wilting by Friday. Mum had sent a box of peculiar lemon-flavoured Spanish chocolates and a bottle of brandy, and had had to be prevented from flying over to look after her sister — her penchant for dramatics would have been strictly against doctor's orders. There had been other gifts, too: a box of books selected by Lysander from his shelves of freebies and sent with a grovelling note that begged an audience with 'the divine Lydia'; a cashmere blanket from Linda Ellery, who begged to know when her former co-star was allowed visitors. The oddest gift though had been a vast hamper of assorted meats from the butchers, mortified at Auntie Lyd's collapse on their premises. Eleanor and I had packed away as much as possible into the freezer, but there was still an entire leg of lamb that we couldn't wedge in no matter how we arranged the frozen peas.

Auntie Lyd declared that she was going to cook it for all of us as a thank-you for our help while she had been ill. Her only concession to our objections had been to agree to Jim helping her cook while she dictated instructions from the armchair he had carried downstairs to the kitchen. She had even suggested to me that I could invite Martin if I liked, but I hadn't passed on the invitation. I had promised him an answer tomorrow, and I hoped that by then I would finally have made up my mind.

I had thought about it. I really had. Especially since I'd spoken to Amanda. Baby, bathwater. Was I going to throw away eleven years just because he had made one mistake? I'd put in all that time and effort and love, and now I was considering turning my back on him — on us — for ever. And for what? It wasn't like I'd been swept off my feet by the available men out there. If anything, the thought of the unsuitable men I'd encountered should have me running back gratefully into Martin's arms. I was nearly thirty; it was time to behave like a grown-up, not the delayed adolescent dater that I had been over the last few months. Did I really want to walk away from a stable adult relationship for sordid encounters with unemployed musicians and teenaged sexters? Like my job at *Country House*, my relationship with Martin wasn't perfect. But maybe it was good enough. Perhaps things could change between Martin and me. Perhaps we could be happy together again.

Everyone in the kitchen was slightly hysterical when I got home from work. I thought they must have started drinking already, but nothing stronger than tea was in evidence, even in Eleanor's cup. She and Percy were lining a complicated-looking fish-shaped mould ('From eBay — can you imagine? Someone was selling it for a song!' said Eleanor) with smoked salmon, and arguing over the consistency of a pale-pink mousse that was to be placed in it. Percy wanted to add more lemon juice but Eleanor slapped his hand away when he ventured near the bowl, and pointed authoritatively towards the recipe book, announcing, 'Do not question Delia.' Rich smells indicated the lamb was already in the oven, while a plaster on Jim's thumb suggested that Auntie Lyd had had him using her lethal mandolin slicer for potatoes dauphinoise. The kitchen table had been cleared of its normal detritus and was laid for five, with Auntie Lyd placed at the head.

'What can I do?' I asked, putting down the wine I'd bought on my way home.

'Nothing at all,' said Auntie Lyd, just as Jim said, 'Open the wine.'

'I'll open the wine then,' I said, and went towards the drawer where the corkscrew was kept, but Jim got there before me. We both reached for the drawer handle at the same time and he nudged me out of the way with his hip.

'Oi, I'm in charge of the kitchen tonight, Dawn. Out.' He handed me the corkscrew and guided me by the shoulders away from the work surface, where vegetables were laid out for chopping.

'So masterful,' I said, feigning a swoon. Since our awkward talk in the van I'd kept my distance from Jim a little, and he from me. The overt hostilities were over now that we were united in looking after Auntie Lyd, and he had resumed his constant teasing, but it was clear that neither of us was keen to repeat our kitchen tête-à-tête any time soon.

From across the kitchen Eleanor shrieked, 'Percy-will-you-get-away-from-that-bowl-with-the-lemon!'

Percy reluctantly handed over the half of lemon that he'd secreted in his palm, and Eleanor threw it in the bin. 'Don't blame me if the mousse is solid,' he declared.

'It's *supposed* to be solid, Percy,' hissed Eleanor. 'Or it will run all over the place.'

'What's for pudding?' I asked Jim, easing the cork out of the bottle of red wine.

'Surprise,' grinned Jim, exchanging a glance with Auntie Lyd. It was weird: I didn't feel jealous of their rapport any more. If I moved out of the house, and back with Martin, I felt grateful that Jim would still be around to help out if Auntie Lyd needed it. Not that I wouldn't be — of course I wasn't going to entirely disappear — but there was a bond there that made me feel that Auntie Lyd was not going to be alone. She had a family — it might not be the husband and 2.4 children that I wanted for myself, but it was a family nonetheless, and she was safe within it. Perhaps in a way that made them my family too.

'A surprise pudding?' I said. 'Mmm, what's it going to be, Jim, plumber's plum pudding with a delicious sauce of grouting?'

'You'll have to wait and see. Like I said, surprise,' he said mysteriously.

Percy and Eleanor were bickering in fierce whispers about who would carry the fish mould over to the fridge, tugging it between them like squabbling toddlers. Auntie Lyd tilted her head in their direction to indicate that I should step in, and I was just about to when the doorbell rang.

'The postman?' asked Eleanor hopefully, looking up from the fish mould. I think we had all hoped that her new addiction to internet shopping might replace Eleanor's early morning whisky habit, but so far she seemed to be able to run both concurrently and quite happily. New eBay monstrosities arrived at Elgin Square daily.

'Not at this hour, woman,' said Percy, pulling at the fish mould again.

'Did you invite someone else?' I asked Auntie Lyd.

'No,' she answered. 'Did you?'

I shook my head.

Jim wiped his hands on the apron that he'd tied around his waist. 'Probably a gift from another admirer, Lydia. I'll get it.'

Eleanor took advantage of Percy's momentary distraction to wrest the fish mould from his grasp and march it over to the fridge. I opened the door so she could place it on a shelf and Percy cast me the wounded look of the unexpectedly betrayed. '*Et tu, Brute?*' he asked.

Auntie Lyd ignored us all. She appeared to be straining to hear the conversation from upstairs, probably hoping it wasn't another gift of meat from the butcher, an apologetic wreath of beef or something. Her face darkened. I started listening too. I knew that voice.

Steps thundered down the stairs to the basement and Martin burst through the door with Jim close behind him. His hair was dishevelled and his face red, as if he'd been running.

'Martin?' I asked, stepping towards him. He

402

looked like someone else — not the calm, ordered man that I knew. 'What are you doing here?'

'I'm sorry to interrupt,' said Martin, breathing heavily. He dropped his briefcase on the floor. 'I've come here straight from work. I couldn't wait any longer, Rory. I needed to see you.'

'Mate,' said Jim, moving cautiously towards him as if approaching an unpredictable wild animal. 'Do you want a drink or anything?'

'I don't want a drink,' Martin said, swatting him away without taking his eyes off me. 'I just need to talk to Rory. Now. There are things I need to say. I can't wait any longer.'

'Martin,' I pleaded. 'Not now. Not here. We agreed we'd talk tomorrow.'

He looked around the room as if he'd just awoken from a dream in which he was somewhere else entirely. The table laid for dinner, the wine open on the windowsill above the radiator, pans bubbling on the stove.

'Well, isn't this lovely?' he said, taking it all in. 'Everyone all together. Thanks for the invitation.'

'This isn't appropriate, Martin,' I said firmly, taking his elbow. Didn't he remember that Auntie Lyd wasn't to be agitated under any circumstances? Although she didn't seem angry. She was looking at Martin with a curious expression; not so much anger as a kind of pity. 'Let's go upstairs and talk there.'

'No!' He wrested his arm away from me and took my hand instead. 'I'm happy for everyone to hear what I want to say to you. It's about time I said it.'

'Martin,' I hissed, feeling the eyes of everyone on us. I couldn't believe he'd burst in here like this, demanding my answer before I was ready.

'I know you, Rory,' he said. 'It was killing me waiting for you to make up your mind and then I realized — you never make decisions about anything. You always wait for me to do it. Remember when we bought the house? You left everything to me, and wasn't it better like that? Don't I know what makes you happy? So here I am. I've decided for us.'

He let go of my hand and reached into the inside pocket of his suit jacket, pulling out a velvet box with a curved lid. He stretched it out to me unopened, bending unsteadily down on to one knee. I could feel myself shaking. Could feel the whole kitchen holding its breath.

'Martin, don't do this,' I said. 'Please.'

'Rory,' he said. He clutched the ring box in his palm so tightly that it looked almost as if he was threatening me with his fist instead of proffering something I should have been glad to see. 'Rory, let me make you happy. Let me make it right. Will you do me the honour of being my wife?'

I started backing away, shaking my head. Suddenly it was all incredibly clear. As if I was seeing Martin properly for the first time. I couldn't spend the rest of my life with him. I wasn't even sure if I could bear to spend the next five minutes with him.

'I can't marry you,' I said.

His smile faltered slightly, but remained, as if resistance was only to be expected. He rose to his feet and came towards me.

'Rory,' he urged, 'you don't have to do this any more. Just let go of the past. It's all behind us now. We've got a future together. You and me.'

'Please don't, Martin,' I said again, retreating away from him.

He dropped his arms by his side. 'Rory?' he asked. He squinted at me as if he might have accidentally proposed to Eleanor or Auntie Lyd, the wrong person entirely; his Rory would never refuse him like this.

Perhaps *his* Rory wouldn't have. But this Rory had.

'What's wrong, Rory?' he said. 'I thought this was what you wanted.'

'No, Martin, this is what *you* wanted,' I said, my fingers bunching into fists. 'Everything is always about what *you* want. If you knew me at all, you'd have enough respect not to come in here like this, interrupting me and my family — '

'Your family?' he laughed, sneering as he looked around the kitchen. 'One dried up old has-been and her half-dead friends? A trades-man? This is what you call a family?'

I saw Percy take a determined step towards Martin, squaring up to a man twice his size and less than half his age. From the corner of my eye I saw Jim shake his head at Percy and mouth, 'Stay out of it.'

'It's more of a family than I ever had with you, Martin,' I said steadily. 'They've been more supportive and kind and loving in a few weeks than you ever were in all the years we were together.'

Martin stepped backwards, bumping into one

405

of the kitchen chairs. His voice was thick with anger. 'After everything I've done for you.'

'Martin. I am grateful. You've been incredibly kind over the last week. But I'm not going to marry you for it.'

Martin went very quiet. The belligerence seemed to drain away as we watched, his shoulders rounding over his deflating chest. He looked down at the velvet box in his hands. 'Don't you even want to see the ring?' he asked.

'No,' I said. 'I don't care if it's the Koh-i-noor diamond in there, Martin, I can't say yes.'

He wrung the box round and round in his hands. 'You've changed,' he muttered at the floor.

I looked at Auntie Lyd. She hadn't stirred from her chair or said a word. She'd left me to deal with this just as I saw fit. Percy and Eleanor held hands beside her. Behind Martin, Jim stood ready to help the moment I asked. None of them would have dreamed of acting for me; they were just here to help with whatever I decided. And I had decided.

'I have,' I said proudly. 'I have changed.'

38

I remember reading in a book once that a turning point in your life only becomes one in retrospect — that at the time you almost always fail to actually turn. You continue living your life, and change creeps in by stealth, by many little turning points that you still fail to notice until — there it is, you've turned. There is rarely a moment of great and shining revelation in real life. It's only afterwards, looking back and trying to construct a narrative for your confused mishmash of conflicting decisions, that you think, *Oh yes. That was it.* That was the point at which I knew things were going to change.

It was like that with Martin. The moment of refusing his proposal hadn't been the turning point at all. Hadn't I known as soon as I went back to our house, all those months ago to collect my things, that it wasn't really my home, and never had been? Hadn't I taken steps to change my life by dating the unsuitable men? And yet I'd continued to dream about getting back together with him, tortured myself about whether to return to the life he was offering, without even seeing that I had a whole life of my own going on right under my nose.

I looked back at the girl I was when I first arrived at Auntie Lyd's, sobbing on the doorstep, as I might look at a stranger: with sympathetic compassion, but also distance and a certain benevolent bemusement. I had thought that I was nothing without Martin, when really I had been nothing when I was with him. My opinions didn't count — not to him but, far worse, not to me. I had felt inferior to everyone, all the time, at home and at work; an outcast grateful to be allowed to play with the other children. Always the anthropologist, taking my assiduous notes on the natives' behaviour, standing outside of it all; believing that to be unnoticed was a kind of acceptance. How had I expected people to accept me when I was so busy studying them that I hardly had time to think about who I was?

After refusing Martin's proposal I felt empowered, emboldened, as if from now on I was going to stride confidently through life in the manner of Auntie Lyd as Destiny Devereux, all shoulder pads and hairspray and ambition. I'd had the confidence to pitch to Amanda for the features editor role as I saw it, not as I thought she wanted it to be. I'd pressed for Unsuitable Men to be promoted to the magazine from the website, but with a difference: I was hanging up my dating hat for now, as far as unsuitables went. I suggested the column be passed on to one of Noonoo's society friends — Kinshasa Norrington-Davies had just split from Timmo Windlesham and was as publicity-hungry as ever. She'd be perfect. I proposed more art history, of course, and the return of Behind the Rope. And, thinking like a journalist, and with her prior approval, I had suggested former television star Lydia Bell as *Country House*'s new agony aunt.

Naturally the features editor job had gone to someone else. Atlanta Beaulieu, formerly of *Tatler*, would be joining the staff in a few short weeks.

Ticky had been personally outraged, as if her three weeks of pencil skirts and pointy-shoed efficiency should have guaranteed her Martha's old job, and mitigated against three years of shameless work avoidance. 'Like, did Maaahn not even notice that I have stayed until at least four-thirty *every day?*' But her dress-for-success campaign had not been entirely in vain. Amanda agreed that Ticky's interrogation tactics should not go to waste — from now on she would be the first-choice interviewer at the magazine. It was enough of a carrot to keep Ticky from backsliding into her old ways. For now, at least.

After the initial shock, I hadn't been especially surprised not to get the job. It would have been too easy a ride to just sail into that promotion after spending so many years fading into the background. Martha got her fairy-tale ending, running off into the Highlands with a billionaire bachelor; I got the real-life version. It was going to take more work before I got taken seriously as a player when it came to my career. I'd been taking it all as seriously as I took myself — which is to say, not very. I'd thought myself so superior to the posh girls who spent a few aimless years on the magazine before bagging themselves a husband and retiring to domesticity in the countryside, and yet I had been just like them:

I'd treated my job as a diverting distraction while I focused all my energies on my boyfriend as the only future that mattered. Now that I didn't have the option of being rescued by a Prince Charming, it was time to roll my sleeves up and get on with sorting out my own future.

But Amanda did agree to restore Behind the Rope as a website feature, and I was relieved of my Unsuitable Men duties once I'd finished writing a final column summarizing what I'd learned from it all. I'd already abandoned several drafts without being able to come to any sort of tidy conclusion. I supposed I'd learned at least that dating wasn't as scary as I'd feared. That sometimes you can have a lot of fun with someone who doesn't tick all the boxes — or any of them. I was an experienced sexter. And I was pretty sure I could now identify a fauxmosexual at fifty paces. I wasn't sure I was any closer to identifying a suitable man though. I'd always thought Martin was the epitome of suitable, and that had been proved spectacularly wrong. I guessed that meant that a truly suitable man might come in an entirely different package from the one I had always expected. Perhaps that was the only conclusion I could come to. It didn't seem like much of an ending.

As for the advice-columnist pitch, I'd assumed by her silence that Amanda had nixed that idea. Until I came home from work one evening to find her sitting with Auntie Lyd in the kitchen, paperwork spread out between them on the table.

It was strange seeing Amanda in my kitchen: a

weird collision of my work and home lives, like coming across a photocopier in my bedroom. Auntie Lyd didn't seem to find it odd at all — she was regaling Amanda with the continued adventure of her attempts to give up smoking, brandishing the nicotine patches that marched up both of her arms, while Jim paid attentive court to both of them. It no longer seemed strange to see him there. Even though the work on Auntie Lyd's house was now finished, he had become so much a part of the household that it was almost strange if he wasn't there when I came home from work. He insisted it was a quiet time of year for him, and that he was waiting for things to pick up, but I had overheard him turning down a job just last week. I think he was unwilling to leave Auntie Lyd's side until he knew she was restored to full health. It made me feel safer to know that he was there, and we exchanged smiles as I came into the kitchen. Even though Auntie Lyd's progress had been amazing, the thought of her collapse, all alone, still haunted me and I was reassured to know she had somebody strong around the house while I was at work.

'Rory,' said Amanda, looking at her watch as I approached them. 'Is that the time already? Lydia, I've kept you for far too long, I must be going.' She stood up and smoothed down the nubbly weave of her Chanel skirt.

'Good to meet you, Amanda,' said Jim, standing up and offering her his callused hand. She smiled back and shook his hand warmly.

'And you, Jim. I do hope we'll meet again soon.'

It seemed an odd thing to say. I wondered under what circumstances they might possibly meet again; unless Amanda had some plumbing work that needed doing. She scooped up the papers on the table and turned to Auntie Lyd. 'Please don't get up, Lydia. I'll take these contracts back to the office and once they've been countersigned by one of the Bettertons, I'll send you a copy for your records.' She held out her hand to my aunt. 'Welcome to the team.'

'Does this mean you're going to have to file your copy to me, Auntie Lyd?' I asked, taking it all in.

'Of course, darling, it's in my contract,' she laughed. 'You're the boss.'

'Interesting,' I mused. 'No chance of late delivery, Auntie Lyd. If only it was as easy to chase everyone as it will be to chase you.'

Amanda pushed her chair back, readying herself to leave. 'True. But could you really stand to share living space with any of our other columnists?' she asked, raising an eyebrow by a millimetre. Wonders would never cease. Amanda had a sense of humour. 'Rory, might I ask you to show me out?'

I translated this as a request to speak to me alone rather than an inability to negotiate the short flight of stairs to the front door, and led the way to the hall with the clack of Amanda's high heels following close behind.

She checked her hair in the hall mirror appraisingly, turning her head from side to side. 'Now I see why you wanted to stop writing Unsuitable Men,' she said, flicking her blonde

412

fringe out of her eyes.

'Do you?' I asked, mystified. Auntie Lyd had had nothing to do with it. It just seemed like something that had served its purpose. I'd thought I'd get over Martin by dating other men, but in fact I'd got over him all by myself. I didn't feel the need to bury myself in ridiculous situations any more, either for work or supposed pleasure.

'Well,' said Amanda, turning around from the mirror. 'He is rather gorgeous.'

'Who — Wait, you mean *Jim?*'

'Of course I do, Rory, who else would I mean?'

'Oh no,' I laughed, a little too loudly. 'Really, there's nothing going on there. Truly.'

Amanda raised one expensively threaded eyebrow. 'Well, why ever not? I saw the way you two were looking at each other.'

I flushed. 'We're just friends,' I said, unable to look her straight in the eye even though I was telling the truth. How had he been looking at me? I wanted to ask. How was I looking at him?

'If you say so,' shrugged Amanda. She took her BlackBerry out of her bag and started scrolling through messages as she walked to the front door. 'Shame. I'd leap on him myself if I wasn't already married. See you at the office.'

I shut the door behind her, leaning my back against it. Although I knew Jim couldn't have heard our conversation without having hung out on the stairs with a hand cupped behind his ear, which seemed unlikely, I felt a sickly wash of shame and embarrassment that stopped me from going down to the kitchen. Whatever Amanda thought, Jim had made it clear that he wasn't interested in me like that. I'd told myself that was fine: we were best as friends, united in our concern for Auntie Lyd. I'd been careful to suppress any thoughts of Jim that weren't strictly platonic. I'd not allowed myself a single daydream about our kiss in the kitchen. No, not one. I averted my eyes from his muscular arms in those terrible T-shirts. I certainly never thought about how it would feel to have those arms wrapped around me. Well, not often, anyway. Oh God, who was I kidding? I thought I'd hidden it from everyone. I thought I'd hidden it from myself, even. And yet apparently it was clear to a casual visitor to our home that I was drooling after him like a lovesick teenager. What if Jim had noticed all along?

He'd tried to talk to me a few times this week, his expression unusually serious, but I'd made excuses to rush away. I didn't need to hear him tell me again that nothing was going to happen between us. That it had just been a drunken kiss. I mean, there's facing up to reality and then there's masochistically putting yourself in a situation where you know you're going to be told something unwelcome. Why would I do that?

I heard steps coming up to the hall, and shrank back into the shadows in case it actually was Jim, come to close match in person like one of the unsuitables from My Mate's Great made flesh. But it was Auntie Lyd who appeared at the top of the stairs. She stopped to catch her breath and I coughed before I stepped forward, in case the sight of me emerging unexpectedly from the shadows made her jump. But she pressed a hand to her heart anyway.

'Oh, Rory, what are you doing skulking there? Honestly. Anyone would think you were trying to give me another heart attack.'

'How else am I going to get my hands on your millions?' I teased.

'If you don't watch it I'll leave every penny to a charity for cats. Won't I, Mr Bits?' She bent down to stroke the cat, and started up the next flight of stairs.

'Where are you going?' I asked.

'Upstairs to my bedroom, not that it's any of your business.'

'Why are you going to bed so early?' I asked, immediately anxious. 'Are you feeling okay?'

'I'm not going to bed, darling, I'm just getting ready to go out.'

'Out?'

'Aurora, please stop giving me that look as if you are my mother. Yes, I am going out.'

'Where?' I demanded. 'Who with?'

Auntie Lyd stopped halfway up the stairs and turned round to look down on me haughtily. 'Not, again, that it is any of your business, but I am having dinner with Lysander Honeywell.'

'Lysander!' I shrieked in a strangled voice. Lysander the pink-shirted gossipy roué of the *Country House* office? And my aunt?

'Honestly, Rory,' she huffed. 'Please don't make a scene. I've spoken to him a few times about the books he kindly sent me and we

415

agreed to meet for a quiet dinner. It's nothing to get excited about.'

This was becoming ridiculous. How much more was my work life going to infiltrate Elgin Square? Was Noonoo suddenly going to appear on Percy's wrinkled arm? Would Flickers be seen squiring Eleanor down Clapham High Street?

'But — but — ' I sputtered.

'If you're about to tell me he's an unsuitable man, Rory, I might have to remind you that you are hardly one to talk.'

That silenced me. She turned to go up the stairs. 'Oh, one last thing. I said to Jim that you'd take him out to dinner tonight — on me, of course; I've left some cash on the kitchen table. We owe him a bit of a thank-you, don't you think?'

'You said what?' I asked. If I'd been worried about how I could hide my feelings from Jim in the kitchen, with the constant chaperoning presence of my elderly housemates, it was as nothing to my horror at the idea of sitting opposite him, alone in a restaurant, with no escape from his scrutiny.

'I'm determined that you two will be friends,' said Auntie Lyd. 'It means a lot to me. Anyway, you wouldn't ignore the advice of a professional agony aunt, would you?'

'But Auntie Lyd, I — '

She interrupted as she continued up the stairs, 'I already told him you'd do it. He's waiting downstairs. Have fun, darling.'

She rounded the corner up to the next floor.

Mr Bits offered me his usual look of disdain before he followed her, although this time I wondered if it might in fact be a look of feline pity for the evening ahead. Of all the dates that I had endured with unsuitable men, this would surely be the most excruciating.

39

'So, Dawn, is this going to be one of those unsuitable-men thingies then?' Jim asked, nudging me with his elbow as we left the square and turned up the dark alley towards the restaurants of Venn Street. I got the impression that he thought our enforced dinner date was all rather amusing. 'You've done the pensioner, the teenage sexter, the dossy musician — now it's time for the plumber?'

Oh great, he clearly thought I'd put Auntie Lyd up to this; begged her to get the plumber to go out with me so I could use him for my column as an excuse to pounce on him again. I cursed myself for looking like such a cliché: just another middle-class girl getting her kicks by slumming it with a manual labourer. He probably got this kind of thing all the time; from his relaxed attitude it seemed he was quite used to approaches from women, taking it all in his stride as one of the hazards of the job. Probably went home and laughed with his friends about it. I burned with embarrassment, glad that we were walking side by side so that he couldn't see my face flaming scarlet.

'I'm not writing that column any more,' I muttered.

'That's a shame,' he said. 'I liked reading them.'

'You read the columns?' I asked, glancing up

at him. I don't know why I was surprised. Auntie Lyd had probably forced him, Percy and Eleanor to read every one.

Jim shrugged. 'Well, since your aunt bought a laptop and went online purely to read it, I thought it was probably going to be interesting. It was. You're funny. Crap taste in men, but funny.'

'They were *meant* to be crap,' I said. 'That was the whole point.'

'So I suppose it's a compliment that I didn't make the grade?' teased Jim. 'Bit of a shame I don't get to be immortalized in prose though, isn't it?' He nudged me again. Even though the alley was narrow, it seemed that he was walking very close to me.

'Oh so you'd like to be, would you?' I laughed. 'Is that what this is about? You're annoyed that I'm not going to write about you afterwards? I will if you like.'

'Yeah? What are you going to say?'

'I won't be able to avoid mentioning your T-shirts,' I said. The latest declared, charmingly,

Not tonight, ladies, I'm just here to get drunk.

'Well, if I'd known we were going out, I'd have got changed,' he said, plucking at the fabric on his chest. 'It's not like I wear these for anything other than work.'

'Where do you even get them from?' I asked.

'Horrible, aren't they?' he said. 'My sister's an air hostess — she gets them for me from all around the world. I've never had the heart to tell

419

her they're not really my thing. She gets offended if I don't wear them though. What else are you going to say?'

'About your T-shirts?'

'About *me*,' said Jim.

'Well, that rather depends on how you behave this evening,' I retorted. Strange as it was to be heading out to dinner with Jim, and uncomfortable as I'd felt when we left the house, I had to admit that he had a way of making me at ease with his silly banter.

'Christ, Dawn, I'd better not hold my knife like a pen or anything, had I? What *would* the readers of *Country House* think?'

'I know what the editor of *Country House* would think,' I said leadingly.

'Amanda? She seemed all right.'

'She thought you were more than all right,' I said. 'She told me she thought you were gorgeous.'

'Did she now?' Jim chuckled. Again that easy acceptance that he was attractive to women. He wasn't even slightly embarrassed by it. He probably had them throwing themselves at him all the time. No wonder he'd so easily dismissed our kiss in the kitchen; he must be so used to repelling unwanted advances that his pursuers all merged into one single predatory female.

The alley opened out into the bottom of Venn Street, where a handful of restaurants clustered around the cinema. Auntie Lyd had left a generous pile of twenties on the kitchen table, which meant we could afford to go anywhere we liked. Attempting to reinforce in Jim's mind that this had been her idea rather than mine, I said that he should be the one to choose where we went; this was his thank-you after all. I hoped he wouldn't choose the cocktail-bar-cum-restaurant that was usually full of couples. There was something very date-y about it that made me cringe a little when I imagined us there. I was going to be bright and breezy, I had decided. Keep up this banter and let him be in no doubt that I wasn't going to pounce on him. This was just a completely platonic dinner between friends.

'I like the look of this French place,' he said as we approached the restaurant where I'd sat and drank wine while, unknown to me, Auntie Lyd was being driven to hospital in an ambulance. There was no need to share this information with Jim. Perhaps going there again would be a sort of catharsis, now that my aunt was better. Now that my aunt was going out for dinner with *Lysander*, I remembered.

'Jim, did Auntie Lyd say where she was going out tonight?' I asked, my anxiety levels rising.

'Relax, Rory,' he said. 'She's meeting Lysander in a restaurant in the Old Town. I already checked. We're not going to run into her.'

'In that case here's fine,' I said, relieved. He held the door open for me and ushered me through, his hand lightly brushing my back as he led me up to the zinc bar.

A sullen waitress regarded us blankly. 'Reservation?' she asked. I was just about to explain that we didn't have one when the owner appeared, bursting out of the kitchen with his hands outstretched.

'*La nièce Devereux!*' he exclaimed, pushing his waitress out of the way. She pouted crossly behind him as he took my hands. 'She is better — *la tante? Oui? Oh, la divine Lydia.* Such a shock — for us, for you! Tell her she must come to see me — soon, soon.'

I promised I would and he pinched my cheek happily as if I was a toddler instead of a woman of nearly thirty. He beckoned over another waitress, who batted her eyelashes at Jim flirtatiously as she led us to a table in the window.

The owner brought round a complimentary glass of champagne each, although, this being a rustic sort of place, it was served in a chunky tumbler instead of a flute. Even so it made Jim's hand look enormous as he held it up to make a toast.

'To Lydia,' he said, touching my glass with his own.

'To Auntie Lyd,' I said.

Sitting by the window was an unexpected bonus. It was still just light outside and Venn Street was busy with cinema-goers and early evening drinkers. That gave me plenty of opportunities to keep up a steady flow of chatter by pointing out people walking past, and dogs, and asking him if he'd seen any good films lately; anything to stop him from bringing the conversation around to anything tricky. I had thought I was doing rather well until Jim put his hand over mine.

'Relax, Rory,' he said.

Which of course made me tense up with annoyance. No one likes to be told to relax. It's like being told to calm down; guaranteed to have the opposite effect. Avoiding Jim's gaze, I flicked my eyes up to the clock behind the zinc bar. It was still only seven-thirty. The waitress caught me looking over, and hurried towards us with her pad ready. I hadn't made up my mind yet, but was glad that her presence distracted Jim for a moment. I was uncomfortably aware of his eyes on me all the time. I made sure to ask plenty of questions about how things were cooked, and exactly what was in several sauces, before I made up my mind to have a *steak-frites*. When she'd taken our order I looked at the clock again. Seven-thirty-five. Perhaps there was something wrong with that clock. Maybe it was running slow or something. I tried to look at my phone without Jim seeing; the display showed that time had not yet stood still. It was seven-thirty-six.

'Checking for more sexy texts?' said Jim, who had of course noticed what I was doing.

'Jim, I think you've got totally the wrong idea about me,' I said.

'I'm not judging, Dawn,' he grinned, and dropped me a cheeky wink that said otherwise.

I felt my face begin to redden again. It was hard to defend myself from implicit accusations of getting about a bit when Jim had been keeping himself more than updated on my stupid excuse for a love life thanks to the *Country House* website.

'I'm really not that sort of girl,' I insisted,

423

sounding ridiculously prim for someone whose very recent sexual partner had been intercepted by Jim the morning after. And then those awful texts from Luke. Was it any wonder Jim thought I was going to leap on him any second?

He just laughed. 'So you say.'

'Look, I know you think I got Auntie Lyd to set this up so you'd have to go out to dinner with me,' I blurted. My cheeks burned.

'No, I don't,' he said, looking surprised.

'Yes you do,' I protested.

'I don't.'

'You do.'

'No I *don't*, Dawn. Because *I* asked her to set this up.'

I gaped at him, my mouth hanging unattractively open. 'You?'

'I've been wanting to talk to you properly for a while,' he said, his brow furrowed.

Oh God. I knew what was coming. I gripped the sides of my chair.

'It's okay, I understand,' I said quickly. 'You don't have to tell me again. I know you're not interested in me like that. And that's fine, actually, just fine.'

'When did I say I wasn't interested in you?' Jim asked. God, he really wouldn't let it go, would he? Did he have to rub it in quite so much?

'In the van. In the van on the way home from hospital. You told me it was nothing more than a drunken kiss.'

'Dawn,' he said, running his fingers through his hair so it all stood up. 'You'd just said you were in love with your ex. I didn't think I should be standing in the way of that. I didn't want to confuse things.'

'But I wasn't in love with him,' I said.

'Well, I know that now,' said Jim. 'But I didn't then. I just said that because I thought I should. It wasn't just a drunken kiss. Not for me, anyway.'

I looked up at him. 'Not a drunken kiss,' I repeated uncertainly.

'Look,' he said, spreading his hands out on the table as if he was going to sketch a diagram with his fingers. 'I'm not saying I was totally sober — I just mean I didn't regret it. Well, not the way you think. I was trying to keep my hands off you, I really was. I knew you were all over the place — your aunt in hospital, your ex back on the scene. But when you looked at me like that, all wide-eyed and with your arms around me . . . I couldn't help myself.'

'You couldn't help yourself — '

'Jeez, Dawn, are you going to repeat everything I say?' he said, exasperated. 'I'm trying to apologize here.'

'Apologize?' I said, and he rolled his eyes. 'Sorry. I just — this is really unexpected.'

'Rory. Are you going to say anything at all?' Jim demanded.

'I — I,' I stuttered, unable to speak. I wondered in panic if I had used up all my words pointing out inanities like passing dogs and the strange hairstyles of people going into the cinema, and now didn't have any left to tell Jim how I felt.

He gave a small, rueful grin as I opened and closed my mouth silently.

'Jim,' I blurted, finally finding my voice. 'You didn't scare me off. I thought I was the one who pushed myself on *you*. I thought you were trying to tell me you weren't interested. That was why I was avoiding you.'

Jim's face burst into a smile. His white teeth made him look more than ever like an advertisement. I felt I would have bought whatever he was selling. 'You seriously didn't notice I was interested in you? I mean, Jesus, has a simple plumbing job ever taken so long? I came up with every possible excuse to be at your house all hours of the day. I've never got up so early in my life as I did to make sure I saw you in the mornings.'

'Well, yes,' I acknowledged. 'I did notice you were there all the time. But you know I thought that was to do with Auntie Lyd. And I was always so horrible to you.'

Jim grinned. 'That's what gave me hope.'

'Hope?'

'Well, Lydia said it showed you weren't indifferent to me. She said you weren't ready to go straight into another relationship and told me to keep my distance until you'd calmed down a bit.'

'Calmed down?' I asked, rattled.

'Stopped shagging buskers and horny teens, that sort of thing,' Jim teased.

I folded my arms across my chest. 'Jim, if you think this is the way to woo me, you are mistaken.'

'I didn't know what the way to woo you was,' he said. 'You were all over the place. Lydia was telling me to keep my distance; Eleanor said I should just go for it — '

'And what did Percy say?' I asked, annoyed. 'Did you discuss my love life with everyone in the house except me, Jim?' I had a sudden vision of them all sitting down to a committee meeting to discuss what to do about their problem resident and her 'all over the place' love life.

Jim had the grace to look embarrassed. 'It wasn't like that, Rory,' he said. 'But they've all got eyes; of course they noticed how I felt.'

'How — how do you feel?' I asked quietly.

'Haven't I been trying to tell you?' said Jim, throwing his hands up in exasperation. 'Jeez. Aurora Carmichael, I think you're gorgeous. I think every time you're in the room it's like there's no one else there. I think I can't keep my hands off you for much longer. I don't know what else I need to say to make it any clearer to you.'

'Well,' I teased, 'surely Percy had some advice, didn't you discuss this with him as well?'

Jim rolled his eyes. 'If you really want to know, Perce gave me a load of advice out of Shakespeare and I didn't understand a word of it, except something about climbing a balcony. And I didn't know if you'd fancy me in tights.'

I laughed, and he pulled his chair in towards the table so that he could lean his face closer. I leaned forward too. I couldn't stop smiling. It was making my cheeks ache. I thought we must look deranged, sitting there just grinning at each other.

'Would you?' said Jim.

'What?'

'Fancy me in tights,' he said.

'Jim,' I said. He twisted his fingers in mine and looked at me intently, waiting for my answer. 'If I can fancy you in those vile T-shirts, I can fancy you in anything.'

'You're not going to change how I dress, are you?' he asked.

'No, but I might stop you getting highlights.'

'I went on holiday to Thailand!' he protested, lifting a hand to his hair. He started laughing once he realized I was joking.

'I wouldn't change anything about you,' I said. 'Not one thing.'

'Really?'

'Really. You're my totally unsuitable suitable man, Jim.'

He leaned across the table and kissed me.

'Do you think I can get that printed on a T-shirt?'

Reader, I hit him.

We do hope that you have enjoyed reading this large print book.

Did you know that all of our titles are available for purchase?

We publish a wide range of high quality large print books including:
Romances, Mysteries, Classics
General Fiction
Non Fiction and Westerns

Special interest titles available in large print are:
The Little Oxford Dictionary
Music Book
Song Book
Hymn Book
Service Book

Also available from us courtesy of Oxford University Press:
Young Readers' Dictionary
(large print edition)
Young Readers' Thesaurus
(large print edition)

For further information or a free brochure, please contact us at:
Ulverscroft Large Print Books Ltd.,
The Green, Bradgate Road, Anstey,
Leicester, LE7 7FU, England.
Tel: (00 44) 0116 236 4325
Fax: (00 44) 0116 234 0205

Other titles published by
The House of Ulverscroft:

LIZZY HARRISON LOSES CONTROL

Pippa Wright

Lizzy Harrison isn't a romantic heroine. She is in no way hopelessly scatty and disorganised — her life is in perfect order. Okay, she hasn't met the right man yet, she's too busy with her job in PR, her packed schedule of improving activities and her diary planned for months in advance. But after her best friend, Lulu, challenges her need for control, it's not long before Lizzy is thrown into the arms of her boss's top client, Randy Jones. Reluctantly, she relaxes her hold on routine and discovers that losing control could win her more than she had ever imagined.